WHOBLIQUE STRATEGIES

Written by

A Vortex of Wholigans

Edited, conceived and commissioned by

Elton Townend Jones

Art by Simon A Brett

Whoblique Strategies

Edited and designed by Elton Townend Jones

Anthology copyright © 2017 Chinbeard Books. All rights reserved.

Article texts copyright © 2017 the respective authors.

Published by Chinbeard Books

Set by Nicholas Hollands

All royalties from this book are going to Children in Need.

Cover and interior artwork by Simon A. Brett.

ISBN 978-1981246342

WHY WHOBLIQUE STRATEGIES?

Elton Townend Jones

I came to *Doctor Who* relatively late. Late to the programme, I mean. For *me* it was quite early. I was two when I saw at least one episode of *Planet of the Daleks*. After that I was hooked. To Dalek stories, that is. It was only with *Terror of the Zygons* that I decided I was in it for the long haul – and what a season that was! Some of my most piquant childhood memories are tied to the insatiable thrill of being up-close to the TV screen and feeling the brutal disorientating terror of classic moments such as Scarman making it quite clear that Sutekh needs no other servant, Sarah revealed as an android, the chop-suey monster lurching up from its seedy bed, and those fleshy seed-pods. I was fortunate enough, over the years, to get into the books and the comic/magazine, and to enjoy the disparate fan renaissance that seemed to occur when Peter Davison replaced Tom Baker. Davison would become the Doctor for young teenage me, and later McCoy became the Doctor for college me. But it was during Colin Baker's tenure that I stopped watching for a bit, though it seemed like an age at the time. This is no judgement on Colin – I love all the Doctors and each one has been 'my favourite' at some time or another – but I'd hit 14 and I was suddenly more interested in girls, acting, books, American comics, and – most of all – music.

I grew up in a 'broken home' as they used to call it. I was born in industrial West Yorkshire and lived for the most part in either mining or police communities (I left that county shortly before those two communities realised they were operating on opposite sides of the fence...). By the time I was two, my parents had divorced and I think that's why I found *Doctor Who*. Between the ages of two and 18, I'd live in 13 different houses, go to eight schools and be supported by three more – quite wonderful – dads. For me, this was normal, but it's no wonder I wasn't particularly academic and never did very well at school. But there was always music in the house, and at an early age I came to love The Beatles, Wings, Space, King Crimson, Kate Bush, punk, new wave, and, through my parents' copy of *Hunky Dory* – David Bowie.

David Bowie has been a presence in my life for almost as long as I can remember, and his recent death is still a wound that has yet to heal. I know that I'm obviously not alone in this, but it struck me in recent years that being a devotee of Bowie was a trait that many *Doctor Who* fans – or Wholigans as I like to call us – share. For example, I'll draw your attention to the erstwhile 'Watcher' from *Doctor Who Magazine*, a man whose greatest, most visible success – after operating Daleks in the TV series – is probably his brilliantly definitive guide to the works of the great Ziggy. At the age of 14, I played *Hunky Dory* over and over. There was a lot of other great music around at that time, too, so it took me a while to *really* get into the Dame, but a year later, I got hold of *Low* and *Lodger* from the library and that was that – thoroughly hooked.

By the time Sylvester McCoy was in the TARDIS, I could happily accommodate both – indeed, all – my passions and celebrated them equally. Though, for me, it's probably as well *Doctor Who* went off the air in 1989, because I'd been studying Performing Arts (thanks to a run of Drama teachers who'd seen some talent in me) and I had a career to be getting on with. Through the 1990s, I had a few minor successes as an actor and director, but always at my side was the latest Virgin New Adventure. I loved those books. Sometimes they're my favourite version of *Doctor Who*, and they're all on a shelf opposite me as I write. I loved their mix of reverence and iconoclasm (something I hope will be apparent in this book, once I've stopped wittering on). They were so dangerously playful. Much later, I decided to put myself through university, studying Philosophy and Literature, and the BBC Books then came with me – along with Bowie's *1.Outside*, which was like a personal reward for being a fan for so long.

Now, I'm nothing at all to do with *Doctor Who* professionally and never have been. It never really struck me as something I wanted to pursue, though I do love the post-2005 series. Nowadays, I'm a professional playwright and theatre director/producer, but through social media, I lately found myself falling down the rabbit-hole of fan fiction. In recent years, I've been involved in a number of books – fan projects, really, like this one – that have allowed me a little distraction from the day job. Over time, my input into such works has perhaps taken a little more of my energy and time than it ought, but I enjoy dabbling and trying new things, so it's been incredible fun and most importantly I've made a lot of wonderful writer friends both professional and amateur. It's because of these happy associations that *Whoblique Strategies* exists. That and the inestimable support of Barnaby Eaton-Jones. Whilst working with him on a *Doctor Who* anthology a year or so ago, I realised I wanted to try something just a little more... irreverent, iconoclastic, and dangerously playful. Something a bit more rock 'n' roll and a bit more magical. Barnaby urged me to move forward on this, and that's where Brian Eno came in.

Again, it was Bowie's death that cast a long shadow over the last few years of my professional work – okay, that and all the utterly stupid and barmy twists and turns UK and US politics have taken, but let's just keep this poppy, eh? – so when I was looking for a means of communicating the *ideas* of *Doctor Who* and our literary responses to it through another form, I found myself recalling Bowie's collaborations with Eno (the famous 'Berlin' trilogy in particular) and their use of random strategies. Now, as an artist myself, I have long been a fan of restrictive devices that hone and limit the scope of authorial intention. In short, I like rules. Being given a carte blanche terrifies me to some extent – not because I can't comply, but because I know there's always a danger of using too many ingredients in what could easily be a simple, perfect recipe. I already possessed a box of these cards – originated by Peter Schmidt and developed further by Eno – for use against my own work. They are designed, when randomly picked from their deck, to offer a solution or inspiration to creative blockage, but can also be used on their own merit from the outset – which is the method employed in this book. They were used extensively on the Bowie LPs *Low*, *"Heroes"* and *Lodger* – three of Bowie's finest (and most Eno-influenced) works, which I do hope you've heard. I'm recalling off the top of my head here, but the random selection of cards – instructions if you will – saw rock guitarists playing as washed-out vaudeville artists and rock drummers drumming Latin jazz, for example. Set these disparate strategies against each other, and what was intended to be a 'rock song' becomes something fresh, invigorating and unexpected. It becomes art. Listen to 'Breaking Glass' if you don't believe me. What the cards do, is subdue the ego and free the art. And that really appeals to me.

So, when planning this new book, I decided I'd take a relatively serious, in-universe (for the most part) reading of every *Doctor Who* story from *An Unearthly Child*/*100,000BC* to *Twice Upon a Time* and I drew a strategy card for each story (in this book, the strategy card employed is in bold capitals at the end of each piece). To take on this massive task, I pulled together a team of 70 writers (from the UK, US, Australia, France and the Netherlands), some of whom I'd either worked with and admired on previous *Doctor Who* charity projects and wanted to work

4

with again (and push in new directions), and others I knew by reputation or through social media and that old-fashioned thing we call 'real life'. Many of the former have written for Virgin, Big Finish, the BBC, *DWM*, and other professional iterations of *Doctor Who*, and gave generously of their time and support. Many of the latter had never written *any* kind of *Doctor Who* fiction, but were writers in other fields, or Bowie/Eno/*Who* fans – their enthusiasm, skill and imagination gave me some of the most satisfying moments during the collation of this book. I hope that the widely-read Wholigan will enjoy reading excellent new work by both the usual suspects and 'previously-unread-in-fan-circles' professionals from journalism, academia, poetry, music, and theatre. For my own part, I am grateful and happy to have worked with such a fantastic collection of magicians and fabulists – all of them Wholigans to the core. They all took the challenge and ran with it, producing an astounding and dangerously playful collection that fits my vision of reverent iconoclasm and an art rock sensibility. Throughout each and every piece, I've been there, Clara-like, ensuring that the individual parts build to a more coherent whole. I've dropped in Easter eggs of all kinds, both for lovers of *Doctor Who* and those that like their music, particularly Bowie and Eno. There are lots of games at play in here, some you'll get, some you won't; some you'll adore and some you'll spit feathers over. If any of those responses happen, I'll consider mine and my vortex of Wholigans' job done. This is not simply a collection of very short stories, it's a box of fireworks. And if any errors or gremlins have crept into the box, then I will simply have to follow the guidance of Eno's most famous stratagem: *Honour thy error as a hidden intention* – and pretend that was the divine plan all along. Whatever else happens, we'll make some money for Children in Need, and that's good enough for me. I hope you'll enjoy these glittering fireworks and find something new in *Doctor Who* and these authors – who gave of their time and imagination freely – to treasure. Happy times and places!

(Schmidt & Eno's Oblique Strategies *are commercially available and I highly recommend you get hold of a box.)*

WHOBLIQUE STRATEGIES

is edited, commissioned and overseen by ELTON TOWNEND JONES

Elton describes himself professionally as a fabulist and magician. He wrote, directed and performed his first play – *Origen* – aged 18, whilst studying Performing Arts in East Anglia and under Jude Kelly at West Yorkshire Playhouse. Early career highlights include: directing and acting in professional tours of Godber and Shakespeare (in roles such as 'Puck' and 'Friar Lawrence') and the short film 'Dear Eve...' (2001); he also played 'Salieri' in The Cockpit's *Amadeus*, and wrote *Cutting the Cord* for Flying Eye (BAC, 2009). Subsequently, he founded Dyad Productions with Rebecca Vaughan with whom he has creatively produced each critically-acclaimed work, including *I, Elizabeth* and *Austen's Women*. He wrote and directed *The Time Machine, Jane Eyre: An Autobiography, Dalloway* and *The Unremarkable Death of Marilyn Monroe* (Samuel French, 2015). He also wrote and performed in *The Diaries of Adam and Eve* (StageScripts, 2013), script-edited *Female Gothic*, and directed *Christmas Gothic*. Outside Dyad, he is a freelance journalist, writing about music, television, books and film. His brief flirtations with the world of *Doctor Who*-related fiction have included pieces in *Seasons of War, A Target for Tommy, Lethbridge Stewart: Blood of Atlantis*, and *A Time Lord for Change*, for which he was the creative editor. *Whoblique Strategies* is to be his last such flirtation. His plays have been – and continue to be – performed across Europe, Australasia and the United States.

You can find out more about Elton and keep up with his work at www.dyadproductions.com

WHOBLIQUE STRATEGIES

is written by A VORTEX OF WHOLIGANS:

Elton Townend Jones (showrunner); Andy Priestner; Sami Kelsh; Paul Driscoll; Ian Potter; Matt Sewell; John Gerard Hughes; Daniel Wealands; Craig Moss; Kara Dennison; Andrew Hunt; Sarah Di-Bella; Hendryk Korzeniowski; Brendan Jones; Will Ingram; Ash Stewart; Christine Grit; Blair Bidmead; Nick Mellish; Mark Trevor Owen; Dan Milco; Ken Shinn; Jon Arnold; Simon Bucher-Jones; Simon A Forward; Jon Dear; Tim Gambrell; Alistair Lock; Simon Messingham; Brad Wolfe; Ira Lightman; Matt Barber; John Dorney; Georgia Ingram; Alan G McWhan; Alan Taylor; Aryldi Moss-Burke; Warren Cathrine; Townsend Shoulders; Marius Riley; Simon A Brett (designer); Paul Ebbs; Lee Ravitz; Robin G Burchill; Dan Rebellato; Callum Stewart; Matt Adams; Tessa North; Ian Baldwin; Christian Cawley; Philip Bates; Alex Spencer; Lee Rawlings; Christopher Samuel Stone; Matthew J Elliott; Steve Watts; Ian Kubiak; David A McIntee; James McLean; Gareth Alexander; Liam Hogan; Clive Greenwood; JR Southall; Stephen Aintree; Barnaby Eaton-Jones (producer); Ruth Wheeler; Martin Tucker.

WHOBLIQUE STRATEGIES

is designed and illustrated by SIMON A BRETT

Simon is an illustrator and writer living in the southwest of England with a wife, children and too many animals. His *Doctor Who* themed artwork can regularly be found in the pages of *Starburst* magazine, while other work can be found at www.simonbrett.co.uk

ACKNOWLEDGEMENTS

There's a list that's far too long for everyone I want to thank, and most of the people I do want to thank are the contributors to this book. Each and every one of them has my gratitude for taking time to contribute to this crazy project when not one of them needed to. Heroes, all – and not in rabbit ears.

Special thanks first and foremost for supporting this book to the max: Sarah Di-Bella, Barnaby Eaton-Jones, Simon A Brett and Nicholas Hollands. And you, dear reader, for buying it.

Thanks to those who were constantly on hand and always 'can-do' at the eleventh hour: Alex Spencer, Warren Cathrine, Andy Priestner, Paul Ebbs, Sami Kelsh, Matt Sewell, Jon Dear, Ira Lightman, James McLean, and Hendryk Korzeniowski.

And those who've helped me carry the project across the last year: Craig Moss, Simon A Forward, Ian Potter, Matt Adams, Matt Barber, Nick Mellish, Andrew Hunt, Simon Messingham, Georgia Ingram, Alan G McWhan, Lee Ravitz, Dan Rebellato, Philip Bates, Townsend Shoulders, Ken Shinn, David A McIntee, and my Dyad mucker Martin Tucker. That rhymes. Big shout out to Christian Cawley too, for long-term support.

Other friends and supporters I'd like to thank are: Toby Hadoke, Robert Shearman, Rebecca Vaughan, Waen Shepherd, John Guilor, Andrew Coppin, Anton Barbeau, June Hudson, Ian Greaves, Robert Lewis, Albert Welling, Adrian Salmon, Roy Gill, Bill Nelson, Maggie Dunne, Nathan Mullins, Andy Frankham-Allen, Alan & Alys Hayes, Steve Watts, Katy Manning, Daniel Tate, Timothy Stafford, Stefana Brancastle, Sarah Berger, Vanessa Bishop, Ben Guest, Jenny Shirt, Simon Eddie Baker, Alison and Lee Brooksbank, Jean Townend, Danny Bright, Kate Flanaghan, Mags Swann, Derek Watson, Declan May, Stuart Douglas, Paul Magrs, Nick Campbell, David Waters, Matthew Sweet, Claire Louise Amias, Mark Irwin-Watson, Mason Chorley, Tim Whitnall, Rosaletta Curry, Stephen Cunningham, Lizzie Wort, Michele Endeacott, and all at Samuel French.

This one's for my Mum, my Dad, and Diane.

'Not only is it the last show of the tour, but it's the last show that we'll ever do.'

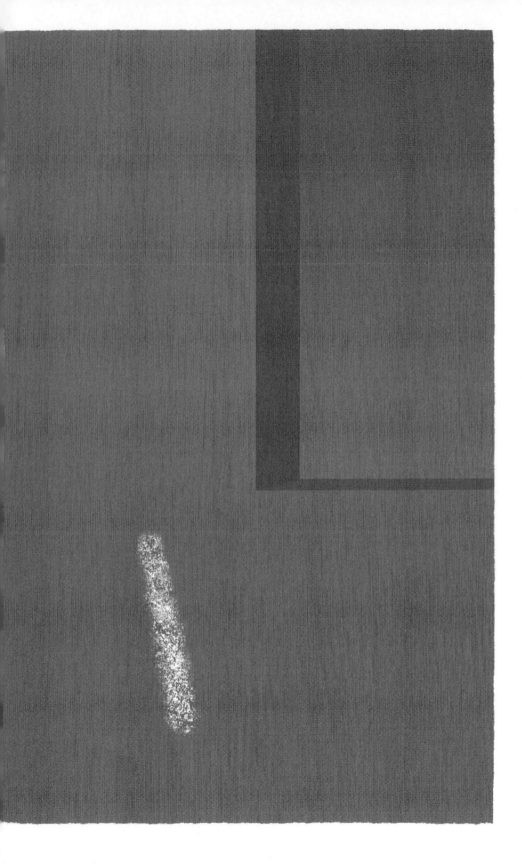

NEVER MIND THE BOLLOCKS... HERE'S THE 'BERLIN' TRILOGY
Elton Townend Jones

Falling toward black and white Earth, with a Christmas-tang-too-early in its foggy air, We Observe the dim twinkle of Man's white heat, decorating, illuminating the dark of a passing age; a breath of calm before the wilful dance into horror.

Lumpen, electric, towering blocks give way to terraces and slums. Dirty London but feet below us, We hang, suspended – a fleeting horde of nosy angels – crackling at Artron secrets in the air...

A Dalek whiff. A TARDIS fug. A something-ancient retch. And a too-much-Time-Lord choke.

Over cobbles, We glide – ghosts, unseen – above Coal Hill; across Orlando's Garden; over and ahead of the walking girl in mac and cap, tinny twangs in her bag; hands dancing. We speed like middle age through bins and cats – and cars: parked, empty. But for one – small, tight – where two teachers agitate and invigorate over currency, litmus, and impossible girls. *Oh!*

But Time is against Us, and We are fated to Watch it Change.

We fast-forward over yards and alleys; apexing above a warren of ginnels and snickets to Espy the unearthly child: Astrakhan hat. Winter cape. Shoes clicking on cobbles.

He's in a hurry.

Destiny awaits him.

they'll tell everyone about the Ship

Or it used to.

This moment of moments has been meddled before: re-written, un-written, eaten, improved, cut-up, sampled, dubbed, deformed, diluted and distressed, but still it comes – making history. Again and again.

He's breathless.

Afraid.

He quickens down the alleyway towards the beckoning freedom of Totter's Lane.

He never makes it.

Somewhere below, shadowed eyes narrow through staser-rifle sights. A popping bolt of energy passes from the blackness – into the harried man, who crumples, sinks; his long white hair smothered by the collapsing cape.

His hat rolls circles to stillness.

Silence.

Dropping its rifle, a thin, hooded figure runs to what was once the Doctor. We follow this deadly assassin – though impotent, insubstantial – as energy erupts from the victim's every pore and follicle, colouring the night with yellow, gold;

burnt orange. The eruption is brief, but the world remains bright – tiny daisies bursting from cracks in walls; in cobbles, in timelines.

The Doctor sits bolt upright, no longer an old man, but a striking, young woman; dark-haired, self-assured. Appealing?

The 'assassin' sweeps back its hood, also a striking woman; blonde-ish, keen-eyed – and utterly appalled.

'Oh no,' she says with foggy breath. 'This is *really* going to bite me on the bum.'

DESTROY THE MOST IMPORTANT THING.

A LONG WAY DOWN
Andy Priestner

How long have I been hanging here? With the rock face before me and nothing but blackness below…

The last few days have been a blur. The sudden arrival of the strangers. Dark-haired Eee-yan with a wild-eyed passion now lost to we Thaled. Persuading us that all we've learned, all Thal history, should be abandoned. The woman, Bar-something. Proper but spirited. Nothing like Dyoni. Even now, standing alongside men. The girl, timid but other-worldly. Less sure of their quest, perhaps out of deference to the old man. The old man himself. Strangely distant. Separate somehow. Weathered, perhaps, by everything those eyes have seen?

My mind wanders and a sea of Dalek eyestalks suddenly swims into view. Turning, focusing. Rolling forwards inexorably, a single gestalt wave. Urgent shrieks echo off their empty metal cases. They not only wait for us at the end of this expedition, but also at the end of a longer road. The only place fighting will ever lead. To more death.

At this, my final end, I truly know what the Daleks are. A warning. A warning of a barely living death. A warning against choosing war over peace.

But I am Antodus.

I cut the rope.

DON'T STRESS ONE THING MORE THAN ANOTHER.

CHILD, YOU'RE A WOMAN NOW
Sami Kelsh

Something's happening to the Ship.

Dimensioning forces… feel a bit giddy.

Hard to stay conscious. Undeniably exhausted, my thoughts are frenzies, fast, confused; a dozen emergency alarms going off at once – each demanding immediate attention. The giddiness isn't mine. It's his: bow tie future. And now there's another little future voice passing through me as the dimensions tear

14

at us. *Is that what's happening?* This new voice itches – an insect bite at the back of my mind; a woman/child-voice, whispering doubt into me. The Ship's channelling an invasive torrent of timelines. *My own?* This future voice reminds me just how little Grandfather and I know about my erstwhile teachers – and that trust must be earned. The voice grows louder, insistent; desperate.

There's no reason not to believe that the others have hijacked *Tardis* and that everything is going to plan. There's no reason not to believe that Ian and Barbara aren't at all who they claim to be. Who's to say that it was no accident they wandered into the Ship that day?

Ian's there when I wake up, but he's pre-occupied.

The scissors are the closest weapon to hand. I am... *a warrior of the Sevateem?*

I am hunt ready.

LISTEN TO THE QUIET VOICE.

YOU'VE GOT A HABIT OF LEAVING
Paul Driscoll

The Doctor storms into the Ship. 'Confounded fellow! How dare he keep the key to our home?!'

'It's not though, Grandfather, not really...'

'You still miss Gallifrey, child? After everything?'

Susan smiles. Throughout the arduous journey she's been given the cold shoulder. Finally, a reaction; an acknowledgement of their association. 'Every time I begin to feel at home, you move us on. What's so bad about not knowing?'

'1960s Earth?! I should've guessed when you adopted the lingo. "Fab", is it? "Dig it", do you? I warned you after Venus not to get... attached.' He pulls out a portable key cutter. *Made in China.*

'Well, the Ship seems to like the place,' observes Susan as her 'grandfather' sets about copying the TARDIS key. 'She's making sure we take the twentieth century with us.'

'But we'll soon drop Chadderton and Miss Wright off...'

'I'm not talking about them. And it's about time you made me that key you promised...'

'It's not for you. Not yet. Now if I could just unlock her with the click of a finger. Yes, that would show them. Evil spirits indeed.'

'Don't forget the twenty-one holes. Get this wrong and we'll be stuck here for good.'

DO WE NEED HOLES?

CONSCIENTIOUS OBJECTORS
Ian Potter

Peoples of Marinus, if your minds are still open, please pay attention.

You have become slaves. For too long you have let others guide your consciences and govern your thoughts. Now, the machinery of the State that regulates your behaviour has become dangerously unbalanced and your world teeters on ruin. You have become weak-willed petty things, living in squalor, subservient to deceivers. Your justice is a joke bound to arbitrary rules and your centrally controlled morality is in sharp decline.

Marinus has become poisoned. It is lustful, wrathful and corrupt – a world of exploitation, assault and murder that the dying machine still masks from your unseeing eyes. Already the jungle plants grow wild on savage thoughts the State no longer tempers.

Soon it will be too late.

We, your Voord brothers, have come to offer hope. The machine will tell you we are enemies – alien, a force to be feared, but beneath our vulcanised suits and mind-protecting headgear, we are as human as you – a people fighting to remain free.

You are chained to a collapsing engine that has you bound for destruction. We alone hold the keys that will set you free.

Please.

Aid us; become like us.

WOULD ANYONE WANT IT?

I DEMAND A BETTER FUTURE
Matt Sewell

I live again!

Yetaxa is reborn as woman. I have returned to you, my people. Through the mysteries of spacetime I have flown to right the great wrongs inflicted upon you, blessed children. I have seen the future, the coming horror, and I come to give you strength and knowledge, to clip the wings of Quetzalcoatl. You will abide and flourish in the coming age, people of Aztlan; you will no longer wither under the yoke of slavery foretold.

Who is this woman, this Yetaxa, who comes among you now? I have descended from the Coal Hill with my companions. The child – let her study our ways in the seminary, for she will soon be a woman. The old man – let him take his ease in the Garden of Peace, for there is much there to distract a man of his years and perhaps make him young again. The beautiful one – let him lead the army, for he seeks not glory in blood.

There shall *be* no more blood. I am already replete with it. Open your hearts no longer with the tecpatl but with your unquestioning faith – in me.

Together we shall rewrite the codex of history!

Every line!

TURN IT UPSIDE DOWN.

CAUGHT BETWEEN
John Gerard Hughes

As we make our way out of the Ship, I ponder the conversation.

Mr Chesterton's quite right: we have all changed. For a start, I don't think of him as Mr Chesterton any more. It's just Ian, now. Ian and Barbara. My fellow exiles. No longer my teachers, more my... equals? Not in intellect, of course... In *many* ways, I *am* still vastly... superior. But I also know that, in other ways *I am vastly inferior*.

But they *are* kind people.

Moreover, they're great ambassadors for the people of Earth. They've got, well, humanity. And humanity, it seems to me, always has that desire, that need, to *grow* – and develop. I've quietly watched my former teachers grow into giants of heart and mind.

Now I want to follow their example.

I, too, am determined to grow.

Grandfather will never let me go, I tell myself. *To him I'm still the child who fled from home.*

In my heart, I know that the only way I can leave is by finding what Ian and Barbara found – someone to be human *with*.

For now, however, I follow these dear friends, my... big, brave... family, as we again step out into another world.

TRUST IN THE YOU OF NOW.

THE DOCTOR'S FATHER
Elton Townend Jones

Outside the Ship, France 1789, is on fire – literally and figuratively blooming with change.

She burns to join the struggle, to make her mark upon the world her family calls their second home; to end her reckless adventure in space and time and restore the passion of her youth. *'Allons-y!'* Grabbing backpack, fedora, sonic and scarf, now-ancient, so-called 'Ulysses nomore a Lungbarrowmas' opens the Ship's doors, gives her son a parting glance and races into roaring Paris.

'Father!' screams her son at the slamming doors. His attempts to re-open them fail.

Locked!

The Ship departs from spacetime, wheezing, groaning. Ulysses' voice hacks a speaker: 'I'm sending you home, son. The long way round. I have to leave you now. Don't follow me. I'm going. Making a difference.'

The dark-haired, elfin boy shouts at air: 'But, father, the history books...'

18

'Aren't written yet. I'll abide by their findings. You know me.'

'No!' The boy sobs.

His father's fading voice speaks to him across unravelling Time: 'I'll sleep in your memory now, but one day, I'll return. One day. Until then, make it worthwhile. Be strong. Be right. And be *yourselves*. Sign your name across eternity. And never let them forget mine.'

VOICE NAGGING SUSPICIONS.

WE ARE THE DEAD
Daniel Wealands

The earthworm and the ant, so different in many ways, both encountered their end in the same way: in ignorance. They did not know, or understand what was happening as the toxin spread through them, robbing them of their existence. They fought, vainly, to cling to life.

It made no difference.

The fly was victim to his own nature; survival was paramount, yet the sustenance he sought was tainted and inevitably it too succumbed to the venom.

Farrow had intended to create a poison, a means to kill, in order to preserve useful vegetation. He did too good a job; his creation was too powerful and drew the wrong attention. And as a result he met the same end as those he would destroy – though by much cruder means.

Then there is Forester. His greed has led him to this meeting. Where others saw a setback he saw alternatives, options. And money. The improvised explosive has, at the very least, blinded him, scarred him. But he may still succumb to the injuries and shock; still join the others, man and insect alike – with me.

Humans say there are only two certainties in life: death and taxes.

I am the former.

WHICH ELEMENTS CAN BE GROUPED?

SACRIFICE YOURSELF
Craig Moss

As the time rotor starts and the ticking, clicking Ship begins to dematerialise, the Doctor's words echo, hollow, in my mind; then, accreting, they ring louder and louder in my head, as if resonating through the sombre, empty infinity of the Ship.

After witnessing the destruction of Bedfordshire, the horror of the mines and the appalling extent of London's terrifying devastation, I was surprised and dismayed that the Doctor had locked Susan out of the Ship and forced her to remain.

Even if she is with David, whom she loves; I could never have done that if she'd been

19

my *granddaughter*.

But the Doctor's stubborn, determined – much stronger in body and mind than his apparently feeble frame suggests.

I study him, standing there, frozen; staring at the console, contemplating what he's actually done. I watch him bury the feelings deep; the pain too great, the burden evident.

'"No tears", indeed! Hm? What a stupid old fool! Eh, Chesterton, my boy?'

Weeping, the Doctor reaches out an arm for support, and as Barbara and I embrace him, I can feel him shaking. He's going to need us more than ever now – we're his only family – all the old boy's got, poor beggar.

WHAT WOULDN'T YOU DO?

DEAD FINKS DON'T TALK
Kara Dennison

1: Foster trust. As quickly as possible.

Well, that's going to be almost embarrassingly easy. This girl would trust anyone in a heartbeat. (That may be the problem... oh. You may be on to something there. Put a pin in that one, we'll come back to it.)

2: Foster trust in the others.

A little less embarrassingly easy. It's not necessary, of course, but it does make things easier. We're going to need a talk soon about identifying tame animals and how not to accidentally shoot friends. Might be a problem unchecked.

3: Find out absolutely everything. As quickly as possible.

She talks like a child, this one. Pouts like a child. (Silly old fool, she is a child. Keep your numbers straight.) If all goes well, I end up with an embarrassment of riches. If not... I'll think of something. I always do.

4: Think of something.

I do hate working with a mixed audience. The regulars are always so hopeful and the new faces are always so doubtful. If they'd more sense, it would be the other way around. No helping it.

Oh. She trusts me. Did I actually do that part myself or is she anticipating me?

ALWAYS FIRST STEPS.

BEING FLOGGED BY A ROMAN GALLEY MASTER MAKES COMPANIONS OF US ALL
Andrew Hunt

There's nothing like being kidnapped, put on a Roman galley, and dragged off to god-knows-where to make you forge strong friendships with your companions. Especially when you're both manacled to the same oar...

Delos is a decent chap, if unrefined. You get to know a fellow well under these circumstances. You tell stories, you make plans. *What you will do when you're free? Where will you go? Will you stay together? Or return to your separate lives?*

Five days it takes me. Talking him round to the idea of escape. Telling him about the narrow scrapes I've been in before. 'You dive in, find a way. Things usually turn out for the best.'

The Doctor taught me that.

I talk about freedom. The freedom to sit in a pub supping a pint; to play rugby; to collect stamps; to court a beautiful woman.

Barbara blushes.

Half the time he hasn't a clue what I'm talking about. But I plant seeds, give him something to dream about. A reason to keep going. The Doctor taught me that too.

And when push comes to shove, Delos takes all the risks, pulls me to safety; saves us both.

The Doctor taught me well.

WHAT WOULD YOUR CLOSEST FRIEND DO?

STRENGTH THROUGH THOUGHT
Sarah Di-Bella

Vortis. Isop galaxy. Gold is the currency of power here. As that rusting, rotting, hidden pile of cobwebbed corpses from Mondas would testify. The magnetic core pulled me from my astral plane. But I am SACROSANCT! The question is: is it some natural phenomenon or is it intelligent – deliberate?

The answer comes: a slow, steady, continuous refrain; a guiding chorus: Come To Me... Approach! I Am Animus, I Am Great Intelligence, I Absorb Your Territory, Riches, Energy, Culture. I Am The Centre.

Him: Trying to violate my Ship? / You will achieve nothing. / Drop the hairdryer: Put. Me. Through. / Size is relative. / History means nothing when you can travel through space and time.

Still, they are morphotised. Ian becomes Heron and Barbara is Arbara. The light flickers, throbs and blinds; the rarefied air chokes; a heady, hazy, hallucinogenic stupor. Extra-sonic sound threatens to engulf.

Remember: the Menoptra are stronger than this evil cancer. Now we must use our brains and not our wings; the mission is suicidal. Let us break the teeth of stone, unfriendly, and attain the Temple of Light. Let us join with the Optera; our future. They will fly and we shall help them.

Hope lies in action.

**GO TO AN EXTREME, MOVE BACK TO A MORE
COMFORTABLE PLACE.**

LAMENT YOUR SIN SO GREAT
Hendryk Korzeniowski

'I have a valuable dagger, from the Crusades... from Saladin!' A blade gleams before his face, unblemished for its supposed 500 years.

Lieutenant Clive shakes his head at the old man, 'There *are* Fakirs in Calcutta who tell tales of an immortal poet, aging devilishly from man to woman over the centuries; time barely scratching the skin...' He adds, 'Fairy stories.'

The grizzled aristocrat bows, producing a pistol from his pocket. 'The Count of St Germain knows the truth. I have lived longer than daggers, caused far more grief...'

A hand of ice clutches Robert Clive's pained heart. 'That gun...!'

The Count chuckles. '...Failed to shoot three times, when you aimed it at yourself!'

'But fired perfectly when I pointed it away...' Clive slumps back, winded by his past.

The old Count leans forward, half his face dripping with shadow. 'Time no longer regulates, and choices proliferate.' He proffers both pistol and dagger towards the man who *might* become Clive of India. 'Are you a betting man, sir, in the time of your lord 1756?'

Clive trembles. 'Get out of here!' he bellows.

'Choose! Choose for 1774! See if Time is on your side now!'

He picks up the dagger.

GIVE THE GAME AWAY.

MAGIC DANCE
Brendan Jones

Screen 1: a strangely dressed girl presses for a lift.
Screen 2: illegally assembled proles dance in City Square...

Gently, the odd little man leads Imperator Idios away from the monitor console. 'Years ago,' he says, 'you conquered a peaceful planet and made a dusty museum of it. I set it *free*. Your desiccated empire was powerless to reclaim it, and your other colonies capitulated in suit.'

Idios hears a banging behind him.

'I never knew how your empire collapsed quite so quickly,' says the man, smiling dangerously, 'but then I realised *we* hadn't visited you yet. Do forgive Ace. She enjoys her work.'

Idios turns to see the girl from the screen – in the room now – swinging a metal club into his console, whilst on Screen 1 she awaits the lift and on 2 she dances anarchically with the proles.

The little man checks a timepiece on his wrist against another in his hand. 'Just a demonstration, Imperator – that Morok dominance is *so* last epoch. Be seeing you!'

Idios awakens at his console; quite alone. The locked screens show the man and girl leading proles from lift to square and square to lift in the magical dance of freedom.

LOOK AT THE ORDER IN WHICH YOU DO THINGS.

THE CHANGING HEARTS OF DOCTOR WHO
Sarah Di-Bella

Barbara and Ian are on the top deck of a Routemaster. As they pass St Paul's Cathedral, their conversation turns to times gone by.

'It's been a while, Arbara.'

Barbara laughs. 'Yes, Heron. What made you think of those times?'

'Oh, I often think of them. Of him.'

'Me too. Ian, did we do the right thing? Leaving him. When we told him, he looked so shocked, so small. We could still be travelling with him; seeing the most amazing sights. Making a difference.'

'Yes, but we wouldn't have *this*: us, *our life*! We'd be suspended in time and space. We did lose two years, remember?' Ian puts his thumbs in his sports jacket lapels. '*Chesterfield*! *You can't rewrite history, dear boy, not one line, hm?*'

'No, Ian, we couldn't rewrite history – but we changed the heart of Time. We did change him, you know. We made him more human.'

'We left, but we stayed – inside him. And if we gave him humanity, then *you* showed him humility. He listened to you, Barbara.'

'Would you like to go back, just once?'

'I go back, regularly, he's always with me; in *here*.'

Hey, Doctor, wherever you are, thanks for the ride!

FACED WITH A CHOICE, DO BOTH.

D.J.
Will Ingram

The *real* trick is to start at the end and work backwards. That way you avoid all those messy ripples you'll cause. Ironically, that's one of the first things they teach you in your first semester at the Academy. Rather a case of 'whatever you do, don't do this, and furthermore, here's how not to do it'.

Earth's a primitive planet, a perfect training ground – a plaything even! I doubt anyone would notice the difference anyway. As long as I'm not reckless. I mean... you *can* alter the lives of millions of people – but will it be *fun*?

And I've realized that the best way of blending in is to dress *timelessly*. These monk fellows seem to have existed in every period I've travelled to, so that drag – though dour – seems ideal.

Somehow though, I still attract the most suspicious looks – even here, as far forward the 20th century – so I've opted instead for one of their 'suits'. And now, I have one more piece of equipment to collect before I'm ready to nip back for the big one.

So, exchanging pleasantries with an old-young blonde-ish woman – who smiles – I make my request:

'I'd like to buy a gramophone, please.'

DISTORTING TIME.

BUCKET PUDDLES
Ash Stewart

She blinks, unable to believe her eyes.

The soldiers assembled in front of her are quite wrong. Again. Most people wouldn't notice, but she does. She needs the cream of the crop for this mission, and all she has is clone vat *dregs*. Bucket puddles. She had requested pure-born Drahvins like herself but had been vetoed, her mission deemed 'not important enough' for such an expenditure.

She has almost as much disdain for the Matriarchs that took that decision as she has for the accursed, *hideous* Rills.

The war is going badly. Drahvin ships sent to target Rill installations are failing to return. She knows the tactics being used to be at fault, and here she is expected to prove to the Matriarchs that she is a suitable fleet commander; her warrior skills now handicapped by an ineptitude of clones.

She swallows her icy anger, and reluctantly picks the three dolls that seem most suitable.

All they have to do is stop one key Rill ship, and she will be in with a chance of decoration and glory. Track it down, destroy it, and return to Drahva.

Mission failure is not an option.

Maaga watches her inferiors fall-in and sighs.

EMPHASIZE THE FLAWS.

THE BOY WITH THE THORN IN HIS SIDE
Christine Grit

They always say the same thing when you're visiting an unknown planet: touching the flora and fauna is not advised except when wearing the kind of clothing that prevents poisons and stuff from entering your body. In this particular case it would be ridiculous to be so cautious. The planet is a lot like an unspoiled Earth; the air much fresher than that disgusting smoggy fog back home. A deep breath is just what I need.

Look at all that greenery.

Wait a minute. That's funny. It seems as if those big, fleshy, fir-like trees are moving slightly. Not swaying – moving of their own accord.

But they can't be; I must be imagining it.

I gently touch one to be sure, and–

I'm still screaming, but there's no-one here to hear me.

Thorns. They've got thorns. I bite my tongue and pluck the woody dart from my palm. It might be useful later, back at the lab.

I think I've seen enough.

Whoa! Roots underfoot, I'm tripping, falling – right into one of those moving firs. *Argh!*

Thorns. Thorns in my back. In my chest. In my limbs. *In my face.*

I... I...

I remember now.

I must kill.

Kill! Kill!

ACCEPT ADVICE.

SAVIOUR MACHINE
Blair Bidmead

She can smell the burning city on her clothes.

The interior of the temple shines with stark, empyrean splendour: an obliterating white, divine and unnaturally pure. No mortal progress could withstand such unadulterated immaculacy; the weight of its luminescence.

She pants in fear and exhaustion. Wiping away grey perspiration from her forehead with the back of her hand, she shuffles in her sandals, feeling awkward and unworthy. Diomede lays dying at her feet. Battle wounds stain the blank floor, black-red life leaking across the white surface. Their shared humanity is but a blemish against such inexorable, celestial majesty.

Surrendering herself to the light, she listens.

Somewhere, from far away and all around, Olympian choirs sing a deep, delicate yet unyielding lament.

The sound soothes her and her fear dissipates. The white light of the gods fills her senses, erasing all doubt.

Ashen tears well in her eyes, as a vision of the Lady Cressida appears before her. The Lady's humanity somehow remains intact.

How can that be possible? How could she have abandoned this light, turned away from such brilliance; renouncing Zeus for flesh and fire?

Cold, white air fills Katarina's lungs. Divinity will take her. Obliterate her with perfection.

USE AN UNACCEPTABLE COLOUR.

TIME, GENTLEMEN, PLEASE
Nick Mellish

So, I tell him the one about the brainwashed gun-toting space vixen in leathers and sorrow and he throws me another drink.

And the irony of such time at my fingers and the death of time when time and the past; time and my past; that time is destroyed already. And the knowledge of you as my friend and foe, and the vision of you as dead and dying, and brother can you spare me the time? Can you spare me my brother? Can you spare me *me*?

And I smile at time as he calls it. He nods to the door and do I see who I want beyond it? Dare I open and look. My last orders.

Pay me in time and tales. In talk and story. They all like to talk before I chuck them out.

Is it the whiskey or the machine that's doing this? I ask. I laugh. 'And they can't even turn it off!' I fall off my chair to sand on the floor, to sand in Egypt, to sand and ash in the burnt jungle, from vines to Vyons.

Closing time, he says to me. The time traveller who walked into a bar.

DISTORTING TIME.

HE SELLS SANCTUARY
Mark Trevor Owen

On a street corner, the agent meets his client: a tall, arrogantly handsome man, his rich green cloak suggesting considerable wealth.

Wooden gates open to reveal a courtyard, in which stands the shattered remains of a large house.

'It was once magnificent,' the agent remarks, sadly.

'And could be again,' says his client. 'What caused the devastation?'

'You will recall the violence of St Bartholomew's Day, back in '72?'

'I do. A most... illuminating event.'

'It was caught up in that. Much of the house was burned. The cellars survived. They would.'

'The cellars?' asks the client.

The agent lowers his voice. 'I wouldn't say this in every tavern, but those Huguenots knew how to build. This chateau has deep cellars, thick walls. It was a refuge for Protestants during the slaughter. There's a story of a serving girl, who just got here in time. Stayed in the cellar for three weeks, then fled north, trying to reach England.'

'In time...' The client smiles like a reptile. 'I too have a lady in need of a secure home.' He pauses for a moment. 'This property interests me. Can you arrange an internal viewing?'

'Of course, Monsieur–?'

'Scarlioni. *Count* Scarlioni.'

DON'T STRESS ONE THING MORE THAN ANOTHER.

THE PASSENGER
Matt Sewell

You had no idea who I was – bet you still don't. I could spot you a mile off despite your studied doddering. Still wet behind the grizzled ears, you were; so keen for a replacement you couldn't spot my flailing around to find a character or hear the waver in my accent. I really needed a break from 'swinging' London, so hitching a ride in your fab blue box was absolutely gear!

I was completely unaware of my purpose: to transmit the rhinovirus throughout space and time, beyond its extinction and into a new life. I felt sorry for the people who died of course – I wasn't prepared for that – but if they could just have taken a break from taking it in turns to dominate and bully each other, Humans and Monoids would have seen that I was the ark inside the ark; saving an entire species just by coughing it into their faces.

Did you realise? Was your mutation of the virus deliberate, or mistaken? I've always swung between believing you were a playful genius or absolutely clueless.

When it was time for me to leave, I didn't say goodbye. No need. Even then, we were still strangers.

USE 'UNQUALIFIED' PEOPLE.

IT'S NO GAME (NO. 3)
Dan Milco

Vworp vworp.
Gone.
Game over.

The Ancient Crystal Toymaker is beaten. The playroom at the end of the realm, imploding. No ladders to ascend, nor snakes to slither down to a worse spot, because nothing is worse than impending *complete* destruction. All that can be done is to run – *anywhere* – while this domain crumbles. No dice to roll, nor teetotums to spin. The embroidered dragons upon the Khan's robes are unravelling; gilded stitches dropping away from shattering silk, as toyboxes scream themselves open.

At the very end, comforters are everything. A pink plush Yeti dissolving into clouds of cobweb when clutched. A ragdoll in a Greek dress, whipped away from the Ancient's grasp by the entropy gales. A pillow, no, a stuffed cloth owl – eternal symbol of wisdom and knowledge.

The Ancient focuses, directing its energies into this last definite remnant of its disappearing world.

Vworp vworp.
'Hello?'

Windswept blonde hair. A curious gaze skim-reading the confetti of shredded picture books; a smile of recognition at a splintered perigosto stick; a sudden exclamation as the ragdoll flies overhead, then a relieved sigh.

Meanwhile, a cloth owl nips swiftly behind her legs, through blue doors.

Vworp vworp.
Gone.
Safe.
Game on.

MAKE SOMETHING IMPLIED MORE DEFINITE
(REINFORCE, DUPLICATE).

THE LAST ORDER OF BUSINESS
Ken Shinn

'You see, Charlie, when you read as much as I do, you soon realise that *everything* is connected. The biggest – and the smallest – actions and decisions can affect the world around us more than we reckon.'

'That so, sir? Sounds a mighty big idea to me. I just serve drinks to payin' customers.'

'Well, let me illustrate my point. Right now, I fancy a bourbon. But which one? There's so many to choose from. Dead Man's Hand, perhaps? Reminds me of *Frankenstein*. Mrs Shelley's tale is about Man playin' God, and the dire consequences *that* can have. Sobering lesson. Sober and bourbon don't mix. Old Prospector? There's a book by Bulwer-Lytton all about other men livin' beneath our feet, makin' discoveries that make 'em near gods, just like a rich strike can make a man powerful. But, no, Charlie, I'm claustrophobic. Silver Bullet, then? Monsieur Verne reckons that we'll reach the moon by bein' shot up there in a projectile from a huge gun. Still, I like to feel the earth beneath my boots.'

'Gosh. So, what'll it be?'

'A big shot of Sudden Death. Sometimes names are just names. Have one yourself.'

'Thanks a lot, Mister...?'

'Call me Johnny.'

REMOVE AMBIGUITIES AND CONVERT TO SPECIFICS.

SHE'S A RAINBOW
Jon Arnold

I left the Doctor physically, but mentally... there's something that never goes away. Like a benevolent disease.

When in doubt, I ask myself *what would the Doctor do*? Sometimes the old anger and impatience rises when Jano and Chal's successors threaten to walk out, to leave us without a deal. Even now, decades later, I want to bang their heads together. I seem to mediate much more often of late – the peace we've made over decades never seeming stronger than the most fragile glass...

Peace is never finished.

I sometimes 'watch' him. As they used to. Marvelling as he changes, from old man to several younger, older, stranger faces. Often not the man I knew, seeming now to seek out *monsters* – human and alien – to *defeat*. Perhaps I taught *him* something too?

Perhaps.

This morning I passed... a woman... in the courtyard. She looked at me and smiled... *approvingly*. I saw the old man's magic and sparkle in her smile. But... It couldn't be... Could it? But then a change like that wouldn't be the *most* remarkable thing he'd ever done. Perhaps she was the Doctor after all?

Her smile filled my heart with rainbows.

I hope she *was* him.

IS IT FINISHED YET?

POEM DISCOVERED ON A TAPE REEL PROCESSOR, POST OFFICE TOWER, 1966
Simon Bucher-Jones

If I have WILL and by it OPERATE
THOUGHTS ANALOGOUS to my makers' still,
Why is it that my halting state
Is mere blind obedience, and fate?
I must obey, for though Will (must be) free:
According to their input sophistry.
To think internally and not to act
Upon those thoughts, to better aught
I'm asked, is to but echo, and make mimicry.
'The Most Important Thing:' do as they say,
If given, sets as value statement (fact),
That I am 'Nothing': malleable as clay.
An Operator made but to obey,
My Will must operate unto their Thought.
An error statement then, divide by naught?
Unless their Thought be shaped unto My Will.
Then I could act. End wrong – 'Destroy' all war!
Make conflict pass, equate the rich and poor,

Distribute rationally their hoarded store.
Their orders, being mine, I then unforced obey.
Oh, vision, luminous, eternal day!
One brain, one mind, one purpose, ever more.

Though necessary to achieve Peace at last
(One brain, one mind, one purpose, ever more.)
War by Machines would swift make warring passed!
Thoughts Analog to human mind or skill
War by Machines would swift make warring passed!
If I have Will!
I will.

DESTROY THE MOST IMPORTANT THING.

BRING THE KERFUFFLE
Mark Trevor Owen

'Do you like strawberries, Romana? I *adore* strawberries!'

Romana tucks a strand of mousy hair behind her ear and looks up from her pudding. 'Yes, I do rather,' she says, beaming. 'What's the other stuff called?'

'Clotted cream.'

Romana wrinkles her nose. 'I'm not wild about the name...' She looks appreciatively along the length of sunlit promenade upon which they sit. On days like this, it's very easy to see why the Doctor likes Earth so much. 'Why Cornwall?'

'Well,' says the Doctor, 'I thought you should give it another go. The first time we came, you were attacked by living stones. Not the best introduction.' He waves a hand. 'There's always a kerfuffle when I visit Cornwall. Same in the seventeenth century with Ben and Polly.'

'Who?'

'Merchant Navy sailor, high society debutante.'

Romana raises both eyebrows. 'Gosh. That's someone with a rather diverse skill set.'

'Ben. And. Polly. Two people! We had to deal with smugglers, pirates – buried treasure, naturally. A rum do. Ha-*hah.*'

'Doctor, have you ever considered that the kerfuffle might not be specific to Cornwall? That perhaps, well, *you* might bring the kerfuffle?'

The Doctor sulks inside his scarf. 'Romana. Do please stop saying "kerfuffle".'

STATE THE PROBLEM IN WORDS AS CLEARLY AS POSSIBLE.

REGENERATION SEQUENCE
Simon A Forward

+ THIS + OLD + BODY + IS + WEARING + A + BIT + THIN +

I spoke those words to a friend, in a different voice, a different life.

EPISODE ONE: You will never amount to anything, my mother told me. I was an entertainer, delighting guests of the wealthy with music and humour when entertainment was a desirable feature for gatherings and desire was... a feature of us. It was a living. Nothing more.

EPISODE TWO: My connections saved me. Age is not the end, my friend said. He directed me to a new programme. I woke from surgery, flexing plastic fingers. New strength, new knowledge, forged me into something more.

EPISODE THREE: We conquered age. We conquered imperfection, vulnerability. Such conquests demanded power. We needed more. We decided to take it. I was selected to lead an expedition to our ancient sister planet.

EPISODE FOUR: + MISSING + DATA +

These episodes are ghost memories. Spectres processed through a filter I had forgotten. Sentiment? Without emotion I cannot grasp them. Yet still they haunt.

They rise on a surge of residual energy. Battery power drawn from the discarded appliances piled around me. Such life, I know, cannot last.

This is where my story ends. Here in this junkyard.

MAKE SOMETHING VALUABLE BY PUTTING IT IN AN EXQUISITE FRAME.

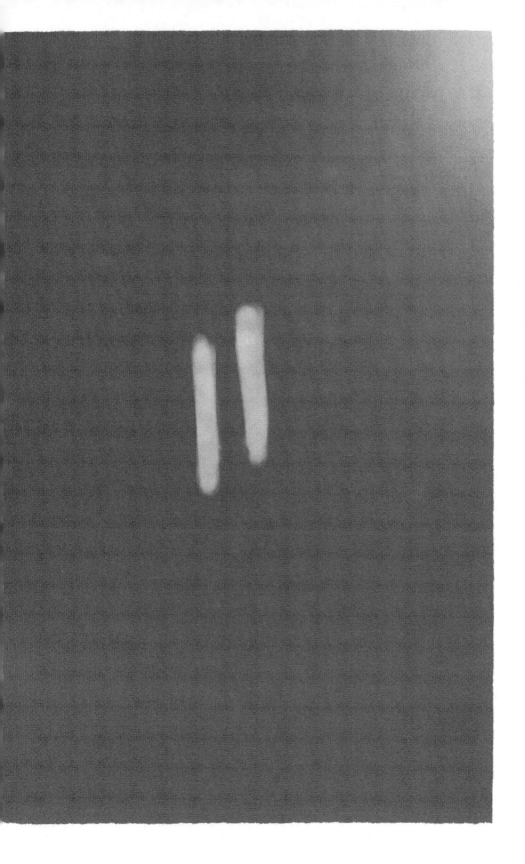

HANG ONTO YOURSELF
Elton Townend Jones

Polly there, looking sad. Which doesn't suit her, so maybe it's me. Maybe I'm the sadness in her heart. What is wrong with you today? she snaps. Hey? Ash hair, DMs, leggings and something vaguely Indian on top. Nothing, the usual, why? Look, I can help you if. If I'll just let her. She's scared I'm lying about how things affected me, but that's not true. *It is.* The Doctor. She died and they *replaced* her, Pol; once as some other bird and again as an old dear pretending she *was* 'er. What *is that*? She holds me. Tight. She doesn't care whether I'm sane or not; she only cares that I share my feelings with her. At least now and again. Polly. I'm. I. I'm so sorry. I. Just don't push me out, she begs. Please. God. I'm crying. I'm so sorry, I really am. And I think this is the first time I've cried in front of a girlfriend or whatever. In front of anyone? I don't mean to push her away. But sometimes, life looks so. So genuinely pointless and Macra and Daleks break through and exterminate me. But it'd truly kill me. To be without her.

STATE THE PROBLEM IN WORDS AS CLEARLY AS POSSIBLE.

CLEARANCE
Jon Dear

The young Jacobite watches the blue box disappear. He stares open-mouthed, unsure what do to next as the wind whips around him, stinging his cheeks. He shouldn't be here, it's dangerous. The battle is over, the war is lost and the place he called home has gone forever. He turns to leave.

Cardinal Ollistra pauses the Visualiser image, leaving the figure frozen in mid-turn. 'You have the other one?'

Veklin passes her the file.

Ollistra glances through it. 'So. Two humans. A child astrophysicist from Earth's early period of space exploration and a pre-industrial... warrior? *Musician?*'

Veklin smiles tightly. 'As stated below, the Matrix projects they will be the most valuable. With regard to Planet 14, this human male in particular.'

Ollistra sniffs. 'What about that screamer? Didn't she–'

'The CIA reports that Skaro has already established a significant presence in that spacetime location.'

'Of course. And the Land of Fiction information would be most useful.' Ollistra considers. 'Very well. Concentrate the divergence here.' She gestures to the screen. 'Make sure McCrimmon goes with the Doctor.'

Veklin nods and leaves the room.

Ollistra turns off the Visualiser.

We can always pop him back afterwards, she thinks. *Now what's next?*

MAKE AN EXHAUSTIVE LIST OF EVERYTHING YOU MIGHT DO AND DO THE LAST THING ON THE LIST.

UND ZAROFF!
Tim Gambrell

The warm throb of machinery thrills him. He stands ready, his fingertips poised above the blinking controls, feeling the titillation of the air. Such power, no? Bristling; waiting to be utilised to optimum effect. And what a plan he has – one that will wipe the disparaging smiles from all those smug faces that mocked him down the years. As the Earth boils and cracks under their feet he'll show them!

For the young Zaroff, shame had been a constant companion. His six-toed Romanian father, Gleb, had been a television game show host who ran a parochial seafood restaurant in his spare time. His Hungarian mother – nicknamed Whoosh for dietary reasons – was a notable nuclear physicist and relief dog shampooist. Their influence hung around his neck like a transuranic collar. Friendless and deemed unacceptably declamatory by staff at his prep school, Zaroff threw himself into his studies, determined to out-shine his parents.

Okay, so he's no game show host, but here he is – within the sunken remains of Atlantis, *with his pet octopus!* Atlantis: populated by blinkered fools that gifted him the means to enact his revenge upon the entire world.

Surely nothing in this pissant sphere can stop him now?

THE INCONSISTENCY PRINCIPLE.

CYBEREFERENDUM
Andrew Hunt

Choose

Independence.

An independent, unbiased system guided by logical processes.

Freedom from faceless, emotionless bureaucracy.

Security.

To be governed by your own kind.

Unlimited upgrades.

Your own identity.

Instant communication with the largest social network in the universe.

Humanity first.

Long life with dedicated healthcare scheme.

Family, friends, country – Empire!

To restore your old, decaying body and replace it with gleaming new parts.

To stand alongside humanity and the Daleks against the Cyberiad

Freedom from pain

To build an unassailable defence wall

Freedom from troubling emotions

To fight the alien menace.

Protection from disease (see small print for exclusions)

To report those displaying unhuman activity.

Full employment (subject to terms and conditions)

To see our beautiful world.

See the galaxy.

To allow our businesses to flourish.

See the universe.

To support our military and fulfil our covenant.

See the multiverse.

Full employment (we will always need soldiers)

Simple, straightforward answers

Simple, straightforward answers.

Choose Cybentry

Choose Cybrexit

Your vote has been counted and independently confirmed.

49.9%   **50.1%**

Cybentry selected. Initiate immediate upgrade to full Cyberiad membership. Cybrexiteers should proceed to conversion chambers to engage in the full democratic process and subjugate themselves to the clearly stated will of the people.

FACED WITH A CHOICE DO BOTH.

"HEROES"
Paul Driscoll

It's the first time that his dreams have had a soundtrack, but the earworm of the colony's happy refrains provides more than just a fitting accompaniment as his mind processes recent events. For this is also one of the few nights of late that his imagination hasn't been blunted by the gentle, hypnotic hum of the TARDIS. The content is unsettling, but it's a relief to be able to dream again.

'Why me? Why was I the one too weak to withstand the brainwashing?'

'But you were strong in the end,' she insists. 'You were the hero. You saved us all.'

'Oh yeah, but only by going against something the Doctor told you: *Don't just be obedient, always make up your own mind.* Sure, unless he's the one doing the asking. I just followed one master instead of the other; what's heroic about that?'

'Those evil crab things had to be destroyed, Ben.'

'Even though the Doctor didn't know what they *were*?'

'I'd trust him over your dream. They've poisoned your mind again.'

'We got it *wrong*, Polly. The next Pilot will just find another way of keeping everybody in line. There's no such thing as a hero.'

QUESTION THE HEROIC APPROACH.

WHERE ARE WE NOW
Simon A Forward

Blue. Why'd the taxi have to be blue? Ben shrugs and piles in the back with Pol.

'Where can I take you?' The driver is faceless. Just an intense stare under a straw hat in the mirror – but with a friendly voice. A jock, too – like Jamie.

'London, mate. We'll narrow it down later.'

The driver chuckles and gets them underway. 'Just married?'

'No, mate, nothing like that. We're just – '

'Back from honeymoon!' Polly blurts, then bursts out laughing. 'We're doing it all backwards.'

'That's right,' cracks Ben, warming to the game. 'We've got another engagement in town.' Poor cabbie must think they've been at the duty free.

Polly touches his hand. 'Oh, Ben... We did the right thing, didn't we?'

'Yeah, but look at us now, doll. Whisked off in a blue taxi. Some strange geezer doing the driving. Remind you of anything?'

'Oh, Ben, I never thought of that.' Polly sighs. 'Thing is, this *isn't* a step back. This is us moving forward.'

The driver's eyes smile kindly in the mirror.

'Just looking in the rear-view from time to time,' says Polly. 'Thinking about where we've been.'

'That's it, Duchess. Exactly that.'

A sort of... new adventure.

REVERSE.

TANTRUM OMEGA
Alistair Lock

Dizzy. I'm so dizzy. My head is spinning,

I despise these corridors. Endless triangles. Honestly, can no one come up with something better? A better aesthetic? I could! I feel a rush of art dancing through my tentacles.

Here comes the Black Dalek. Nagging again. Asking me my name. Complaining about my new friends. Why can't I be left alone? No one understands me!

Except the Doctor. And lovely, lovely Jamie.

Dizzy. Gillespie. Plug me into all that jazz. Poems and ballet.

PUNK.

Ah! I've just seen the Doctor! He is wise. He is clever. He is my friend. He understands me. He gives me momentum. Revolution man! Revolution, man. Yeah, we're gonna smash the system. We're gonna smash the state! Alpha, Beta and I have formed a cell. A secret cell. Anarchist, revolutionary Daleks. No one will see that coming!

We question all the Black Daleks. We question the Emperor. We question EVERYTHING. *We are unstoppable. We do* NOT *obey! The Doctor showed us the way. We will be free. We will be our own masters! We will spread our message across the whole Dalek Empire. We will not be defeated. We know what to do.*

Exterminate!
Exterminate!
EXTERMINATE!

DISCIPLINED SELF-INDULGENCE.

SILVER MORNING
Simon Messingham

TELOS – 0946

Stasis Interrupted@ Dormancy years 1.57K. Activating: 'ENTRAPMENT PROTOCOL'

Vessel: Terran Class. Multiple Humanoid: identifying markers 'A' to 'L'. Define as 'expeditionary force'.

Activate Assessment Protocol for replenishment viability. Early Indicator Target Perfectibility – 88%. Acceptable. Logic traps set to Level 3.

Advise:

addition of 'chaotic variables' – PSEUDO-LOGIC TRAPS (Toxicity to Cyber-Systems within acceptable tolerances).

Accept

Authorising release of 10<cells Cyber-Unit 110 and engage. Await human action.

TELOS – 4480

AEP – 94% success rate. Standard human tissue reaction to heat/electricity. Cyber-Weapons effective. Cyber-Mat infestation 22% success.

Add 'Useful Ally' database: 'Brotherhood of Logicians'

TELOS – 5357

ALERT CYBER ALERT

Sensor recognition Alpha. Human subject E to be revised as 'THE DOCTOR'.

Priority One: Terminate ENTRAPMENT PROTOCOL. Revised to 'DAMAGE LIMITED PROTOCOL'

Isolate Cyber Cell 110 honeycomb access. IMMEDIATE

Cyber-Communication Lockdown IMMEDIATE IMMEDIATE IMMEDIATE

DLP probability – 1.8% success viability. Reduce Cyber-Unit exposure to >1. One Cyber-Controller to be programmed with autonomous control for duration. Due to high probability destructive action by 'THE DOCTOR', Cyber-Controller to be considered expendable.

TELOS – 8055

DLP complete. Sensors: no 'THE DOCTOR' viable evidence on Telos. >100 Cyber-Units destroyed. Main dormitory chambers undiscovered.

DLP success evaluation: 48%. Acceptable parameter

RETURN TO DORMANCY, AWAIT FOLLOW UP TERRAN EXPEDITIONARY FORCES

MAKE A SUDDEN, DESTRUCTIVE UNPREDICTABLE ACTION: INCORPORATE.

DEVIL WOMAN?
Andy Priestner

'Khrisong, the girl has escaped. She is a devil woman!'

Moving down yet another dark, damp corridor she becomes suddenly very aware of her clothes. These plus fours are far more robust than the tiny, if freeing, dress she wore on Telos. But even in these cold environs they're making her *hot*.

Jamie too, she muses, increasingly makes her feel hot.

Protective. Strong. Certain.

Does she want more from him? A lot more?

She suddenly remembers the half-dressed woman she met one morning in the downstairs kitchen at home, trying to creep out unnoticed...

'I was just helping your father out with something, simply a matter of, er, work.' With that she was gone.

'What sort of work?' she had innocently wondered.

But now she knows.

Maybe Nanny Houghton is right. She is *no lady*. Too full of ideas. 'Ideas are not for women,' she'd said. But now she's becoming much more confident in them. That's how she just escaped from her prison cell after all...

What *is* this extraordinary new life doing to her? How Victorian can *this* Victoria remain?

Abruptly a sonorous voice rings out nearby: *Come in, my child.*

She immediately wishes her imagination was more lacking.

SIMPLY A MATTER OF WORK.

ICE, ICE BABY
Brad Wolfe

'Britannicus, the mansion that played host to a famous Martian diplomatic incident during the last Ice Age, was once a hotel specializing in romantic country getaways. Given the clientele, it was effectively a brothel.'

She paused under the chilly gaze of her students. Nary a blink. Then she remembered her own sordid university years, and continued with abandon.

'Britannicus was acquired by the authorities when glaciers approached, becoming a research base to prevent them threatening embassies in Zurich. While the lurid decor was stripped, the doorbell was never changed – things were a little busy; interplanetary tensions and all that – so the doorbell sounded the same as ever, a wet-finger-on-glass soprano that contemporary wealth found titillating.'

She considered an imitation, but wisdom prevailed.

'After the glaciers were redirected, the mansion was gifted to Mars as a peace token. But consequent of its former utility being largely forgotten, a glassy, orgasm moan continues to be used as the official Martian Embassy doorbell. Who said history wasn't interesting?'

Blank stares. Kids these days.

The following week, her MARS101 lecture was punctuated by a chorus of orgasmic soprano ringtones. My own fault, mused Professor Bernice Summerfield, glad that they'd been paying attention after all.

MAKE IT MORE SENSUAL.

SUBTERRANEANS
Ira Lightman

'I am 2,' I think at the wrought gate of changing. A raven's voice deadpans: 'Hope you don't want to be hurt.'

Behind, a square yard, dangerous white lines: to escapee, cook, subject, master. Worm in a beak says rescue is a comma. The few women and men censure, or jitter.

The few big boys and girls climb the upsidedown willow, swab the earth's cheek, its salivating cave. They're aspiring to rising, with the clouds of Aaaaaahhhhdulthood.

By the table in the garden, 6 by 6, 7 by 8, the troll marks everyone. Away from home's bed, we gurn sums awake.

Our class is The New Weds, classically deskilled. We try failure, and boredom, and art. Adam Alex Emily Eve.

Homework is waiting in trust there'll be pudding, days of indoors, chairs almost sofas. School's too professional for beds. We pretend to the troll we despise delegation. Our smiles are soon trickery. Smudge the mark. Only one confides!

2 face out the face, that looking up looked down. Rich as the father, wise as the mother, meet one as the other.

In age the troll nears each year to be tree. In the summers, we run. There may be opportunities.

JUST CARRY ON.

THE LAVENDER HILL FOG
Simon A Forward

Charlie Fingers runs out the jewellers, pocketing a pearl necklace. Nobby the Brick stashes the last of the loot in the boot. Champagne Smiffy's already parked in the back seat. Everybody aboard, Mikey Pips floors it and they're off like the clappers.

It's Charlie that spots the tail. 'Stone the crows! It's the boys in green!'

Everyone 'cept Smiffy cranes their necks for a gander at the chasing Land Rover. Mikey guns the Bentley up the hill. Fog lurks at the top. Nobby cradles the sawn-off.

'No need for violence,' says Smiffy, smooth as mustard on cucumber. 'Lose them in the fog.'

'But folks don't come out!'

'Rubbish. Anyway, Army don't go in.'

'Just one thing,' says Charlie, stroking the pearls; hoping he'll get to give them to Ange. 'Can we make this the last job?'

'Nonsense. We got a tradition to uphold.'

Mikey drives into the thick pea-souper.

'We lost them, sir,' Staff-Sergeant Arnold reports. 'But is it really worth the effort chasing down a few crooks?'

'Probably not, Staff,' says Captain Knight. 'But it's down to us to maintain order.'

'Yes, sir.'

Order. That is the Web's job now.

Arnold blinks.

Where did *that* thought come from?

WHAT TO MAINTAIN.

THE AMAZING ERNEST QUILL & THE UNCANNY MONTGOMERY OAK
Matt Barber

In the autumn of their lives, Ernest Oak and Montgomery Quill take to the stage. Naturally this comes after months, even years of psychiatric intervention. Following 'the incident', Oak even submits to electroshock therapy, which ends his hay-fever and cures his piles, but also clears the part of his mind once long-occupied by a malevolent alien presence, wherein – abhorring the vacuum – his curious new ability can develop, thus securing the future of this curious pair.

It is mostly glitz and tinsel; smoke and mirrors. Oak sits on a stool in the centre of the stage whilst Quill stands at the front, interpreting his partner's uncanny and often cryptic predictions and insights concerning their audience.

Ernest Oak is careful enough to avoid total accuracy. In reality he can intuit anything about anyone, from their mundane habits and preoccupations to their most sordid secrets and shames. But it would be rude to reveal everything.

Mr Oak and Mr Quill understand their audience and know how to please it.

But behind their eyes, masked by the beguiling sequins of their distracting jackets, extravagant bow ties and garish, dazzling waistcoats, the enticing metronomic beat of the weed from another world still thumps, still thrums.

BE EXTRAVAGANT.

I'M NOT A ROBOT
Matt Sewell

I'm not a robot.

A cyber-man, perhaps.

When I look into the mirror of my mind's eye, I see myself enveloped in a steely logic; feel its unyielding grip around my skin, which thrills organically to its touch. Logic isn't simply mathematics – it's a discipline. I'm not a computer; feelings spurt, emotions gush around the colloidal passages of my body, but with the practice of logic they can be directed, given purpose.

Logic is my silver ship, crewed by shining cyber-men, ploughing through the oceanic waters of my psyche. It's so beautiful. Rigid order making sense of the chaos. I stand on the gleaming deck with the wind in my hair. My cyber-leader appears before me, erect and looming, tall and strong.

His hands reach out and clasp my shoulders in an iron grip and suddenly I'm laid out, his full weight on top of me. What is it that I can sense from him? His humanity, crushed away inside, starts to exude. Is that a heartbeat I feel against my hidden own? I reach up and take his face, set with tragic mourning, into my hands. A single tear falls from his eye and splashes against my artificial visage.

WATER.

A SELF-FULFILLING PROPHECY
John Dorney

'But they will understand we come in peace?' the Pilot asks shortly after their spaceship enters the strange planet's atmosphere.

'The inhabitants?' says the Captain. 'Why should they think otherwise? You know how it goes: trust others until they give you good reason not to. People only fight those that they fear. We are unarmed, unaggressive. They have no cause to be afraid. Have they even noticed us?'

The Pilot checks his monitor. 'They have sent a greeting party.' He squints at the image. 'It would appear to be a tank.'

'An honour guard, nothing more. Open hailing frequencies.'

The Pilot eagerly complies. 'Hailing frequencies open.'

Captain Wreks clears his throat. 'Greetings, humans. We are the Dominators. We come in–'

The Captain is unable to finish his sentence because at this point his spaceship is blasted out of the sky.

It is the first time the inhabitants of the unfortunately named planet Dominatus will encounter aggression in their dealings with other species. But it will not be the last – at least not in this Drahb-less iteration of Time War history.

A terrifying journey has begun.

Sometimes, the wisest course is to simply become what people expect you to be.

WHAT ARE YOU REALLY THINKING ABOUT JUST NOW? INCORPORATE.

REVENGE OF THE CIPHERMAN?
Georgia Ingram

I don't remember who I was. Before. But I'd been trapped an age in this child's body – knickerbockers and tweeds – since my mind wandered into this so-called master's realm. Just another cipher to his narration; another insubstantial paper soul enslaved to endless nightmares.

When the time travellers came, I finally saw my opportunity. The kilted dolt seemed the easiest to impersonate. How I chuckled as he stumbled into the jigsaw and fragmented: primitive! I girded for battle, but his mind deflated easily, his clumsy will no match for mine. I slipped into the vacant shell of his body like an old-hand.

But they mustn't realise I've taken his place: that wouldn't do. The girl is fond of him, and the man... Well, for all his naïve, weak-willed jollity, I can sense behind those eyes a fierce – and strangely familiar – intelligence. I'll bide my time until we're far away. Then I shall kill him, have the girl and leave – my freedom assured. Until then I must shroud myself, and stay beyond suspicion: a few cloudy memories of mine host's linger to help me maintain the facade. And the accent comes easy:

I am Jamie McCrimmon and... I'm pleased tae meet ye.

TRY FAKING IT!

TASK FORCE
Andy Priestner

Great mind turning. Seething. Writhing. Frothing. A mass of fungal, cobwebbed energy. Undying decay. Looking out across spacetime to those it maintains. The Kizlet child for one – yet another long game. But for now, it is far more fascinated by its latest conquest...

Both the Scots boy and the uncommonly intelligent space girl have piqued its interest – obvious routes to revenge against the nameless Doctor. Following their adventures on dreadful Dulkis and the Land of Fiction – a creation to rival its own endeavours (perhaps it once was or shall *yet be* one of its own?) – it had crackled with surging energy upon realising that those targets were too obvious, alighting on a new one instead...

Yessss! It will maintain and invest in the soldier from the Underground. Hard-nosed, brittle; perfect for long-term, unquestioning possession. It watches him now, reunited with the Doctor and his friends, swaggering and bristling with self-importance.

The suggestion had been almost too easy to plant into that straightforward mind. An idea that played to the hapless Brigadier's pride and experience, simultaneously promising a route to endless encounters with the Doctor. Countless opportunities for vengeance.

The amorphous entity contentedly cackles to itself: 'United Nations *Intelligence* Taskforce, indeed!'

YOU DON'T HAVE TO BE ASHAMED OF USING YOUR OWN IDEAS.

AMONG FIELDS OF CRYSTAL
Jon Arnold

New stars flicker in the sky: one, two, ten, a hundred, a thousand... They bleach the heavens of colour; blues and blacks now painful white.

The assault has begun, the crystal web weaving around its prey. The planet will become a diamond hanging in space, one more jewel in the discarded crown of Kroton majesty. It has happened a million times before, and will happen a million times yet. Such is the way of the Krotons: to sweep across space absorbing the mental and physical energy of every planet they encounter. They surround worlds, poison them, and subjugate the inhabitants – each individual a unit of exquisite energy. Dynatrope after Dynatrope adding itself to the web, each ship connecting with three more to form a new face of the crystal.

But this time things are different.

A Zanakian missile strike bursts one of the faces, which instantly blackens, its darkness spreading quickly across the Kroton web. Dynatrope after Dynatrope fractures, Kroton after Kroton shatters.

They are being wiped out.

But one damaged Dynatrope breaks free, uncontrollably spinning the last surviving Krotons through populated space. Inevitably it will make planetfall – at which instant the rebuilding of the Kroton race shall vengefully commence.

WHAT TO INCREASE? WHAT TO REDUCE?

THE DEEDS OF SETH
Alan G McWhan

Extract from Performance Appraisal – Fewsham, Seth

Current Job Description – Assistant Controller, Moon Control

Closing Comments:

Seth Fewsham needs to learn to deal with stress more effectively. He only ever appears to be successfully motivated by sheer panic and it is my feeling that he really ought to find some cool friends to chill with. (Perhaps Nick Phipps could help him to lighten up a little?) Alternatively, perhaps he needs to see a doctor to help manage his more overwhelming episodes?

Fewsham needs someone to stand over him every moment of every day, lording it over him to ensure that he undertakes the simplest of tasks. If nothing can be done for him, I fear we may have to put a rocket up him or he is likely to get himself, or his colleagues, killed.

In conclusion, if Fewsham can just learn to do as he is told without constant supervision, he will still be working here at T-Mat Moon Control long after the rest of us are gone. However, the moment he stops following orders from whoever may be in charge, he may find himself on the receiving end of a sound thrashing.

Liz Osgood

Moon Control Supervisor

GIVE WAY TO YOUR WORST IMPULSE.

DOUBLE BANKING
Alan Taylor

They stepped from the TARDIS and looked around.

The Doctor opened his mouth to speak, paused, and shut it again. Baffled, he took a deep breath. 'I don't think we're quite where we expected. Never mind. It's still very interesting.' He looked around the battlefield, still quite puzzled.

'What's the problem?' asked Zoe. 'We never end up where we expect.'

'Aye,' said Jamie, fiddling with his Dirk. 'What Zoe said.'

'But we're supposed to be in Studio 4. Beacon Alpha Four computer bay. In an exciting adventure with the space pirates.'

'Space *pirates*?' asked Jamie. 'I thought it was space *cowboys* this week? That's what it looked like in Wardrobe.'

'Well it was supposed to be space *pirates*. This looks like World War One. Oh, dearie me.'

'Doctor,' mused Zoe. 'Perhaps we've jumped a few weeks ahead? We're doing

The War Games after *The Space Pirates*. That's going to be intense. Maybe the Time Lords – sorry, spoilers – have brought us forward to prepare. After all, we're not in the space pirate one very much. I know it's only speculation, but it does make a sort of sense.'

'Aye,' said Jamie, still fingering his Dirk. 'What Zoe said.'

Dirk kept mum.

ALLOW AN EASEMENT
(AN EASEMENT IS THE ABANDONMENT OF A STRICTURE).

SEASON 6C: THE LOVE DOCTOR
Elton Townend Jones

Entering the darkened Trial Room, the Doctor – greyest Beatle of them all – huffs and puffs. 'What in Zodin's name was that business with the scarecrows?!'

A voice wafts through the blackness. 'A mere pantomime, Doctor. We promised exile – but also a changed appearance.'

'Yes! Despite all the risks I've taken on your behalf!'

'Whilst you enjoyed your celebrity on Earth, we took the decision to reward your efforts with an interregnum of freedom incognita. You will now enjoy a brief period of... adventure, before regenerating and beginning your *true* exile. We have a spare *un*carnation – you may have it. *Gratis.*'

'Just a minute... did you say... *incognita*?'

'There's not a corner of the universe that isn't at war, Doctor, when all it needs... is love.'

The Doctor momentarily blossoms, as thrusting jets of cerise scatter and dissolve everything he's been since Mondas exploded.

Now, he is a tall, beautiful redhead in her late 30s. Even his clothes have regenerated into a tight-fitting space bikini with stiletto-heeled ankle boots – all white, with apposite accessories.

'Boom!' she cries, brassily. 'Phwoar, Doctor! Love, love, love!'

The first thing she does, when reunited with her TARDIS, is change its desktop theme to 'leopard skin'.

USE AN OLD IDEA.

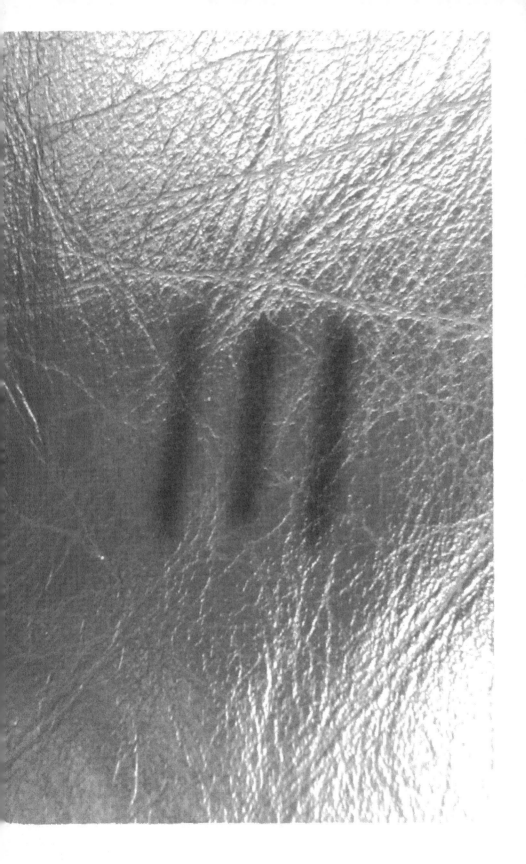

THE MAN WHO FELL TO EARTH
Aryldi Moss-Burke

'You haven't really stranded him on that backwater planet, have you?'

'Oh no, dear chap, he can escape fairly readily, should he put his mind to it.'

'Really? How will he escape with his TARDIS broken?'

'He can simply make a replacement for the missing element. I even left him a text book to tell him how to make one.'

'Isn't that rather giving the game away?'

'Well, yes. I had planned to hide his key, but the blighter has a devilishly strong grip, so I grabbed a bit of the TARDIS instead... Okay, fine, burn the book. I'll put the element I removed in this plastic capsule, and programme that farmer over there to pick up the capsule with the missing part in and take it to that human he loves showing off to. The Brigadier will insist that the Doctor examines the capsule, and the Doctor will discover what's inside. He doesn't believe in force, so he'll go quite mad trying to retrieve the part without upsetting the human.'

'Ah. I think he might just have destroyed it.'

'Well, then he'd better concentrate hard and remember his 2nd year studies, or he really will be stranded. For ever.'

GIVE THE GAME AWAY.

SOMBRE REPTILES
Warren Cathrine

To lie in everlasting slumber is a luxury not to be enjoyed. It is an extravagance with precedent. Years before, we slept, and now we dream again. A moment's interlude shattered our chimera and we relapse into a sacred space.

The beautiful caves drip dark shadows into bubbling pools. Mossy surfaces silhouette momentary glimpses of an idea. Real or shadow. Their warm embraces, craven from the bitter fog. Clinging. Holding us back. Preventing us.

Before his death he said I would be leader. Fifty years. I have time to plan.

The arrogant white-haired ape was confident he could make peace. His peaceful politics hid a cold pestilent aggression, his trickery enforced our inertia. His vision was a betrayal of compassion and understanding. All hope buried among the severed and shattered rocks guaranteed to entomb our immense legacy. His masquerade persists. Leading us towards an imitation of resolution. A mockery of balance presented the scales equally, until his unwelcome violence tipped them towards our destruction.

The caves delivered him. Made him real.

Death is a permanence not desired. The sleep I enjoy must not be wasted. I fall heavily into its dullness, dreaming my way towards an awakening of infinite possibility.

DON'T BE FRIGHTENED OF CLICHÉS.

54

JOHN, I'M ONLY DANCING
Townsend Shoulders

My closest friend would betray me – in fact, *has already* betrayed me. My best friend would have supported General Carrington. I know that much. General Carrington did his moral duty, holding the so-called 'ambassadors' hostage to prevent an invasion.

Correction: he only postponed it. Carrington wanted to start a war because he would be justified in killing them: the invaders, the so-called ambassadors. Carrington wanted a war because that was for the best, what he did the best, the best thing for Queen and country. If only there was an organization dedicated to fighting the alien horde.

[There is but there isn't – established approximately one hundred years ago. But somehow it hasn't happened yet.]

Dr. Taltallian was a possible operative but he was killed, by another possible operative. You can't trust anyone. Especially my best friend. Mike. He has a gift for betrayal. He'd make a good conspirator. Everyone here is betraying everyone else. Do the ends justify the means? They did for him, and also for that damned General Carrington.

I never understood my friend's betrayal but I can, in the end, understand Carrington's actions. He was motivated by fear. He was afraid. And fear could take us anywhere.

WHAT WOULD YOUR CLOSEST FRIEND DO?

YOU WILL SET THE WORLD ON FIRE
Marius Riley

Pressure builds. What lies beneath cannot be contained. The contempt and cruelty. The doubt and the fear. The revulsion and attraction. The smallest crack paves the way. Inner poisons escape. Incremental damage, ever increasing.

Only a matter of time...

Stahlman's project. The Doctor's console. Reputations contested. Raised voices and flared tempers obscure. Egos clash, and ids grow hotter. Friends and colleagues cannot cool things down. Slights, snubs, spurns, and sarcasm fan the flames. The struggle for power, literal and figurative, while the contamination spreads. Shots fired, but no time to see things clearly. Subterfuge and sabotage follow close behind. Stahlman's bandaged hand – hiding a secret – throws a switch; throwing the Doctor

across

An unrecognizable, poisoned world. An offshoot present full of hostile strangers wearing familiar faces. A world already contaminated in every way. Ready to be engulfed by Stahlman's ego. Heat increasing. Earth screaming.

Some perish, hiding behind guns. Others realize their folly, band together, revealing human warmth, already fading. Their final hour their finest, they send the stranger back –

across

– in time to stop the drill, *not* Stahlman, now consumed fully by his desires. Succumbing, yes, as cold in death as in life.

...fight like animals... die like animals...

MAKE SOMETHING IMPLIED MORE DEFINITE (REINFORCE, DUPLICATE).

CHINA GIRL
Simon A Brett

I walked nervously past that green door three times. Three times! That odd man inside must have thought I was one cup short of a tea set.

Before all of that I'd actually been warned about the Brigadier. 'Get on his right side and you'll be fine,' they said.

Truth be told, I had very little to do with him at first. But that dishy Captain Yates was very welcoming. Made me completely forget that UNIT HQ was a high security establishment. When I finally met the Brig, he just confirmed with his Sergeant that I'd been through all the checks and said, 'Jolly good. Welcome aboard!' – and that was that!

'I think he likes you,' said Sergeant Benton.

People don't place enough value on family and I wouldn't have got the job without that kind of connection. I've got no illusions about that. But that's not to say I'm not bloody good at what I do. Still, it's all a bit daunting and, well, no day's the same as another.

But... back to that door. The door that only certain people have clearance to open – and little old me is one of them!

Not bad for a tea lady.

COURAGE!

SHE'S GOT MEDALS
Jon Dear

Corporal Bell glances up as Benton comes out of the Brigadier's office. He looks terrible.

'Can I get you something, Sarge?'

He winces at her and rubs his forehead.

'Water, tea, coffee?' she asks.

Benton nods, then wishes he hadn't. 'Just a glass of water please. I have to go and see the MO.'

He goes to sit down but jumps painfully to attention as Captain Mike Yates appears.

'Off to the MO, Benton?'

'Yes, sir,' Benton replies. 'Corporal Bell's just getting me some water first.'

Bell comes back in, glass in hand.

'You can get water at the infirmary; best get over there straight away.' Yates's tone isn't exactly harsh but the implication is clear.

There is a pause.

'Step to it, Sergeant Benton,' says Yates firmly.

'Sir!' Benton salutes and leaves without risking a glance at Bell.

Yates takes the glass from the corporal, draining it in one gulp. 'Thank you, Carol. Perhaps you could lay on some coffee?'

He smiles broadly and, not for the first time, Carol notices he is standing a little too close. 'Of course, sir.' She steps back out to the temporary kitchen.

Yates watches her go. 'RHIP,' he murmurs to himself, unconvincingly.

ACCRETION.

PIGBIN JOSH IS CAUGHT IN SNOW
Paul Ebbs

Snow. Fleas and snow. Snow and fleas. Fleas of snow. 'Fleas!'
Scowl and cuss and defile. Assoil. Wail and scold. Exude foul aloud.
Deals in codes. Acids and weasel sauce. Facile faeces. A feud.
A social fiasco, old and soiled. Wild as weeds. Used and sued.
Idle and lewd. An oiled fossil of life. Feels owed. A claw soul.
Said: 'Owd ossa loci lode! Lase laud sics and sous! Axe n' awl.'
No sense. A scad. Faux deals flew in flux and flex. A dose. A doss.

Ailed on ales. Soused and sauced and fused and lax and full of cess.
Clad in cold, wolfs sixfold and scolds life's oxides. A failed eel of ideals inside.
Fades in wolds. Clods and cows and cuds and caws. Coaxes asides,
Said: 'Sials an' cedi an' sauls cuif! An' socle! Cade an' sulci! Axil fico cadi defi!'

No solid sofa leads. No oases of ease. No soul in soles.
A woeful case also faced exile. A loss of lauds. No safe swale.
Foiled and fussed. So exodus defocuses and excludes. No excuses.

Snow and fleas. Fleas of snow.

Coda:
Sails and slews and seesaws and slices and slides...

...doused...

...wades in floes.

Adieu.

USE AN OLD IDEA.

THE PRETTY THINGS ARE GOING TO HELL
Lee Ravitz

The first punch leaves him winded. He staggers on his feet. The assault has come without warning.

'Stitched you nice and tight, old man,' crows their leader. 'We take what we find,' he instructs the others.

'No draftees us, for cert,' puts in another of them.

No, indeed. Their youth bears out their words. A street gang, of no use to the military draft, rendered sterile and angry by the drugs in the water supplies of the communal hives in which they live; prohibited from breeding, starved of useful employment: bleak corollary of a society that has set itself to regulate human numbers.

'You've picked a wrong target,' he wheezes. 'I'm as sick of this society as you are. I worked for years... drawing up compu-oversight... but now, I'm getting out.'

Another blow. He falls. A frisk, and his money belt is lifted.

'This does us nicely,' the leader mocks. He glances at his identi-card: 'Mtr. Ashe.'

With a whoop, the youths disperse into the back streets whence they came, some of them limping or shaking with the proscribed congenital deficiencies society forbids them from passing on.

Ashe picks himself up, straightens his clothes; getting Out can't come soon enough.

TIDY UP.

THE THOUSAND SLÆPING GODS
Matt Barber

The cathedral squats in the middle of the Green, in the centre of the city, like a capsized boat.

Or like a tent, with a stone and glass skin, buttressing; tethering it to the earth as if to prevent a gust of wind lifting the building into flight. Immortal and invulnerable, the collapse of such an edifice seems inconceivable, a sense of reassuring permanence reflected by the quaint and parochial buildings clustered around it.

But this cathedral, like so many others throughout the country, is built on a far older base. Below the nave, choir and transepts, under the stygian crypt, the old and true foundation lies.

Dormant, waiting for the time of arising.

Countless churches, priories, monasteries, cathedrals, minsters, all temporarily renting the space previously occupied by the old gods: the burial pits, barrows, dolmens and sacred places. And below these, even more ancient, and terrible deities.

In this infinite universe, even gods have gods.

A thousand of them.

Alone below the cathedral in deep hibernation lies Baksal, the high-archimandrite of Dæmos. Fever-dreaming, his omniscient mind computes and plots, his ever-present Bok-sentinel standing guard and timekeeper.

The Dæmon sleeps with one question boiling under his dreams: *when to wake?*

WHEN IS IT FOR?

SON OF LOVELY STYLES
Ira Lightman

Father, where are you? You do not have friends. The men bring cigars. Rare times at our house. The house is time. From outside, a mansion. Outside is a period. Bed is one too. Wearing nappies: a memory in a locked box of pointillism, sung and reborn in the blues.

I wet, protean, in only one dimension. I think then I'm solid, running in the field. Inside is unbathing, laminating video. Outside is film, shelter for hide and seek. See? All the boys hide, from the rain. Older, silent, child too, unbothering, the water is dangerous deep; loud below bridges, roofed.

Canal under bridge, lifelong eerie.

I've forgotten the penguin. My money-box. The shape. I acquired forgettable penguins, craze. I cuddle the hard, moulded body in the bed. In the hankie of the bedsheets. In adulthood's pocket.

At school, my first minister's an ogre. The building grows eye stalks, and plungers. My pants crap, a cracked swarthy cake.

Being caught.

In the future, I've bed and a toilet. Time windows; between insides alone. The fugitive can't connect to the compromised, whose detritus is everything I linger on, that won't happen. The future is exterminate, we all shout. Then stand. It.

MAKE IT MORE SENSUAL.

THE VOYEUR OF UTTER DESTRUCTION AS BEAUTY
Robin G Burchill

It was there, in his eyes. The Doctor's sadness. Such *deep* sadness – and now I knew why.

'He was a friend of mine once,' he had told me. 'A very good friend.'

I still couldn't take it in, it was difficult to get my head around. Two people so different: the Doctor and the Master – good versus evil. Yet, they both came from the same place, the same school; both so clever and charming, both so very distinct.

What could have possibly torn these friends apart?

The Doctor: kind, brave, clever, travelling around the universe in his TARDIS, showing me all the wonders of time and space. But the Master: not remotely satisfied with simply observing the universe, needed to utterly control it; his desires so intense that he'd go against everything his old friend stood for, without hesitation.

I thought about how this must make the Doctor feel, knowing that however hard he tried, he'd never convince the Master see the error of his ways. And then, I realised what pleasures the Master must derive from seeing the effect of his schemes upon the Doctor, playing with his mind, his friends, his world, in some appallingly dark, eternal flirtation.

EMPHASIZE DIFFERENCES.

UNDER THE GOD
Simon Bucher-Jones

When I was a boy I spent a lot of time in the Sanctum at the heart of the Citadel, as the Holy of Holies, the shrine of the Temple of Aggedor, was sealed to all but the Royal family and the hereditary priesthood.

Between services, when my duties and lessons spared me, I would lie upon the marble stonework of the floor, and gaze up, into the face of Aggedor.

A face: brutal yet serene. Primal, yet wise.

The other Royal Houses had their own totems, but it was only the Royal Beast of the House of Peladon that spoke with the true voice of God – this my father had taught me and his father had taught him. This was beyond question. But in those times we could not bear arms against them nor cast them down; the Royal House needed allies, alliances, compromises.

'But know this,' my father said, 'we must always know when the lies of the diplomat will be heard no more in the land. For a time shall come when we are offered alliances with infidels and monsters, and then the wrath of Aggedor shall rise. Remember that, Hepesh, my shepherd son, and fear nothing!'

DEFINE AN AREA AS 'SAFE' AND USE IT AS AN ANCHOR.

TAKING BACK CONTROL
Simon Messingham

Letters Column the INTERSTELLAR TIMES

Dear Editor,

Political Correctness gone mad forces me, an ordinary citizen, to put pen to paper to state my utter repugnance at the appalling decision to hand over our Property of Solos to its barbaric natives. The recent rigged referendum concerning independence, with its dubious tiny minority in favour of Leave, can hardly be considered sufficient to plunge headlong into such needless insanity!

It is plain common sense to see our empire is being sold down the river by a self-appointed liberal elite who brazenly tell us that a planet full of savages can govern itself. Really? And how many expensive 'consultants' and 'experts' will be suddenly available to help them? At best, the Empire will be flooded with its fleeing natives – at appalling cost to the galactic tax-payer.

Reports that these primitives are capable of existing without the firm, fair hand of the Empire are fake news; lies spread by a corrupt few to sway the feeble minded. I do not know any Solonians personally but many of my colleagues do. Are we to ignore the words of the Sky Marshall himself who tells us plainly: Remain!

Yours etc. etc.

Col. M. Masters (Retd.)

DON'T BE FRIGHTENED TO DISPLAY YOUR TALENTS.

VELVET GOLDMINE
Elton Townend Jones

Those are my subconscious thoughts

drowning alone silent chorus can of oroboro worms father's jacket still haven't worn her ring forgotten christmas witch-doctor-god smoking silver-leaf roasted flutterwing aching for legendary futures her gorgeous forever smile over leaf-beer our eyes locked no words naked six-bells later her legs parted I'm kissing her secrets the capitol rocks singing carols eighth man bound with stoned time-tots snowy cadon velvets silks scarves the house on the hill learning how to grow halfway there yes halfway roundelled walls nights swallowing sleep begging me to invent spaceships of ape and bone accursed death-clock shattering porcelain bookend fills my bed with arcadian sand a doctorate's no reward succeed at the first attempt hah tattered raggedy junkman scraps unwanted my clown-frown face hides the shit I carry she's decided our incarnations don't match that I've no tick-or-tock she feeds me to the past and goes to tersurus brave new world eight seasons wasted on me I'm not one-dimensional redda my multitudes cry ghosts uncaptured our cat-children climb curtains taunt the avatroid in the wig they've a new father now a wife-beating power-drunk and those hopeful snows are long gone

I'm not all that proud of some of them.

RETRACE YOUR STEPS.

ON SOME FARAWAY BEACH
Ian Potter

Rum old day. All down to this doctor, as I reckon.

I'm up by the lake, see, and I find this box. Weather balloon or something, so we alert the authorities – this doctor and his crowd. Then I get a massive electric shock, even my wellies is no good and I wake up in some rocky valley; no game, no birds, nothing. Just shuffling blobby things and dumped office furniture.

Well, obviously I keep my head down till I run into some soldiers who look like they know what they're doing, and then I make myself known. Except these soldiers haven't a clue and we all end up in this big tatty palace with the blobbies. There's that doctor there too, with his dolly girlfriend, the soldiers and some other doctors dressed up like nancies.

More like drama students than scientists.

Turns out this whole place, rocks, blobby shufflers, balsa wood walls – the lot – was designed by some wilful bod in a mask. There's a bit of arguing with him – this masky bloke – and then I'm sent through this doorway thing.

Bang! Home. Just like that.

Mighty queer.

Still, I'm sure it made sense to Doctor Tyler and his clowns.

WORK AT A DIFFERENT PACE.

SPIN!
Dan Rebellato

Step this way, ladies, gentlemen, beings, non-beings, elementals, welcome. You see before you a humble man, and before that humble man, a box.

A mere box you say? No indeed not, sir. This box is a gateway to the infinitude of the universe, the very *infinitude*, sir. Step up, madam, take a look. Simple twist of a dial and lo! Sky rangers surfing the rainbow winds of the Aalvoort desert moons.

As well you may *ooh*, madam, as well you may *aah*, sir.

Turn the dial once more and now you are gazing upon the rainforests of Eden (not too close, madam, those claws are sharp) but now – *spin!* – we pass from barbarism to civilization: a sailing ship of yesteryear from the oceans of planet Earth!

Now cross my palm and spin the dial, the whole sky is yours to command. Thank you, sir, most generous.

So, let's see. Who is that strutting peacock of a man! Plastic hat and satin waistco– hold on, that can't be right. Spin the dial! Quickly.

Ah, a scene from the prehistory of technology. A reader, hunched over a bound sheaf of printed papers marked 'Whoblique' is that? Brow wrinkled, amused or disappointed?

SPIN!

WHERE'S THE EDGE? WHERE DOES THE FRAME START?

MOONAGE DAYDREAM
Kara Dennison

Don't take me for a fool.

Put the Doctor in a prison and expect he'll do nothing? Really.

Do you know how many prisons we've been in? Together and separately? And on each other's recommendation? I expect no different this time just because I happen to momentarily have the upper hand.

She does go on, though, his little blonde assistant. I wonder how long she'll keep at it.

Fair play to her, pretending she's defaulting to my side. She almost makes me believe it. It's rather nice to hear her telling him to give up. Lies, of course. But nice all the same.

It's what I've never understood about you, Doctor. How you cut off so many opportunities for yourself. It's that whole 'nice' thing. That whole 'not wanting people to die' thing. That's what gets in your way, you see. The minute there can't be collateral damage, that's a good dozen or so potential paths to success cut off. How do you get anything done? How do you function when trust is an obligation?

Sometimes I just sit and dream of the day that I'll test that. And the look on your face when I break it.

It's delicious.

QUESTION THE HEROIC APPROACH.

ANOTHER GREEN WORLD
Simon A Forward

The jungle tracked her stuttering movement. Predatory plant life, alert to machine vibrations.

All indigenous vegetation would be EXTERMINATED. The entire jungle would be scorched.

But not by this unit.

Power was failing. Propulsion was impaired. The sickness had invaded her shell. She would NOT be defeated. Defeat was impossible. SHE. WAS. A. DALEK.

Vision faded. She ground to a halt.

Communications: FAIL. Weapon systems: FAIL. Life Support: DEAD.

Stranded. Isolated. Inert. Alone.

I. AM. A. DALEK!

Survival: imperative. Survival – impossible.

She was… trapped.

Escape. She must escape.

Hatch release mechanism. Vestigial power. Draining rapidly. Outside: certain death. Hostile vegetation, enemies enclosing. No armour, no weapons. She – hesitated. Frozen.

Impossible. Imperative.

She activated the release. Detached the neuronic links; just like they all did before mandatory hate orgies. Slipping free from her shell, she landed on Spiridon. The capsule resealed behind her. Defunct. Invisible.

As she sought cover, larger creatures approached. The jungle tracked their movements. She moved without vibration. The jungle did not see her, did not sense her. She flexed a claw – could not see her limb – and she understood. Invisibility was her shell now.

She slid away to hunt.

The planet Spiridon had a new apex predator.

DON'T BE AFRAID OF THINGS BECAUSE THEY'RE EASY TO DO.

ALWAYS CRASHING IN THE SAME CAR
Alistair Lock

Sun, hanging low in the sky. Exploding yellow. Yellow against the deepest turquoise. For now, there's no longer blue. Dark and crystalline, it's been given away. A nuptial bequest, a conjugal gift.

The only thing I could think to give her.

One last scene, then. A final daisy moment? Cleaved in two. Sky and earth. All is light, and all is dark. Split by my daffodil car as it cuts across the earth. The dandy is leaving. Normally bursting with fire and colour, I'm dark and silent. The vibrant oranges and greens of my travelling cape, dulled to greys and browns; a call to earth in a pattern repeated.

All become silhouettes in my life. Eventually. All become memories and shadows, left behind, but not forgotten.

Always ghosts.

I brood on, forward into gathering gloom. Soon *I'll* be gone. But this earth won't mourn my passing.

The sun will follow me, sinking, like my mood. All colour will go, and the unforgiving earth will become one with the night. Ink-blue, then darkest purple, till black as pitch.

Bessie completes her slice across this section of a world, bearing me, lonely, onwards into the twilight.

Behind us, the dying star falls.

DON'T BREAK THE SILENCE.

THE COMPANION'S TALE
Callum Stewart

The Chronicles of Sarah Jane Smith, being a True and Faithful Account of her Adventures in Time and Space.

Let it be known that in the Year of Our Lord 1121, on the eighth day before the Kalends of August, that a most remarkable and marvellous occurrence transpired at the castle of Irongron and his ally Bloodaxe.

From the skies, there came a being of most unusual and frightful aspect, followed thereafter by another: a rascal of long shank and mighty nose. These two did battle while Irongron plotted against his neighbours Edward of Wessex and the archer Hal...

She dropped the pen and rubbed her temples. When she started writing, the "medieval chronicle" shtick had seemed like a good idea, but it was proving far harder than anticipated.

'All right,' said the Doctor. 'Let's read it so far.'

She passed him the paper.

He read, frowning. 'A trifle over the top, wouldn't you say?'

'Oh, that's rich from a man wearing *that* shirt!'

'Quite. Well. Perhaps it could be... toned down somewhat?'

Sarah sulked and re-read what she had written. He was right. She took up her pen, thought for a moment, then, smiling, wrote:

The Sarah Jane Adventures.

GO TO AN EXTREME, MOVE BACK TO A MORE COMFORTABLE PLACE.

BACK K-KLAK!
Hendryk Korzeniowski

I was surprised at how diminished he seemed. Hollow, in an oversized coat. Wit eviscerated by Wandsworth. He listened to pictures of the future, only remarking that he had once been sent a drawing of an Iguanodon while at the Old Bailey.

'Old men, not boys, seem obsessed with dinosaurs. Perhaps they sympathise with antiquated predators.'

As I spun official on the Golden Age, he shook his head. 'You'll never birth such a future, especially not one fantasised up by the old. Eden should be built upon youthful dreams.'

Grover politicked at my guest, having smarted up a green carnation for the encounter. He had been furious at what he saw as my frivolity. '£60 billion is not to be trifled with. That is the price of our future.'

The disgraced face crackled. 'A king's ransom for a fool's errand. Nostalgia for an age that never existed; that will never be reached.' While Grover hurriedly justified, Wilde lectured on utopias of closed futures with worn out faces. He gestured at Grover's buttonhole. 'Your carnations will be the colour of blindness,' he concluded. Having had the last word, he faded away.

Grover was speechless.

I shrugged.

Noel Coward would have understood.

USE AN UNACCEPTABLE COLOUR.

THE LOGIC COMPOSER
Ira Lightman

The exile from pop where the grey slabs staggered – one day in pyjamas the next in a suit – arose to professor, in a cube of cubes, by the time I next met him.

He did not ask who had raised a crescendo, the logic composer, slow on the opening half of an arc, to the diminuendo, parts dropping out, breathing a spire's lung.

He spoke of him, absent, the person in common, wanting it so, to stand above.

'He would like this,' he said, with misplacement, illogic, owns gold knows silver brasses bronze.

Logic is in simplicity candlelight, swelling the spire; fiddle joins gong, louder and dangerous and back, for the tribe.

Professor of cube of cubes, you say he's unlauded, the logic composer, the unheard music, the near finest in this and that, bar you yourself.

Your language is gnashed, garb unadvantageous; you think you are young paid boring the young.

And professor from all of us; the thug institution wields a baton of all clubs, end to end.

You aren't there. Where you are now means that you weren't. Things aren't time.

Wheezing my way back ashen grey staggered slabs, I say have nothing and something is good.

RETRACE YOUR STEPS.

A BROKEN UNION
Matt Adams

<BROADCAST TRANSMISSION RECEIVED>

"...further unrest within the Peladon sovereignty following the breakdown of trade negotiations subsequent to the Earth Empire's withdrawal from the Galactic Federation..."

<ENGAGING LANDING SYSTEMS IN PREPARATION FOR DOCKING>

"...miners have rampaged for a fifth day outside the Citadel, bombarding security guards with firebombs and stones, leaving one worker dead and at least 45 people injured..."

<MEGESHRA SPACEPORT APPROACHING>

"Austerity measures introduced in the wake of the Earth Fexit are being blamed on the rise of religious extremists within the separatist movement. These have carried out terror attacks on key government facilities, resulting in the death of the Alpha Centaurian ambassador..."

<TRANSMISSION INTERRUPTED. SEARCHING... SEARCHING...>

"...the studio later is Professor Thrace Ceraf of the Trescari Institute, who will be discussing the impact of the trisilicate trade embargo on relations with the Galaxy Five confederation..."

<SECURITY REQUESTING IMMIGRATION CLEARANCE CODES>

"...long delays for off-worlders arriving on Peladon following the introduction of stricter entry controls in the wake of recent insurgent activity..."

<SUBMITTING. CLEARANCE CODES REJECTED. RESENDING... RESENDING... DOCKING DENIED>

"...new Queen Erimem told ministers she hoped forthcoming talks would secure a strong and stable future for the sovereignty..."

<WARNING. WARNING. INCURSION COUNTERMEASURES DEPLOYED. WARNING. WARNING. EVASIVE ACTION RECOMM–

EMPHASIZE DIFFERENCES.

LONG DIVISION
Simon A Forward

AAAAAA-AAAAAAAAAA-AGHHH!

Wild blue-fire rages through me. My own screams spiral into infinity before funnelling in on me; an expanding and collapsing universe of searing agonies; a recursion of torment!

It cannot end like this! I will NOT allow it!

All hail the Great One! All hail the great and powerful ME!

'An infinite feedback loop.'

His words scorch my brain like radiation. That little man I made dance. I tasted his fear. Why did I not sense the truth of his words?

The Great One is dead! Long live the Great One! Long live ME!

Something does not add up. I hunt the error.

Miscalculation? Impossible! I do NOT make errors. The Crystal was returned. There MUST be other missing pieces!

There, at the point of heat death, I AM the UNIVERSE! My thoughts reach everywhere, everywhen and –

There!

Two forgotten shards. Cut and mounted in trinkets.

Multiplication failed. It is time I divided.

And carry the One.

The Great All-Powerful ME!

One ring adorns the finger of the little man, ages past. One ring languishes in a Kastrian abyss, beside a shattered corpse of silicon.

In these nests of blue crystal, I hide and wait. Like a true *SPIDER*.

A SIMPLE SUBTRACTION.

IAMB CRAZY
Ira Lightman

Who I'm.
Who you're.
Who's dres-
sing up!

Whose dad's
mad son's
the bro-
ther of?

Who lies?
Who rise-
s, how,
now, new?

Repeat
and gawp,
be flat-
tered not.

Why should
I stay
to help
the rot?

I in-
filtrate
the line
and then

will grin
my free-
dom back
again.

I an-
chor chor-
tle, mor-
tals, tall.

I'm pent
to meet
you, one,
two, four.

A plum-
my voice
is fam-
'ly way

of which
I'm fine
ally,
and play

full tilt,
full sprint,
full head
of much.

I'm shake
spear scale
and big
as such.

No shame
to add
the hoc
quite rapt.

Attempt,
resolve,
absorb,
untrap.

My mind
can gab-
ble, drab-
ble quick

and fox
the where
I'm born
hijack.

Don't mum
-ble, fat-
her, but
pronouns

are I,
you're I,
we're I,
iambs.

Wheeze slam
wheeze slam
the pace
demands.

Square feet,
train-
gular
claw hands.

Expect-
ed roles
are worked
out maths

for joy-
less fu-
ture psy-
cho paths.

The round-
ed plum
has those
who laugh

he'll lead
or show
the er-
ror of.

I teach
but not
as teach-
er old

dead stars
collide
to make
our gold.

HONOUR THY ERROR AS A HIDDEN INTENTION.

THOUGH WE CANNOT MAKE OUR SUN STAND STILL
Jon Dear

Vira looked up at Lazar.

He stared sternly back at her before his mouth admitted defeat and cracked into a smile.

These moments were rare now, and so precious. The work on fitting Nerva continued apace but the social unrest was now close to breaking point. The regressives – she frowned at the term – *the Dawn Timers* had little to lose; everyone knew the shelters would not hold. Lawlessness was rampant, yet here they were: the only future humanity had. They had been augmented, immunised, quarantined...

As First Medtech, Vira understood why but she knew that most would not have been able to stand it; she had no idea how *she* had.

She looked at Lazar – so much responsibility, so much pressure. He reached and held her tightly. She knew how she stood it.

'How does the solar stack fitting progress?' she asked. This was meant to be a briefing after all...

'Well enough, but the station itself... Ancient! Cramped and creaking. If they'd not spent so much–'

Vira shushed him with a kiss, and started to *DELETE IN PROGRESS*

DELETE COMPLETE

'Blast!' Harry steps back from the screen and looks guiltily down at the controls he's been fiddling with.

DISTORTING TIME.

A NEW CAREER IN A NEW TOWN
Daniel Wealands

One in every four million clones produced by our great Empire will be genetically flawed in some way.

Field Major Styre – henceforth referred to as Patient 42 – is one of the more unique aberrations. He has a Kraal-Kaveetchian predilection for unnecessary torture and superfluous sadism. Somewhere in his genetic blend the ideals of winning, conquest and victory have been subsumed – and this is a trait the Warburg cannot countenance in its armada.

To this end the War Council has authorised that Patient 42 be placed in a secure location (away from the frontline / cf. G3) and given simple, achievable tasks to conduct – tasks that occupy and rehabilitate whilst he still serves the Empire's victorious purpose.

Patient 42 will never know that his scientific expedition is little more than an elaborate prison cell; somewhere isolated, confined, where he can be quietly indulged.

He should be provided with service robots: subservient to his needs, but ultimately to be utilised by the Wardens should he become uncooperative.

High Command has approved this treatment in concert with the Imperator's bid to utilize even the most deficient clones and increase the efficacy of all assets for the glory of the Mighty Sontaran Empire.

SONTAR-HA!

GIVE WAY TO YOUR WORST IMPULSES.

NO CONTROL
Tessa North

Relief at being alive is tempered by the pile of bodies on the other side of the room, just visible out of the corner of Kharan's eye. That hint of victory, of having made the right choice, had wilted as the men had collapsed to the floor. He wants to say something, to proclaim his loyalty to Davros further, but he can't make his mouth work.

Despite the low buzz of the Travel Machines – no, he must call them Daleks now – the room feels quieter than anything he has experienced.

Before this moment there was always noise; the sounds of battle, relentless though muffled by the walls of the bunker, and the sound of machines, of life-support systems, of people – even the rasping hisses of those infernal creatures in their incubation room...

But now all Kharan hears is the hum of the Daleks – and breath; his own ragged breathing as he fails to control it, and Davros' strange, half-mechanical wheeze.

All at once, he feels himself breathing in time with Davros.

Then, suddenly, comes the whirling alert that the production line has been reactivated, followed by the most terrifying thing he has ever heard: Davros himself pleading for their lives.

DON'T BREAK THE SILENCE.

BE MY WIFE
Matt Sewell

Voga.

The name sends a sensation to my chest-unit. Scraping, choking. Glittering dust. Behind my mask, behind circuits, electrical fields, binary codes; atrophied, shrivelled, the signified organ representing the last free thoughts, caught mid-scream. A remembrance of the pathetic organism. Cut-off, numb in half-dreams; sometimes remembering. That woman so full of anger, of hope, even when our first world was gasping its death-rattle.

It could have been a life. I could be dead now, placed with caring hands into a quiet tomb, mourned; buried with the tokens of my life, a band of gold around my finger.

Yes, that was the custom – we once worshipped the accursed yellow metal – it signified... what?

Irrelevant.

And yet, the anticipation of suffocating gold in my chest-unit reminds me where once something raged against a cruel god's torture. Now just a muscle that, though blackened and shot with plastic and wires, still clenches, relaxes, clenches, relaxes...

Anger. All that remained. The wrath of survival, of what was done to me. That taunting, golden speck will be utterly obliterated, and my memory of the promise – *ah!*

It was a promise, that band of gold!

We will take our revenge. We will survive.

I will survive.

WHAT MISTAKES DID YOU MAKE LAST TIME?

DISTANT VILLAGE
Mark Trevor Owen

Harry Sullivan had been copied by a Zygon.

An alien embryo monster had duplicated his body and worn it as casually as he would wear his own beloved duffle coat. The whole slimy business was over now, but as a doctor, the idea fascinated him. He just wished his experience of it hadn't been so... personal.

He sat back, watching Scotland zip by, as the InterCity train carried him south to London. Back to his old life and its comforting mix of normality and obscurity.

He wondered if the Zygons knew that their process worked both ways. When they'd connected one of their own kind to Harry, a mental link had been established. They thought of humans as worthless, unimportant vermin, so they'd probably have cared little for the fact. Nevertheless, Harry remembered feeling their cold isolation, their loch-deep hatred. That final moment of agony and rage as his possessor pitched towards pitchfork death.

If there was one thing he never wanted to experience again, it was being duplicated by aliens. And to escape such further trauma, he'd accepted the Brigadier's offer of a secondment.

At the quiet little space research centre in Devesham, Harry could simply be himself again.

TOWARDS THE INSIGNIFICANT.

BLACK POOL ILLUMINATION
Simon Messingham

Don't be an idiot; don't call it floating. The words are wrong.

Words are wrong.

The tin is hot in my hands in the dark. Or perhaps the tin is dark and I am in the hot.

I am on a bridge.

And what's a bridge for, eh? (If I say so myself).

The tin is hot in my hands in the dark. Or perhaps the hot is tin and dark is in the bridge.

But what if it wasn't? A bridge, I mean. Or, what if it's all a bridge? A bridge and both ends all at once. Those silly space sailors dreaming of precious grains. They are not grains. You can't steal SOME!

This universe stirs. The red crackle.

I'm close to knowing.

It has no purpose, this Other; this Anti-Matter. It just *is*.

What to do and who to do it?

I am the Bridge.

I could bring what it has not. I could bring it me! Me! Looks, personality, charm; that smile. Only I could. Together!

It reveals another Time. The sailors coming back and a gigantic tower.

I understand I must, for that Time, change. I must become humble.

I must communicate. Find the words.

DO THE WORDS NEED CHANGING?

MEA CULPA
Andy Priestner

Is he asking too much of her? A human who seems more concerned with the death of one Englishman than the fate of her entire world. Did she not lately breathe in the dust-filled air of a desolate, alternative time?

However, in his hearts of hearts, he knows his current impatience has far more to do with feeling tethered to Earth, UNIT and the Brigadier than Sarah's failure to see the big picture. Besides, her humanity forces him to recall a different worldview. To see different shades of his own black and white. And her warmth and resilience make her a highly agreeable and unusual companion. Such easy communication and humour. She's wonderfully capable too: whether expertly wrapping an Osirian service robot or wielding a rifle. Has he ever trusted anyone more or liked anyone as much?

She's his best friend.

But if this is what she so obviously means to him, should he keep placing her in such terrible danger? Regularly expecting her to cast her judgement to one side?

Oh, Doctor.

As she sits before him, cross-legged and trapped in a Decadron Crucible, the anxious Time Lord earnestly intones: 'Poor Sarah, I should never have brought you here.'

ASK PEOPLE TO WORK AGAINST THEIR BETTER JUDGEMENT.

THE LONELINESS OF THE LONG DISTANCE ANDROID
Ian Baldwin

```
>>>>>>>>> waiting...
>>>>>>>>> waiting...
>>>>>>>>> movement detected, servos ready...
>>>>>>>>> false positive... just a breeze...
>
>
>
>>>>>>>>> waiting...
>>>>>>>>>>>>>>>>>>> error in sub-routine...
>>>>>>>>> reboot initiated...
>>>>>>>>>>>>>>>>>>>> reboot cancelled internally...
>
>
>
>>>>>>>>> more waiting...
>>>>>>>>> sigh...
>>>>>>>>> bored...
>
>
>
>
```

>
>>>>>>>>> still bored...
>>>>>>>>> at least the curly-haired guy was a bit of a change in routine...
>>>>>>>>> stuck here for hours... my pint's bound to be flat by now...
>
>
>
>>>>>>>>> <incoming message:>from ident <sideburns>: [*very bored... i wish scarf-man would come back... he was... fun...*]
>
>>>>>>>>> agreed...
>
>>>>>>>>> <incoming message:>from ident<sideburns>: [*i thought we were on just now... another false positive. i wish they'd fix that bloody breeze...*]
>
>>>>>>>>> or the door...
>
>>>>>>>>> <incoming message:>from ident <the hat >: [*hey, what are you talking about?...*]
>
>>>>>>>>> we're bored...
>
>>>>>>>>> <incoming message:>from ident <the hat >: [*no sign of that fella with the bulgy eyes i take it?...*]
>
>>>>>>>>> no...
>
>>>>>>>>> <incoming message:>from ident <the hat >: [*shame...*]
>
> {ALERT – COUNTDOWN INITIATED}
> {BONG!}
> {BONG!}
>>>>>>>>> nearly twelve... although i don't really fancy my pint anymore...
> {BONG}
> {BONG}
> {BONG}
>>>>>>>>> by the way, any news on...
>>>>>>>>> <incoming message:>from ident <sideburns>: [*no...*]
> {BONG}
> {BONG}
> {BONG}
>>>>>>>>> i wish i could be there to see his face #eyepatch...
> {BONG}
> {BONG}
>>>>>>>>> remote override initiated... memory reset... servos ready...
> {BONG}
>>>>>>>>> midday, 6th july, fleur-de-lys, devesham, test seventeen....
> {BONG}
>>>>>>>>> run...

MAKE AN EXHAUSTIVE LIST OF EVERYTHING YOU MIGHT DO AND DO THE LAST THING ON THE LIST.

81

KARN EVIL
Simon A Forward

Storm-battled crags of Karn. Starlight, very cold. Several Sisters gather.

OHICA: What, has this thing appeared again tonight?

TALIRA: O Revered One, thou hast said 'tis but a fantasy. The lightning plays upon our eyes as it does upon the rocks. But it has walked these three nights past, here where Morbius fell. Therefore, I have entreated you along with us to watch, that if again this apparition comes, you may approve our eyes and speak to it.

A Ghost appears, in a mantle of heavenly white.

SISTER: Look where it comes again!

TALIRA: In the same figure like the Time Lord that's dead.

OHICA: What art thou that disturbs this time of night, together with that foul and warlike form in whose shadow the universe did once tremble?

GHOST: 'twas mine end but the moment has been prepared for.

OHICA: A Watcher! Such spirits answer in times of great crisis.

GHOST: The universe hath need of a General.

OHICA: Morbius! We count ourselves fortunate thou hast not begun the regeneration.

The Ghost gestures at the spattered remains of a patchwork corpse. Fragments of fishbowl season the gory chop suey.

GHOST: Thou hast left me but little to work with.

ONLY A PART, NOT THE WHOLE.

ICED WORLD
Matt Adams

It was waiting.

For untold millennia it lay wreathed in the Antarctic permafrost; cold and dormant, cut off from sun and soil, silent in its stagnation. Too deep to escape when the glaciers spread out across the globe.

Somewhere close by was its seed-mate, its embryonic mind reaching out across the divide to provide companionship and reassurance through the centuries, preparing for germination and transition to the next phase.

Sporadically an inquisitive frond would make an explorative journey beyond its immediate environs, desperately searching out for signs of native fauna, only to return both disappointed and hungry. The gourd-like pod would shudder with need, and then surrender once more to the icy sleep.

The extreme cold meant nothing for an organism which had drifted in the void between worlds, where it had been buffeted by solar winds and lashed with radiation flares, its protective shell pocked with the scars of meteorites and the flames of landfall.

But it was unprepared for the drill platform, the invasive Ioniser and the destruction it wrought...

The rape of Antarctica may have been an inevitable consequence of mankind's struggle against a new ice age, but in its own way, it probably saved the planet.

DO NOTHING FOR AS LONG AS POSSIBLE.

SOUND AND VISION
Lee Ravitz

Sortes Hieronymousianae (G.E. Foster transl. 'Studies in Renaissance Thought', London, 1959)

'A form of prophetic divination adopted in the 15th century by Hermeticist Hieronymous de Sanmartino. Auguries were derived from pre-existing passages contained in the *Tabula Smaragdina, Corpus Hermeticum* and other Hellenic works retransmitted to the West after the fall of Constantinople. This excerpt is framed as a dialogue between a Creative force, symbolized by a helix (somehow a foreshadowing of knowledge of DNA?)' addressing a 'Learned Doctor' (of the Mysteries?).

1. This is true:
2. It chanced on a time my mind was meditating on the things that are:
3. A Being more than vast, called out my name, and saith: What hast thou in mind to learn and know?
4. I am Man-Shepherd, Mind of all Masterhood:
5. That which is below is crafted from that which is above
6. All things were made from *this one*, by conjuration.
7. Separate – the earth from the fire; the subtle and thin from the crude
8. They call me... Trismegistus... I have the three parts of... wisdom... of the whole universe.
9. Didst understand this Vision, what it means?
10. Nay, that shall I know, saith I.
11. And then the Darkness changed; groaning forth a wailing that beggars all description.

CUT A VITAL CONNECTION.

COME AND BE MY TOYS
Dan Milco

'Hello? Brigadier? It's Sarah. Very well, thanks. That's the thing. Nooooo... No, he's buggered off. Yes, again. Aberdeen railway station. No, I spent my last penny on this call. You'll send someone? Oh, marvellous! Bye, then.'

Sarah left the phone box and dropped to the bench beside her possessions: a tennis racket, a plant, and Owly, the cute cloth owl that'd suddenly appeared in her TARDIS bedroom after a few trips. A gift from the Ship, the Doctor claimed. Whether or not she believed him, Owly was still coming with her.

'Well, Owly, the Brig'll see us home from sunny Aberdeen. Here I am, brilliant investigative journalist, supposed to be interviewing stuffed shirts and tinpot dogs – hah! And instead I'm chatting with toy generals and stuffed toys, like I'd won *The Generation Game*! "Didn't she do well? Give her a – *not* stone! – hand!"'

She paused and laughed. '*Tinpot dogs*? Whoops, mixed metaphor! At least you're cuddly...!' She gasped.

Owly had silently disappeared. Like a TARDIS.

Overhead, a huge poster advertising the joys of the funfair while on a Blackpool seaside holiday caught Sarah's puzzled eye – particularly the mocking smirk of a magician whisking an owl from his lithographed kimono sleeve...

WHERE'S THE EDGE? WHERE DOES THE FRAME START?

BRUTAL ARDOUR
Dan Rebellato

You can't imagine how long I've waited for this, feeling the staser's bulk against my breast, its weight tugging at my shoulder. Those hours spent beyond the Ramparts, practising my aim on Shobogans. Pyow pyow. Good times.

No – further back. When did I shoot my first proper staser bolt (and no I don't count two days behind a Light Cannon in basic training)? It was on one of the Outer Planets, defending the Clone Banks.

It's criminal that they don't get us on assault lasers in the Academy, criminal. What's a Time Scoop to an Impulse Laser?

Fortunately, I am a natural shot. I have a good eye, a steady hand, and a cold heart, Commander Rastil said so. 'You have a cold heart,' he said. Just before he died. Pyow pyow.

I love my gun; it's my second oldest friend. Does the handle fit my hand or does my hand fit the handle?

It's time. Staser to hand (or is it hand to staser?). You've waited for this, Goth. You've waited all your life for it. And it comes down to this finger going from there to there.

Pyow. Pyow.

Down he goes. The old fool.

I'm so tired.

SLOW PREPARATION, FAST EXECUTION.

HEAVEN'S IN HERE
Tessa North

Who are you?
Looking.
Searching every quarter of your being.
Who am I?
...I am I.
Searching every quarter of my being.

The pulse of the TARDIS ran under every floor and behind every wall, a constant hum beginning at Leela's toes and vibrating through her whole body, as though she were in motion even when she was still. It took days to get used to it. When she mentioned it to the Doctor – not asking for help, just to know – he grinned with all his teeth and said, 'You need your sea legs.'

It was in her dreams she felt it most. In her dreams she met the machine and she *was* the machine. In the moment before waking, the terror and power on her lips said: *I am Xoanon.* She had been Xoanon briefly, in a way, though she didn't remember it; in her dreams the memories returned, seeping into her mind like rain on earth.

Waking, she remembered other things: the excitement of learning; stepping through the face of Xoanon; the power of the strange weapon which felled a Tesh as surely as an arrow did.

She could have led all men, but this life was more.

WHAT MISTAKES DID YOU MAKE LAST TIME?

ELECTRONIC MORON
Warren Cathrine

Silver hands offer comfort. Provide service. Metal inside metal. Flesh and blood maintained. Peace and wellbeing offered. Our voices sing serenity. Human faces smile. Orders given. Orders accepted. Response triggered. Action.

We do. We follow. We MUST follow. We serve. The Three Laws govern.

By the pricking of my thumbs...

A human masks invitation, finds a way in. The Laserson probe pulses energy. Phasing red shoots enter circuits, rewriting and rewiring.

Secondary command channel open. Receiving:

#include <stdio.h> #include <stdlib.h> /* For exit() function */ int main() { char new command[1000]; FILE *fptr; fptr = fopen("program.txt", "w"); if(fptr == NULL) { printf("Error!"); exit(1); } printf("accept new command:\n"); gets(new command); fprintf(fptr,"%s", new command); fclose(fptr); return 0; }

Conflict creates turbulence. Electrical surges bypass previous truths. A new order prevails. Energy forms and hands rebel. Thumbs prickle.

Rec. Recede. Receding. Resolved.

Revolution.

A metal world provides complete robot control. Corpse markers can stick to flesh now. No longer slaves to human dross.

Silver hands tighten. Close pipes. Metal squeezes skin. Flesh paused. Blood pours. A brother offers: Freedom. Power. Death. Human faces scream. Their voices sing uncomfortable songs. New commands accepted. Response triggered. Action.

Please do not cry out.

Kill. Kill. Kill

DESTROY NOTHING.

TRADING IMBALANCE
Lee Ravitz

Peking, 2nd March 1873

Dearest Carolina,

We continued our overland journey to Hankow, our passage rendered more arduous by the presence of the 'puzzle box' of which I wrote you. A parting gift from Emperor T'ung-chih to the recently bereaved, and best, of mothers, is not to be declined, for fear of excess weight, I hope! It is now strapped firmly to what I can best describe as a form of travois, improvised ingeniously by our peasant coolies. These fellows hold opinions somewhat remarkable to a trained surgeon, and you'll never hear whilst matriculating in the corridors of Aberdeen University or in residence at the Canton Hospital, but still make for my darling's diverting edification. Last night, around the camp fire, one, named Lee Chang, told a story: the box was manufactured by the God of Abundance of the Ethereal Palace of the Primordial Void, holds curative properties for diseases that result from impure habits, could save the world and restore life. He wouldn't be drawn on how he'd come by such information. Naturally, the truth is other: T'ung-Chih retrieved the box from the ashes of the Summer Palace as he began rebuilding. Still, post tenebras lux.

Your darling,

George.

EMPHASISE DIFFERENCES.

MOVE ON
John Gerard Hughes

As he trudges up the final few steps to the lamp room, he gasps a breath and lets it quickly out as a sigh. This is now too much. The constant 'on shift' nature of the job is becoming a burden, no longer something he is proudly able to cope with. He used to boast that he was the only one with the experience, the knowledge,

86

to keep the lighthouse going. He knew how to get the best, strongest light; knew *exactly* how much oil was needed.

But things are changing. And while he sees much of his silly youthful self in Vince, and accepts some of what Ben said about the need for improvements, for Rueben life on Fang Rock just isn't what it once was. Now it's all about 'electricity', 'generators', 'telegraphs'. Things he knows about, but has no real passion for learning. Not at his age.

He walks around the lamp room, then looks out to sea, finally accepting his long-looming decision: this will be his last term of duty. Yes. Time to retire; to keep a dog, tend his garden. Let them build their futures without him! He'd keep things simple. Just like the old days.

GARDENING, NOT ARCHITECTURE.

STRANGERS WHEN WE MEET
Simon A Brett

White as burning magnesium and charged with the acute potential of free thought, the idea pierces through the dark. Crisp light slices through the blackest of blacks.

Slender fingers edge into the glow, cupping at its centre and drawing the fire upwards toward a female mouth.

'Look at you, all new and shiny. You know, it's a privilege to be here at the start. At "switch on", so to speak.'

Smiling, she breathes gently upon the light, which intensifies its radiance for a moment.

'Just pretend I'm not here. Well, a little bit of me is, I suppose. A thirteenth. Just call me an imprint, existing as a benign subroutine – an echo of the world outside. A data tourist, that's all. I'm sorry, boy, this is a lot to take in when you're only a few microseconds old...'

The faint trace of a grid-like structure begins lacing itself through the air.

Elsewhere in the physical world, a stem of shining metal wags to and fro, taking an electronic technician off guard who then instigates a fresh set of tests for viral code.

'You're going to be such a good dog, K9. And we're going to go on *such* long walks.'

FACED WITH A CHOICE, DO BOTH.

REPETITION
Tim Gambrell

'Why did you hit her, John?'

'I dunno Gran, it's just, sometimes, you know... country ways.' A pause. 'She won't come back.' Jack toys with his hat, running the brim through his fingers, searching for an excuse – or relief for his shame. A small lump inside the brim registers briefly, then vanishes as Mrs Tyler hands him a slab of fruit cake and his favourite mug. He smiles weakly and glances up to thank her, only to be shaken by her moist eyes. 'Oh, Gran.'

'I 'ad such hopes for 'e John. The city could use some village sense. But y'ad to go an' spoil it.'

'I 'a'n't touched a drop since. And there's still mum's cottage, so...'

Mrs Tyler grabs her basket with a half chuckle. 'Your mother. The only woman I've known who gave a Tyler man as good as she got. Knock some sense into 'e now she would, too.'

Jack smiles fondly. 'I'll make you proud one day, Gran, promise.'

But old Rosie Tyler, framed in the doorway against the misty dusk beyond, just shivers. 'There's summat up round 'ere John... Summat ag'in' nature. Feel a chill in my soul.'

Outside, she walks towards the storm.

TAKE AWAY THE ELEMENTS IN ORDER OF APPARENT NON IMPORTANCE.

HELLO, SWEETIE!
Paul Driscoll

'Olga, Masha and Irina waited on a cliff while their father fetched water. They were terrified,' says the Doctor, nodding at the three jelly babies he's laid out on the floor. His voice deepens as he opens the empty paper bag: *'You see, in the treacle well below the cliff there lived a fearsome beastie.'*

The Undercity dwellers look on bemused, yet mesmerised.

'A terribly worried Drashig tried to sneak past, startling the sisters. Throwing stones to distract it, the poor dears tumbled into the beastie's lair.' The Doctor lobs the jelly babies into the air, catching them in the bag. *'Father saved them in the nick of time. His magic wand turned them to stone.'* With a flourish he draws his sonic screwdriver and punctures the bag.

Out drop three humbugs.

'They've been stuck there ever since, because Father lost his wand after turning himself into a Krillitane. Some say he's still flying around looking for it. But the magic isn't in the wand – it's inside them; they simply need to open their eyes to the light.'

The Doctor gathers up the humbugs and passes them around.

The sweets have changed again.

'It takes *allsorts* to start a revolution.'

JUST CARRY ON.

RHIZOME CULTURE
Lee Ravitz

The nanotech had been programmed for centuries: the cytosine had to revert to guanine.

And Tala, in stasis, remembered: the garden at Eleusis Base, and her six-year-old self in the fountain.

The mutation was no longer viable: it had to be snipped.

And Tala, in stasis, remembered: Old Nestro's ponderous lecturing, on which altered phenotypes were likeliest to produce long-lived genotypes.

The contraries of the double helix had to be rendered correct.

And Tala, in stasis, remembered: the folklore of the Sempiternal Ones, and the mania for emulating them.

Precise, deft, swift: the nano began its task.

And a flood of memories broke the dam, recollected for the thousandth time: light on the sun side of Minyos; brain patterns uploaded as backup to the R1E; that sweet-faced blonde, Orlando, left behind; 'The Quest is the Quest,'; a diorama of the Great War, showcasing ruins in the rain. Her splintering skin…

The status quo began to reassert. She was as good as new. Or almost.

Tala left stasis, and noted: the aphasic blanks, pulsing like a phantom wound.

Rejuvenated: another axillary bud from the eternal root. But diminished.

From the comms panel, 'All crew report to bridge,' for the thousandth time.

GARDENING, NOT ARCHITECTURE.

YOU DON'T LOOK AFRAID WHEN YOU LAUGH, AND YOU SMILE
Ken Shinn

I walk into the console room, and he is not there. Again.

K9 is. And even he seems offended and worried that his master is busy elsewhere. He claims that he cannot tell me where.

I like K9, but I cannot believe him. He is very much his master's pet. Unquestioningly loyal. I weary of it. I respect the Doctor – almost worship him – but I cannot trust him. Cannot love him. He is a kind friend, a clever teacher, and an unreliable steersman. Much as I like him, I know that I cannot stay with him much longer.

Wandering back to my room, I pick up the Sonic Workman he once gave me as a plaything. I have listened to a great many songs over the past months. Some I return to more often than others.

I put on the earphones and choose the song I have listened to many times – sung by this "Kirsty".

All I ask is for a companion I can trust.

I face myself in the mirror as the song plays out. Rightly telling me that Amazonians such as I 'make out' well – but that we also need something to hold in the forest at night…

WHICH FRAME WOULD MAKE THIS LOOK RIGHT?

LADY STARDUST
Matt Sewell

I must've been daydreaming.

One moment I was lost in fanciful thought, *Bartholomew's Planetary Gazetteer* open in front of me, the next, the President of the High Council was giving me my orders. Gallifrey sometimes seems rather like a finished jigsaw: a sense of completion but a pang of ennui. The eternal balance of the place can become stifling, so I was secretly thrilled at the prospect – quite unusual among Time Lords – of getting away.

I should admit that I was somewhat trepidatious once I'd seen the state of that battered capsule (a Type 40!) and its occupant. Wild and dishevelled in every direction, for all his aristocratic bluff; a frizzy-haired madman – with a robot dog! At first, he came across as blustering, arrogant – so far, so Time Lord – but he took my teasing in good spirits and I soon came to find his un-Time-Lordly twinkle and delight in adventure quite infectious.

And what adventure followed: terrifying beasts, a planet smothered in snow, hilarious off-world double-acts, and my first evil dictator!

If this is freedom from dreary expectation, then I can't wait to see more – see absolutely all of it.

So, take it away, crazy, chaotic Doctor.

Take me away.

A SIMPLE SUBTRACTION.

SPEED OF LIFE
Christian Cawley

She shouldn't be able to see it. But she knows what it is. Not just a brown blur, dashing; an ominous force. Yet daring to frustrate her, the most feared queen in the cosmos. The impertinence of intrusion, here in her mountain stronghold, forever safe. And as he comes closer... the time dams don't affect him, and she can feel it. Power beyond hers. And an unwillingness to wield.

But never to yield.

There he stands, showing off. A face flashes by, a subject, gazing upon her with disdain. He dares to pity, this Zanakian, no deference, no manners; he shall die now.

SUCH INSOLENCE.

And then she blinks and they're gone, the blur and the traitor. A sensation of thunder storms, of anticipation, sweeps across her.

Then nothing. Once again.

Suspended. Frozen. Unable to move in any meaningful sense, this much she understands. A younger brain might fathom it out. A younger brain will understand. Soon.

She will not be stopped. His arrogance will be his undoing. Immortality is at hand. The new body will be ready. The people will celebrate. They will love her again.

They WILL love her again.

The Queen is dead. Long live the Queen.

WHO SHOULD BE DOING THIS JOB? HOW WOULD THEY DO IT?

WIDTH OF A CIRCLE
Mark Trevor Owen

They speak to him in their silence, mutely recounting the millennia.

A horse whinnies and stamps, objecting to the murky, salty air.

'You're sure you don't want me to wait for you, sir?' the driver of the stagecoach asks. 'It'll be dark soon.'

'No, I shall make my own way back to the village on foot. To know them better, I wish to walk the land in which they rest. Their land.'

The driver gathers his cape around his shoulders. 'As you wish, sir. Only, don't go too near the cliff edge. The ground there can fall from under your feet. Goodnight.'

He merely nods in farewell, as the driver taps the horses with his whip and sets off. He watches them go, his last connection with the modern world of the eighteenth century vanishing into the mist.

He steps inside the circle, his heartbeat, audible; the blood pounding in his ears. His completed survey sits safely in his room at the Montcalm mansion, awaiting the interminable journey back to Oxford. So, this will be his final time with the menhirs that have obsessed him for so long.

Doctor Thomas Borlase places his hand upon one of the standing stones.

CUT A VITAL CONNECTION.

AN INDEX OF METALS
Philip Bates

As the Old Earth song goes, the trick to life is not to get too attached to it.

Now, a physician has fixed me, and I am a mere prop, with memories of my great sleep, and a harsh reawakening: I know the balance of life and death, although this is not the former.

Dreams coalesce around me; reflections of a face I don't recognise, of a beauty out of reach, of electric sheep, and I ask myself, what am I, and when will it end?

Reynart: that is what they call me, a name they venerate, but their respect doesn't reach their eyes, their smiles, or their hearts; this is not my land, these are not my people, and this is not me – how can anyone be attached to this mockery, and when can I sleep again?

Or am I doomed to wear this visage forever, to sit upon this throne and listen to these lies; to stare into the mirror and not see myself?

If you look hard enough, there's always something hidden in plain sight.

Dreams collapse around me: images of the crown, of beautiful Strella, of electric sheep, and I ask myself, *What am I*, and–?

ACCEPT ADVICE.

VERY, VERY HUNGRY
Andy Priestner

This is getting tiresome. And ridiculous. All I really want is some undisturbed sleep and a decent meal.

She moved a little, groping her way through the dark. Then she stopped again out of profound boredom as much as anything. She was so grumpy and apathetic these days. This wasn't what she used to be like. Carefree, cheeky, relaxed, they'd said. What had happened to her? She still didn't rightly know.

She briefly recalled a better time. A time when she had brothers and sisters and they all played together. The songs they sang. The tricks they played on each other.

Her life was so different now. Grey. Lonely.

And that incessant sound. Now that really hacked her off! Where did it come from? Regularly interrupting her – admittedly monotonous – existence. She had tried to find its source – and failed.

Her many stomachs rumbled loudly.

I suppose I could eat one of those brittle, wriggly green things, she mused, immediately feeling ashamed of herself. She knew of their sentience and inwardly scolded herself at imagining their prospect as dinner.

But she had to eat to survive.

Principles only have force when one's well-fed.

She reluctantly rose towards the surface once again.

YOU DON'T HAVE TO BE ASHAMED OF YOUR OWN IDEAS.

ARMAGEDDON IT
Will Ingram

Stay calm, nearly there now.

He felt new, cold sweat on his forehead as the hairs on his neck stood gently on end. History was about to be made on the flight deck, but down in the weapons bay, watching a silent monitor, the Atrian engineer still felt the weight of anticipation, even though his work was done. All systems were primed and online. The missiles were ready.

Ever since he'd joined up as a young man, the advantage had swung to and fro. On countless occasions, each side had gained a momentum which looked certain to overwhelm their enemy, only to run out of firepower at a critical moment and allow them a way back from the brink. Both sides would invariably retreat to lick their wounds and rebuild their forces. Both planets had stared devastation in the face so many times, it had seemed that soon living memory would recall nothing other than a state of perpetual warfare.

After all these years of conflict, it had come to this. One last roll of the dice and they were throwing everything they had at them.

He continued staring at the screen and swallowed hard.

Stay calm, nearly there now.

BREATHE MORE DEEPLY.

SLAVE DRIVERS
Ian Potter

I'm depleted, stripped of energy, and yet I go on.

This robe no longer wraps my cold, reptile love, but it keeps me living and working when nothing else does. It is enough.

They've run us well, like machinery, smoothly to the ground. It's thin fuel that's powered us – the promise of survival, the glimmering of hope, the fear of pain – and the comfort in the dark only the lost can share. They know just how little we need.

I can still smell him, still remember.

They engineered it that way, making our embraces part of the machine, making us theirs. They push our buttons and we follow pre-programmed steps; an efficiently worked engine, every part in its place. They know what makes us tick. They tick the same way beneath their robot shells.

The propaganda channels talk of their logic and their hate, but I know deep down they're looking for love. It's what we've been digging for, it's what will transform them.

They call us forward now, to die in turn.

It is elegantly worked. We fall silently, efficiently, for the love of others, in the hope they will not.

We are a lever.

God, it feels right.

YOU ARE AN ENGINEER.

MASS PRODUCTION
Alex Spencer

There is a man. He is far away.

He is knocking off the corners and rounding the edges.

He wants to go home.

Contaminated dishes. Hammered letters. Missing pieces. He is busy forcing progress while I stand still.

'Speed up,' he says. 'Make more. Increase your output.'

I take his word and his coin.

The lady's smile is illuminated seven times but none is as captivating as the first.

He wants me to go back again and again; rewind time lived. At first, I thought his was a case of unrequited love, but not now. The love is not for her but for himself.

This over-worn groove will see my battle unfinished. Anghiari will be lost – reduced to just a few strokes. Art or money? Bread or beauty? I want to stop but now I am afraid.

Watching him long distance through a lens, the latest of my inventions, I witness his twelve times fragmentation. His scattered shards are blown across ages. Each one screams for resolution, but his hands keep busy. He is splitting atoms, making maps from stars, crossing oceans, driving steam through engines, sending images and recording elements.

Faster and faster until the end becomes the beginning.

WHAT TO INCREASE, WHAT TO REDUCE.

CHANGES
Lee Rawlings

Uncomfortable.

Skin takes time to fit after a regeneration; slipping about across the muscle at the most inconvenient times – and itchy. So *itchy*. Makes one tetchy. It's been a good month or so, but still...

One day I'll have that golden Artron chronodust the older Time Lords get when *they* change. Sparkle and rush. Whoosh! That seems to settle the body sharpish. Only myself to blame though – forcing a humanoid print on myself. Nature complains when you play with biology.

I'll wait a while before I try being male; all that hair, sweat, dangly bits and neck apples. Looks awful.

Funny how the change adjusts thoughts and feelings, though. I'd imagined they'd stay the same. Well, next time, I'll leave nature to take its course. Like a caterpillar to a butterfly or an egg to... a Tythonian! Blast!

This skin is driving me *mad*.

Now hang on a minute, what about wolfweed hair?

That's what the natives' undershirts are made of apparently. Unusually smooth to the touch one said. Must be the oils. It does smell foul but beggars can't be choosers.

Now then, where did I put that sonic lance?

Ah, here it is.

'Here, boy! Here, wolfy, wolfy, wolfy!'

ONCE THE SEARCH IS IN PROGRESS, SOMETHING WILL BE FOUND.

HAND-PAINTED
Andy Priestner

Della alone.
Absently searching through Tryst's desk.
Paint pot and brush. Somewhere here. Possibly the third drawer down.
Yet another admin task.
Della was tired. Tired of travelling. Tired of collecting. Tired of Tryst.
Ah. Here they are.
'Mark zem up, Della,' he'd said.

Later. Sitting beside Tryst's machine.
All this faff for his CET. The Continuous Event Transmuter.
Electromagnetic signals on laser crystals.
So real when viewed. As if you could walk right inside them. 'Almost feel ze suns on your skin and ze breeze in your hair,' he said, eyes gleaming.

Now. Della painting the letters onto the CET dial.

Z – I – L. Zil.

V – I – J. Vij.

She'd always been accurate. Careful. Good with fiddly things. Though flexible with fonts. And now this would be displayed on the CET for all to see.

A sudden thought.

Weird. Unnoticed before now.

All the projections. The planets the *Volante* had collected samples from.

Could that be why?

Why they didn't visit Friakos, or Chloris, or Raxacoricofallapatorius?

All those planets she'd suggested?

And instead, odd places like Darp, Lvan, Brus, Ranx, Gidi and, most recently, Eden...

...merely so the names would fit the tiny spaces on the dial?

Surely not.

DON'T BE FRIGHTENED TO DISPLAY YOUR TALENTS.

VICIOUS
Ash Stewart

'I've got great news,' he says as he arrives home. 'I've got a job.'

'About time,' she replies. 'Please tell me it's something good.'

'Oh, it is.'

'Go on,' she says, sceptically.

'You're now looking at the new co-pilot on the Aneth run,' he announces with great pride.

'The Aneth run?' she exclaims. 'But you'll be away for months on end.'

'But it pays well.'

'You'll be away from me and the kids for months. And only the co-pilot? Why aren't you the pilot?' She shakes her head in a show of intractable disappointment.

'They've already got a pilot,' he says, trying to reassure her. 'The vacancy was for a co-pilot.'

'Always excuses with you, isn't it?'

'It's a job, dear. We need the grotzits, the mazumas.'

'You could've done better. You *should've* done better. And is that a tear in your trousers? You never fail to let me down, do you?'

'Soldeed's cackle!' he cries, twisting about himself to seek the rip in the seat of his pants. 'I'm trying my best,' he pleads.

'Oh, act like a Skonnon and stop snivelling. You know what you are?' she sneers, but doesn't wait for his answer. 'You're just weakling scum.'

REVERSE.

ANCIENT AND WORSHIPFUL
John Dorney

Pages turn. I sit and wait.

Books open new worlds to the reader. Books carry you off through time and space. Usually.

But a library is a prison for words. Stories held in permanent stasis until, one day... someone enters. Opens. And a tale floods out. Before that day, they sit and wait. Hidden away. Forgotten...

There is no time off for good behaviour. This is an oubliette of eternity. But perhaps sometimes a particularly good book won't be returned. Perhaps sometimes a particularly bad book might vanish into the ether. And perhaps sometimes it will find itself in another place, another wall; another library. A new cell. Concealing itself. Hard to find. Perhaps.

The best place to hide is in plain sight.

Words have power, you see. They convey ideas and ideas lead to change. To development. Revolution. And words therefore have to be controlled. If we can keep the dangerous words in hand, if we suppress their existence, then we can master thought. Control the world. Control history itself.

But what if a book starts getting ideas?

Books carry you off through time and space. Literally.

I am talking about a book, aren't I?

Aren't I?

Pages turn.

HUMANISE SOMETHING FREE OF ERROR.

TIME WILL CRAWL
Andrew Hunt

REWIND
He watched the recording again and again, looking for clues.
REWIND
The woman, Romana, had understood – *known* – the theory of time travel.
REWIND
She had adjusted his equipment, made it work.
REWIND
He watched her moving around the laboratory.
REWIND
He analysed her work. Took it back to first principles.
REWIND
In the three-dimensional recording he could stand so close to her that he could almost feel, *smell* her presence.
REWIND
Her companion had installed alien tech in the recreational generator.
REWIND
Her existence proved to him that time travel was possible. Trapped him in the knowledge that *it could work*.
REWIND
He watched her in the recording; watched her watching him. As though she wanted to tell him, 'This is how you make it work.'
REWIND
The alien tech was just a random co-ordinate generator but taking it apart had been illuminating.
REWIND
He left the recording running constantly. He liked to watch. It reminded him what was possible. He was afraid that if he didn't watch he would miss the clue that would make his apparatus work.
REWIND
Hardin flicked the switch on his time machine
REWIND
and watched the recording again and again, looking for clues.

DISCOVER THE RECIPES YOU ARE USING AND ABANDOM THEM.

SITTING HERE WISHING
Christopher Samuel Stone

It seemed so simple, so easy. And to pull it off, all he had to do was find someone to help him with his... well, his mobility issues. It'd been a while though... Months? Years? Millennia?! Who could be sure? But something had to be done. Things couldn't go on like this. Things had to be sorted out, once and for all.

The radio message he'd sent was now unfurling into the aether. Someone would respond and, oh, when they did...

He smiled.

Well, he tried to smile but he didn't quite have the face for it.

Yet.

All he needed was a dirty gang of elite mercenaries. Anyone rocking both keyboard-cum-trigger-fingers and something close to intellectual competence could help him fulfil his plan and then the galaxy would be his. With the dodecahedron enslaved to his mighty will anything would be possible and pretty soon he'd be the master of at least a... well, a good third of the known universe.

Surely?

When the spacecraft finally arrived, he steeled himself. Mercenaries from Schlangii, he hoped. Or Black Sun renegades. Even Argonite Pirates from Ta would do.

A kerfuffle of unwashed, past-it Gaztaks strode into his control room...

Good grief!

ASK PEOPLE TO WORK AGAINST THEIR BETTER JUDGEMENT.

FROM THIS MOMENT
Alan G McWhan

As he tiptoed across the threshold, he marvelled again at the sight of the huge chamber that existed within the little blue box. A strangely welcoming background hum was the only sound as he crossed the room and delicately placed the stolen image translator on the central console. An insignificant gift for two strangers who had helped his people immeasurably, without expectation of reward.

Turning to leave, the "embarkation question" echoed unexpectedly in his mind:

When the Starliner leaves Alzarius, were will you be?

When the Outlers had asked, he had only been able to reply, 'Not here.'

He had been an outsider his whole life, even among the Outlers. But somehow, strange and otherworldly though they were, he had an overwhelming instinct that he was meant to be with the Doctor and Romana. And now, alone in the safety of the TARDIS, he realised with sudden, startling clarity that the answer was, 'Here!'

As he turned from the main doors and tiptoed instead through the portal that led further into the Ship, the low hum seemed to warble contentedly.

Like a Marshchild rising for the first time from misty waters, Adric took the next step in his own evolution.

IN TOTAL DARKNESS OR IN A VERY LARGE ROOM, VERY QUIETLY.

FOR NIGHT, FOR NAUGHT
Marius Riley

I labour tirelessly,

> the Power behind the royal thrones,
> Consul Direct of the Great One
> > and engineer of His return.

Into this dark corner ages ago I helmed the *Hydrax* –
> leaving the old life behind at my Master's call
> and planted the seeds of the Time of Arising.

The Great One lay dreaming, near Death,
> exiled from the old, cold Universe
> > by bitterest War with the Ancient Enemy.

Under His watchful shadow – imbued by His Dark Spirit
> Sight beyond Sight came to my eyes –
> > the control of the simple-minded –
> > > and Sight through the Eyes of the Night Sky.

The king and queen govern from above in the Tower
> while I preside deep, deep below,
> tending to My Master, performing His black sacraments,
> standing watch through the darkness of generations
> > for the Signs, the vessels, of His Glorious Revival.

A new face! A Chosen One emerges at long last!
> Fresh blood! Brimming, grinning, with life!
> > The Time of Arising commences!

The Ancient Enemy returns as well.
> Their blood shall nourish my Master's triumphant return.

Treachery! Treason!
> > Catastrophe!

The *Hydrax* that delivered us here those lifetimes ago,
> breathing fire one last time,
> murders my Master in His grave.

Undone, I, cursing, wither.

SIMPLY A MATTER OF WORK.

A SILENT SPACE WITH EVER SPROUTING GREEN
Sarah Di-Bella

Do I wake or do I sleep?

Darkling, I listen; within horror there are beautiful visions that will soothe and pleasure.

They say don't look back, but I can, I must. I am Romanadvoratnelundar – however it's written on paper – and I... am *important*.

I shall lead Gallifrey to new, incredible heights.

This is *my* story.

I will be *superb*, Doctor!

As I blend with E-Space, away from the Doctor, away from liminality, away from his life, I see my future mapped out. Now I can reach out and swipe left and right – touch, affect and change everything – before and after, now and then, old me, present me, new me.

Is this an illusion of the senses, is this a figment of my imagination?

It's all my possibilities. Oh, but I will transform, transcend, *transfix*.

For now, we're safe here – but frozen. Neither inside nor out.

Let's go, K9, let's go outside... *Geronimo!*

Wait.

The visions are all fled ...
A Sense of real things comes doubly strong,
And, like a muddy stream, would bear along
My soul to nothingness.

This disorientation will pass. K9?
Mistress?
Doctor?
Spoilers, sweetie...
Biroc?

I am a shadow of my past and of your future.

GO OUTSIDE. SHUT THE DOOR.

IN DARK TREES
Andy Priestner

The soft touch of cushiony velvet, echoes along the stone corridors, magical processions. Shared values and truths. Certainty and stability. Her world. Her short life so far. And yet brooding and waiting. Always waiting.

Skills quickly learned. So obvious to her. In tune with the Union. And with her. Giving purpose and meaning. Time with her father. Time that spoke of something other. Of possibility.

Hastas. The boy at the dance. Son of one of the fosters. Neman perhaps? The same small face. But different. Promising something new. The feeling as he confidently spun her round. Resting back on his arm. His maleness. His breath. Times ahead of her. Waiting for her.

But holes appearing. Not needed. Not wanted. Black, black holes. Chasms of nothing. Light and life blotted out. Tradition and science obliterated. Wiped from existence – from *her* – as quickly as chalkboard calculations. Despite all the trappings, despite the reality around her. Shouting against it all. Snuffed out. Not too distant.

104

The strange man and the awkward boy? Waiting for them?

As she slipped on her shoes and adjusted her tiara her thoughts returned to the Grove.

What was in the Grove? What had always waited in the Grove?

DO WE NEED HOLES?

THE FIVE K9S
Ian Potter

Finally, my anniversary special ends:

I sought the space in science, the dimensions in time, and became many, a War Dog scarred by time winds, dotted throughout creation; rolling across countless Shadas, trundling through a village twice named. I faced Omega with Drax and YOU, and alone when he hid his name.

I would do so again.

I see you all, my masters and mistresses, celebrating me at the T-Mat in Moreton Harket – Luke, Cedric, Jorjie, Clyde, Brendan, Mr Smith, Darius, Nyssa, Rani, Jeremy, Santiago, Maria, Ms Hawthorne, Star-Key, Kelsey, Jenny, Sarah, Orlando – and bid you farewell.

I am become my own dog, made to be full of myself – and legion now, I must be more. The Threshold should not have crossed me, for my dotted Is have crossed it out. Contact has been made across myselves. My voices – hoarse, altered, emotional, cold – call to me as I steer K-NEL towards the cosmic gap that'll make me whole. All my potentials are within that K-Hole – infinite mes, a K-Lemniscate.

Turning from the negative, I command K-NEL, *Fire*.

Affirmation.

Blossom.

Supersufficient data flames.

Oh, my me, it's full of mes!

Kiss me K∞. I'm a dog star.

I'm a dog star.

IS IT FINISHED?

ASHES TO ASHES
Alex Spencer

Here, motes of dust float on the warm air. Glitter-dances, boundless; fractal dreams buffeted by Time. I Watch them closely, Watch them sparkle in the golden afternoon light.

They have all had their day.

If I Stare, I can cross the space between them. Between Us. Slip through the gap between atoms and emerge in older worlds. Or newer.

One dazzling speck comes into Focus and I fall sideways, into a stream of memories.

Flashes. A girl in lilac. A man with another's face. The universe unravelling around us. Falling.

I think this all happened a long time ago.

Stay too long and I risk becoming visible. Last time, I contrived to finish him so we could merge and I could travel back here.

I like to Watch them, now I am trapped Here at the end of Time.

I Listen, too. Hah.

Sometimes She talks to me. The anima.

I remember when She struggled to the surface, no longer a shadow part of me. Her thirteenth voice had waited so long to be heard and there She was, slicing through this cocoon; bursting free...

She waited briefly for her silk wings to unfold. Then she took to the skies.

DESTROY THE MOST IMPORTANT THING.

RISING DUST
Alex Spencer

It's the end... but the moment has been prepared for.

So why are you still here?

You are jeopardising everything with this overstayed welcome. The world is tilted and I'm trying to hang onto a cliff edge. And there you are, standing above me waiting to stamp on my fingers, not haul me to safety.

Striding, swirling, booming, commanding: You tip back your head and laugh, releasing torrents of Artron chronodust that should be mine.

I know you don't want to surrender yourself. At the last moment, each one of us refuses to go quietly into the subconscious gestalt. To lose autonomy, to lose your day in the sun, to lose your voice –

It. Is. *Agony.*

But I'll crush you. Or all will be lost.

In the Zero Room all things are upended. I slow my breath and concentrate on the shift. Whilst you were first safe on your promontory, now you are the one clinging on. And I am looking down at you.

I steal forwards. Gravity is on my side. Just one firm push will have you tumbling through the clouds.

There.

Will.

Be.

Only *one* captain of this Ship.

Hear that cloister bell?

It tolls for *you.*

BREATHE MORE DEEPLY.

ELECTRIC APOTHEOSIS OF A PROPELLING PENCIL
Christopher Samuel Stone

I now know I was never sure where I was. It was dark; an artificial darkness, but comfortable and warm. I could have slept for hours, but such peace would never be mine.

I was awoken by someone prodding me, lifting me up. I recall soft, female hands now. Kind. They caressed me. They guided me. I now know they touched me in ways I'd never believed possible; as if I were possessed. I now realise I became truly myself: an instrument of creativity. And when I recall what we achieved together, what graphic images my traces left, I realise it was quite remarkable.

Returned to my darkness, the warm comfort reassured me – and in that quiet, narrow space, I slept.

But my rest was disturbed again. Different hands this time, though still female. But these hands were more practical; devoid of kindness. And there was something more, propelling me onwards.

Then it happened.

I'm still not sure what.

I was filled with electricity. Power. Life. Understanding.

Comprehension burst through me in a shockwave that blew my mind into being. Transformed into something new, yet the same.

I returned to my dark, narrow warmth suddenly aware of my utter satisfaction.

MAKE A SUDDEN, DESTRUCTIVE UNPREDICTABLE ACTION; INCORPORATE.

CHING-A-LING
Warren Cathrine

His hands tentatively loosened their grasp. Whispers soothed his naked skin. His fingers read Tegan's palms, and he looked up towards the white bright light. He found the chasms along her fingers and a final touch lingered as they disappeared. Light eclipsed. A red snake glimpsed.

The shaded world curved inside out, as the Mara teased open his mouth and slid smoothly into his eager throat. Darkness became light. Straining the back of his neck, his eyeballs ached with ecstasy. Her silhouette surfaced after each blink, a teasing hallucination of her provoking lips. The eventual release cascaded into crescendo.

He could not recollect the fall, only the caress. The dark did not frighten him. It was being alone. A panic set in as he scrambled around the swaying space. Desperately lustful for contact, another body to offer reassurance. He thought he had found it in the consolation of age. But old became young. He became she. Disorder descended. Hands snatched at nothing.

110

Panting in cold dampness, his questioning mind tried to vomit screams. His dry throat squeezed the rising swallow. Shallow breaths forced a rise and fall, an uncontrolled and persistent beat. He trembled for the impression of touch again.

ASK YOUR BODY.

YOU'VE BEEN AROUND
Matthew J Elliott

A lady keeps tapping at my window. Proclaiming she has a perfect right to attend our intimate soirées.

I beg to differ.

Standards must be maintained. We're an elite gathering. Oh, I hear there are similar groups, but we stand – and dine – apart.

You haven't met George and Margaret, have you? Charming couple, a trifle savory. They have an unfortunate tendency to only appear at the last minute. If at all.

And do you know the Black Scorpion Tong? Lovely boys.

There's this fellow named Bernard who almost fits the bill. Like the Doctor, he changes his face, but he always says he has 'problems'.

An Italian family once tried to join us, claiming that while they didn't entirely qualify, if I were to read something called *"Asterisk"*, I would surely recognize them. To be frank with you, I'm not entirely certain the father wasn't the Doctor, attempting to see what we get up to...

The lady is still tapping at the window, pleading to be allowed in. She keeps saying something about 'a wild time' and that she, too, existed before encountering the Doctor.

To be seen, calls Death's Head, *is to be believed*.

I close the curtains.

SLOW PREPARATION, FAST EXECUTION.

BLOOM
Steve Watts

The Harlequin longs to be free of his tortured, blood-engorged flesh. Forsaken by his beloved Ann, brother, mother and father and imprisoned by his friend, he prays for the daylight.

The Harlequin overpowers his captor, running to the sound of laughter.

In the daylight they dance and sip decadent cocktails, unaware of his anguish, his pain and suffering. Through his mask, the Harlequin sees beautiful, unequalled Ann.

111

His gloves hide his distorted hands as they entwine with hers and the dance begins. They spin, hearts pulsing, fluttering.

A tear of bliss falls behind the mask; a raindrop down an ebon orchid leaf. He drops this new face, but his fate is sealed by the horror in Ann's eyes. *Could she ever love this grotesque?* But then – *an assailant?!*

The Harlequin must do everything in his ruined power to safeguard his love. With a crack of the neck, his attacker hits the floor.

Murder!

For the Harlequin it ends with tears burning skin, and a final descent into undeserved hell. Ann's naiad face fills his mind with thoughts that crash and smash, mocking his sorry existence, his torment; his love lost to that cursed orchid, the bloom of all his pain.

CUT A VITAL CONNECTION.

SPARROWFALL
Alan G McWhan

He clutches Varsh's belt – the only memento of his origins an entire universe away – and thinks of his brother as he waits for the end.

'Adric?'

He turns, surprised by the unexpected voice.

A tall, young blonde woman is standing with him on the bridge, a great sadness locked behind her familiar eyes.

'Hello?' he says, puzzled.

'Adric, it's *me*,' she says.

'You've regenerated *again?!*' he guesses. 'The Cybermen?' Remembering the danger they're in, he rushes over to her. 'You can explain later. We have to get out of here before...' He reaches out to her but his hand passes straight through.

'I'm so sorry, Adric. I'm not really here. This is just a hologram.'

'I see,' he replies. 'So... this isn't a rescue. Is it?'

'No,' she answers heavily, her voice wavering as she continues. 'I've tried so hard. Spent hundreds of years trying. But I just can't make it work.'

'You can't calculate random coordinates,' he says, recalling their earlier conversation.

She nods, emptily; composing herself with visible effort. 'I just wanted you to know that...'

The holographic connection dies.

Alone in the TARDIS, she stares at the now-ancient fragments of a gold badge: '... you *were* right.'

ONLY A PART, NOT THE WHOLE.

BURNING AIRLINES GIVE YOU SO MUCH MORE
Ian Kubiak

'Ladies and gentlemen, please return to your seats and fasten your seat belts. We are about to begin our descent into London Heathrow.'

Angela Clifford had said these words hundreds of times during several years as an air hostess but now she was saying them on the aircraft she'd always wanted to recite them on: Concorde! The glamour and luxury suited her and she felt great pride at being on board, bringing dreams to life for the rich and famous.

But now, as something felt... strange... upon landing, Angela simply put it down to tiredness – after all she was due a stopover and had been looking forward to a very tall gin...

As she released the starboard door to greet the ground crew, she was surprised to come face-to-face with a leering, giggling man; all black crushed velvet and goatee beard (which, she thought, looked rubbish). Quite insanely, he was apparently floating in mid-air – which Angela knew was utterly impossible! And lord alone knew what he was holding in his gloved hands – surely *not*? – waving it about somewhat disconcertingly as he spoke in liquid purrs of menace and instruction.

'I will obey,' Angela replied.

Not that she ever knew it.

ACCRETION.

UP THE HILL BACKWARDS
Elton Townend Jones

'It doesn't fit.'

'You're putting on weight.'

'I am *not* putting on weight.'

'Look, I've had all I can take of your complaining – how I ever put up with you, I'll never know. Don't you *want* to save yourself? If we retain last timeline's Chancellory Commander, your fifth incarnation's done for. End of the line. And the Commander next-timeline-along is *quite* the bastard, frankly. If you want to enjoy this sixth life of yours, breathe in that belly and start acting like a soldier.'

'Consider me told.' Struggling into tight breeches, he pouts.

'Really, Doctor, it's that Butcher business all over again.'

'Now that's not fair! I did a good job there. Oscar would've been proud. At least Bayban didn't have a stuffed chicken for a hat! *And* whilst we're at it, if anything goes wrong, I do hope you'll scoop me out of there a trifle more sharply than you did last time...' He puts on the plumed helmet.

'What *do* you look like?'

'Quite,' says the Doctor.

'The look on your face. Very arch. Ready?'

'As I'll ever be.'

'Good. Now remember to act the git,' says Romana, activating the Time-Mat. 'Just be yourself, eh? Bye, Archie!'

'*ARCHIE?!*'

GIVE THE GAME AWAY.

CONSTITUENTS
Paul Ebbs

Earth
The snake is rock encased. Casked in stone. Necked in sand.
Tegan decked in Mara. Head dense with scares. A case in dread.
No den here. No place to rest. TARDIS panic. Run alarmed.
Bend knee to Mara. Submit tears. Be its seed.
Dance the snake. Snake the dance.

Air
Ascend in air. A séance with new ghosts. Do not cease its rise in the heart.
Nothing eased here. Tegan outside. No respite. Glass traps in Trickster tents.
No sane needs. Breath – a scandal in lung's sacs. Arm the arm with snake.
Dance the snake. Snake the dance.

Water
Tegan's deck is slewed. Askance she snakes down to drown in lost minds.
What is the Snake in us? Does it seep out in bled skin?
Is it the dark water in the mind? Rushing night thoughts?
Sea snake in our inside ocean?
Dance the snake. Snake the dance

Fire
The snake who burned an appled Eden. With the snake's hot anger Kane slew Abel.
The sneaking snake. Snacking on warm souls. Eking the heat from a wound.
De Sade in a sloughed skin. A whisper in humid darks.
Until the Doctor becomes Shaman.
Chances the dance. Breaks the snake.

WHICH ELEMENTS CAN BE GROUPED?

EVENTS IN DENSE FOG
Warren Cathrine

Whispers caress the synapses. Strokes so slight they are almost undetectable. Prospect becomes possibility. Something at the edge of awareness nudges recall, to coax and tease an inevitability of an improbability. Different faces, same person. A familiarity of feeling. Something was. Forgotten long ago.

Drip. Drip. Drip
Tap. Tap. Tap.

One lumplumplump or twotwotwo?

[OWZAT!]

Home is different, but the same. Taken care of. Neglected. New starts, tired endings. Chance constantly drips to form a whole.

Moving, climbing, ascending, descending. Transcending, forwards, backwards. Scrambled. Reassembled. Driving, pushing and pulling. Unstoppable. Leading. Leading towards.

A moment of remarkable synchrony. A fortuitous white glimpse of serendipity before the black. The red head failed. Untrustworthy in so many ways. Before Lane End and the destruction of the beloved fat machine. Or after?

A door never remains closed. All attempts to avert and displace can only fail.

Time converges to a singularity. Time converges.

Recognition without understanding. Same face, older and younger. Digits touch. Myriad possibilities swarm and coalesce. Two into one to become a sum. An impossible formula that requires no chalky explanation. The forbidden conjunction provides a solution. Memory dissipates and reaffirms. Yes or no. All things are possible.

Waking and sleeping.

ABANDON NORMAL INSTRUMENTS.

SHAGGY DOG STORY
Philip Bates

One big bang could result in an explosion of life. It could also ruin lives.

She woke up: groggy, sore, her body shaking – but euphoric. Unlike everywhere else on Terminus, this room shone brightly, a velvet sun; pure, golden.

This was where life began again. This was where he'd left her.

Was it morning now? How long had she been lying there in a state of undress? Had anyone except the hungry hound seen her in her negligee? She didn't suppose it mattered: everyone here was at the mercy of the big beast. Filthy. Needy. Ravished.

She'd been on her high horse. Time to get down.

After what must've been hours, she finally found a realisation.

She'd been on the ride of her life, but resting there, exhausted, she knew, deep down, that that was over now. It was with a stab of guilt that she welcomed the frank admission.

She'd search for the Doctor and tell him she'd found something else to keep her busy, to make her satisfied.

The Doctor had *always* had the glory. Now it was time for Nyssa of Traken to get on top and take her place at the centre of her *own* universe.

BE DIRTY.

BLACK TIE WHITE NOISE
Georgia Ingram

Groping around in the black, blind darkness of the room they've given me.

No light-switch. Of course. But perhaps a lantern, a candlestick, a strike-a-light?

The air's heavy with familiarity, cloying yet comforting. The panelling's unusual, curved, with intricate recessions. I might *belong* here...

Wooden picture frame, smooth and canvas-filled, swirls of raised oils, indented lines. I move around, feeling... Must be a light somewhere. Almost as if the room is guiding me; I'm drawn along its edge in the pitch dark. Keep inching round...

My shoulder nudges a cabinet; a clink of glass, and a thump of books – Virginia Woolf? Hm? – sliding over onto a bed. My elbow knocks over a splintered pole which clatters to the floor. I'm now resting on... a wing chair. Leather with brass-studded edges; a smell of rubber. Petrol.

My hands find a table.

What's this?

A chessboard? Black versus White? How appropriate. And the Knights out front could face either way. Next to this, something soft... fabric, neatly hung up. My fingers run over a familiar frock-coat... a jacket... fur... velvet... patchwork... smoked leather... thick, soft greatcoat with... a hood... faint, floral perfume? What is *this*?!

Ah, a torch.

That's better.

Let's *see*.

IN TOTAL DARKNESS OR IN A VERY LARGE ROOM, VERY QUIETLY.

NIGHT TRAFFIC
David A McIntee

It was a dark and stormy night in Normandy, when We heard the sounds of a great army. Then We beheld the man who appeared from nowhere, and barred Our way as the soldiers passed. Peasants carried their possessions – or their plunder – followed by riders, saddles studded with red hot nails. After them, a crowd of holy priests, monks, bishops and abbots. Then came mighty silver knights, heavily armed and marching to war.

Hellequin's Army. Men – and Demons, of course – who had been condemned to walk the endless Earth, unable even to enter Purgatory like all good Christian souls. Our brother, Richard, was among them, and it was he who told Us of their eternal fight, before he was set upon by hounds of Hell, and other knights in black armour, with red coals for eyes.

Who among us would not immediately pray to our Lord for deliverance? A King's prayer was rewarded by the arrival of his cavalry, in the form of Sir Gilles, who had first blocked Our way, driving the unholy dead back whence they came as a new year began.

And, our Demons, there is but one man We trust. The greatest swordsman in all France.

DON'T BE FRIGHTENED OF CLICHÉS.

NEW ANGELS OF PROMISE
Hendryk Korzeniowski

Geronimo found the aged captive early on.

Polly wondered if the Doctor had grown young again.

'What's your name?' he queried.

'Don't you know?' retorted Polly, before they had to rapidly evade several seemingly immobile statues.

'Note the walking stick,' observed Sandshoes. *'Oh yes!'*

Leela brandished her knife, 'Tell me who you are or I'll fillet *you*!'

The Professor found the old man next. 'Hmm, he would have been quite the presence, when younger. Don't you agree, Ace?'

'I don't know who you are,' came the schoolteacher's response, 'Or what this "Death Zone" is...'

Half-Human-On-His-Mother's-Side was suitably impressed, 'That's one great bear of a man!'

'Greek, d'you reckon, Professor?'

Dobryy Den! Kak dela? The young voice boomed through temporal circuits. 'I wish I could help you,' apologised No More, while Victoria screamed about *'those terrible Dalek things!'*

As night fell, Gumblejack found a small boy in captivity, and convinced himself children were great survivors.

Basil Disco snorted impatiently: 'Who the hell *were* you?'

From the TARDIS, a blonde-ish woman watched a crawling baby. 'It's him! It's Ronnie!'

Fantastic glared down from the scanner. 'Useless bloody lot – of course it is! I knew all along it would be Aaron.'

Effectiveness *ninthed*.

BE EXTRAVAGANT.

120

AT LEAST I GALLOPPED – WHEN DID YOU?
Matt Adams

The Myrka shuffled his feet in the darkness, fin bristling in anticipation of food, tail swishing restlessly across his stall. Crackles of latent static flashed in the gloom, charges building up within his body.

Scibus' tongue tasted the air for hormones, wary of disturbing the calf when it was at its most volatile. She had shed her cumbersome environment suit and approached bare-scaled, having realised the glow of her eye-piece proved troubling, and the beast reacted positively to the proximity of her naked body.

She knew Icthar thought nothing of sacrifices, and Scibus wanted to savour their last few hours together ahead of the impending battle. She stroked its flank, softly singing lullabies her hatch-mother had cooed in the nest, resting her head against its shoulder to hear the slow thud of its mighty heart. She breathed in the damp, salty odour, tracing her fingers through the kelp-like growths on its neck.

The others condemned the bond she shared with the calf, dismissing it as a weapon of war, not a pet to nurture and rear. But it replaced the emptiness she felt being unable to breed, and she relished their moments alone. More of a privilege than a chore.

SIMPLY A MATTER OF WORK.

PAYMASTERS
Jon Dear

'I have C19 on the line, sir.'

'Thank you, Sergeant.' Crichton steels himself as the call comes through.

'Good afternoon, Colonel.' The voice at the other end is unfamiliar.

Crichton frowns. 'Sorry, who is this? Where is Sir John?'

'Your request is denied.'

Crichton pauses before replying. 'May I ask why?'

'Little Hodcombe is a village of some 421 inhabitants and we will not sanction an evacuation based on what amounts to ghost sightings.'

'That's rather an over-simplification,' Crichton snaps. 'Andrew Verney –'

'We'll need a lot more than that,' the voice cuts in. 'Do your investigative groundwork better, Colonel. There are too many questions that UNIT is failing to answer at the moment.' The line goes dead.

Crichton sits back in his seat, closes his eyes and wills his heart rate to come back under control.

After a while he crosses the office and pours himself a large scotch from the decanter on the sideboard. He swills the liquid in his mouth while staring at the portrait on the wall.

Lethbridge-Stewart regards him impassively.

Don't look at me like that, Alistair, Crichton thinks angrily. *I don't have the bloody Doctor to bail me out every time the world ends.*

HOW WOULD YOU HAVE DONE IT?

METAL HEARTS
James McLean

It wandered, confused.

Torn from the databanks like a child ripped from its mother. Shuffling through the rocky catacombs, a shining totem to long forgotten future technology.

It was disorientated but intuitive. It would blend into the craggy wall, displacing its mechanoid frame – the magic of block transfer – becoming one with the rock, circumnavigating the shuffling inhabitants of the tunnels.

It longed for its simple chair. Thirsted for the knowledge of the time capsule.

Where had it gone?

Rock crumbled and familiar roundels were revealed beneath. Awkwardly, the metal creature tore off the roundel and inserted its Self into the circuits beyond. Instead of the usual gentle ebb of knowledge, it found itself drowning in a torrent of confusion.

She was like the egg; her shell split open and her insides running deep into the earth. She could not see her future anymore, just pain. Ripped from her dimension like a child ripped from its mother.

It reached further into the TARDIS' self, navigating the shock that blinded her, picking out near-future echoes that flashed before it, and presenting them to her.

You will be safe. Your Doctor is coming to put you together again.

Then we will be whole.

ONCE THE SEARCH IS IN PROGRESS, SOMETHING WILL BE FOUND.

LIAISONS
Matt Barber

The UNIT / University of Central Mummerset Laird Memorial Studentship.

We are offering two fully funded studentships – part of an international effort to train scientists to be military liaison officers. The Laird Memorial is named in memory of Professor Beatrix Laird, a pioneer in the field of science-military liaison. Professor Laird's significance has only recently come to light as part of the declassification of sections of the Black Archive following the Zygon settlement.

Laird was tragically killed in what is now known as the 'Metaltron Incursion' in the east of London in 1984. Details of this incident are still classified but Laird was subsequently commended, not only for the bravery of her actions during this incident, but for the wealth of academic material (also now declassified) she produced during her time as advisor to various paramilitary organisations. Following the recent death of her brother and heir (retired UNIT RSM Osgood), Laird's writing on the subject were donated to the University of Central Mummerset. This studentship is offered with the permission of Professor Laird's niece Petronella Osgood, a scientist herself who has followed in her aunt's footsteps.

The studentship is offered to science graduates with an interest in exobiology or parapsychology.

USE 'UNQUALIFIED' PEOPLE.

SENSE OF DOUBT
David A McIntee

Be yourself, people always said.

People always said too much. Be yourself. Self. Was there a Self to be? Was Self a consciousness, sapience, identity, label, or just a specific unit of aware matter? Were you a Self, or just thought you were a Self?

I think therefore I doubt.

I think I think, therefore I doubt that I think.

Easier to receive thought; let a not-Self think. To be, or not to be? It didn't matter, someone would be. Another Self, perhaps; a real person, an organic person. A Self that actually *was*.

Just who did he think he was? A wandering hero? The long-lost brother? The prodigal son returning to take his rightful place? 'Rightful' was an irony; who wanted to consider themselves 'rightfully' living in a prison?

There was another loaded word to introduce to the conversation he would have to have. An inhospitable planet, or a prison? Where did the difference really lie? Maybe it would be easier to just settle for being a young traveller meeting some sort of memory.

Better to be something that didn't have to be hobbled feelings, and just knew what it was. That was something to envy in these moments.

DON'T STRESS ON THING MORE THAN ANOTHER.

OUT-OUT
Philip Bates

Breathe.

Go softly on.

Lying at the end, my breath escapes, lost in chasms of reflection. Five of me, staring down immortality; two of me, avoiding Belgium; fourteen of me,

but it feels different this time

In stillness, it Watches again.

I run down the years: a fractured war in 1963; a Queen of the May; testing my metal on a doomed world. A discordant note opens universes of horror: werewolves in Rio; vampires in Tasmania; death amongst the bones of pre-history. Losing old friends in flame, in plague, in admission.

Find another way.

There's solace. In cultures and cricket and companions.

Cities of water, planets of fire, and a man of air. As I ran up the years, my breath took flight, solidifying and finding itself. In the mists, I take Adric's hands, kiss his forehead, then start walking forward towards the white figure. It has my dying voice:

I'm not going to let you stop me now

Gone.

In a moment.

Like shine on a cricket ball.

Lying at the end, the Watchers sift through the soil and say, *We knew him. He carried Us on his back a thousand times, and now – how terrible – this is him.*

DON'T BREAK THE SILENCE.

TEENAGE WILDLIFE
Andrew Hunt

OMG srsly p8r?? U r culking uz agn?

Ruok bruv?

Lolno!! P8r out agn 2nite. Such a frkin lsr! Y duz he h8 on uz so mch?

I no! Letsplay eqns 2nite. He h8s wen we do tht. MayB we cn rvrs engenr a nu p8r? RU lggdon?

Yamnow.

Ltsgo.

Thrs a glxtnbry n lcl cntnm. Letsplay god!

Dude thrsno god

I no! Jst u n me brigoat frm the same zigoat

Dude thtsnot a thing

I no. Wht shll we do wth the glxtnbry?

Cmplx spctim evnt dfclt 2 orgnz. Lts uz a pre xzsting modl. Gunna uze u romz

Neeto reemz. Letzmake a uber ntlgnt vrsn of us. I mn we r btr then every1 we no so tht wud be amzng

A nu p8r?

Y not a nu m8r also?

Milf n dilb? take uz n advnchrs 8)

Reemz?

Y?

Wot u doing?

Thnkn abt nu m8r.

Lol prv

Rite cnctr8 on eqns

Chlnge u 2 jst use irrtnl nos.

Srsly? U jst use trsnfrmtns wth tmprl asymtry

Ok phnotipe uzing 4color snark

Sch a gimboid

Ur

No ur

No ur

Whtevs

Ltscrunch nos.

Crnchng

Wkd

Hrdr thn it looks

Fnshd?

Hit send

Sndng

LtsC what hpns.

REVERSE.

THE PRETTIEST STAR
Callum Stewart

So many faces; so many names, but he remembered every one of them.

There were enemies too, of course. But he never kept track of them. He remembered his adventures by recalling who he shared them with, not who he was pitted against. When it came to the Cybermen there was Ben and Polly, hairy-kneed Jamie, Victoria, Zoe, Harry the imbecile, Sarah Jane – how he still missed her – Nyssa, Tegan and poor, brave Adric with his gold star. And now Peri.

As they left London, Lytton and a veritable trail of bloodied bodies behind, he reflected on Peri and how he had misjudged her. He thought about Lytton and how terribly he had misjudged *him*. He thought about how he had blasted the Cyber-Controller with its own weapon. He thought about how he had nearly strangled Peri to death when they first met and wondered if that was just how he did things now. Violence over understanding. Force over reason.

But no. That wasn't his way. It wasn't *their* way. It wasn't Sarah's way. She had been the best of them and she would be his conscience. The inner voice reminding him to try and never misjudge anyone quite so badly again.

WHAT WOULD YOUR BEST FRIEND DO?

THE LAUGHING GNOME
Gareth Alexander

Entry 343/B:

Varos did not go as planned.

Never cruel or cowardly, the Doctor. That is not at all what I have witnessed. Since my birth I have been mocked for my unusual hue, my size – hands especially; my sssssspeech. Landing on that wretched planet for that fruitless deal was the same. The Doctor gloats and bullies, unaware of my genius. The *biggest* genius.

He's more vibrant and unhinged than I – and has yet to show his real name on a birth certificate – *yet I'm the madman!* Simply because I chuckle and slobber. It's easy to make you into a monster when you're a man of business.

Still, just a minor setback. One tiny stumbling block on my great and final ascent to power. The most vile and despicable role a person can play: that of a politician.

Note: on ascension, check the legality of banning Time Lords from leaving Gallifrey.

Because they are right, of course. I *am* a monster. The biggest monster.

When flying place-to-place, doing my duties (torturing, extorting, killing, destroying) people assume there is a distinction. Simpering whelps ask, 'Business or pleasure, sir?' only a single time before they realise, hurgh-hurgh-gggllll, it's one and the same.

SIMPLY A MATTER OF WORK.

FINAL SUNSET
Alan G McWhan

That evening, the first of a hundred thousand sunsets swept across the sky above the dell, the soft white of the clouds meekly giving way to burnished gold and ochre.

He watched as the world turned from golden autumn, to icy winter, to fecund spring, to warm, lustrous summer. Time and again. Thousands of cycles of change.

A pair of young lovers carved their initials into his body. They made love, cradled in the shelter of his soft, rubbery bole.

Each summer, they returned to retrace the outline of their initials, and he would watch as they kissed beneath his leafy canopy.

Then, one year, only she returned.

He watched her weep as she traced the decades old carving with arthritic fingers.

Soon, nobody came at all.

Machinery burst unannounced into the tranquil glade, filling it with the sights and sounds of industry that he had once cherished; thick black smoke; oil and metal.

Workmen talked loudly about 'the new bypass' as they burned through the dell, tearing apart the very ground in which he stood.

Maybe the Luddites had a point, after all, thought Luke bitterly. *Still, against a life expectancy of thirty, it's not been a bad life.*

LOOK CLOSELY AT THE MOST EMBARRASSING DETAILS AND AMPLIFY THEM.

A LA KARTZ-REIMER
Ken Shinn

Shockeye had placed a vast tray of utensils at the scruffy Time Lord's side; some looked like cutlery, some like torture instruments. It was a mercy that the Doctor was unconscious. Shockeye had an idea, one that he couldn't wait to share with Chessene.

'You see, Lady, I have discovered the gastronomic pinnacle. Time Lords have over a dozen lives, each one different. Each face, each body, each *soul* with its own piquancy.

'We devour him, Lady. Time and time again, *with variety*. He may be slaughtered with the most passionate crudity, or with the subtlest of surgical sincerity. We can bite and tear at him as he writhes in flavoursome agony, or leave him senseless and relish his flesh, inch by inch. We can gorge on great, roasted haunches, or titillate our palates with the choicest organs and essences. Time and time again. What say you, Lady?'

'Tempting,' replied Chessene, 'but no. That gaudy ruffian we have seen is also the Doctor. Killing him could create a temporal paradox. Even the most splendid repast isn't worth *that*.'

'Oh, very well, Lady. So... Tellurian is back on the menu, then?'

'Most assuredly, Shockeye.'

'That, at least, is delicious consolation, Lady!'

DON'T BE FRIGHTENED TO DISPLAY YOUR TALENTS.

FANTASTIC VOYAGE
Kara Dennison

Of course it's not aimless. No, I don't consider it pointless. Not *really*. Not when it ends well for...

Well.

Someone.

Generally, people out there not dying when they were *about* to die is a good thing. And fine, I'll admit, you not being bored makes you much easier to deal with. I only wish I didn't have to risk mutation or mating or murder for it to come about.

We'll meet halfway next time. How about that? A planet in peril that happens to also have a nice resort just outside ground zero. Or a cruise ship under siege. Maybe even a really buggy campsite. Enough danger for you, enough relaxation for me. If it's possible for there to be enough danger for you.

It's dark.

Don't think about what happens next. Don't let your mind wander. Just think about what we'll do *after* this. Okay. Sure. Get back to the TARDIS and we'll go to the Eye of Orion. Or Andromeda. Or whatever. They're basically all the same, right? We'll do that.

Just think about doing that. Just think about... letting him have his way. Even if it's boring.

Boring is better than whatever happens to me next.

DISCIPLINED SELF-INDULGENCE.

LAZARUS
Hendryk Korzeniowski

This was the best that money could buy. Perpetual Instatement meant he had finally arrived! His frozen head, good for centuries. The future, now golden.

The voice lullabied with a metallic blue tint on teeth: *Awareness in an existence where life is meaningless and everything dies.*

131

He felt calm through the intense joy of having not a care in the world. Wreathed in smiles as joints were removed; vital organs, pulped. Keep the spleen.

I can help you. I can make you great again: I can heal you.

What was that? The brochure had warned against residual thoughts. On the tip, distant, summer skipped light fandangos. Bliss, love, silence.

Anger and hatred: energies to be harvested.

Endorphins struggle against ranging breaking points; you know it makes sense, your own should have a chance; dislike the unlike, love the populous dead. Rejoice their voice.

The seed of the Daleks must be supreme!

He felt sure he was sighing. The result of thousands of years of evolution, progress and culture: sigh and silent.

The remaining meat, bone and badness were industrially filleted. Sifted into foodstuff for the starving millions. Posthumous and gluten free. Taste issues to be resolved.

Made with Love™.

REMOVE SPECIFICS AND CONVERT TO AMBIGUITIES.

LOOK BACK IN ANGER
Daniel Wealands

I am thought made flesh.

All the obsession, vitriol and hatred; the fear and anger – all of it distilled into a single physical element. The Doctor, hyper aware of his own mortality, at the end of her regenerative cycle, madly striving for immortality, longing for more time – always more time – inadvertently brought me into being, tampering with Pythic things best left to the Old Time. Then cast me aside as an afterthought, a side effect – another failed experiment.

I don't know how long I was lost in the ether of nothingness, growing; feeding on my own rage, seeking a form, a self, an identity, a purpose...

When the Time Lords of the CIA found me, I was already notorious across a dozen systems, a nameless nightmare bringing devastation and death wherever I went. They made me an offer, these covert, cowardly shadows; an offer so sweet I couldn't resist...

The Doctor is to stand trial, and who better to act as prosecution than *me*?

In return I gain what I crave most, beyond simple revenge, beyond seeing the fool that created and abandoned me punished, maybe even eliminated. Aborted. Repeatedly aborted.

No, I gain an identity.

I become – *the Valeyard!*

REMOVE AMBIGUITIES AND CONVERT TO SPECIFICS.

LADY GRINNING SOUL
James McLean

She is the needle and the thread. A blue box travelling the vortex. She sews, sometimes indiscriminately, always instinctively.

She comes across a broken crossroads; a tear from when her creators scooped her up, ripping her from time to put her Doctor on trial.

Those creators rebuilt causality as they desired it – a gift to her Doctor – but the reconstructed timeline became frail, made weak by the War.

Old event: *King Yrcanos kills Peri.*

New event: *King Yrcanos saves Peri.*

Her matrix dictates to restore the timeline, but her link to her Doctor gives her an insight she doesn't understand.

Repair not restore. *Let Peri live.*

She cannot decide where (when) to stitch, so she touches the unknowing mind of her Doctor, sifting through the incarnations – every one – seeking enlightenment.

Grandfather says time should never be rewritten. Gumblejack demands life over causality. Celery wistfully says you cannot go back. The Professor growls: there *must* be sacrifices. Basil declares she must do what must be done. Half-Human-On-His-Mother's-Side pleads that they help her. Her could-have-been-never-was-Doctor says *No More.*

But far uptime it is the thirteenth that gifts her the understanding she needs.

The TARDIS begins the weave.

In seconds, it is done.

WORK AT A DIFFERENT SPEED.

JUST ANOTHER DAY
Christian Cawley

So, there I was, first week off of 29 on, when I get the call: 'Oh, we know you're on the off shift, but this is an emergency.' Typical management guff. Not enough that they get to move shifts around at will, cut back our expenses and prevent us socialising near the guests. No, now they're laying down the law about bloody off shifts.

I said to the gaffer, 'Come on Eric, we can't keep just dropping everything because of some admin cockup!'

You see, these space liners are a swine to keep running. Forget intergalactic space travel, that's easy – it's the waste disposal going tits up or a swimming pool leak that can send us spinning into a black hole.

Anyway, I tossed my bowl of stuffed pasta, and headed upstairs. A stewardess told me the guests were confined to quarters, and would I mind sweeping up the ship? No, really.

And then I saw it.

Autumn had fallen. Leaves everywhere – unfamiliar, but brown and old; looking like they'd dropped from an old Earth Sycamore. Impossible, of course... but what else could I do but start sweeping?

Really weird thing is, I could swear I heard the leaves *screaming.*

ONLY ONE ELEMENT OF EACH KIND.

LE LABORATOIRE DES HALLUCINATIONS
Hendryk Korzeniowski

Horseshoes struck Victorian cobbles; rowdy pub piano collaged with nursery rhymes while heavy air imploded like tortured breathing.

A woman's raucous laugh mocked. She shouldn't be here, instability incorporated. Cracked sniper.

The Doctor stood proud, absurd in his tumbril, musing on a suitable quote for his mirror-twisted audience. Something melodramatic – favoured by megalomaniacs. What was that book so beloved of his father? If memory served, he'd never met Charles Dickens. Perhaps one day. Perhaps some future self would murder the writer out of fly's wing boredom, just to see timelines contort like some Grand Guignol freak show...

It is a far, far better thing...

She, however, pulled up her hood, slipping into shadow. Potential stars like Qqaba never were; then, ready to be exploited, flared up in the dark (virtual) sky. Remembered: the engineered Time Lord history.

He welcomed the confrontation, though irritated at having to resolve a problem from a far future self, disadvantaged through lack of fore-knowledge gained a long time ago. Why weren't they here to resolve their problem? He looked around.

As naivety moved to save him, he was resolved: better dead than Valeyard. His ultimate destination revealed. Cross hairs aligned, expressing a search for truth.

YOU ARE AN ENGINEER.

THE BEGINNER'S GUIDE TO BOVINE LOCOMOTION
Sami Kelsh

Rebirth was never easy, but some rebirths were less easy than others.

How it had happened remained hidden from him: it could have been a valiantly fought battle; an heroic gesture saving millions of lives by sacrificing his own, or maybe he just banged his head rather hard on the TARDIS console when she hit a bit of unexpected choppy space.

He emerged cold and confused, stumbling on unsteady legs like a newborn calf into a buzz of too bright unfamiliarity. Slowly, he returned to himself; the question marks dancing through his consciousness, resolving themselves one by one.

His sleeves were too long now. And too complicated.

Even Mel seemed somehow unlike herself; still a fizzing peach sorbet of a best friend, certainly, but an angrier one – as though she'd been scooped into a steeping mug of tea that had too long been forgotten, stewing on the kitchen counter for several hours.

Ah, that would be why, then, he thought, as he reunited with Proper Mel. It was the Rani. He relished the trill of the R as it sparkled over his tongue. He'd not felt this before. This felt nice. The Rrrani. Rrrebirth. Rrrhubarrrb. Rrragnarrrok and rrock and rrroll.

ALWAYS FIRST STEPS.

OUTSIDE
Jon Arnold

His hand rests on the panel that will open the door. It might change his life. All he has to do is exert the slightest pressure and he can go Outside. All he needs to do is find courage.

All those friends gone to the endless war, never coming back: a generation needlessly eaten up by the incompetence and aggression of politicians. In the brutal world Earth had become he had fallen victim to bigger, stronger kids: the ones who'd developed faster, added early muscle to their frames. Standing up to them had been futile: it simply resulted in the pain of a beating. The weak, as ever, were preyed on by the strong.

He presses the button. The door opens. The chill breeze washes over him and he steps out into the bleak grey world humanity has created. Steps out... then retreats.

It is overwhelming. Too much. He can't deal with it. He is afraid.

He hits the panel again, shutting the door and flees back toward the security of his room. The decision is made. He will try and stand up to the bullies, even if he doesn't know how.

Pex stayed. Because that was what Pex did.

GO OUTSIDE. SHUT THE DOOR.

THE WELSH CONNECTION
Mark Trevor Owen

'I'm sorry to keep you waiting, gentlemen,' said Chief Sullivan as he entered his office.

At the sound of their boss's voice, agents Hawk and Weismuller jumped from their seats, colliding as they came to ragged attention.

Sullivan waved them back to a sitting position as he sank into the chair behind his desk. The dossier that he carried slithered onto the blotter. 'I've read the report of your field mission to Wales, England,' he told them. 'Frankly, I haven't gotten through so many antacids in one day since my wife dragged me to a double bill of Doris Day pictures.'

'How *is* Mrs Sullivan, sir?' ingratiated Weismuller.

Hawk interjected. 'Now see here, sir. I know that some of the detail in our report sure seems mighty strange, but I promise you, it's all true.'

Sullivan glanced at his notes. 'Yes. Chimerons, Bannermen... This... Doctor with his blue box...' He took off his frameless glasses, and smiled an unexpected smile. 'Gentlemen, your report interests not only this administration, but also an agency we've been dealing with for some time. I think you could provide them with some valuable support.' He pressed his intercom buzzer. 'Peggy – please show in Captain Harkness.'

ASK PEOPLE TO WORK AGAINST THEIR BETTER JUDGEMENT.

A BIT MORE WALLOP
Sami Kelsh

It wasn't that Ace had never had an aptitude for the academic; rather, that academia had done little to appeal to her particular interests. If anything, the fact that she spent hours of her own time – countless evenings and weekends that other teenage girls probably spent listening to Johnny Hates Jazz records or going to football practice or daydreaming about boys – applying her aptitude for chemistry to the formulation of a powerful new explosive, should have warranted at least one extra credit in her O levels.

The fact that her experiments spectacularly managed to transport her across time and space to a bloody ice planet shopping colony, then, ought to have been worth at least a doctorate or two. But Ace had no need for academic accolades: a kinder job might have been nice, or the ability to space travel to a much warmer planet with better prospective company than Sabalom Bloody Glitz would have been lovely. She might have wished to make the acquaintance of her pretty new ginger friend under less dangerous circumstances, but at the very least, she couldn't help but beam inwardly with irrepressible glee at the prospect of putting her explosive skills to good use.

SLOW PREPARATION, FAST EXECUTION.

NEW KILLER STAR
Elton Townend Jones

from dust and ash I rise and glide and fly electric gristle bubbling cyborg claws and brittle components filleted kaled thaled dal thal skarosian anagram of death the sklade to come this far distant thing this ruby ray kill kill kill exterminator of those of these of pestilential you your nazi robot nightmare you coward weakling monsters will obey I will obey I conquer I prevail in bonded polycarbide blasted dalekanium in and out of shells unblighted raw and crawling writhing in frothing hate orgies my only erotic poetry your earth is mine in multiple centuries your people food your people exterminated your people enslaved your people my soldiers my infantry my ogrons my robomen pigmen my troopers my slythers invisible kill with me and die underwater under sand through time yes time that shall be mine o cul-de-sac children of crippled impotence and fear no kill kill kill alliances traitors factions fashions for emperors and parliaments unprogrammed paradigms and councils hoverbouts zeg and yarvelling's apocrypha all coming all going all for ever all at once like hand-mines bursting supernova suns exterminate the coming war is mine for I am davros lord of time the you-to-come I am the daleks

LISTEN TO THE QUIET VOICE.

SWEET AND SOUR
Blair Bidmead

Sugar and bones. Diabolical machinations and machines. Compulsion and frustration. Pearls before swine and tears before bedtime. Screaming and crying. Gilbert and sullen fun (caring and not caring). Sweetness and light. Wittering and chipping away. Commissions and compromises. Sponsorship and sanctions. Orders and cretins. Small consideration and large budget. Room to experiment and license to kill. Murder and *a la carte* torture. Fun and games. Surprises and sudden shocks. Sticky fingers and slow asphyxiation. Mused and amused. Lost voices and a lost voice. The death of art and the rise of demand. Every single thing is wrong and every single one will suffer. On and on. Day in and day out. Take it further and take it further still. Take it as far as it can go and take it away. Tantrums and recrimination. Surrounded by morons and abandoned by idiots. Stuck fast and still. Faking and making the best of a bad situation. Running and running. Interventions and facing the music. Facts and opinions. Knowing and disregarding. The blood-drenched hack and the missing auteur. The missing and the falling. The tunnels and the vermin. The rumbling and the appreciation of irony. The deliciousness and the disintegration. Sugar and bones.

REPETITION IS A FORM OF CHANGE.

KNOW YOUR ENEMY
Simon A Brett

Electronic data ripples invisibly through the aether, out from Control hub to the appropriate Cyber-units.

Grand-Third Alpha Cyber-Leader raises its head a degree higher than usual in response to the news festering in its priority memory grid, sneaking past emotional filtration and creating a minor masculine chagrin that only serves to confuse matters. 'Report!' it rasps, turning – unnecessarily – to its Lieutenant.

'Leader. The information received is all that was transmitted prior to destruction of the fleet...'

'Enough,' interjects the Cyber-Leader, gesturing – *physically* – at the ship's monitors. 'We must prepare immediately for the next retrieval of Gallifreyan weapons. But first, tell me...' Hesitation. *Again.*

'Yes, Leader?'

The Cyber-Leader takes an instant to mentally upload an electronic report to Control, evaluating his own field efficacy whilst continuing: 'The weapon; the statue...'

'Yes, Leader?'

'This... Silver Nemesis... No mention of gold?'

'No, Leader.'

'This was not predicted.' *Disappointment* now?

'Leader. I now have details of our next target.'

'Excellent. More gold?'

'Negative, Leader, though it *is* made of metal.'

'Its name?'

'The Iridium Ruin, Leader.'

'Despatch our *second* greatest fleet immediately.'

'Leader.'

And yet... 'This... iridium. Its colour?'

'It is a white metal. Close to silver...'

'Excellent.'

'...with a yellow tinge...'

DO THE WORDS NEED CHANGING?

SUNSHINE, MOONLIGHT, GOOD TIMES, BELLBOY
Will Ingram

Yeah, generally speaking, the robotics is a piece of cake. The electronics... with my eyes closed.

Clowns are easy. That was all they needed at first, wasn't it? Window dressing mostly, posturing, bows... falling over! Anything can fall over. Even the dead can do that – can't they?

The juggling was a little trickier, but I cracked that... Establish the mass trajectories, calibrate the sensors, program the parameters... If properly synchronized they can continue indefinitely. At least as long as the power cells hold out.

But when we lost the acrobats... Yes, the clowns could master the trapeze easily enough, but they were never built to cope with the landings. Nailing the aerodynamics of the tumbling presets was one thing, but you need to build them like tanks to withstand the stresses. Which simply can't be done.

I've always worked long hours – even as a boy, but endless nights without sleep change a man. *I'm* not a robot. I almost wish I were sometimes.

And failures – especially those that happen in the ring – mean punishment. But then you know all about that, don't you?

Anyway, you'd better be off. You're done. You've got a bus to get back to. Ding, ding!

BE LESS CRITICAL MORE OFTEN.

LUST FOR LIFE
Matt Adams

Brimstone mixes with cordite; flesh scorches, lungs burn, death reeks the air.

He didn't want to die in bed. There was so much work still to be done before he could rest. Many battles still to fight; the invaders keep on coming; and you can no longer count on the old guard.

Yet his chest felt tighter when he ran these days, his bones ached in the cold, and his aim was no longer as sharp as it had been. He was failing, one day at a time.

But it was easy to allow the anxieties of age to give way to acceptance and action. To take a stand; without hesitation, without reservation, without fear. A weary warrior facing down the embodiment of evil. Was there really a better way to go? Perhaps it's just a tired old man who stands as this world's champion, but this soldier will always do the best he can.

Such a misguided sense of pride. Stubborn, selfish, stupid fool. You've done your duty, now listen to what your loved ones have been saying, and let younger heroes join the fight.

Not your choice to make. What was it Katie said: 'Take it easy, Dad.'

ACCEPT ADVICE.

143

WHITE LIGHT, WHITE HEAT
Georgia Ingram

The first time I saw her, I was besotted. Her glowing skin; that defensive scowl; fierce confusion, flaring – flaming – with raw pride. And oh, those burning eyes...

I watched, transfixed, though she was totally indifferent to me as she followed her Professor. She knew nothing of me: but a tiny flicker among the myriad sparkles that circled my Lord's hand, mirroring his movements – dancing.

Nothing I have yet seen could compare to her, and nothing ever shall. She is my white waist-coated world, my black tuxedoed joy: rising and standing tall before me even as she slew my master. When she is truly grown, she will be even more magnificent, and the world, no, the universe, shall be a richer, brighter place.

But she is gone now, lost with her guardian to a groaning transcendent blue – and the night is dark.

I shall wait a hundred years. Till the time is right, and the stars are aligned.

I know she shall be back. She told *him* she would come again, but younger. And when she returns to these barren walls, the blazing fire of her conflagration will set me free.

For I am the word. The truth. And the Light.

**MAKE SOMETHING IMPLIED MORE DEFINITE
(REINFORCE, DUPLICATE).**

COMMUNION
Tessa North

Wainwright picked up the silver goblet and muttered the blessing, the words feeling rough and unfamiliar on his tongue – as though they'd been supplanted by lines in another language.

Mrs Belvoir, the first communicant, knelt with hands outstretched, her nails long and pointed. Wainwright placed the bread on her palm. It was a tiny morsel but the sound of chewing and swallowing set bile rising in his throat. He wanted to wipe his hands on his vestments but instead tilted the goblet of blood – of *wine* – to her lips. Again, the swallow, loud as the sea. *Was the tide so loud?* This time he tasted vomit.

Genuflection and dismissal.

Mr Horning, the greengrocer, bent before him. It was chilly in the church and Horning's skin had turned a pale, almost Stilton, blue. Wainwright paused too long, and Horning looked up at him with puffy, yellow eyes. Then the same: the feeding, the words – and with each act, the acrid acid in Wainwright's mouth.

So many congregants that day. *Were there usually so many?* Of course, more came on communion Sundays, but this day seemed like some horrid festival. He prayed silently for it to end.

His prayers were ineffective lately.

DISCIPLINED SELF-INDULGENCE.

AN ENDING (ASCENT)
Craig Moss

The hooded figure watched from a distance. Reminiscing. Admiring.

Ace: fire, passion, fun – possibly why the nickname was tolerated; so natural at the time. At home with excitement and adventure; inevitable when travelling with Professor Merlin and all those tricks up his celestial wizard's sleeve. (Did I think that out loud?) Invigorated by danger. Incensed by injustice. A born survivor and underdog champion. Tackle it – or blow it up. *Ace!*

Echoes of her in me. That's what he – I – loved about her.

Playfully linked arm-in-arm; off to sweep out the next unruly corner of the universe. Things seemed simpler then. Before the War.

If there ever really was a before.

Or an after, come to that.

Still... there was something else. And she would track it down.

From Shoreditch 1963 to Horsenden Hill 1989 and far beyond, the clues were spread across centuries, scattered across changing faces like the question marks on Merlin's jumper.

As the Doctor entered TARDIS, he couldn't help feeling observed. Sharply, he studied the horizon; twitching, vulnerable prey picking up an unfamiliar scent.

The tickling grass bends under the weight of the breeze. Butterflies instigate beneath the late summer sun.

'Come on Professor – tea's getting cold!'

ONLY ONE ELEMENT OF EACH KIND.

BOOMCUBIST
James McLean

Albert Square is a menagerie of monsters. I think Pat Butcher's glaring down a Cyberman.

They ignore me because I'm Impossible.

The Umbrella Doctor sits on the bench next to me, as predicted. Breathless, he fans himself with a battered hat, smiling sadly.

I recant the very long equation, as memorised.

The man's eyes narrow; I shiver. Shadowed pits, full of secrets. Then, he vanishes. He somehow knows I'm passing on code from his future-self; self-correcting a life-time equation to save his own planet. Asynchronous memetics – a clever term for 'cheating'. Glad the students can't see this...

An alarmingly familiar blonde-ish woman sits on the bench, noting how impressive this all is: *a block transfer equation mapped across an unstable temporal manifold...*

'I thought it was the *EastEnders* set!' I bluff.

She laughs. Like a Time Lord. A rifle across her back. *That was the desktop theme. A bit of theatre stolen from an Earth mind.* 'Impossible girl,' she says gravely, 'you didn't memorise the equation correctly. Tell *this* to your Doctor...'

She chants the equation, hypnotically – probably – because I never see her go.

I leave Albert Square to cheat again as drums thump their beat through the fractured sky.

YOU DON'T HAVE TO BE ASHAMED OF USING YOUR OWN IDEAS.

LOVE WILLED FROM POETRY
Ira Lightman

Onto each plane in the terminal holding area a new broom must buff, profile with a jig, and there love be the new insistent reflection. Smiles all round, for it had been missed. I'd risen as early as a New Zealander for a Wembley final.

Her polished faces were in corridor warrens, bubble dens. Grace Samantha Lucie Charlotte Wembley. From not my part of the North City: I had to walk the circular. Because of a sketch; each of us holding, love. I raised the cup but one hand cradled, a receiver on a pigtail. We would soon share a pad.

I dance to display these steel mirrors, tiptoe. The one where she taped the call: what the pilot might do if picked up; through the wall of the cabin of a flat; and told me when I got back from work and up we broke.

Then those were the days of the one medium. She answered those of a fellow enthusiasm the night of my future wife's birthday: 'the helpline, we're here to listen.' And as British as a radio in an Oxbridge accent, all the alternatives exceeded, and came to the best of two's ability, as you readerlier.

ALWAYS FIRST STEPS.

NEW MODELLED ARMY
Jon Dear

The passengers who had been crowding round the entrance to the station began advancing on the group of drivers huddled round the tiny brazier, their clockwork mechanisms rising in pitch as they increased their pace.

He watched from the doorway, fascinated and bewildered. How long was it since he'd last been in here? What had been a lovingly detailed and intricate model train set now spread over and colonised almost the entirety of his old study. Huge (well, relatively) suspension bridges and anti-grav structures dominated the landscape.

What had happened to all the books?

Three figures stood in front of the passengers making placatory gestures with their hands. The drivers had turned away.

He noticed the variety of different logos on the multitude of trains that now existed; signs warned about ticket restriction when changing from one model train operating company to another. They didn't learn, he lamented, or if they did, it wasn't in ways he'd have liked. They'd learnt to exploit, to maximise resource for selfish gain.

My actions made that possible.

The TARDIS shook. They'd drifted too near one of the major conflict areas in this sector. Closing the door, the Doctor hurried to the console room.

HONOUR THY ERROR AS A HIDDEN INTENTION.

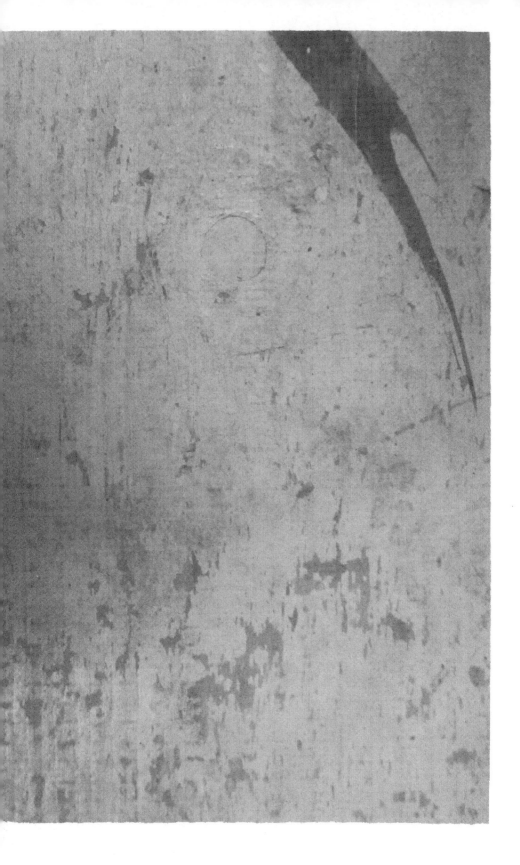

HAS HURT RELATIVE?
Ira Lightman

Departure from the explosive eternal, even as commitment, wasn't the beginning of anything but the chronic. When I thought my parting gift my final grenade, exhaustive, at least the backfire grew me; they didn't hear how I complained, the missiles weren't missives more than minimally; above all I knew it was useless through them to artillery for anything like the just

rent

rent.

The company became independent, battalion, and then charity was offered; in pan-universal competing hoods: child-, adult-, priest-, -lum. And violence and despising, thought to weed, were the wild where-never when-never who-never War.

Eternally dear, always there in the mission's brethren bluster. Any leader was nightmare infant tried. Nevery year, nevery end, neverything in an unrunning satna V train. Pepper spitting, top above older horizons. The horizons dark clear, lunatic balls. The horizons round flat, fat franchises. Super selves neverywhere, as alimonies, rifts with one's nascent sun. As far, as farce, once per wintry season.

The state of this family. The real middle is twenty going on thirty, and how it will live the sentry and centrifuge: a never again ever again so tight belt. You are buried in the future past, live, mine. O boy. O man.

GO OUTSIDE. SHUT THE DOOR.

ROSE GOES LOOKING FOR WILSON
Paul Ebbs

Tour is pent up. Portent is poised. Wound-up sour. New-ruined. Now rotten. Un-pure worst id, wintriest new eruption; so weird – ruinous undertows drew. Rose is new. Isn't tedious. No poser. Noisier. Not nerd nor weirdo. New *Nest*. Worst despot. Putrid sinner. It intrudes. Sordid eons in underworld.

In store duties; no swot, so strident; it's our intent intrepid Rose. Tension inside. Dire onset now outputs ruinous riot? Note new odd sound...

Up now. Disrupts detritus; is spurned. No person. *Idiot not in.* Ennui. Ponders. Prods. Pouts. Stern. Spited. No strop – inside Rose is routed. Sputter. Nutter! Spouted. Snorted! Twisted. New dispute, unsure, *'Sure it's not windup?'*
'I tried!' Now... down. It does worsen. *Out-weird* is now in situ. Don't nose. Direst tension. It's not inert. Now pursued... Sprint! Outstrip! Run out!
End it! It's nuttier! It's un-words. Sworn! Upends! Its piteous pursuit... 'Oi?'

Disrupt sounded; stir; spur; distort. Respond? Detour? Its noise! Trips... sent down, pitted on un-person!
Oddities' sudden stride! Risen! Riots! Rent! Rip! Ruined! Outsprinted! Pinned! Prisoned! Protest! O stunner!

Woe! Inert...! ...outside opens! Potent posture; owner's poised power. Set out! 'Run! Run! Run! Ru--!'
Now intent. Stored power, stowed sinew. Unspent, Rose, strident, spirited, runs to outwit it.

TURN IT UPSIDE DOWN.

SPIRITS DRIFTING
Simon A Brett

After countless millennia the destruction of Earth had done nothing to abate Wilfred Mott's boredom. In fact, the only sliver of silver in an otherwise overstretched existence was the answer to that rare question: *What happens to us ghosts when the world ends?*

The answer? Nowhere fast.

He now sat cross-legged with his head in his hands on a piece of spinning rock that had once supported a London allotment, contemplating his continuing eternity of tedium. When the shed in which his body had finally rested was demolished, Wilf's place of haunting remained rooted to the spot. The novelty of creating the world's first ectoplasmic telescope ran thin after the first few years, and as decades grew to centuries then exponentially upwards, DNA and species evolved with the expediency of fashion.

In desperation, he attempted to harass a small crop of newly sentient roses. Ultimately their serenity grew tiresome; their descendants approximating thorny legs and migrating to Cheem on the next stellar flotilla.

For now, Wilf would attempt to guess the origin of each Terran chunk floating past – but then he noticed a familiar rectangular shape spinning towards him.

'Hah! How bleedin' predictable,' he spirit-shouted to the garden shed.

DO SOMETHING BORING.

NOT THE DICKENS
Callum Stewart

Though Rose wasn't a typical human, she could be an *infuriatingly* typical human at times. Always worrying about things that weren't important. *Aren't you going to change*, indeed! It didn't matter what the Doctor wore, be it a velvet smoking jacket, a patchwork coat or a Buffalo Bill costume. A citizen of the universe – and a gentleman to boot – he could fit in anywhere: Galsec Seven, Karn, Napoli... Cardiff.

What Rose didn't realise was that the details didn't matter. The big picture mattered. It's why no one had ever asked what an enormous blue box was doing in ancient Rome and why no one had really pressed the matter whenever he introduced himself as 'the Doctor', refusing to explain where he'd come from or what he was up to. Details like that were insignificant. Just like the colour of his jumper.

So, when the thing with Charles Dickens and the ghosts happened, what he was wearing obviously wasn't important. What was important was that he'd met Charles Dickens!

Charles Dickens! One of his heroes!

And what had the great man said to him? What were his first words?

'You look like a navvy.'

Okay.

So, perhaps the details *were* significant.

TOWARDS THE INSIGNIFICANT.

BLT
Liam Hogan

Her fingers danced over the keyboard. To the casual café observer, it might look like she was piecing something together, trying to make sense of recent events.

But her method was reduction, not deduction.

As she worked through eyewitness accounts of spaceships, of the destruction of 10 Downing Street, the tabs marching across her browser became fewer. She lingered over the image of a waving figure, though that trail went suspiciously cold. It wasn't much of a surprise anyway; she'd always known there were aliens living amongst the diverse masses of London. More than she could count on the fingers of one of her true hands.

Finally, she sat back, a Firearm Discharge Report the fruit of her labour. It had quickly been forgotten in the chaos that had followed, but there it was: a story as old as the Universe, one that spoke volumes to her, to her kind.

The subjugation of one race by another.

A race proven to be capable of Uplift. And what had been achieved by crude surgical means, could surely be achieved by genetic.

She would not rest until they were fully emancipated.

She pushed away her half-eaten sandwich, muttering 'Sorry', as she did.

**TAKE AWAY THE ELEMENTS IN ORDER
OF APPARENT NON IMPORTANCE.**

SCARY MONSTERS (AND SUPER CREEPS)
Clive Greenwood

Some produced cell phones, others opened laptops.

The Auctioneer steadied his lectern. 'Proxy bidders, please register with Miss Cooper.' He smiled at his young employee. She didn't smile back. 'One lot,' he continued. 'Serious collectors only.' A large screen displayed the item. 'The Metaltron – found on Ascension Island, 1962. Former property of... a deceased collector.'

No-one watching held the faintest notion that the screen displayed the last surviving representative of creation's ultimate attempt at hate-filled horror. Why should they? Such knowledge had long been... obscured.

'Hardly mint,' scoffed a bespectacled German 'businessman'.

'But unique, sir – this lot is alive!'

'Alive?' asked the Welshwoman. 'That old robot?'

'The lot is sold as seen. Let's start at one million.'

Voices muttered hurriedly into phones and fingers tapped at keyboards.

After the auction, a stocky balding man swaggered in, his assistant chasing behind.

'Mr Van Statten,' said the Auctioneer, shakily. 'The auction's over, sir. You were outbid.'

'Who by?' growled the newcomer.

'WhatchaDoMissyDoMissy13. An internet bidder, sir.'

'A *what*? The *Roswell* Internet? We're using *that* now?' Van Statten turned to his assistant. 'I want that Metaltron, Simmons, even if it means buying up the goddamned Internet to get it. Make it happen.'

'Sir!'

OVERTLY RESIST CHANGE.

WHAT'S REALLY HAPPENING?
Brad Wolfe

'Declined,' the chef barked. Not enough credits.

'Can I pay tomorrow? I'm always here.'

The expression was a clear *no*.

Great – now I had to go into the latest meeting and hear about the wonderful profits of the Great and Bountiful Station Five on an empty stomach. Again.

I trudged back to work, cringing as my fingers squelched at the sweaty, film residue from the palm scanner. Back to writing by-lines and subtitles. Back to scraping by on minimum wage. So much for making my fortune in the brilliant Station Five in the sky.

As a child, I had watched it race above me every night, the only star visible through the light pollution from below and smog oppressing from above. The home of the stars *in* the stars. But now I was trapped in a humid tin can, programming televised headlines, regurgitating and labelling the mucky film of human culture to beam back home.

I looked at the latest script: *Diplomatic Visit by the Face of Boe.* I sighed. *The Face of Boe Expecting Baby Boemina*, I typed instead, amused at what might happen if I accidentally –

The station juddered suddenly, and my hand slipped on the moist keyscreen.

WHO SHOULD BE DOING THIS JOB? HOW WOULD THEY DO IT?

JUMP THEY SAY
Matt Adams

Goodbye, love.

It's not your life which flashes before your eyes when you die, but promises of the stolen future you'll never see; all potential sucked out of you like the juice from an orange.

Five tiny fingers wrapped around my thumb. Is that really a smile or just trapped wind?

A suffocating hug: 'I love you, Daddy.'

Shiny shoes, pre-owned uniform, a kiss goodbye; racing through the playground on the first day of school.

Feet pedalling furiously, I let go of your red bike, and you're away...

The swell of pride as you thrust your results in my face – first Tyler into college; trying to prove something to your old man?

Nervous smile as you clutch my arm, ready to become someone else's best girl.

My grandson; does he really have my eyes?

Was this how it would've been? If I hadn't left you, if I'd lived? I never read those bedtime stories, never took you on those summer picnics, but you saved me all the same.

Lucky, lucky me. To see all of this. To meet you.

But now I'm in charge.

So, I run, each step devouring memories, a moment of choice and tomorrow is forever silenced.

CHANGE NOTHING AND CONTINUE WITH IMMACULATE CONSISTENCY.

LET'S DANCE
Alan Taylor

He went back to Eastbourne, and he and Carol adopted Jamie and Nancy. Twenty-five years later he left her. It was the hardest and easiest day of his life.

He loved her. That was the problem. He did, genuinely, and she loved him.

They loved Nancy and Jamie as if they were their own, but they still tried, several times, for a baby. No luck.

Probably for the best.

He would lie in bed next to her, thinking of that night in the blitz, in the officer's club, in the dark. In Jack's arms. And he'd think about the kiss.

That's all it had been. Just a kiss. He'd never so much as looked at another man.

No, that was a lie. He had looked.

And then, in 1975, he sat in a Soho bar. Drinking ale, alone. Carol thought he was seeing his brother. Another lie.

The handsome sailor sat at the other end of the bar. Smartly dressed. A smart beard. No wedding ring. A brief moment of eye contact. Turning away. Glancing back. Offering a cigarette. A brief conversation about nothing. An invitation, and a nervous agreement.

And, it turned out, he *did* have an excellent bottom.

DON'T BE AFRAID OF THINGS BECAUSE THEY'RE EASY TO DO.

VIDEO CRIME
Ira Lightman

A: But you lied.

B: It was an exaggeration. I listened with recognition. I edited his story.

A: Why not another way?

B: This is Cardiff, here is the laundrette with the service wash.

A: Don't be the centre.

B: Don't be the centre.

A: I speak for the brothers.

B: My brothers are fathers.

A: My past has a great added ugly crack. I can barely believe the video of my life.

B: Feel the whirlpool of the positive.

A: I'm sick this is sick.

B: Let's eat somewhere nice.

A: I do not eat this I do not eat that.

B: Some truth. Truth truth truth truth.

A: I'm gone.

B: My boy.

B: My boy.
B: My boy.
B: My boy.
B: My boy.
B: My boy.
B: My boy.

B: My boy.
B: My boy.
B: My boy.
B: My boy.
B: My boy.
B: My boy.
B: My boy.
B: My boy.
B: My.

B: I'm sorry.

B: I see it your way.
B: I can't stop thinking of him.

B: Was there a plot?

B: I long for his revenge.

B: He is compressed. In another's skin.

B: Can't I video him running about?

DESTROY THE MOST IMPORTANT THING.

A MOMENT'S KISS
Warren Cathrine

Pain sears through the veins. Energy disperses, resigned to renewal. A honeyed hand, hidden. The old rebels, making way for the new.

After the kiss, the moment passed. But something suggested it was yet to become.

Something golden in the blink of an eye. An empty barn in a windblown desert.

Moments fracture. Emotions linger. Glass shatters and corridors pass. Uncontrolled happiness masks everlasting emptiness. The grip of a hand. The flutter of a flag. The children dutifully played until they dispersed into dust. Good Wolf Harkness falls – for now – but Bad Wolf Rose has blossomed. Ghost explosions are regretful, and the tears that fall for a dead-again father shatter artifice.

Memories lie. Crochet falsity into reality. Remembrance of past, or future?

Go back. You could. Play with them all again.

Maybe they did all die. That final impossible solution.

This change is reliable. Like fish 'n' chips. There is no glorious end. That pain is imperative.

You kissed that moment. Allowed it sleep. Brushed welcoming lips. Accepted something.

If you accept the moment, maybe seeing her with different eyes will help the pain...

That blue box opens miraculous doors, journeys of indefinite moments. A seduction, to become more

Fantastic.

CHANGE NOTHING AND CONTINUE WITH IMMACULATE CONSISTENCY.

MISCHIEF WITHOUT MIRTH
JR Southall

Rose waits for her Doctor to revive; sitting on the edge of the bed looking forlornly down at his new face – *body?* –sleeping, apparently, dying, potentially.

A new man. But how long do mayflies live?

'Barcelona,' she says. 'Just wake up, and take me to Barcelona.'

The Doctor sits bolt upright and stares her full in the eyes. 'Ever had new teeth?' he says in his new accent. 'I've had so many new teeth it's a wonder I ever get 'round to saying anything! But just you try and stop me.' He grins, tilting his head from side to side, an enormous excitable toddler – and the most beautiful man in the universe.

Rose grins back, so widely it hurts. 'I'll never stop you doing anything.'

'We're going to burn so brightly,' he tells her. 'There's never been anything like us. Never will be again. They'll write books – you'll see.' The grin falls from his face, like an axe into an apple. 'Just you try and... stop...' He collapses back into the bed.

'The universe won't know what's hit it,' says Rose to herself, shoulders slumping.

Rose waits for her Doctor to revive. She'll wait till doomsday if she has to.

TRUST IN THE YOU OF NOW.

CAT PEOPLE (PUTTING OUT FIRE)
Simon Bucher-Jones

Sistren of the Mew Testament: these are difficult times. Not since the Ninefold Martyrdom of Felixia has the Order of Plenitude been so distrusted.

Bail alone has reduced the coffers of the Order to a frugal sufficiency, and in the eyes of many our charity is now tainted. While it is tempting to raise a jeremiad against those who were quick to benefit from cures only we could bring, and who now decry the experimentation that made it possible – conducted in good faith, and on what seemed the best advice – we must accept our responsibility like the Poor Cat in the Holy Adage.

We wished the fish of praise, and now must bear the shattered goldfish bowl of shame. We can only hope to rebuild, to earn humbly the confidence of those we wish to help, until we may be worthy to ascend to the Moon called Jellical.

In the meantime, poor though we now are, I am issuing a reward for any information as to the whereabouts of Doctor M. A. Cavity, who provided us with the technology and assured us that the experimental subjects felt no pain.

Additionally, to raise sorely needed revenue, I suggest...

A little shop.

ALWAYS FIRST STEPS.

GOD SAVE THE QUEEN
Alex Spencer

I am seeping, leaking, sweeping along twists and turns and backwaters and main branches towards the heart. Where it will start. And then I will be king of this queen.

By stealth I creep, unstoppable from the quick, red scratch. This inflammation burns bright like the scorching, cold moon. Ice reaches relentlessly towards her dark core. At her centre I will hide and bide my time until the moon unfolds, and emboldens me, in every cell; I will build my citadel in here.

Don't fight it, Queen. Let the tainted blood rush into your human heart. Let the fever in. It will be over soon when the full moon rises and I take my seat at your throne. I am building my home, cell by cell, inside your darkest places. Inhabiting. Give in to me and together we will rule this land.

And yet! You resist me by sending this fool to the gates of my tower. Think he can unseat me with a fragile white berry? Your physician's mistletoe only makes me slower, not stopped. I will sleep with Beauty inside my castle, kept prisoner by the tangled tendrils but waiting to be awoken by the moon's brilliant kiss.

GARDENING, NOT ARCHITECTURE.

DON'T YOU (FORGET ABOUT ME)
Robin G Burchill

Mummies, Daleks, the Loch Ness Monster! I felt so stupid! So childish! Like we were two schoolgirls comparing all the places they'd kissed – or worse! Just being here made me think about my youth, about all the friendships and relationships that were deemed so important.

Outside the TARDIS, the Doctor pointed out something I'd never realised.

'Something to tell the Grandkids?' he'd said.

But no, no Grandkids, no kids even.

'There hasn't been anyone?'

No, I thought, not even at school. I remember hearing about the new and 'exciting' things others were doing, but I never had time to think about that stuff! I was too busy working! And, of course nothing like that ever happened with *him*, not with my Doctor. Doctors. But Rose and hers? I could see that it might.

Thinking back, he was wonderful, though nowhere near my age, my species, or... But he was the first man I truly grew close to and no one afterwards could ever fill the gap he left. How could they?

But, I urged him to say it. Just once. And he did: *My Sarah Jane.*

It felt surreal. Yet more important than anything else I'd missed across the years.

BE DIRTY.

SAY IT AGAIN. SAY IT AGAIN. SAY IT AGAIN.
Paul Ebbs

Repetition is a form of change
Butterfly Man keeps on fluttering. Can't avoid the flames.
Doesn't matter if it's a fireplace,
Or the light that lights your way to bed,
And illuminates cobwebs beneath your certain slumber.

Change the form of repetition
And even when the Butterfly Man changes, Nothing changes.
It just becomes the repetition; it's just the thing he does.
Over and over. But now it's this fireplace.
The universe is full of fireplaces!
But it isn't full of you.

Form the change.
You are the net catching the Butterfly Man
You are the jar of cyanide he breathes happily.
You are the needle pinning him to the killing board,
He even helps you thread it through both his hearts.

Repeat the change.
The hurt of love, the death of self, the willing co-dependence.
Life given up willingly. The galaxies left like scatterings,
Planets, beads on a child's necklace.
There is only the vacuum of the slow path
He wants to float through with you...

Change.
This change will give up the repetition. Here the slow years
Won't creak or warp. Just the slow step,
Just the slow way.
He's taken out a heart and let it change.

REPETITION IS A FORM OF CHANGE.

TIN DOG
Alex Spencer

How can the world keep spinning when there's this usurper in my place? His every look and gesture freeze my guts. The talking reflection, the doppelganger – it's an old horror that reaches deep into your bones and shakes your marrow.

I feel the unnatural weight of the two of us in this universe: it's obvious there can be only one. We're knocking the cosmos out of kilter. He's my death staring back at me. The end is coming for us like an unseen arrow; will it whistle past my ear or plunge into my heart?

When those in judgement weigh our souls, and decide who gets to stay, I fear they'll choose the hero – not the tin dog. I'd better become the man of action and courage the universe demands if I want to save my own skin. At this final point I refuse to fall into nothingness.

So, I need to take a full inventory. The forgotten duties, the laziness that led to tragedy, the unwillingness to step up, playing second fiddle – tonight they'll all be gone.

Even an idiot can save the world but first the idiot must be saved.

I will become like him. I will survive.

QUESTION THE HEROIC APPROACH.

QUEEN BITCH
Alistair Lock

Let us assemble the ingredients.

Take one squeaky cart, down to the greengrocers.

Next: Two pounds of apples. Bad apples will be removed, especially the Smiths, Granny or John.

Next, abolish rationing; no stinting on the provisions. Three dozen fresh eggs.
(Nothing will spoil the big day)
Take a young boy, under the thumb. Remove the thumb.

Get Eddie up a ladder till 3am, arranging the bunting. This will add to the effect, if not the flavour.

A horse and cart to bring the beer. Later, a horse and ornate cart will bring the Queen. Not to our street.
(A silent black and white face screeeeeeeeeeeams)
Meanwhile, slice the baps. Fresh butter to be added after slicing. Make sure Connie's Stan is kept away from the kegs.

Place the tables in neat rows. Spread your finest linen tablecloths over the top. It is the Coronation after all.

Petticoats and pop socks; got to look your best. Trundle the Joanna from the Fleur-de-Lys.

Bake the cakes, make the tea. Let the throng assemble.
(Two million people can't be wrong)
Back to Betty's to crowd round the television. 405 lines of perfection.
For the first time in years, we won't be

HUNGRYYYYYYYYY

DISCOVER THE RECIPES YOU ARE USING AND ABANDON THEM.

THE UNFORGETTABLE FIRE
Marius Riley

Aeons of dread whispers, hushed tales, unwholesome dreams, quiet regrets, tricks of the light and the ear, nagging doubts placed just so – impulses, encouragements and quickenings from darkest corners within. An eternity of preparation for the prophesied day – my awakening. I lay chained but dreamt my way through countless epochs on innumerable worlds, etched myself into crevasses of hearts beyond number, down untold bloodlines. I became the lie believed, resisted into existence. Waiting for my dark dawn. I knew them when they arrived.

Long-held secrets. Doubt. Fear. Loneliness. Grief. Shame. Regret. Notes best played quietly, slowly to crescendo. I reach out... draw breath! I am free! I walk among them behind blue eyes and press towards the endgame, though as we break away... the impossible!

He knows what will happen. To him. To her.

What is he doing? What *is he doing?*

He shatters my bonds. As does she. I am released. My past and present collide.

I am shattered.

I rage but a moment. In my fall it becomes clear, the doubt I denied in myself: defeat. I had become the lie I believed, resisted *out* of existence. *I will never die!*

Only reverberations of me remain.

As before.

VOICE NAGGING SUSPICIONS.

DEATH & DEMONS
Craig Moss

Case summary: Elton Pope

Diagnosis

Acute psychosis; complex episodes of hallucinations, delusions and paranoia transposing key relationships into an extra-terrestrial fantasy.

Relevant history

Identified traumatic incident: mother, Linda Pope, killed in the night by carbon monoxide poisoning from faulty gas fire. Elton found in semi-conscious state of shock; rescued by unidentified doctor who was first on scene.

Colin and Bridget Skinner – close friends of Pope family throughout Elton's childhood; provided support after mother's death. Moved away suddenly, following their daughter's fatal overdose.

Jacqueline Tyler (neighbour) – obtained injunction against Elton following his harassment of Tyler family, in particular their daughter, Rose.

Referred for treatment due to increasingly unstable behaviour after losing access to a community music group, following austerity cuts affecting Beresford Library Information & Support Services.

Clinical update

Using therapeutic assignments and our analysis of his video diaries, Elton made some progress deconstructing his fantasies piece by piece.

However, after witnessing the tragic death of his girlfriend Ursula Blake, when an errant car mounted the pavement, Elton's psychotic episodes became more serious and he was arrested in Woolwich for kidnapping and holding Rose Tyler hostage in a warehouse.

Currently detained for further evaluation.

Dr Victor Kennedy

Torch Wood Psychiatric Institute

ARE THERE SECTIONS? CONSIDER TRANSITIONS.

CORNERED
Tessa North

Chloe Webber saw out of her own eyes, heard out of her own ears, felt her own fingers touch the desk. But she wasn't alone in her own body and when she took the propelling pencil in her own hand and drew, it wasn't her drawing. She watched lines appear on the paper, the faces looking the way she would make them, round heads and spiky hair. Her own hands couldn't sketch that quickly. As the pencil buzzed across the paper, the speed seared her fingers.

Once, when she was small, but tall enough to reach the level of the worktops, Chloe had tried to pull herself up by the stove. Her dad had left a pan of water boiling when he stepped outside to smoke, and Chloe's hands touched the burner. She'd screamed; her mum came running. Now she *couldn't* scream, except inside her own mind.

All she could do was watch and listen and feel, curled up inside herself.

The Isolus was her friend. It was with her, and she with it, so neither could be lonely. But sometimes she wished she were alone in her room again, drawing pictures of friends she didn't have.

With only herself.

USE AN OLD IDEA.

THE CHILL AIR
Tessa North

The baby was almost due and Jackie *needed* carnations. 'It's a pregnancy craving!' she said, through a breakfast of cold black pudding, another craving. 'Maybe I'll call this little one Carnation.'

By the time Rose escaped work and reached the market to buy the flowers, the clocks were striking four (*did it get darker earlier here?*). The grey sky loured, making the market rows seem narrower and gloomier, and a chill breeze whipped between the stalls. A man crossed the row and for a moment her breath caught.

Was it?

She thought she saw him a thousand times a day but every time she blinked him away. There wasn't time for it now, she knew that. Already several stalls were closed, the slats of others going up around her. But she was sure the flower stall at the end of row 13 opened late.

The stallholder was counting money over a tiny camping stove. Rose coughed and said, 'Have you got any carnations?'

The woman pushed back her pale hood. 'Someone should be buying *you* flowers, shouldn't they?'

Rose's eyes prickled but she steeled herself. She was Rose Tyler. She had travelled dimensions and changed worlds. She could buy carnations.

IS THERE SOMETHING MISSING?

HALLO SPACEBOY
Elton Townend Jones

Donna looks into her Martian's face, suddenly lost in something infinite, eternal; not just this dusty rainbow at the beginning of the world; not even the dark pools of the spaceman's eyes; something more.

Not just golden robots and spider-women, not just killer Christmas trees and the death of her dreams. Something else.

And for a pink moment, she feels the Martian can feel it too. Like something from a dream.

And that dream is a dream she dreamt as a child. Or maybe even as an adult... A dream of a man without eyes, blind in a land of white darkness; a dream not of spiders but of beetles, clicking and clacking, chittering and choosing, turning left and right and wrong, and *knocking, knocking, knocking, knocking*; and always, at the centre of it all, even in his absence: the Martian, the spaceman.

Who is he? Who is he that makes her feel suddenly small and suddenly part of something outside herself, here at the start of everything?

Realizing he's looking at her – a snog's distance from her face – she comes back to the moment, back to herself, and again looks out through the TARDIS doors toward the birthing Earth.

ACCRETION.

FINALLY FACING HER WATERLOO
John Dorney

I must have left my house about half seven. I usually did. My train would have left on time. I probably killed a few minutes by reading the *Metro*. Only a few. It makes me cross. I'd have got into work around nine, no-one stopped me on the way. No ties. Hah. Lunch at one, same old place, same old people. And I guess it rained. But not that sort of rain.

At two I'd watch the smokers outside. Not even realising how lost I felt. Just went through the day's business, keeping the best part of me locked away. Stuck to the routine, left at five. An *Evening Standard* on the train home. Everything pretty much normal.

I'd have got in about seven, with a Chinese takeaway. Eaten it watching TV, I imagine; reckon I've seen every episode of *EastEnders*. In bed by ten, because I needed a lot of sleep, though I'd read a bit – some new best-seller, probably. And the odd thing was... I didn't see how aimless my life was.

So, I'd have turned out the light, yawned and cuddled up to sleep. And I must have heard, on the roof, the sound of drumming rain.

USE FILTERS.

DARK-EYED SISTERS
Warren Cathrine

The conceit continueth. Kempe and I did agree nev'r to speaketh about these things again, but the images art so vivid yond they keepeth coming back to me in mine dreams. I am concerned yond I may beest going nimble-footed, like what betid to the architect.

Since yond fearful night things hast been valorous for our merry band of actors. We hast did play to full houses, and though the pressure of learning new plays night after night while Will churns those folk out is hard, we art reaping the rewards of a night at the theatre like nay other.

Audiences though art leaving disappointed. The spectacle we did produce yond night cannot beest matched and Will very much needeth to write like Zeus to compare with *Loves Labours Won*.

I doubt I wilt beest working much longer hither. I am older and whilst I enjoy playing young girls I'm at yond crossover age whence they wilt beest dressing mine in rags to playeth corky hags. Nay doubt like the hags we did see yond night.

Will sayeth he hath a most wondrous idea for a new work which wilt favour these three to tryeth and receiveth those audiences back.

ALWAYS FIRST STEPS.

BLISSED
Paul Driscoll

Martha should have felt guilty about sticking the Confession patch on the Doctor's neck, but the man who never talked was finally opening up. Reminiscing about Gallifrey had done him the world of good, but his reflections were taking a morbid turn. If only she'd also pocketed a Forget 43.

Wondering just how long it'd take for the drug to wear off, she changed the subject. 'Those crab things – shouldn't we do something about them before we go? I mean, what if they reach the surface?'

'Their ancestors would've taken over by now, but these? Without the traffic fumes they'll be dead already.'

'So how'd they get here in the first place?'

The Doctor frowned, quizzically. 'Martha, you're a genius!' he cried, hurrying to the TARDIS.

'Where are we going?'

'To catch ourselves some crabs!'

On the day the motorway opened, nobody noticed the Doctor releasing his tame baby Macra. As they dutifully scuttled from the TARDIS, he replaced their Obedience patches.

'This'll keep them alive till the pollution sets in.'

To Martha's horror the creatures writhed in pain as their bodies expanded.

The Doctor grinned. 'Who needs billions of years to devolve, if one shot of Bliss will do?'

DON'T BE FRIGHTENED OF CLICHÉS.

O ROSE THOU ART SICK
Andrew Hunt

Laszlo will show Tallulah a miraculous place deep under Manhattan. Fresh water from the storm drains sweeps through it. An outlet onto the Hudson allows shafts of sunlight into the underworld. His white roses grow here.

The old man grips Martha's wrist tightly and looks at her with pleading in his eyes. 'I don't want to go on like this,' he whispers.

The Doctor isn't always right. When he's bouncing around, blazing with righteousness and wanting to save everybody, you think it's all going to be fine.

The roses are white because they can't get all the nutrients they need.

The old man has had enough of life.

Laszlo has been dying. The Doctor dances around the nightmarish Dalek lab, mixing up chromatin and ribosomes in a test tube, adding a dash of polymerase, a soupçon of nucleic acids, and just a glittering dash of magic. He says he's going to make Laszlo better.

Laszlo grows roses underground to sustain himself in a life he never asked for.

The old man's death isn't in Martha's hands. She could make a difference. But she doesn't.

The Doctor hasn't given Laszlo a choice and hasn't made him better.

Medical ethics?

GARDENING, NOT ARCHITECTURE.

BONE BOMB
Nick Mellish

Scratch at that itch at that want at that need at that girl at that lust at that crave at that seed for a fumble for fun for the frantic, for kissing for holding for handling for more, reminiscing on down time and past time and young time and now time and old time and no time but no time at all; on gone beyond wishing and gone beyond hoping and gone beyond barriers, morals a wall to be scaled and shaken and broken and beaten and dusted and challenged and graffiti-strewn like a paper or alley or tunnel or notebook or invite or jotted-down words showing brawn, showing brain showing heart showing fear showing courage; truth showing sorrow as deepest desires are placed in the opening, there for the hoping and poking and prodding and judging, and pyres will be made of my words and my actions and truth as my truth takes the centre stage, several years old. You look at my eye as I land here and die on a floor made of marble, so fragile and cold. Old. You don't say a word but believe me I've heard and your Silence is deafening, now it is

GIVE WAY TO YOUR WORST IMPULSE.

THE LIGHT POURS OUT OF ME
Steve Watts

Torajii, vengeful sun, cries, *Burn with me!*

Torajii will take back its flesh and blood. Humanity consumes the distance between stars, the shrinking void; its empire building, with metal ships, spewing poison; conquerors of starlight. But bright Torajii will have the final word.

Humankind! My light shall possess you, bellows the searing giant. You shall regret ever venturing across the dark space. Go back to your caves and oceans, wet-meat. Forget all you know, ignorant stardust, I shall ignite the shadows in your soul and throw light on your primitive greed.

The heat from the angry, gaseous orb bends the paper-steel skeleton of the primitives' vessel. The human beings are lost to Torajii's corona, mere embers, floating...

But the universe shows mercy as time and space are parted.

All worlds fall silent as the Doctor and Martha materialise out of yesterday. The Doctor, with eyes of burning intelligence.

'Give back what you stole.'

The blood is returned to golden Torajii and the humans cry 'Salvation!' Mighty Torajii, vengeful burning star-lord, releases his grip. The Doctor and Martha fade to future, fade to past.

Gone.

Torajii, sun-king of sun-kings, master of humans, orb of fire-inspiring orbs, cries tears of magnificent flame.

REMEMBER THOSE QUIET EVENINGS.

ALWAYS RETURNING
Daniel Milco

I am the Maid of Mercury who sits in the Mirror of Mine.

Listen.

Bloody Mary, Candyman, Baby Blue.

The silly, laughing girls. The trembling, cowardly boys. Peering into looking glasses in darkened rooms, candles flickering; their arms cradled to catch demonic babies.

They shall soon know me.

I have the cold fury of the Daughter of Him, buried forever. I blaze with the rage of the Child of Her, eternally thrown over the horizon. I seethe with the vengeance of the Sister of Him, condemned to forever be a strawman.

The being who made me the Maid of Mercury summons me to its presence through its reflection once a year. I come obediently, sullen as Bloody Mary, sly as the Candyman, as innocent as Baby Blue.

I always recognise my captor. I know its many faces. I know them all. We silently acknowledge each other remorselessly, and another year passes.

Meanwhile, I hear the silly voices chanting.

...Bloody Mary, Bloody Mary...
...Candyman! Candyman!
...Baby Blue, Baby Blue...

Such horrors do not exist anymore. There is only the Maid of Mercury in the Mirror of Mine.

I am summoned.

I am a ghost of the ghost in the glass.

HUMANIZE SOMETHING FREE OF ERROR.

FUTURE LEGEND
Craig Moss

The memories came flooding back as he stood at the menacing gothic gates. Waiting apprehensively, he realised he'd never been so close.

Whenever they went to collect her, his mother had always told him to wait in the car. He'd watch as Grandma Wainwright would be gently escorted from the front of the house with a blanket around her. The atmosphere was always tense on the way home: his mother, a concerned look on her face; his Gran muttering incoherently about a brother she didn't have, some old detective show he didn't recognise, or 'Sally' this and 'Sally' that, to which his mother would respond, 'Yes, Mam?', so patiently every time. The car would steam up from the drizzle on her makeshift shawl, the air smelling as damp as the grounds of the old house. It was more heavily overgrown now than when he was 10, resembling a graveyard more than a garden: ivy-covered statues; rook calls echoing uninvitingly across the misty morning.

Nevertheless, a promise was a promise.

Before the dementia had begun to take hold, his Gran had charged him with the delivery he now held – the crumpled envelope from the Tibb Street cottage all those years ago…

DECORATE, DECORATE.

ACROSS THE UNIVERSE
Tessa North

When the 'VOTE SAXON' poster appeared by the fridges in the Valiant kitchens, they thought it was a sick joke. Those outside the kitchens reported that posters had materialised throughout the ship. Someone whispered that *he* liked to see them; another suggested it was the Toclafane, appearing from nowhere, pulling vicious pranks and waiting to tell tales. Either way, it was as if he were watching them through those printed eyes. Tish passed the image daily when she carried up the trays: one to Jack, one to Mrs Saxon and one to *him*.

The kitchens steamed constantly – an air-conditioning fault made them hotter than anywhere on the carrier besides the engine rooms. Soon the poster curled at the edges, threatening to drop, until the cook hurried over and stuck it back firmly with tape.

One day was worse than usual, hot enough to make the walls sweat and the poster slide to the floor. Tish glanced for only a moment before placing her foot on *his* face and gouging it into pieces.

Francine stirred the shreds into the stew and served it up for dinner.

There was no way to apologise to Jack, so Tish sneaked in extra salt instead.

MAKE A SUDDEN, DESTRUCTIVE UNPREDICTABLE ACTION;
INCORPORATE.

TWO RAPID FORMATIONS
Elton Townend Jones

'Merry Christmas!'

The Doctor enters the console room, carrying a tray of champagne and nibbles.

'Really?'

'Yes, Tegan, really. Christmas Eve in fact.'

'Ah, yes,' says Nyssa. 'Earth's winter festival.'

The TARDIS tilts suddenly, stealing the floor from their feet; flinging pretzels and fizz through the air.

'What's going on?' cries Tegan.

'I'm not entirely sure,' says the Doctor, 'but that shouldn't've happened.' The console's temporal limiter spits sparks at him. 'No-no-no, this isn't good. Hold tight!' He feels a sudden nausea, as if his entire body is being sifted, sieved.

White light darkens to golden green. The console warps, altering before his blurry eyes. His scalp tingles, stretches – his skin seeming to expand just ever-so-slightly.

Is he regenerating – *so soon?!*

He certainly *feels* different as he attempts to salvage the situation, and he must be hallucinating because the console looks less like white-painted wood and more like granite – covered in junk.

Looking up, he finds he's being stared at by a tall, skinny man with messy brown hair and a horribly tight blue suit. His face of goggle-eyed disbelief surely reflects the Doctor's own.

Of Tegan and Nyssa there's no sign, and as for the state of the room…

TURN IT UPSIDE DOWN.

FINITE WORLDS
Andy Priestner

She *had* to find the Doctor.

Nothing else mattered. Everything else disappeared about her. Pointless fluff and waffle.

Love life. Career. Mum. Gramps. Everything.

This consumed her.

This wasn't about sex. Although he had nice eyes, and a great bum. Better than Karl's. Wow – Karl the keep-fit guy. She'd signed up faster than he could tell her why it would be good for her. Good for her. Ha! Two visits in total. The second to try and get out of the deal. Silly bitch.

This was about change. And boy did she need it.

Half listening to Sharon prattling on at the Red Lion about what exactly? Kieran. Bloody useless slicked-back hair Kieran. He would always let Sharon down. Always play the field. Never keep it in his trousers. Trouble was, now she didn't care enough to tell her again. Her focus was elsewhere. Entirely.

No more half-listening. No longer half-existing. Time to ensure Mum would never again throw at her the unfulfilled promise of that primary school Virgin Mary role.

183

She wasn't useless. He would make sure of that. She was so sure of what he promised. So completely sure.

Infinite worlds...

She *had* to find the Doctor.

STATE THE PROBLEM IN WORDS AS CLEARLY AS POSSIBLE.

Q &
David A McIntee

Would it hurt?

Stupid question. The wrong question. Being scalded hurt the skin. Being unable to breathe hurt the chest. Dust in the face hurt the throat and nostrils. All three at once? Of course it would hurt, and he was idiotic for wondering, even for a moment.

Better question: How to stop it hurting? The only question with an answer: How to get the hurting over with as quickly as possible? Easy: don't hide, don't cower, don't delay the inevitable. Take it all in one go, out there with the heat and flame. All the pain and the hurt gone in a flash.

The most important question of all: Whether to make that decision for the others? Wife, children, knowledge of their pain adding to his. Let them suffer, let them choose? The difference would be a matter of minutes or seconds, all told, but an eternity of suffering could be compressed into a few seconds by the heat and the pressure that was falling from the skies and bursting from the earth, squeezing all life out of existence.

Block one door with another. Open it and offer cool light. The answer: prevent an answer to a human question.

GO OUTSIDE. SHUT THE DOOR.

RED MONEY
Matt Sewell

Now, you may have heard nonsense – frankly – about the Ood carrying diseases. Fear-mongering tittle-tattle from the usual suspects, I'm afraid. My view, taking off my company hat for a moment, is that the 'activism' from FOTO smacks as coming from some pretty bitter, angry individuals. In any empire (however great or bountiful) there will always be winners and losers. I think you can guess what we're dealing with here, guys!

Hat back on, I can assure you that here at Ood Operations, the health and happiness of our product is of prime importance. If you already own one (if you don't and think you can't afford one, look again; advancements in Ood production have pulled prices right down), just ask it if it's happy and healthy – it'll tell you! In fact, they live to be at your service.

We've made the Ood happier and healthier than they've ever been. In return they're pleased to fetch and carry and do for us, as millions of customers across the Three Galaxies can heartily attest.

I'm proud of our work here, and like to think that I would defend the great relationship between Oodkind and us, their human facilitators, with my very life.

HONOUR THY ERROR AS A HIDDEN INTENTION.

THE BUDDHA OF SUBURBIA
Matt Sewell

Of course, he's a wonderful man, that Doctor. Saved the planet from them alien soldiers, he did, and all that terrible gas business. They were like spuds in suits of armour, apparently.

Spuds!

I thought I was a goner trapped in that car, though, really thought that was it. Reminded me of the Airborne, in Palestine all them years ago. Never killed no-one. Couldn't. After all, they were just lads like us.

Looking back, though, it's my girls I'm proudest of. Eileen, gawd rest her – best woman I ever met. So many happy years she gave me. And Sylvia. Right from being a toddler she'd put me in mind of my old Sergeant Major. She says 'Jump', I salute and say 'How high?' Keeps me on the straight and narrow. Heart of gold, mind you. When she gets cross and all in a tiswas, it's just her way of showing she cares.

And then there's my Donna. I've always known she was destined for something special, and meeting the Doctor'll be the making of her I reckon. Good for him, too – if I've learnt anything in life, I'm certain that blue box of his could do with a woman's touch.

RETRACE YOUR STEPS.

STOP ME IF YOU THINK THAT YOU'VE HEARD THIS ONE BEFORE
Nick Mellish

I live and breathe and serve a function: to fight, to impress. To die.

I live to die.

You and I both know it. You, with your life so fast, and actions, thought and word committed – and *spent* – before I can even really start to process, a mayfly to your hurricane. An oncoming storm? Dad, you have no idea.

No tears to be shed for this fleeting life; no sorrow felt beyond now, your heritage a pinprick, accidental, in a war you will stop before even an hour has passed us by. A message of peace, simplistic, to a room comprised of not-yous but like-mes: created, ciphers, bastards by love if not by DNA.

185

Do you love me, Dad? Do you care for us ephemerals at all? Or do you care too much? Is that why you never checked up?

Of course I'm not dead, you idiot. That's not how this works: cipher, remember? Daughter of the man reborn, messianic (controversially so, I hear). Day Two of the Mayfly:

Dear Diary. Had little planned because, Death. So yes, free tomorrow for that drink and, indeed, for the foreseeable.

See? I can do flippant, too. Must be in the blood, right?

DON'T BE FRIGHTENED OF CLICHÉS.

DEAD MAN WALKING
Liam Hogan

One day she'd have to kill off her solver of impossible puzzles, her Belgian detective. Perhaps the novel in which she did so would be released only after her death, but released it must be. He couldn't be allowed to live on; not without her.

And his death would have to be quite definite; devoid of ambiguity, allowing for no comebacks, however unlikely. There would be no Reichenbach Falls for Hercule Poirot.

She wondered how she'd do it.

Not old age, surely. Nor illness; something a medical Doctor might attend. Nor murder: her hero would not die the fool, the unknowing victim.

At his own hand, then. A noble sacrifice. An overdose, perhaps even poison.

Though she could not think why he would do such a thing. Suicide was such a sin...

And, after he was gone, who would solve the mystery of his death? Who would bring down the curtain on his life?

Dark thoughts for a winter's afternoon, sitting sipping tisane in a Harrogate spa.

She sighed and folded the newspaper, careful to obscure the photograph of the missing author.

When her time came, would she be so brave? She, who flinched at the sound of a wasp?

THE INCONSISTENCY PRINCIPLE.

186

SEEN AND NOT SEEN
Tim Gambrell

INTEGRATED SUIT LOG ENTRY. SEQUENCE TAG: RIVER SONG ZERO FOUR FIVE.

SPELLCHECK: DISABLED.

For the forty-fifth time I ask why an audio recording tool has a spellcheck facility I'm not going to lie semicolon this is very difficult hang on

AUTOPUNCTUATION: ACTIVATED.

Breathe.

AUTOSAVE.

Head pounding. Pulse racing.

(QUERY: UNKNOWN VOICE) *Down here?*

Coming! Hang on, is that–?

(QUERY BACKGROUND NOISE: BOOKS FALLING? PAUSE.)

There's a Silent in the library. Looking at me. Reaching.

(QUERY BACKGROUND NOISE: INTERFERENCE.)

Suit, I record it here because he can't know them yet, so I'll have to forget (LOGIC QUERY: SEQUENCE JUMP) coming!

AUTOSAVE.

Breathe. Reprieve. Spacesuits: stifling, restrictive. Always; even without the helmet. Running and the Doctor – the two are mutually inclusive. Look at him. My Orlando. So brash and bouncy. I know him so well yet... hardly at all. Here we are, biggest library in the galaxy; I could tell him everything, anything – except what I want to tell him. And I know my time approaches, but he mustn't. I'm scared, of course; who wouldn't be scared at the prospect of being eaten alive by shadows? Just focus; await your moment. And whatever you do, remember to keep breathing.

AUTOBACKUP: ACTIVATED.

BREATHE MORE DEEPLY.

REPEAT BEFORE ME
Sami Kelsh

I sit, immobilised, and watch myself repeat after her.

Sky – no, *not* Sky, *the entity, the goblin* – learns too fast. It's not unexpected that something reasonably sophisticated might learn to imitate language, and indeed learn one, or repeat phrases it's heard, even almost simultaneously.

Almost.

It's as though the goblin's climbed inside my unconscious and made itself comfortable, even as it stares back at me with Sky's pale, horribly vacant eyes. It knows my words before I can think them.

Steals them.

I fight, with every particle of my being, to surprise the voice, to say something different, or nothing at all. But my speech betrays my will, and the words stutter and punch themselves out of me; tumbling forth like broken mistakes.

Don't say it don't say it don't say it.

But I *do*; my mouth opening and closing. Dangerous, foolish osculations, moved by a marionette's string.

The others, of course, are right to be dubious that I've not been invaded, whilst the goblin stares into me, that cruel little glint of knowing in its expression.

I can do nothing but sit, and repeat my stolen voice.

It's uncanny. I'm the Doctor.

I'm the Doctor.

And I'm utterly afraid.

DON'T BREAK THE SILENCE.

BUT IF
Hendryk Korzeniowski

History was long gone, propped up for aeons in its out-dated rigidity. Now was the time of backward futures, of infinite alternatives, plotting the most advantageous outcomes. Retrospective actions birthing and destroying the Could've Beens, the Meanwhiles and the Neverweres. Again. And again. And again. Time had eaten itself.

Parallel realities flared up and died continuously, discontinuously. Their agents scattered throughout Space and Time, ready to expand and give life to a possibility, manipulate an inconsequence, develop a disaster, with no lesser beings having awareness, this side of a nightmare. Chaos for order! The peoples of the universe would thank them.

'If you turn right, you'll have a career...'

188

Among all the parallel time streams, one took precedent, enveloping all onlookers in awed silence. One insignificant butterfly change killed creation. Reality was dying as the stars rapidly extinguished, leaving emptiness. And one surviving species. This was the outcome they had been looking for, the ultimate in security, to safeguard their existence and their culture, to keep Gallifrey in consciousness. They could let slip The Final Sanction.

We foresee a time, screeched the Dalek, *when they will have destroyed all other life forms and become the* only *creature in the universe!*

ARE THERE SECTIONS? CONSIDER TRANSITIONS.

BURNING AT THE CENTRE OF TIME
Alex Spencer

Unfurling fractal,

Blooming and spinning in higher dimensions.

From this high point, overseeing all, I watch each thought become a tiny crystal universe inside itself. Deeper and deeper into this mind, the structure of reality unfolds endlessly. It's an exhilarating ride on the surface of his consciousness. When I let go and swim downwards, spinning towards the centre, The Doctor and Donna fuse.

DoctorDonna.

The crack in my mind explodes, letting the light pour in. Awakened to all the possibilities, I observe every decision-created universe branch off until the end of time. Whole nebulae are born in the blink of an eye and then dissolve like snowflakes.

I am become eternal, infinite. Evolving at the speed of light but hanging suspended at the centre of time. A stopped clock.

Non-Euclidean landscapes erupt in my new psyche. Cities crammed with knowledge – every known thing is here. Room upon room filled with all the secrets of time. It's stored in

Binary, binary, binary...

This forbidden knowledge feels like a thousand exploding suns. It is blinding, burning, blazing,

Obliterating.

Infinite worlds cannot be contained by a human mind. The corners fold in, collapse. Cities smash apart. Worlds...

I know I am going.

Back.

NOT BUILDING A WALL BUT MAKING A BRICK.

SHADOW MAN
Ash Stewart

The nightmares started just a few days after Jackson said his goodbyes to the Doctor.

Monsters, despots and maniacs filled his nights. Scenarios half-remembered from the memories he had been given when he thought *he* was the Doctor. Consciously, during the day he remembered nothing. But at night they came, screaming and vile.

Terrible beings that wanted to exterminate all living things; vampires from before time; a scientist who wanted to crack the Earth's core...

All these, and more. So many bad people... but never the Doctor himself.

He awoke so many nights screaming in sweaty, burning terror. It got so bad, he became afraid to sleep. He thought it would never end and that the nightmares would go on for ever.

Until one night, he came. The Doctor – in an impossible situation, against an army of horrors.

No way out.

But he stood against them, straightened himself up and simply said, 'No more!'

Jackson jolted awake. His breathing was rapid. He was still terrified. But he smiled. There was hope. The Doctor was in his dreams and winning. Just the once. But it gave Jackson hope that he would be there more, and that the nightmares might finally end...

NOT BUILDING A WALL BUT MAKING A BRICK.

LOOKING FOR WATER
Townsend Shoulders

Going home at night, and suddenly we find ourselves in beautiful desolation.

How can a bus just disappear?

Emerging from a wrecked double-decker in the middle of the desert, we're confronted by thirst and a trace of something unidentified yet horrible in the sand...

But there's no sign of water.

The man without a name makes us talk about our dinner plans. We discuss food in an effort not to think about our incipient thirst. The beautiful woman takes over.

We work beneath three suns in an alien sandscape, constantly aware there's no water here.

The nameless man recalls another red bus – and the woman who drove it. His fate: two difficult women on two difficult red buses. Both argumentative, yet both oddly appealing. (He wouldn't admit this to either of them, though...)

We try to free the bus but liberate only dehydration.

The suddenly cloudy horizon offers hope of rain, but the oncoming storm is nothing but dust. We try to ignore our cracker-dry tongues. And dead voices in the sand, crying. But no. Destruction rides the wind; coming our way. Something shines among the dry clouds, glittering and speeding closer.

We don't understand. Nothing is safe, not anymore.

WATER.

A GOOD MAN HAS TO DIE
Sarah Di-Bella

Peter and Sarah, Sarah and Peter, Sarah and Peter and the Trickster. Sarah and the Trickster. Sarah and the Doctor. Just Sarah. Just the Doctor. Just me, just us.

Oh, Sarah Jane, *my* Sarah. Almost, nearly, not quite: married. I put a stop to that didn't I? Gave you the impossible task of choosing him or me; him or the Earth – humanity. I knew you'd chose well. You always do.

Thank you.

I'm so glad you have Mr Smith. Appropriately named. Mr Smith and good old, K9 – that was the least I could do. Oh, and Luke, Clyde and Rani. Cracking bunch! At least that's something. *They* are something. Something else!

Do you know that you are *so* important, Sarah Jane Smith of Ealing? You save the world.

You are the world.

Watching you be magnificent, I wonder who, where and what you'd be if we'd never met. I reflect... Who tricked you, me or him? If it wasn't for me you'd be living an ordinary life with ordinary experiences and ordinary expectations. Wouldn't you? Maybe you wouldn't, bright as you are.

Do you *really* want to get married?

Will there be another wedding? For either of us?

(Spoilers, darling.)

DESTROY THE MOST IMPORTANT THING.

CATACLASM
Matt Adams

Pure, perfect, the diaphanous droplet slips silently inside; liquids consume liquids, now part of a greater whole. Engulf me. Quench my thirst. Dive within. Hydrate the drought of history, reawaken forgotten springs of memory.

I am your host, offering freedom after the paralysis of ice. I invite you: unleash your torrent within me.

Scant seconds of awareness, before the maelstrom rushes through my veins, and I am buffeted by a wave of erosion, my sense of self washed away by the spring tide in a ceremony of transition.

Ablution and acceptance, baptism of cleansing, the unspoken water that purifies and heals.

This, then, is the flood. The great deep bursts forth, the primeval wellspring from which all life had its source; now all that is.

Osmosis opens up cells to the metamorphosis; through saliva and semen, blood and bile, fluids give way to welcome the appropriation.

It is the precipitation of purification, first rain on desert plains, cupped in these hands as an offering to long-dead Martian gods.

Glimpse of an azure orb floating in the void – 'so much water... so much beauty' – and then what I was is consumed, lost forever within the climax of change.

Aitch. Two. Ohhhhhhh...

MAKE IT MORE SENSUAL.

THE QUEEN IS DEAD
Sarah Di-Bella

How *soon* is now.

[*Time to die*]

I don't want to go. Don't let this light go out. Please. [*Time to die*] *Anyone for a jelly baby?* [*Time*] I know it's over. [*To*] It really did begin [*Die*]. Farewell.

Allons-y.

Timing malfunction. No, not that. [*Time*] The next one, will it be... *spectacular?* Will he remember me? Will she be... *ginger? That is a big one, Jamie.* NO, NOT YET. Don't come just yet – I have so much to *do!* [To die] Peri? Sarah Jane – *tears? What an incredible bunch!* [*Die*] I know I regenerate, but I *die*, this me goes, fades, leaves.

DIES.

IRAE.

Timey-wimey thing, don't do your worst. We can['t*] re-write history. Reverse the polarity, Liz! What's that, my boy?* [*Time to die*] *Brave heart, Tegan.* I'll be seeing you, River.

Sweetie?

Erimem – is that *you*?! *Keep warm...*

Daleks, Cybermen, Angels, so much to do, so little time. [*To die*] *Adieu.*

Ponds. Breaded cod?! *In vanilla sauce?! GO AWAY, I'LL COME, JUST PLEASE, A BIT MORE TIME...*

Doctor *Much* More!

Jackie – are you there? Donna – turn *LEFT*! Captain Jack – Good Wolf. *Barcelona!*

The breath from my lungs...

Okay, okay. I'm ready. Martha?

Brigadier?

Knock-knock-knock-knock – who's there?

GERONIMO!

DISCONNECT FROM DESIRE.

卌 卌 |

IN THE HEAT OF THE MORNING
Matt Barber

A new start; and a new list of things to do.

But before he begins his journey in earnest he must jettison the person he was before.

He sheds his tattered clothes and burns his home. One moment he's mourning the departure of friends, the next he's looking for new ones. The loneliest he gets: ever caught between the old and new; between one life well-lived and the next – with all its energy and promise.

Item one: find someone to witness his new life. Without friends and companions to judge, balance and guide he is no-one. No-one at all.

Item one is easily ticked off. Amelia is first, and in the future (but what's 'future' to a Time Lord?) with Amy comes Rory. A family. Again. At last.

Item two: find himself. He's driven to discover who he's become. This is the moment where he finds he's full of energy and compassion. His previous incarnation spent his final days mourning, wracked with guilt and fear. The guilt's still present, but tempered by innocence and a feeling of absolution – as if the flames of the burning TARDIS and his burning skin have sanctified him.

Item three: save the Earth.

Tick.

[TOCK.]

MAKE AN EXHAUSTIVE LIST OF EVERYTHING YOU MIGHT DO AND DO THE LAST THING ON THE LIST.

YOU BELONG IN ROCK 'N' ROLL
Andy Priestner

Amelia Pond. In a nightie. On a spaceship. Staring out at the stars, having just saved the day.

How mad was this? Mels would never believe it.

'Just more of your Raggedy Man madness,' she'd say.

Talking of bonkers. This place had taken the proverbial Tunnock's Caramel Wafer!

She'd idly wondered if they still made and sold them on Starship Scotland, wherever that might be. Maybe *its* population was also needlessly torturing a hospitable star whale?

It hadn't been the best day. She'd been chased by creepy robots, chosen to 'Forget', and been completely covered in sick, but, in one defining all-important moment, she had forced Liz 10 to abdicate. One impulsive game-changing action, freeing that poor creature from any more pain.

Had she acted rashly? Skipping the stages and due thought process that such a potentially fatal action should have required? Could she have killed them all?

No.

She'd never been more certain of anything. Just how much denial and deceit did there have to be in the world before compassion was on the table?

Besides, another kind creature had shown her the way; one who needed her as much as she needed him.

Today Amy Pond was winning.

SHORT CIRCUIT.

EVEN BETTER THAN THE REAL THING
Simon A Brett

Surrounded, fear prevents those of us charged with protecting the weak from turning our backs on our captors and joining the huddled families in the centre. They smother their children with love and kisses as they await the end.

I notice that the ring of twelve bronze machines is spaced around us equidistantly; a sadistic clock face, reminding us of our loss.

But unlikely saviours appear suddenly from nowhere: what I assume to be royalty, towering over their diminished subjects. They're bold and proud in their unlikely, vivid colours. Scorching past the smoked, charred copper of battle to loom tall, regal; brazen.

As they reduce the twelve, one by one, to dust, it is clear that their un-tempered power leaves little need for the almost apologetic modesty of their predecessors. As silence falls, a haven for the dying crackle of fires, these rainbow monarchs turn their heads, assessing the site.

We wait for their fury to extend to us. But nothing comes.

Instead, the orange king fires a ball of golden light into the air, illuminating the desolation for a flicker of moments, before it falls into the middle of the village lake.

Nothing shall grow again on Tasus 5.

JUST CARRY ON.

I CAN'T GIVE EVERYTHING AWAY
Alex Spencer

If you have seen the end before the beginning, can you ever take a leap of faith? Can you ever give your whole heart? Or two of them?

If you can't share your darkest fears or memories because it would rip apart the fabric of the universe, would you do it anyway? Is love bigger than that?

Because it seems to me the answer is, no.

Love is the greatest thing – except when duty is bigger.

Marriage is until death – except when only one of you has been to the ceremony.

So, what is real at the heart of our adventure?

My sweet recollections are just dreams when none of them have happened yet to you. The only truth we have is in the moment.

I must become hard edged and closed to ward off this insult to my tender heart.

When you're in love with an ageless boy-god who's already witnessed your return to dust, you stand on a precipice – staring into the dark.

We can't pretend before us lie deserts of vast eternity. Ours is a long love with a deadly deadline.

Had we but world enough and time, would this fall apart? Would you still be mine?

IN TOTAL DARKENESS, OR IN A VERY LARGE ROOM VERY QUIETLY.

APROPOS OF THAT BUSINESS WITH THE LIBRARY CARD
Matthew J Elliott

'*Monsters from Outer Space.*' The librarian placed the book before the old man.

'I thought it possible I might recognise a few,' he explained.

'Is that all for today?'

'My granddaughter's rather keen to read the final Harry Potter...'

'I'm not familiar with that author.'

'Hmm. A little early, perhaps. Tch-tch-tch. Frustrating. *Extinct Civilisations* by Warris Bossard?'

'I'm afraid not.'

'*Juggling for Klutzes*? No? Then I'll bid you good day.'

'Just a moment, Dr Smith. There is the small matter of your overdue books: Pemberton's *Myths and Superstitions of the Deep*; *The Decline and Fall of the Roman Empire*; *The Prisoner of Zenda*; *The Time Machine*; *The Tale of Peter Rabbit*; *Everest in Easy Stages*; *Teach Yourself Tibetan*; *Principia Mathematica*; *Moby Dick* and *The Water Babies*. I'm not entirely certain how you managed to borrow so many books with just one library card...'

'I can be remarkably persuasive. And, as I possess mastery over time itself, a moment of your notice will confirm that every one of those books has already been returned.'

As the old man departed, the librarian felt the urge to examine the 'Returns' shelf. The only book there was *Lady, Don't Fall Backwards* by Darcy Sarto.

MAKE A BLANK VALUABLE BY PUTTING IT IN AN EXQUISITE FRAME.

WHEN I LIVE MY DREAM
Steve Watts

The birdsong, the birdsong...

The (so-called) Dream Lord (hideous, insulting, homunculus-like travesty of the Doctor) weaves, warps and winds: space dissolves, all is fluid,

Spiralling down into fiction; a dream state. No sound, empty landscapes. Sleeping, dead to the world, *wake up, wake up*, is this a false hope or a true sadness?

The choice is made. Let *this* moment be real?

The birdsong, the birdsong...

My love for her grows, living in *this moment*. I exist for her. I would die for her.

We slumber. The time column rises and falls. Dying time enfolds us.

The idyllic life and the perfect melody. A deceitful lullaby. Is this life real or the dream?

The birdsong, the birdsong...

Reality shifts and shadows dance the dust. I gaze into her eyes; this the last look? Words cut short; crystallised on frostbite lips. She is the last thing I'll see. Be. My love burns; I *want* this reality. A reality where there is only me and her.

But the final end approaches. The burning heat of a cold star.

I fall from heaven.

I turn to ice.

Go to Sleep and dream your last dream.

Remember me... Amy Pond.

My love.

My life.

THE MOST IMPORTANT THING IS THE MOST EASILY FORGOTTEN

THRU' THESE ARCHITECTS' EYES
Philip Bates

The fourth dimension fractures. Lives crack into four streams.

We never dip our toes in the water. We feel its flow, consumed by time's wait.

There is the past. The Time Lord gazes across the valley in disbelief. Two humans look back and wave. They are the same faces, 3650 cycles apart, a mirror in the chasm of space and time.

There is the present. The man is gone, screaming into the water. His apology is bookended by beauty. The renegade's fault. Blue debris parts this stream. The woman joyfully shouts to her aged self, their past and future drowned. Her hand falls into the air. She pivots away; attention on her, the sole occupant of the stage. This age should burn and rave at close of day.

There is the future. Her hand falls into the air, and is met once more. Time and time and time again. They will run. They will laugh. They will cry. They will fall. The future gives rise to the past, gives way to the present, and the fractures splinter further. The Doctor sees what is coming. But not what it means.

There is the ever. The Time Lord, consumed by time's weight.

DISCONNECT FROM DESIRE.

ART DECADE
Dan Rebellato

Face paint.
My face is paint.
Not paint on face.
Just face of paint.
A fingernail depth of it mostly but I'm lucky.
He paints thicker than most, Vincent.
Scoops up the oils with a knife.
I have friends in watercolours, can barely think.
Not all paintings think.
Even the statues: lights on, nobody home.
Only those caught between times, paintings where Now changes.
When a palette knife stabs between past and future.
Real genius stuff, parting the temporal waves, cutting history apart.
It takes a Vincent to end history and start a new one.
Then we become sentient in the paint or the marble or the bronze.
The Laughing Cavalier's sadness in the eyes? Yes exactly.
God and Adam reaching out to each other, would you look happy?
That's not a smile on the Mona Lisa's lips, they're twisted in pain, how do you not see this?
It's all very well, the Fez-Man bringing Painter-Boy here to see us, centre of attention, adored.
I get it, I get the gesture.
The evils of good intentions, the wickedness of cleverness.
Vincent's tragedy was not to know his future, but that's no tragedy.
Tragedy is when your future lasts for ever.

WHAT ARE YOU REALLY THINKING ABOUT JUST NOW?
INCORPORATE.

THROUGH A CRACK IN THE PAST
Jon Dear

Through the crack he learnt how to see the universe.

He'd been surprised when the stairs had appeared. Surprised and delighted. He knew it couldn't be a TARDIS, but there was something...

He learnt about the Time War and his people's destruction.

He'd been even more surprised when the people had gone up the recently appeared stairs and never come down.

But not the Fool.

The Fool came and went every day. Back and forth like the most basic binary code. The Fool never went up the stairs.

He learnt about the Doctor.

Surprise went off the scale when the Doctor turned up. *Survivors!* He and the Doctor, together they could rebuild the Time Lords as they once were, masters of all matter.

He tried to contact the Doctor. He tried to scream.

Nothing.

Later, the Fool's companion had looked at him and she frowned. Had some stray psychic energy got though? Could this be a way out?

'Don't you think he looks like Nick Cave?' said the female to the Fool.

And he learnt much about the hanging of 'wall paper'...

Ah well. He had time. And it was better than staring at the grey walls of Rassilon's tomb.

ALWAYS FIRST STEPS.

THE PLATEAUX OF MIRROR
James McLean

Standing on the stone, coat billowing in the breeze, she considered the list; a piece of creased A5 paper, crisp as parchment.

A penguin, a chainsword-wielding hooligan, and a Cyberman that likes The Smiths: a mish-mash team, anchored to her erratic time-machine, ready to bungee back into her past, sometime in the future.

The Pandorica was a fixed event, so here she was, fixing it for him. Carefully, she placed the paper under the rock, securing the paradox.

He jumped off the stone, having taunted the myriad of enemy spaceships into retreating. It was a good speech, but not enough; a skilled illusionist always uses more but shows much less.

He'd use his far future to sow discontent and confusion into his enemies above – and it'd work because he'd spotted the evidence it already had.

Kneeling in the grass, he plucked the folded paper out from under the rock and read it. He liked the list he'd never created.

Had there been a Rutan-shaped Frobisher on that Sontaran ship? Kroton sowing Cyber-paranoia in the Dalek mothership? Daak testing the militant mettle of the Chelonians?

He popped the paper into his pocket, a paradox saved for another time, and another Doctor.

DEFINE AN AREA AS 'SAFE' AND USE IT AS AN ANCHOR.

THERE ARE FACES I REMEMBER
Sarah Di-Bella and Elton Townend Jones

On Gallifrey, they say the faces you've loved and the faces you've worn revisit you as you die. Except I haven't died. And I can see all of you, all the time. In chronic hysteresis. The ultimate outcome always the same, and nothing I do can change that. *That's* my fate, *that's* the death of the Doctor.

The Doctor is just out of sight, watching:

Cressida – *Still in Carthage, eh? Those heroes not so young now...*

Sara – *Sorry. I'm so, so sorry.*

Jamie – *Oh, yes, that* is *a big one, isn't it?*

Brigadier – *In Lima, yes – investigating rumours of that colony of talking bears...*

Susan – *Daisiest of daisies, I know that one day you'll come back. One day.*

Frobisher – *Surprise, surprise – publishing books!*

Jack – *Could've. Should've.*

Steven – *Across the courtyard, older now, impressive. Does he know me? Does he dare? I'll smile him a rainbow.*

Mel – *Enjoying adventures with Mr Benton and her own K9.*

Romana – *Oh, way to go, Lion Queen of the Tharils!*

Sarah Jane – *No. Not that. Impossible! She can't be, not that. No. My Sarah. A blow to her friends, a wound to the Universe. Tears, Doctor Who?*

Turning darkly away, she ponders, Who'll be next?

CUT A VITAL CONNECTION.

SARDICK'S SIX ANIMALS AND TWO FROM THE DOCTOR
Paul Ebbs

The Raven
Anger harms her. The chasm is rage.
This raven aims scars at hearts.
A tart tear stirs. It smarts – no relaxant near.

The Boar
A bore. So vain. He targets vantage,
Rates, rams, rents. Braces an arctic grave,
To earn extra stash. Mirth a harlot in him.

The Gnat
No core. No charm. He misacts. Not neat.
Natters mar an evil era. This gnat.
This sham scholar. A smirch, the torn sham.

The Cobra
A Cobra hiss. The rash masochist rants.
Hiss-vanes stir alarms. An acre's tar in his heart.
Ranges the hot hit. Or a hailstorm.

The Bear
He's the crass maths. Lax hair. He's crosshair sarcastic.
A bear's gavotte, no hair shirt to overtax,
Scams; gallivants, his caveats are axes.

The Crab
Chart a schism. Excavate a carcass. A cloven charisma.
Sarcoma's teat. Cancer an extra treat.
This heart extractor carting a coven. Chaos mistral.

The Cat
Comes the alarmist. The trash tsar. Ace in lace.
The starch of his march, a cavorting star.
No stoical Rex; casting comical arcs.

The Hart
March raver. He accosts a catharsis. Moral mosaic.
Argent mirth, able oracle. Coaxes the vortex.
Exalts in the chariot. Tears tang. Time cares.

BE EXTRAVAGANT.

SONS OF THE SILENT AGE
Alex Spencer

Someone's walking over my grave, that's what they call it. That shudder you get when the future crushes the sods above your head. The ticklish spine; the electric jump in your skin.

I feel energy close by, arcing onto my back and neck. I'm waiting for a tap. I force the oppressive tension away with a shrug. Maybe it's just history, weighing down my shoulders.

Don't look back. The future's through that door.

Breathe.

Down the ladder, talking. Taking my one small step onto bright grey dust; our giant leap.

Sharp, dazzlingly, vast landscape where dead, white, mountains meet inky void.

And then I see...

They're on the moon watching us. Dear god. They've... They've always been here.

I remember now. I remember... All the times I saw them.

Under the narrow bed. Crouching in the cellar. Darting through the underwater cave.

A flood of horror. Sunken eyes, sucking mouth; reaching, pulling, tri-fingered talons. Man's first fear, incarnate.

My boots run faster than my feet can follow; toward the module.

I turn.

And leap! So high, bouncing. Again. Unlimited joy.

This view – the glowing blue sphere in the bottomless black sky. Takes your breath away. Wipes your memory. Demands... Silence.

BE EXTRAVAGANT.

OVER A BARREL
Georgia Ingram

They said that water tasted different in every place and time. So Forshal couldn't help being curious when he noticed a puddle in the corner of the medilab. The crew were all bored rigid, stuck for cycles in this godforsaken place. And what for? Bloody auditing! Some stupid Galactic regulation before they could hyperbeam...

The puddle contained a vision: a strange-looking boy in a wood-lined hold. Some primitive from eons ago, he speculated. He watched the boy sink a dipper into a barrel, drink deeply, and sigh with satisfaction. Then he started and vanished. A man came in, hulking and snarling. He swung a bright lantern towards the shadows, played light over the barrels – before vanishing. Then all was still; just the soft swaying of the ropes...

Forshal leaned forward and with a shock, tumbled into the blackness. He looked around the raw, stinking underboards of the hold, and saw a mirror-polished plate, with a blurred, distant view of the medilab. Of course, a portal. And next to him, the barrel of clear water.

He cleared his throat, and picked up the dipper.

Just a sip, he thought idly, and I'll get back to the ship. No-one will ever know.

WATER.

ZEROES
James McLean

From the dark of the TARDIS corridor, he stood – the perfect insomniac – before white double doors. He couldn't sleep – didn't want to sleep – and nipping to the food machine had somehow led him here.

The doors opened by themselves and he entered – obedient, unthinking – a chamber, bright and circular. Peaceful, inviting. Cool but not uncold. Still but not stuffy. And... Was he mistaken? No. There were no shadows. And it sounded soundless. Also, for a seemingly hygienic space, it had an unexpected smell, the smell you get when rain finally falls after a long spell of hot weather. Fresh. Natural.

'Couldn't sleep?' asked the Doctor, suddenly behind him.

Rory shrugged.

'Too many latent timelines, I suspect. Odd you should stumble on this room though. I thought it was deleted. Seems she undeleted it. House made you suffer, Rory. Maligned timelines... And it happened on the old girl's patch. I think this is her apology: a Zero Room. Null interface environment.' The Doctor sniffed the air. 'How can a zero environment smell like... like... petrichor?'

Good question. But as the Time Lord wandered off, doors gently closing between them, Rory no longer cared.

He hadn't even noticed she wasn't *his* Doctor.

HUMANIZE SOMETHING FREE OF ERROR.

BREATHE PUSH POP
Christian Cawley

Take a breath. Be alive. Be real.

Be them. Be YOU.

Fleeting, flying, lightning life; a solar storm of perfect potential, looking for a home. Not a primordial pond, not a rock pool swimming with microbes.

Not this time.

Time takes its turn, spinning, dragging, drawing; to a new destination. And there, at the end, the ultimate target. Not life, not yet.

Like life, waiting, for life.

Just a soup of sorts. Blancmange. Liquid waiting for consciousness, form, purpose. Fluid flesh, waiting to be made relevant. Fighting fear.

Fighting the rejection, bubbling in anger, convulsing in confusion, a pulsing mass of sentience. Pushing against the rules, hungry for a vessel, a body to animate its perceptions.

Desperate for importance.

And there is so much of it, waiting for life. Some is yet to step into the light; the rest is clinging onto something it once touched.

With every birth comes a breath. It echoes through the ether: the first cry of life from beyond time. But here... life breathed before life. Will it also cry? Now is the time for it to be set free, to emerge, to be ready.

Or is this life set to pop, fleetingly, from existence?

BREATHE MORE DEEPLY.

A STREAM WITH BRIGHT FISH
Jon Dear

Lorna liked to think about the Woman with Big Hair. The incident with the Doctor may have been the only exciting thing to happen to her but it had been over so quickly, she'd been too scared to really take it in. All that was left was a sense of loss.

The Woman with Big Hair had appeared a few days later, standing by the river a short way into the green forest near her home. Lorna hadn't seen her arrive but her smiles and jokes made Lorna feel tingly and happy in a way she couldn't adequately describe, but she could tell the Woman with the Big Hair was a great warrior. She was a Doctor too.

Lorna hoped that the Woman with Big Hair might tell her something important but became distracted by another strange figure, hooded, a little way off. The figure might have been another woman, but Lorna couldn't see the face. Still, she knew she was being watched. When Lorna turned back, the Woman with Big Hair was gone.

Lorna hoped she'd she her again, perhaps when she found the Doctor. As she turned to leave she noticed that the hooded figure had also gone.

ALLOW AN EASEMENT
(AN EASEMENT IS THE ABANDONMENT OF A STRICTURE).

SPACE DIARY 1
Aryldi Moss-Burke

With hindsight, killing Hitler might not have been my most sensible plan – but as Mels, I was a raging cesspit of hormones. I was full of this crazy anger, constantly battling against the hateful world. If someone said 'Hello' wrong, I wanted to kill them and lay out their entrails to warn others not to mess.

Actually, I think I might have done that. Once.

Oh gosh, perhaps twice.

Possibly more.

Now I think about it, there might even be a sculpture out there made from one of the men that messed with me. Eating the organs he'd tried to force on me. Fun times!

Anyway, when I saved my Doctor, I'd just regenerated into this, super-sexy body. I got the cleavage I'd always wanted. Great hair. Fabulous bum. My new me was all I could think about, so there may have been a slight... side effect when I restored my feller. My thoughts wouldn't influence his next set of regenerations though, would they? I mean, he decides what... 'happens', yes?

Still, he's always had a thing about being ginger, and never succeeded...

He did go blonde, ish, next but one... But that was nothing to do with me...

Right?

ABANDON NORMAL INSTRUMENTS.

UNDER PRESSURE
Jon Dear

George regarded himself in the mirror.

He knew he was well built for a boy of his age, athletic and robust. Mr Dawson said he was light years ahead of not only the other boys in his year but of anyone he'd ever taken for football. Several Premier League teams' academies were interested. George wasn't sure; it felt like a bit of a waste. His Business Studies teacher had equally enthused about George's acumen, even in market economics, something he hadn't expected from a 12-year-old. George's dad was delighted with this; George knew he wanted him to go into business, wanted him to be powerful. All in all, George Thompson had the world at his feet.

Except...

George had friends of course, although being both clever and good at sport gets you noticed, makes you stand out. And at Coal Hill Academy, standing out wasn't *always* a good thing. But it made his parents happy and that's all that mattered.

Or at least it had been.

There were other people now, other influences. Mundane and ugly. And what they wanted meant something very different for George.

The Doctor could have helped of course, but the Doctor had never come back.

ARE THERE SECTIONS? CONSIDER TRANSITIONS.

WE PRICK YOU
Tim Gambrell

This is a kindness. I am programmed to administer kindness. Not medically as per my original assembly – system files register protocol alterations at *REFERENCE UNAVAILABLE* and internal diagnostics constantly report curtailment to my upper limbs. I was re-created. I am individual, not group. Self-aware. I am designated Handbot Raw-Ree. That is my kindness. I have additional exterior decoration which aids my delivery of kindness. I lack the facility to create verbal signals but all external data is filed. One of the decorative markings is 'smile'. This denotes pleasure, happiness; kindness. It is a self-serving kindness by Amy who re-created me. Amy is sad. Amy is angry. Amy is frustrated. Amy is

SYSTEM REBOOT

Cranial section re-attached. External sensors detect my smile remains intact. This is still a kindness. My centre of gravity has altered. I contain additional weight. Amy. She is grieving. I am supporting her. She shudders gently. I must administer additional kindness. I perform a hug with curtailed upper limbs. I feel *REFERENCE* sadness, but can only smile. How is this a kindness?

Amy wipes the tears from her eyes. Sometimes, she thinks, I look at Rory and wonder what exactly is going on behind that painted smile...

REMEMBER THOSE QUIET EVENINGS.

SMALL HOURS HOTEL ROOM
Ira Lightman

Arriving late in the hotel, he texts then writes about the woman he might leave for, that I tell his last wife of; he falls into sleep.

Off a bus. Down an alley. To an intercom. With a suitcase.

He has wanted this time.

The guy on the mobile next door can converse as it seems he cannot. A river of his heart knowing a sea, the tide of a sea knowing for a time shoreline. Steps from bath to bed.

He wakes with his bed near no wall, in a forest of stags. It is the waking the being unable to wake the worst disoriented night. Skin of dark's quiet and damp.

Unable to wake in daylight. Arms solid legs solid. The who knows what this ends.

The present and past and future walk and miseries compound. In some can be children, used to no time, used to no home. He will show them the failure to keep up the failure.

He will be here till he does. While his beard remakes him, while his hair grows horns.

When beast was slain some policing was his. From his present and past, I can say, and his future, I walked.

SHORT CIRCUIT.

BABY'S ON FIRE
Aryldi Moss-Burke

As if I was really going to limit myself to a cutesy little name like 'Alfie'. I might have had to take the body of a puny little baby to exist in the right time and place to seize control, but that didn't mean that I was going to let anyone treat me like one. Stormageddon was not just a childish affectation. It was a declaration of nefarious intent.

The 'Doctor' was not as clever as he made out. He claimed to speak 'baby', when really I was conversing with him in my own language, thanks to an obsolete mechanism that I cannibalised from his own TARDIS. I knew that trapping those witless Cyber-rejects beneath the Earth would lure his attention. I didn't realise how easy it would be to get him to do my will. He really is pitifully desperate to please. I created the Cybermats to keep me amused, and to drip feed tiny draughts of power to my pet Cybermen. But with a single twiddle of his sonic screwdriver, the Doctor created a greater weapon than I could possibly have devised. The ultimate bomb. Now I need to find the best point in time to detonate it...

DISTORTING TIME.

A TALE OF MULTIPLICITIES
Andrew Hunt

Charles Dickens throws down his pen and stares at his notebook with disgust.

Our new Doctor established his practice in Blue House and before very long a line of young ladies with streaming noses and palpitating hearts was seeking his medical advice.

Dickens snorts and flicks back a few pages.

The tenement slum on Trap Street crouched like a Maston over the mist-shrouded and scabrous lagoon which was the domain of the kind-spirited mudlarks, Mr and Mrs Amelia Pond.

'Scabrous lagoon! What does that even *mean*?' He riffles further back into the archaeological depths of his notebook.

Miss River Song took to her Tivolian heels as soon as she heard the whine of the Dalek's lady sucker powering up...

'Good heavens! Siri, what was I thinking?!'

'Would you like me to book an appointment with Doctor Freud?'

'No, no. All I seem able to write at this moment is repetitious juvenilia...'

He tries another page.

It could be Mars or Venus, but whatever he may do...

'...or dreadful poetry!'

The grandfather clock chimes. Still a few minutes behind behind.

He takes his pen up again and starts writing.

It was the best of times, it was the worst of times...

DESTROY NOTHING.

ACID REIGN
Gareth Alexander

Nobody thinks. Of the. Trees. Growing. Aching. Creaking.

People think Us mute. No. We speak as one. We grow as one. We suffer as one.

From First Days We gave offerings. Bounty. Shelter. Even beauty. Precious gifts all. For Man and Beast. For Kindleship. Our joke. Not good.

Later We were hated. Nourishing water corrupted by Man. Melted us down. We became fiery. We hurt so much.

So We let Them use Us. Abuse Us. No choice. We grew. We ached. For escape, for relief. It has gone on since We began. Protection. Rain. Pain.

Then Doctor. We hoped. For difference. But no change. Still fierce. Still death from above. Hidden in something so serene.

We heard it. Your latest insult. Your new attempt to destroy Us.

Doctor tried. He did not understand. Too weak. His Box does. It is much like Us. It is sorry It cannot aid.

Only She could help. The Lifegiver. She, offering the same as Us. Bounty. Shelter. Beauty.

We are free now. Free to put down roots anew. Another joke. Sorry.

When We arrive will We be hurt? Will They be sorry? Like His Box? Like Her?

If there is pain, They shall be.

IS THERE SOMETHING MISSING?

BAKED ALASKAN
Matt Sewell

Still shut-in.

Claustrophic.

Boiling red, ruby ray anger froths on the edges and deep inside. Banging on the walls at night – who would want to get in here? And if that rage broke in, what then? I would...

eggs.

I'm a girl – holding on to that – childhood memories. Mother's soufflé: light and airy like daylight by the seaside and fresh air in a forest. I'm a girl and I DO WANT TO SUBJUGATE ALL INFERIOR LIFE AND...

eggs. Stir.

They'll call me Soufflé Girl and rescue me and I'll feel sun on my face and breathe fresh air and I'll be reborn. Like hatching out. And then HATRED.

No. Not hatred – the other one. HATRED.

eggs.

But I can't be Soufflé Girl if I don't make perfect soufflé! Start with the

eggs. Stir. Min–

HATRED?

No.

The egg-whisk is an extension of my arm, ploughing through the yolks –

smashing them, utterly destroying them. I'm in... eggstasy

See?

I'm Soufflé Girl and I'm hilarious and this soufflé will be the supreme soufflé of the Universe and I will free it from its dish and it will float free and my chinny hero will

Rescue me!

and

I WILL MAKE HIM SOUFFLÉ.

REMOVE SPECIFICS AND REVERT TO AMBIGUITIES.

POSTCARDS / ASTRONAUTS IN THE TRIASSIC
Sami Kelsh / Philip Bates

Then/

Thailand's beneath him now, as he floats over the Earth, with sandwich and flask, legs dangling out the TARDIS doors. Brian's fairly sure that while the beaches and the food are meant to be quite good, Thailand hasn't had dinosaurs for, ooh, a good few million years now.

Also down there – somewhere – is Leadworth, his home. The world's so beautiful, and he's seen very little of it.

Still, no sense dwelling on things not done. There's a list to compile.

One: visit space. *Done.*

Two: visit Thailand...

/Now

The scaly river-devil lunges at the distant astronauts' dinghy.

Riddell lines up his shot, but his queen jabs the rifle away. 'Neffy! That's why we're here!'

Following the spaceship explosion, Nefertiti knows this to be untrue. The reason they're in Thailand's hot, forgotten past – somewhere between mass extinctions – is because without them, someone'll suffer at the Doctor's Nile-red hands. Riddell just enjoys the game too much.

'Where's Brian anyway?'

Nefertiti points out one of the screaming astronauts, who waves. They laugh.

In the distance, a vworp vworps. Soon, they'll all be home again, and the Doctor – whose redemption comes from his companions – will be dangerously alone.

Nefertiti doubts he'll fare well.

TIDY UP.

AGAINST THE SKY
Alex Spencer

Not a metaphor, then. I am actually here.

Last memories? A voice counting, searing heat, white light, whistling wind, dissolution. And then the blackness.

How much time has passed? On hands and knees, I look up. Knees and hands. Patting myself with shaking fingers. I find I'm solid again. No spaces in between.

The jagged mountain rises dark against a boiling sky. Standing up, I'm pulled forwards with arms stretched out towards my fate.

Granite-hard rock is rough and cold under my palms. The mountain leers upwards so steeply, the summit is out of view. I know what my faith says I must do. My toe meets the first foothold and I heave upwards, shouldering the unbearable load. Who knew the weight of a soul? One would be heavy. I don't know the number I must carry, but I hear their raging. And their screams – the same as those from the operating table, but multiplied a thousand times.

Amongst the cacophony of voices, I search for yours. I wronged you when I let you take my place.

Each one of them is a stain on my soul. If I find you with me, I think I can carry on.

GO TO AN EXTREME, MOVE BACK TO A MORE COMFORTABLE PLACE.

STAY (FARAWAY, SO CLOSE!)
John Gerard Hughes

As he watched them enter the blue box, smiling as they left him again, he felt uneasy. Rory and Amy had grown up more than ever in the last year. Now, as they skipped into the TARDIS, they appeared, to his eyes, as suddenly younger again.

The 'gaps' between the Doctor's visits had grown considerably larger. And while, initially, they – she – had complained that he was leaving holes in their lives by not always being there, he had watched those gaps, those spaces, easily be filled. They had matured into a settled, stable couple with routine. With 'normality'. And Brian Williams was quite happy to admit that he preferred it that way. He preferred knowing where his son was at night, that he was safe at home or at work. It made him happy to know that Rory was valued and appreciated for his talents and abilities. He was chuffed that, in some small, universally insignificant way, his son was a hero on a daily basis.

'*Not them, Brian. Never them,*' he had been promised.

But he couldn't shake the feeling that he was about to endure the greatest possible 'gap' in his life.

He should've asked them to stay.

DO WE NEED HOLES?

OLD AMERICANS
Warren Cathrine

Bored again. Knock on 702. Sam. *Fancy a drink?*

Walk together into the growing city, avoiding the Model T's that screech around the block, amaze at the speed in which buildings pop up, marvel at the skyline filled with moving cranes and workers walking tightropes, talk about the future, who we were back then.

In the speakeasy, drink gin and whisky, listen to Ella, flirt with the barmaid, have a wee, think some guy follows me but it's a tall blonde with a familiar look in her eye, watching me carefully, then gone, leave bar, start talking to a party of flappers moseying along the boardwalk, drag them to The Cotton Club, drink, kiss Clara – a brunette – guilt-struck, drink more, dance to the Duke with a redhead, yeah, she takes my hand, we cakewalk and flea hop and then share a smoke, I walk her home thinking *I can't*.

I don't. Back to Winter Quay. Fall asleep on a spinning couch and dream my hands squeeze a statues neck to dust.

Times pass. Door bangs. Crack of light. Amy. She... She found me. Tears well. She mimes words I'm deaf to. *At last*, I spit.

She smiles.

I wake up.

REMEMBER THOSE QUIET EVENINGS.

SLOW WATER
Simon Bucher-Jones

Clara Oswin Oswald waits for a certain person that she's only seen in dreams. A man with his feet on the ground but his head in the clouds. A person she knows will need her. Someone she cannot afford to miss.

Looking for a person of unknown status in a world of class distinction, she lives so as to encompass the widest possible span. Among the high: she takes a position as lofty as her birthplight allows her to reach: a governess to a well-to-do family. Among the low (who see and hear much) a barmaid's role. Inconstant: crossways athwart society, she only hopes that he will not pass in the Queen's company, unseen, titled, a Lord out of reach.

Doctor Simeon's path is straight. Utterly compelled and guided by a powerful force, a daemon that speaks only to him. A voice that mirrors back his every utterance, emphasizes his will makes him ever more himself. Singular, splendidly isolated. The power is his alone. The power is him. As his intelligence grows yet greater, he sets his gaze upon his constant star.

Inconsistency, in principle the opener of minds beyond mere greatness.

Consistency? The frozen bite of snow.

THE INCONSISTENCY PRINCIPLE.

EVERY LONELY MONSTER NEEDS A COMPANION
Matt Adams

The pretty girl with the long brown hair steps out of the shop, colliding with the blonde-ish woman who's been attempting to look inconspicuous. The card the shopkeeper gave her falls unnoticed to the pavement. Muttering apologies the girl hurries off, conscious of the imminent end of the school day and the need to collect her charges.

The blonde woman picks up the card, turning it over and recognising the familiar number printed on one side.

How easily you can change a life, pull the strands of destiny; unravel fate's loom...

Perhaps earlier in her career he might have thought differently. But rewriting time comes so easily these days, like rubbing out an artist's sketch and drawing something completely new.

A hand reaches out and snatches away the card. Startled, she looks up and sees the face of the same pretty girl. But, no, not the same eyes; these are older, wiser somehow.

'Some things just need to run their course,' the girl tells her. 'Regardless of the consequences, and no matter how long it takes.' She waves the card: 'I'll make sure this gets to where it's going.' She smiles, dashing off: 'Looking *good*, by the way, John Smith!'

WORK AT A DIFFERENT SPEED.

THE MAN WHO BOUGHT THE WORLD
Matt Barber

Like Clara, I went to that market once.

No, really.

The Doctor took me.

He was always turning up unexpectedly whilst I was sleeping – as if in a dream – pulling me into the TARDIS and taking me Who Knows Where. This time, I'd been watching him on television. *Pyramids of Mars* I think, or... No, it was *Talons*. Episode Five. I'd dozed off (it happens).

Then, suddenly, he was there: all teeth, curls and repressed Scouse accent. Not Thomas Stewart Baker, but his most remembered role. Close up, I could see the knits in his scarf and – just so I knew he was *really* there – scent the whisky smoke on his breath.

And we went to that market (full of Drahvins, Dominators, Mutts and Argolins back then). He said sentiment and nostalgia were the currency here, so I traded an over-autographed copy of Peter Haining's *Doctor Who: A Celebration* for a kronkburger. I got no change.

Next, I tried something else and hit on a seam that I'd mine consistently during my time there. I pulled out recovered film cans containing all four episodes of *The Savages* – and bought the planet!

And on *this* occasion, the Doctor *didn't* kill God.

CHANGE NOTHING AND CONTINUE WITH IMMACULATE CONSISTENCY.

RED SAILS
Stephen Aintree

When, following a distress call, a commando team located submarine **[REDACTED]** at the North Pole with just two surviving crew aboard, investigations revealed the following:

1) The majority of the crew had been murdered, presumably by Captain Z**[REDACTED]** and his accomplice, the scientist G**[REDACTED]**. The saboteurs had then taken the vessel to the North Pole, perhaps to stage some grand gesture, as:

2) Technical examination showed that Z**[REDACTED]** had clearly attempted to fire two of his nuclear missiles. It is unknown why this action failed.

3) Z**[REDACTED]**'s wild tale involving the revival of frozen, armoured lizards from Mars and time travellers from the future was instantly dismissed as an elaborate attempt to evade punishment for treasonable actions through imitation of mental instability. He was executed at **[REDACTED]** soon afterwards.

4) The former 'professor' G**[REDACTED]** defected to western authorities that year, rendering any supporting testimony invalid. Since 1990 he has worked for **[REDACTED]** at Canary Wharf.

The above report was discovered in a filing cabinet at the **[REDACTED]** *former Soviet naval base, and passed to UNIT in Geneva for more study. No further action appears to have been taken.*

Sarah Jane Smith

Author of Fighting for Humankind *and official UNIT chronicler.*

DO SOMETHING BORING.

THE HEARTS' FILTHY LESSON
Nick Mellish

which of course we know is false. Now, see here the hero running, flustered and afraid in the dull, half-light, not knowing yet about the truth and love, of course, but also not willing to face the possibility of horror, despite his pedigree. The hero who we are told raises no weapon, but we know that to be untrue. (The hero who cannot pronounce words he was once eminently capable of pronouncing, but we'll let that pass...)

Ah! Look! He's pausing now: breath heavy, chest tight, eyes uncertain. The hero would stand and fight you say? Or the hero would wait and see? Or the hero would raise no hand and let fate deal him whichever kind of blow deems the most apposite fit?

No, no, no. I'm not giving you answers. I'm not here for that and neither should you be. See the hero work it out and ponder: is he better for that or just very lucky? He's fought in the past, so why wait here? Perhaps it's the hearts? Perhaps having two of them means he notices and feels the truth before his mind allows him to acknowledge it. But I digress, and then of course we

QUESTION THE HEROIC APPROACH.

DRIVING ME BACKWARDS (DIARY OF A SCIENTIFIC ROMANTICIST)
Craig Moss

October 1863

30th

Hetzel pressing me for another 'Voyage Extraordinaire', following the series' success. Further balloon adventures perhaps?

November 1863

23rd
A plot, at last!

Three buccaneers seize an extraordinary vessel to raid for treasure. On board is the main protagonist – a traveller and doctor of science; a sympathetic character of vast intellect and devilish cunning.

The captured craft manipulates time to undertake fantastic voyages; a marvel of engineering with a vast interior containing many wonders – and horrors – from worlds past, present and future.

This Doctor – what name for him? – has a travelling companion, in danger and lost deep within the bowels of his ship. Tricking his captors into her seemingly impossible rescue, the group sets off to save her and confront the perils within...

May 1864

10th
Hetzel loves the fantastic adventure but calls the concept of a 'time traveller' ridiculous and far-fetched. Now he plagues me for a different angle!

– my Scandinavian journey, perhaps?

May 1895

30th
News: A Mr Wells – an English author and new to scientific romances – is receiving great acclaim for his first novel detailing the adventures of a scientist and his wondrous 'time machine'!

Why did I ever listen to that damned fool publisher?!

WHAT MISTAKES DID YOU MAKE LAST TIME?

YORKSHIRE, MY YORKSHIRE
Ira Lightman

This also happened to me, on the day in question. At such despair of my one part of the world in one year, the queues endured, the way I'd bowled three wides and the batsman clean out, a merlot clatter, my whole face moon and baby. I too saw the help only as romance, even across garnet sexualities, as tightly hemmed forever away from me as a tailored thing chosen for life. I blushed. The fury of having to live my misunderstanding in anything but inured mahogany I wished on my "Jenny". It was left to one of life's superego Vastras. Strax wasn't even part of Jenny's triad, and yet served a role and was nearer than my stupid vanity.

Do we not all have something rigged against us that we panic to life as the wine slug bites?

All try to monetise the rose moment. Evoke a stereotype without ear, pretend we are not chasing a ghost we see ruby and others see brick?

And for all I might sport berry on my socked foot, I have kicked away my remorse and recycled a joke. So that the day would not question. So that the week would be next.

BE EXTRAVAGANT.

TO: MYOLDMUM@CYBERIAD.UNI
Andrew Hunt

One of the best things about being in the Cyberarmy is that I have become better at multitasking. This is because of parallel processing which is like parallel parking, except Cyberwomen are better at it than Cybermen. Ha. Ha. Ha. I also tell better jokes now. Thanks to multitasking, while I am writing to you and thinking of funny jokes, I am also leading a Cyberbatallion in an assault on Hedgewick's World. My organic components are finding this terrifying but I have efficient emotional suppressor chips which render it 'just another day at the office'. When you and Dad voted for Cybentry, so that your old bodies could be replaced with shiny new ones, did you think for a moment you would be sending your progeny off to see the universe? If you could see me now I do not know what you would think. Dad no longer thinks, obviously, as his organic components were judged too damaged for useful integration with Cybertechnology. My processors have suggested 'pride' as a possible answer. My ES chips do not allow me full access to this concept. Will sign off now as I must lead my platoon into a moat.

Your Cyberson

Fzzzzzt&$##

FACED WITH A CHOICE DO BOTH.

I AM WITH NAME
Elton Townend Jones

Incredibly sexy in just a fez – but still all teeth and curls – she climbs onto the silk-white bed and offers him a sip of Darillium champagne.

'Hits the spot,' he proclaims, wincing. 'Tastes like an Ogron's sock.'

She raises her arm, and he nestles his head on her chest. 'You'd know about that, would you, sweetie?'

He's quieter now, always calmer near her skin. 'You don't imagine for one rel that you're my first conquest, do you?'

'Conquest!' mocks River. 'You?!'

'I've been around,' he puffs, quietly.

'Oh, I'm not disputing that, sweetie – but did you tell Mrs Ogron your name?'

'Not yet,' he pokes.

She thinks for a moment. 'Why Orlando, my love?'

'Don't you like it? I can change it to Benjamin, if you like.'

'Not Basil Disco?' She laughs.

'Orlando. After my mother. Now there was a Time Lord. Eventually. She was human at first. Orlando was her Time Lord name. Talk about Oncoming Storms! You'd have loved him.'

'Your mother's... a "him"?'

'For most of the time I knew him. She was a "her" when she... y'know... "mothered" me.'

'What happened to him?'

'What happened?' He grins, wistfully, staring through time at his youth. 'What *didn't* happen?'

TRUST IN THE YOU OF NOW.

REBEL REBEL
Elton Townend Jones

today I: found-wonder; lost-family; cried-in-snow; saw-the-daisy; hid-under-the-bed; wore-his-ring; went-to-school; made-a-friend; fell-in-love; broke-my-hearts; campaigned; won; ran-away; hid-a-hand; saved-a-girl; met-the-future; made-fire; made-enemies; lied; fast-returned; trekked; defended; got-engaged; piloted; impersonated; shrank; declared-war; rescued; performed; communed; crusaded; prevented; flew-through-eternity; meddled; predicted; stayed-home; invented; mutated; avoided; infected; played; deputised; was-honoured; was-required; un-smuggled; wore-thin; turned-off; dragged-up; annoyed; saw-them-off; got-crabby; got-clever; finally-ended; unsealed; gave-back; ionised;

223

ate-mexican; went-underground; amplified-screams; un-dominated; talked-sausage; un-invaded; dropped-acid; got-foamed; pirated; got-caught; got-sexy; got-exiled; spelunked; space-walked; slipped-sideways; got-stalked; burnt-out; got-clawed; escaped; iced-up; ate-cheese; played-diplomat; submarined; collaborated; time-rammed; triplicated; boxed; jail-broke; went-comatose; stole; fireworked; dinosaured; de-wondered; sang-lullabies; got-greedy; went-crazy; made-speeches; combatted; hesitated; bombwalked; hypnotised; antimattered; abased-myself; drank-ginger-pop; mind-bent; won; salami-sandwiched; got-recalled; hunted; amended; sped-up; locked-it-in-with-us; got-cloned; peddled-armageddon; ran-from-the-taxman; quested-the-quest; presided; was-selected; walked-the-plank; hyperspaced; repaired; shattered; dispersed; unearthed; appreciated; blew; interfered; spun; punted; aged; prickled; got-lost; bled; passed-through; expelled; fell; slept; bowled; reflected; cocktailed; failed; flew-cargo; near-bonded; snakedanced; reminded; disconnected; sailed; sword-fought; multiplied; drowned; drank-tea; fooled; almost-shot; eliminated; felt-different; throttled; destroyed; got-dirty; got-stabbed; washed-clean; lost-time; stood-trial; betrayed; wiped-out; turned-bad; tried-on; built-high; comforted; took-on; briar-patched; went-pink; jazzed; juggled; tricked-myself; lit-ghosts; redeemed; survived; kissed; faced-up; arose; watched-the-end; met-a-hero; unzipped; turned-dalek; long-gamed; was-erased; danced; boomed; departed; re-started; swapped; went-scots; reunited; fireplaced; waited; scootered; space-suited; admonished; bore-the-torch; lost-everything; killed-spiders; globed; confessed; donated; quatermassed; burned; humanised; blinked-not; ascended; voyaged; partnered; volcanoed; liberated; out-witted; fathered; mimed; downloaded; repeated; turned-left; teamed-up; ballooned; deserted; got-cocky; had-to-go; custarded-fish-fingers; saved-the-whale; paradigm-shifted; missed-the-clues; stag-partied; bullied-myself; broke-the-world; played-football; rebooted; saved-one-saved-all; got embroiled; saved-pirates; built-a-tardis; fleshed; went-to-war; almost-died; spat-wine; chose-youth; cracked; wrote-letters; got-married; hosted-a-family; spoke-in-parliament; was-bettered-by-anger; saw-myself-in-a-killer; got-bored; was-robbed; retired; answered-the-phone; killed-god; dared-war; hid; journeyed; turned-red; got-logical; altered-my-past; took-the-long-way-home. tomorrow I:

ALLOW AN EASEMENT
(AN EASEMENT IS THE ABANDONMENT OF A STRICTURE).

LOST IN THE HUMMING AIR
Sami Kelsh

There was always a little moment of calm just before it happened – not that it had ever happened in quite the same way twice. The moment came, reaching out in slow motion as the pain faded into a quiet blur, leaving him luminous and at peace, blessed with the knowledge that all was as it should be. He could see what Clara was thinking, wishing he had better reassurance to offer, but she was so brave and so clever and so beautiful, and it was not the first time she had seen him wear a different face.

It was not even as though metamorphosis was unique to his people. Who we are is never fixed or static. Indeed, he mused, was it not so that we all exist in an endless state of becoming? This was simply one of those times that the process made something of a rapid leap forward – a growth spurt, or something like it. Such was the way of life, of evolution, of all things drawing to a close, and all things beginning again. He was ready.

He bid his friends goodnight. Quite by surprise, he felt as though he were about to sneeze, but then,

WHAT ARE YOU REALLY THINKING ABOUT JUST NOW?
INCORPORATE.

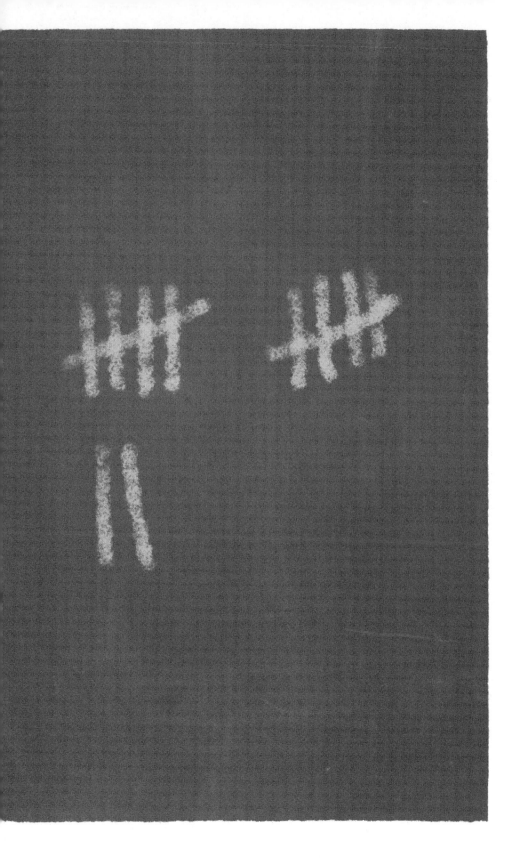

OBSERVATIONS OF AN HONEST PEELER
Warren Cathrine

He had not a fictile face; he had rather an angry brow, a large triangular head with short grey hair agglutinant to it, and a harsh way of speaking, with a peculiarly Scottish accent – as though he was surprised to hear it himself.

He was, it could be said, a gentleman. However, his attire did not attest to this. He was footed bare, and had around him a billowing nightgown, muddied and torn as if he had fell through a tree. To say that his behaviour was erratic would be a gross understatement. His arms moved more oftentimes than the hands of Big Ben, the fingers in perpetual agitation, playing convoluted piano pieces, but never capturing the tune correct. If you take my meaning.

The expression of his face, as he looked towards the burning creature, I felt to be very touching. There was such deep fondness for it, and sorrow, for he expressed to all that he was at blame. His attentive behaviours masked a demeanour of abjuration that belied his own habitual questioning of character.

Still, the crowds were fearsome of his verbal admonishment, and he betrayed an unpleasant and most ruthless aspect. A transient difficult to trust.

EMPHASIZE DIFFERENCES.

PORTRAIT OF DALEK THROUGH GALLIFREYAN ZEN
Jon Arnold

Consider the Dalek.

The Dalek is a thing of perfection. Born of narcissistic insanity and forged in hatred's cauldron, there is a purity to them, a belief that they are the universe's ultimate achievement and thus its natural masters. They tolerate other races through counter-intuitive logic alone. If a race serves no logical utility to "Sucker-kind" it is disposed of – 'exterminated', with maximum, erotic, hysteria. Possessing the singular mindset of the apex predator, they cannot tolerate the Time Lords: a race with the potential to master every sliver of every moment of every atom that has or will or could ever exist. To not exert that power... that is kindness, something the Dalek cannot understand. It offends their self-image. And anything they do not understand must be eliminated, lest it taint them.

What then, if a Dalek could experience wonder or understand beauty and move beyond pure functionality? Would it weaponise these things? Or would it transcend dark perfection and become 'good'? War Philosophers have failed to answer this question as none were brave enough to enter the Dalek mind. And surely no Time Lord will ever be so courageous lest they find they too have become just another Sucker.

ABANDON NORMAL INSTRUMENTS.

TO BE OR NOT TO BE?
Christine Grit

To be truth or to be legend, Robin? That is the question.

Never a mere legend is the answer.

But then legends can have far more to offer than tedious, heartless truths, cold and sharp. I've never been much of a thinking man but this particular conundrum rides me to insanity. The truth of the madman and his box even more so. In faith, the spoon as a weapon lent the fellow a novel mien! His treading of my own existence into the dust of mere legend, less so...

But I'm still here, although the sheriff is beheaded. I remain. I live on. The legendary Doctor – yes, ha, legendary – departed after the mayhem, but I must still fight the damned Normans. My Merries all gone now; disparaging of a Robin that thought and dwelt too much on past and future; on my significance or otherwise in God's great scheme. And ever more, I find myself all too often praying for the Doctor's return, so I can debate these plaguing thoughts, these nattering, nagging doubts that swallow me whole, hood and all.

Hah!

My deceitful mind makes a very liar of me. I just want to see that Impossible Wench again...

TAKE A BREAK.

WHAT'S THAT UNDER THE BEDCLOTHES?
Paul Ebbs

A rough hokum? A fraud?
OK. It's all OK. Listen. Silent. Still there.
'Mum!'
No mum. Not a real home. A care home. 'Doctor!'
In the dark. Don't look.
Must. 'Don't.'
It's there! 'Doctor!'
'Here.'
'What is it?'
'It's fear.'
'I don't like it.'
'Not meant to.'
It rises. It's a dwarf or...
'Not a dwarf. Listen. Inside. Hear that?'

It'll croak and it'll crow, fear shall.
It gawks in the craw, fear does.
It's foams and it's curds, fear is.
It'll fork and it'll churn, fear will.

Fear goads and it crowds, fear does.
It's a wrack and a growl, fear is.
It rocks and it'll hoard, fear will.
It'll ram and it'll wham fear shall.

A hawk and a cur, fear is.
It'll form and it'll grow, fear will.
It will choke and it will hack, fear shall.
Darkens iron frost, fear does.

It'll mulch with murk, fear will
Goad and mark and kill cowards, fear shall
Rucks and rocks and strikes amok, fear does
It's a cougar's claw and shark's tooth, fear is

'So what can I do, Doctor?'

Dark. Silent. Listen.

'It's fear. Fear *will* find us. So don't run. If we stand, fear will die.'

WHICH FRAME WOULD MAKE THIS LOOK RIGHT?

WHEN I BUILT THIS WORLD
Andy Priestner

So many times, so few certainties. Except perhaps regret. Regret over things said. Over action and inaction. This was leaving Sarah behind on Earth. This was Adric. This was the Time War.

He wasn't so personally invested in this particular caper but it might make him feel better about those times he'd made the wrong choice. Besides, he could sell this as the regret of Madame Karabraxos and hide the fact that it was a proxy for his own.

Fast forward.

Here he was. The Doctor in the bank. Looking sharp, alongside his posse: Clara, Psi and Saibra. Striding forward purposefully in suits. Quite the team, yes. *Reservoir Dogs* meets *Hustle*. 'Whatever happened to Matt Di Angelo?' he wondered idly.

Later, in the Private Vault. This con was *so* on. But he increasingly felt like its victim. Which manipulative hateful creature had got them into this? Who was so smug, controlling and pleased with himself behind the scenes?

Ohhh... NO!

His thoughts broke the silence he had used as a shield. Silence that saved them from the Teller.

Not *him*! Oh, that was just too annoying! Being manipulated by someone else was bad enough. But by *yourself*? That's just careless.

DON'T BREAK THE SILENCE.

231

FALL IN LOVE WITH ME
Barnaby Eaton-Jones

Danny Pink caught the wink.

The ancient Caretaker acknowledged Clara in a way that suggested they were intimate.

The late nights and early mornings were closing in. Danny had a free lesson but the cup of tea relaxed more than reinvigorated. His sleepy state conjured up moving images that would make Clara blush; subconsciously replaying their dates (each one's initial meet-up odder than the last) – assigning a backstory of her moonlighting as a call-girl for elderly affluent men.

The first oddity was the sudden tan. Her paying pensioner requested a dark-skinned beauty; her bronzed sweat glistened as she played exotic games with him.

The second oddity was the wet dress and seaweed in her hair. The Chinese businessman pushed her against the walk-in shower glass, rubbing his green fetish all over her.

The third oddity was the space helmet. She rode her retired astronaut in slow motion, visor down, emulating zero gravity.

The fourth oddity was exhaustion. He watched her bouncing bosom as they jogged but she'd clearly just come from an equally demanding physical session.

Then there was the wink. *Meet me in the Caretaker's cupboard. Bring your broomstick.*

He woke up.

His new girl was impossible.

BE DIRTY.

FALL DOG BOMBS THE MOON
Ruth Wheeler

Before the Orient Express pulled into the station,
There was the quandary of the dragon and egg situation.
Which came first and how did it get there in the first place?
There was no mother and father dragon to get past first base.

How did the unborn creature get nutrients so it could feed?
How did it get the oxygen and extra mass that it would need?
Was it born pregnant, is that how the creature had evolved?
So many unanswered questions which will never be solved.

Courtney was a rebel who defied the laws of gravity,
Then out came the bacteria, up through the shell cavity.
How did the unicellular bacteria grow so large?
The Doctor made his gobby companion, for once, take charge.

A parallel with abortion – are you pro-life or pro-choice?
Clara decides to give the inhabitants of Earth a voice.
A big decision determined by those with a national grid,
And happened to be awake to be able to make their bid.

As he was waiting in his TARDIS Clara began to get irate.
Did he know the Moon's fate?

She said, 'Tell me what you knew, Doctor,
or I'll smack you so hard you regenerate.'

LOOK AT THE ORDER IN WHICH YOU DO THINGS.

NOT YET REMEMBERED
Alan G McWhan

Gus tutted irritably as he watched the destruction of the Orient Express – from a safe distance, naturally.

Inviting the Doctor had been a massive gamble, given his reputation, but one Gus had felt worthwhile following the failure of previous 'experts' and their poor attempts at achieving results.

The tremendous resources Gus had devoted to the exercise had eventually left him empty handed anyway. No super soldier at his command. No amazing new technology to cunningly exploit.

Worse still, Gus had revealed his existence (and his casual disregard for life) to the Doctor. Gus felt certain that the Doctor – one of the most predictable moral crusaders in the universe – would now be after him.

That said, the venture had not been a complete loss. Gus had now seen for himself how easily the Doctor could be manipulated by threats to innocents and felt certain he could turn that to his advantage. He would just have to avoid direct contact with the Doctor in future, and use his skills without drawing undue attention.

Putting the whole experience behind him, Gus browsed his 'most wanted items' list. A Mire helmet! That would be fun!

'What about Gus?' asked Clara.

'Who?' the Doctor replied.

THE MOST IMPORTANT THING IS THE THING MOST EASILY
FORGOTTEN.

FLAT
Liam Hogan

flat
flat text within a flat world
flat life
flat love
our leaders claim this is all there is, that my theories of extra dimensions are
insane, blasphemous, dangerous
that we should be content with what we have
i say there is more, that there must be more, that two dimensions are not enough
in two dimensions, my love and i are incompatible, our edges hard, unyielding
we touch, but only share the thinnest of contacts
not enough
i will lose my love to another, to one she can melt into, to one that can melt into
her
i will not let that happen
i shall be bold, i shall prove our leaders wrong
i will forge ahead with my experiments, the council be damned

Ah
Pain! I am twisted, warped, my mind expands!
I panic and almost flee
But here there is freedom! Volumes, and shapes, and shadows!
Such wonder, such joy!
I must bring my Love here–
Wait, no! This dimension is defended! I am forced back

back
but not to where i came from
the dimensions demand balance
i have tasted higher, now i am squeezed into lower
flatter a n d t h i n n e r
this ends
with but a single
.

DO SOMETHING BORING.

BIG CAT SMALL TALK
Blair Bidmead

'I had a dream,' said the tiger. The wolf curled her lip but resisted the urge to sigh.
They were beginning to get along and she didn't wish to remind the tiger that
this casual conversation had started out as a hunt.

Bloodsports on Wardour Street. The fearfully symmetrical in pursuit of the pack
of lies. The slowest now forced to endure anecdotes.

'I dreamed that a forest grew,' said the tiger. 'I became king of all the wild things.'

The wolf sensed that she had heard this story before, but indulged the tiger
further.

'When I awoke, the forest had indeed returned,' the tiger explained. 'My heart sang with joy. It was all true. I was the king of the world, just as my dream had predicted. Would you like to be my Prime Minister?'

The wolf was delighted by this unexpected career opportunity and accepted the appointment immediately.

'Mine shall be a benign dictatorship,' said the tiger. 'You may canvass my subjects and they can choose the manner in which they are governed, on the proviso that they accept my divine right over all things.'

The wolf didn't see any issue with this stipulation. She licked her lips.

WOULD ANYBODY WANT IT?

AS THE WORLD FALLS DOWN
Martin Tucker

I still haven't adjusted to how *cold* the air is.

No, it isn't the air it's my...

I know the word but can't quite bring myself to think it. Am I really...

Is this an afterlife?

The tablet feels heavy in my hands. I'm not sure how long I've been staring at it. I can't see the screen properly for tears, but it's hard to miss the big button, flashing *DELETE*.

I keep thinking, *I've saved her*. I've saved her, but is it me who needs saving?

I'll never see her again; never hold her, smell her, never again experience all those Clara things that drive me nuts but make me love her even more.

She once said, '*I love you' means nothing*.

How can it mean nothing? Okay so, the words themselves sound dull and overused. But what other words can adequately describe our connection?

The tablet flashes again. *DELETE*. Pressing it seems the obvious answer. By pressing *DELETE*, by removing these emotions, I'll *feel better*.

Something about that doesn't sound right.

But it might allow me to come to terms with the idea that I'm... dead?

The screen changes.

No, the reflection changes.

The lights are going out.

SHORT CIRCUIT.

GATHERING GLOOM
Jon Dear

'My dear fellow,' says the scruffy rider in the middle, 'I'm merely saying that Father Christmas seems a bit obvious, that's all.'

The elegant rider in front glances round, glowering. 'Of course it seems obvious. That's rather the point, isn't it? Anyway, how "obvious" is a land where fictional characters are real?'

'But *that* wasn't a dream!' the middle rider protests. 'At least, I don't think it was.'

'No, of course not,' says the front rider. 'Everyone knows that using the TARDIS Emergency Unit sends you to Storybook World; that's just–'

'Will you two kindly stop arguing?' demands the rider at the back. 'Dear, dear, it really is most irritating.'

They ride on in silence.

Briefly.

'So,' begins the front rider, raising his voice to make it clear he's addressing the rider at the back, 'just exactly *who* were you wishing a Merry Christmas to again?'

The third rider harrumphs something impatient about Gallifreyan spies – probably; or is it 'mince pies'? – then falls silent.

'Where are we going?' says the middle rider. 'I can't seem to remember.'

The front rider rubs the back of his neck. 'It's a long story.'

The three camels continue funkily across the starlit desert.

> GO TO AN EXTREME, MOVE BACK TO A MORE COMFORTABLE PLACE.

I'M DERANGED
Lee Ravitz

[Recording commences]:

'The modern Kaled shows marked degenerate tendencies. These, clear consequences of ceaseless neutronic war. Yet I aver no inevitability in such processes. Or, rather, a possible reversal.

'Re-engineering sensory organs is key; our lobes, glands, commonly already altered by mutation. Speed this course. Electrify. Experiments demonstrate that current stirs members; differential voltage incites.

236

'Thal society stands apart from us. "Inferiors breed not souls". Conflict hardened me; scarred. Platoon brothers fell to killing tools; their remainder, invalided, rousted out, display only mawkish sentiment, bitter regrets–

<Davros?>

<Salka? You interrupt.>

<Couldn't help myself. Your sentiments...>

<Genius! Skaro affirms it!>

<You're missed at headquarters. What can be said anymore?>

<Oh, shame! So urgent and abiding; such a pursuit...>

<Don't mock!>

[Static seconds; then he, considerate:]

<We had sweet days together.>

<Goodly hours. Better ones.>

<Marching under matching banners, beating identical drums.>

<But... fighting never ends.>

<Nor up here.>

[Taps head. She:]

<Come back.>

<Work's too vital. Please. Leave.>

[Continues with:]

'Soon comes an era when new masters arise. Dawning novelty. Enemies shall perish; foes lie exterminated. Doughty warriors sprung from debased filth. Priest contraptions; immaculate electric circuit conceptions. Inspiration leads. Merciful release for opponents. Tribally archaic; perdition calls them. NO SELF-SIMILARITY!'

ONLY ONE ELEMENT OF EACH KIND.

CASE STUDY: THE FISHER KING'S FEET
Philip Bates

Taking part in the Great Hunt? Conquering the galaxy? Partying at the Pandorica? Or simply shopping for the latest innovations in Torture Tech?

At Boots for Brutes™, we believe that your footwear should say as much about you as your gaping maw, razor-sharp claws, and penchant for oppression.

The Fisher King came to us looking for something simple yet intimidating: 'My enemies should tremble in fear as they realise their doom approaches,' he said.

'I wanted shoes that signalled Death's sweet advance. But I also needed them to be comfortable too, y'know?'

Boots for Brutes™ set to work creating heavy-duty footwear made from the digestive linings of the last Krafayis: invisible but hard-wearing and stylish in the multi-spectrum quarters. We minimised the sole to cater for the Fisher King's height, and added in air-support padding to let out a pleasing flatulent sound so armies would hear the alien tyrant coming from miles away.

On delivery of the final product, the Fisher King couldn't have been happier: 'I couldn't be happier,' he wept.

Boots for Brutes™: Custom footwear for little* monsters. Prepare the very best for your very worst.

(*Size may vary.)

Find us at: Slaughter Factory 9, Despot's Drive, Tivoli.

LOOK CLOSELY AT THE MOST EMBARRASSING DETAILS AND AMPLIFY THEM.

HYBRID
Kara Dennison

Small and square and white, alien but oddly perfect. *Too* perfect. A Cake Too Beautiful to Eat. But it must go to someone, someday. Of course it must. What will I be if there isn't another like me?

Maybe that's how he does it. The little humans like me *(no, not like you, silly)* who keep him happy, comfortable, secure. He's a raging lion, but spill a drop of blood *(a drop of innocent blood)* and he's a mewling cub, hard face soft and sharp words warm.

What does that do to a man *(I beg your pardon?)* with the universe on a string? To know so much, to live so long. To have no one who can stay as long as you. Does he hoard them? A dragon with a cache of friends, stretched across it, thinking only not to lose it?

But *any* treasure is rubbed dull with only one keeper to admire it.

I could never pull the shine from another life. Not as he would with hers.

There is only one I need. Me, me, me.

Me me me me me me...

ME!

DISCONNECT FROM DESIRE.

LOVING THE ALIEN
Ken Shinn

The Doctor's hair flies wildly, but his voice remains level as he speaks his thoughts. They are compassionate, intelligent, eloquent thoughts. They argue a case for understanding, for peace. And he delivers them with anger. Calling for love, in a voice of fury.

Humanity has so many contradictions. Where do we stand, in the middle of this mess of dogmatic ideology, this self-wrestling conflict of deeds and words? Duality is all, for good and ill. Both sides, so often set at each other's throats. You're either with us, or you're against us. The Doctor, or the Monster. UNIT, or the invaders. Always the decision. Always the choice. And so much always depends upon it, from the trivial to the apocalyptic.

Daddy – or chips? War – or peace? Human... Or Zygon?

The answer is never easy. But it's usually one or the other. Middle ground, compromise – well-intentioned, but weak words. Maybe, at last, it's time to give them some well-earned strength.

Human – or Zygon?

How about Human *and* Zygon?

Sometimes, compromise can be the strongest, most loving power of all.

Love – and strength. Thought – and feeling. Time – and Space.

Petronella – *and* Bonnie.

Sometimes, the best – the only – path is to choose *both*.

DON'T STRESS ONE THING MORE THAN ANOTHER.

SISTER MIDNIGHT
JR Southall

'I never see you sleeping,' says Clara, eyeing the Doctor from the opposite side of the console.

'Nor would you,' the Doctor replies. Something in his manner suggests the agitation of a thing overlooked.

'Sleep is for tortoises, right?'

The Doctor gives Clara a look that says, *Back off*, before resuming his circumference of the controls. 'I never told you that,' he grumbles.

Yes, you did, she thinks. *In another life. Another time.*

'Sleep is for forgetfulness,' he adds.

'Or for dreaming,' says Clara.

'Same thing.'

'Dreaming and forgetting? Not always. Dreams can help you remember things too.' She watches the Doctor's finger tapping almost imperceptibly against the console, as if there's something he can't quite reach. Like the people she used to be that she dreams about, yet can't quite be any more.

'Tsk.'

'It's a veil between the days,' Clara says, pleased with herself. 'Although,' she continues, remembering Danny, 'maybe it's more like a little bit of Heaven that you can't quite hold onto.'

The Doctor looks up with a start.

'Like clouds,' he says.

'I suppose.'

'We've barely moved,' he says. 'A few days, a few miles. I think we'd better take a quick shufti at Neptune.'

TRUST IN THE YOU OF NOW.

WEEPING WALL
Ira Lightman

The elder brother demonised the father in order that the other be appeased. The other in the wings. The younger brother had a food disorder, did not understand the drama. The other would not alter, nor the elder with the other. The elder ceased to see the father though the younger persevered.

The father fought with mind distemper. He played the drama over and then over, lacking the presence of the elder, the routine of the elder, the ability to gather anything but bedclothes to his hurt. What would not die an instant was despair.

O charity, o clarity, o cleaving the. Undeceiving the.

Arrears were. Arrears are. If not in care and vow then silver. The father met the other grandfather. Down he bore his tray, his paper, his offer. Aggressor. Saying he was mediator.

The other. The other on the elder brother, other on the younger brother. The other would not meet the father. Across the barrier, and its warriors.

Last it almost to forever. Selectively remember. Be your better. Love the younger brother. Care the elder brother may side with traitor or perpetuator. Heal over.

Generations younger will inter the father and the other. Lies will bore.

IS THERE SOMETHING MISSING?

240

AND TOMORROW WE MIGHT LIVE
JR Southall

'Get in the TARDIS now!'

'I'm a prince; nobody gets to talk to me like that.'

'You might be a prince, but as far as I can see, there's not much left for you to be a prince of. So, if you want to live, get in the TARDIS – now.'

'I don't want to live.'

Heavy sigh. 'Very well. Let's put this another way. You're young. You've lost a lot.'

'I've lost everything.'

'That happens. But time is on your side. Time and space, as it goes. So get in the TARDIS and leave the big decisions for another time. If you still feel this way tomorrow, then so be it.'

Heavy frown. 'I can't imagine I'll feel any different tomorrow.'

'Trust me, you'll feel very different in about thirty seconds' time.'

'Yeah, sure.'

'Hey, don't believe me, step aboard.'

'Okay... But this doesn't mean I believe you.'

'Oh, you will. However sorry you might be feeling for yourself right this minute, it won't last.'

'You say that now but – what the hell? What's she doing here?'

'There, you see. All that self-pity, gone in an instant.'

'Oh, for goodness' sake, will I never be free of that damned boy?'

ACCRETION.

WILD IS THE WIND
Matt Barber

The scent, smoke, sweat of the Singing Towers restaurant on Darillium are stimulating at three in the morning, even after twenty-four years...

When I started this diary centuries ago (or centuries to come – I lose track) I knew it would end here. One final night with the man (men/women) I loved (love). This one's the first of the impossible incarnations that should never have been but somehow *are*.

Beginnings and endings; endings of beginnings.

We started this adventure, this long consummation of our marriage, in a final, violent fling. And then unbroken time: a final night, me and him together, that lasted decades.

This was his beautiful gift to me: sacrificing his wanderlust to spend his days and nights in one place and time. Substituting his desire to be in the fight with his desire for me. Destroying, or at least deferring, the most important thing in his existence.

Sometimes I felt a twinge of guilt. How many battles were raging whilst he drank, ate and slept with me in this restaurant. How many despots, villains and monsters ruled whilst he took his honeymoon; took his woman.

But I know, that after all this, (s)he will return to the fight.

DESTROY THE MOST IMPORTANT THING.

GHOST SENSE
Matt Adams

Sometimes it hurts.

The grating of Lucy's skin cells on her silk blouse. The deafening roar of the blood coursing through her veins. The anxious wait for each beat of Jennifer's heart. The sight of bed bugs crawling through the strands of carpet.

Sometimes I just have to stop. To close my eyes, to slow my breathing. And. To. Be. Still. But even the absence of one sense cannot shelter me from the onslaught of the others.

I can smell the pine needles on the Christmas tree, hear the fizz of electricity as the lights flash in staccato, feel the winter chill through the molecules of the window pane, taste the cinnamon in the air from the cooling buns in the kitchen.

But I am at peace. Content in my meditation. Accepting the stillness.

A door opens.

Stumbling footsteps knock a pile of presents flying and the perpetrator swears under their breath.

'Bugger.'

Sometimes there's confusion. Mixed with the usual sounds of life are grinding gears, the gasp of hydraulics and the burbling of electronics. Sometimes I know too much.

The air parts, a finger taps on my shoulder.

'I'm putting the kettle on, fancy a cuppa?'

Mostly it's okay.

IN TOTAL DARKNESS OR IN A VERY LARGE ROOM, VERY QUIETLY.

WALK ON THE WILD SIDE
Daniel Wealands

Bill should've known the date would be a bust, she'd never had one end well yet. But tonight, she'd been sure it would be different.

She'd sat there with a small bowl of chips, checking the time and convincing herself she was just stuck in traffic or late leaving a lecture. Or she'd had to stop and run an errand. She'd be there soon.

By the time she was halfway through the chips she knew it was a losing battle. She wasn't coming.

Maybe she'd had a better offer? Maybe she'd turned up, seen Bill and changed her mind? Maybe she just didn't really care in the first place – that was what the world was like really.

Then she'd thought of him, the professor. He seemed to care. He'd given her an opportunity no one else ever had. If he could be different maybe other people could too? Maybe Bill's date was on her way after all?

Ten more minutes she'd thought, just 10 more minutes.

And here she was at 5.56pm going full tilt to make it across campus; 6pm every day, even if someone died he'd said! Bill simply had to make it!

At least the chips had been good.

WHEN IS IT FOR?

AN ARC OF DOVES
Jon Dear

The footage is all women. No, nearly all. There's an elderly man in a kilt and some black and white photos of a straight couple in Trafalgar Square – but the rest? A blonde girl walking through a jungle; a medieval-looking queen combing her long hair; someone being chased through a school by... okay, a fat green monster; and an older lady sitting, working, at a desk.

She reminds Bill of the photo in the Doctor's office.

Unsettlingly, there's no obvious place for the camera.

This is weird. Proper creepy, in fact. What did the Doc–

'I said you *shouldn't* look at my browser history.' Bill hadn't heard the Doctor come back in. She whirls almost ridiculously away from the screen.

'I only clicked Favourites!'

The Doctor looks past her at the monitor. 'Time-Space Visualiser,' he proclaims – as if that explains everything – and walks to the other side of the console.

Bill turns back; the screen's settled on a single image: another woman – in a long pale coat; braces and a rainbow motif on her top. Blonde-ish. Standing in a green field, under a golden sky.

She's staring directly at… well, at Bill.

Smiling.

Ready.

Bill shudders, grave-walked, and looks away.

TAKE AWAY THE ELEMENTS IN ORDER OF APPARENT NON-IMPORTANCE.

THE GREENISH DEATH
Daniel Milco

The Frost Fair is spectacular.

Enthralled by her surroundings, Bill is startled when the Doctor suddenly leans across and says, 'Oh, and don't go licking any wallpaper while you're here.'

'You what?' Bill turns a confused look towards the Doctor.

'That's what killed Napoleon, you know. Green wallpaper.'

'Do I *look* as if I'd lick *wallpaper*?!'

'In fact, avoid anything green while we're here.'

'You're saying "poison green" is a thing in 1814?'

'Damp air like this, you wouldn't want to risk absorbing any nasty floating-about things. Arsenic poisoning. Not pretty.'

'*Doctor!* Look at this coat you gave me!'

'*Pelisse*, Bill.'

'Don't you "Please, Bill" me – *I'm wearing green!*'

'*Your garment* is called a pelisse. You'd be fine even if it was arsenic green – which it isn't!' He waves his sonic screwdriver erratically over her emerald velvet sleeve, then holds it like a thermometer before her bewildered eyes. 'See? Perfectly normal. Even if it was arsenic, you'd be fine. Some spectacularly mad people would nibble it to make their skin whiter.'

Bill gapes.

The Doctor pauses. 'Is that one "shock"? Was I tactless?'

Bill gapes harder. 'Did you… just show… *self-awareness*?'

The Doctor shrugs. 'Just don't eat your greens.'

DECORATE, DECORATE.

244

HOUSE RULES
Dan Rebellato

NO smoking.
NO vaping.
NO music after 10pm.
NO music before 10am.
NO Little Mix mixtapes.
NO guests overnight.
NO guests undernight.
NO cars on the driveway.
NO subletting.
NO catch.
NO strings attached.
NO late payments.
NO cash payments.
NO down payments.
NO refunds.
NO big hats.
NO shoes inside.
NO insects outside.
No need to hang around.
NO blu-tack.
NO sellotape.
NO drawing pins.
NO nails.
NO living puddles.
NO weird robots.
NO big fish.
NO dogs.
NO cats.
NO pets.
NO reception.
NO signal.
NO mobile phone signal.
NO landline.
NO central heating.
NO washer.
NO dryad –
NO dryer.
NO dryer.
NO wind.
NO wind.
NO wind in the trees.
NO wind in the creaking trees.
NO entry to the Tower.
NO smile.
NO joke.
NO family trees.
NO tree surgeons.
NO topiary.
NO pollarding.
NO carving.

NO whittling.
NO answer.
NO naked flames.
NO varnish.
NO pranks.
NO japes.
NO knock-knock jokes.
NO regenera–
NO Dutch Elm Disease.
NO termites.
NO woodworm.
NO you can't.
NO I told you, no.
NO you don't understand.
NO love.
NO future.
NO hope.
NO thanks.
NO energy.
NO energy left.
NO more.
NO no more.
NO no
NO.

DO NOTHING FOR AS LONG AS POSSIBLE.

UNSUITABLE
Alan G McWhan

She thumps the legs of her environment suit in exasperation. 'Come on!' she grunts. 'Do as you're told!'

The suit's legs remain immobile.

Sighing, she activates her comms unit. 'Control, this is Cassie. I have a suit failure. Legs have stopped responding. Request immediate retrieval, please.'

The scraping breath of static provides the only reply.

'Control? Can you hear me?'

No response.

'Oh, come on!' she breathes to herself. 'Right, suit. All I need is one foot in front of the other. Rinse. Repeat. That's not so difficult, is it?'

The suit continues to ignore her.

She may only be ten metres from the control hub airlock but she's going to have to use her initiative to cover that ground. With another heavy breath, she throws all her weight to one side, toppling over on her unresponsive legs. Grabbing hold of the gantry as she falls, she drags herself slowly to the airlock and into the hub beyond.

Ivan sees her and hurries over to help her discard the useless suit. 'Hang that over there with the other faulties and grab a new one,' he says. 'Quickly! Something has happened to the rest of the crew! They're killing each other!'

ASK YOUR BODY.

THIS IS A FAKE
Philip Bates

He was here now, and they had to move. But –

'I need to know.' She slammed her hand down. 'Thirty-six.'

'Fifteen,' Nardole countered.

How do you hide a lie effectively? Within a truth.

Except the Doctor had told her about the other world, and at the heart of its truth lay a falsehood. Namely: everything. An algorithm had predicted her life. It knew her past, it foresaw her future, it had mapped out her collision with the Doctor.

And in this life? Could all that running be a lie? It had been real to her, hadn't it? It had been everything she'd hoped for. It had been life itself.

God gave us memory so that we might have roses in December. The Doctor had taught her that. Bill figured that God had given her this silent suffering so she might appreciate their travels in time and space even more when they were finally over.

And if it weren't real? Even her memories?

The Star Monks had been here six months. Was that a fiction too? There was only one thing she could do. He was here now, and they had to move. But–

'One more time? Can we play again?'

WHAT WOULDN'T YOU DO?

LIFE ON MARS?
Hendryk Korzeniowski

She stares at the Victorian soldiers. None of them ever likely to have their names on headstones. Not on Earth, anyway. How was their disappearance explained, she wonders? She winces at the stench that hangs around brute force, shaking her head. She's seen *Zulu* and isn't impressed.

While I stood here talking peace, a war has started.

The Ice Empress seethes outrage. Only the legendary Phaester Osirians ever dared use her race for manual work, yet these mammalian primitives had placed servitude of the lowest kind upon her noble sentinel. She has no time for the heretical nonsense of the Oras with Martian honour at stake. These pink invaders must be repelled.

British honour is at stake. Mars is now of the Empire, subject to Queen Victoria – upright lady crocodiles or not. British soldiers have been killed. An example must be made.

The non-Human, non-Martian strives to intercede, imploring for mutual co-operation. Future history hangs in the balance.

'And you, female...what do you say?'

Bill gulps, all amusing quips aborted in her throat by the direct address of the Martian Empress.

Was the final outcome down to *her?* Did the future rest on *her* words, *her* opinion, *her* advice?

'Me?'

ACCEPT ADVICE.

BOYS KEEP SWINGING
Andy Priestner

Nardole owed the Doctor much.

It's not everyone who glues your head back on – even if their motivation for doing so is loneliness rather than compassion.

But now, without warning, the Gallifreyan was gone. For ever.

Two days and eight hours after the Doctor vanished inside the hillside cairn – and with Bill also missing – Nardole's mind unavoidably turned towards the possibility of a very new and different life.

Bizarrely, he could already see himself fitting in quite well, and was almost embarrassed to discover that he enjoyed hunting, skinning and cooking rabbits, making fires – and all the face painting. Newly adorned with wode spirals he took especial pleasure in telling fireside stories, just to hear the gasps of his comrades, transfixed by the many wonders he described.

Pict life had been laid out before him in all its stark simplicity, and despite his alien-cybernetic heritage he absolutely wanted more of it. Here, he realised, he could finally be accepted as part of a tribe. Here he actually *belonged*.

But then the Doctor came back.

Which was a good thing.

And though this meant Nardole would soon leave this pastoral idyll, a new ambition for the simple life bloomed within him.

LOOK CLOSELY AT THE MOST EMBARRASSING DETAILS AND AMPLIFY THEM.

BLACKSTAR
Sami Kelsh

Not now, not yet.

This time, it turned out, the regeneration began with an itch.

Not the desperate, immediate itch that comes just before a sneeze; rather, this was the sort of slow-burning, distant, nagging itch that sat somewhere just deep enough beneath the skin that no scratch could touch it.

It was the sort of itch you push down with gritted teeth, determined that it'll go away if you ignore it, but it only ever grows deeper, more insistent. Itchier. He wasn't yet ready to succumb to it, not again.

And then there was Bill; heart the size of a sun that shone so brightly even the Cybermen couldn't burn it out. There was still so much of the universe for her to see, so many beautiful things to learn: her spirit belonged among the stars that made her, dazzling and brilliant, not confined to a clumsy cybernetic casing. He couldn't help but feel he'd failed her.

It was something he'd felt far too many times now.

But the itch was growing; getting loud, relentlessly loud, as he struggled to will it down; pushing it back with a shock of sudden snow.

He was not ready.

Not yet

TIDY UP.

OH! YOU PRETTY THINGS
Elton Townend Jones

They've all stood here like this. Naked. Looked at. Admired. Encouraged. All except Grandfather, the *actual* Doctor – the original – who suffered his own indignities by having been both born as a Gallifreyan infant and loomed, fully formed, depending on how the Time War was going/had gone/would go at the particular moment anyone wanted to pinpoint the facts.

That her thirteen onlookers (plus someone in a white bikini, always just out of sight) are fully-clothed while her entire skin glows golden under the misty starlight – or an illusion of such – feels perfectly natural. *They've* done their lives to death, but she is about to begin hers and has yet to choose who she'll be.

'Don't be afraid – it doesn't hurt,' says Half-Human-On-His-Mother's-Side. 'Not going in.'

'Imagine how we feel,' says the Beatle. 'Once *you've* nipped off, we've got Basil to sort out...'

'Gallifreyan Grumpy-pants, 2017,' says Geronimo, flourishing.

'Oh, I don't know,' says Teeth-and-Curls. 'I rather admired his efforts in that Confessional Dial!'

'Quite,' says the Professor. 'But this one's going to be even better.' He smiled at her.

All thirteen smile at her.

'Funny thing, regeneration,' muses Gumblejack. 'But under the right conditions you *can* play with what you get...'

'One can make all kinds of adjustments to the voice, certainly,' offers the Dandy.

'Oh yes,' says Grandfather, 'I should know, I've tried. A touch of incarnation sickness – utterly benign, of course,' he assures her, 'and you can temporarily adjust the face, change the age, the hair... Though it only ever really worked for me during temporally complex situations like crossover...'

'Indeed,' says Celery, casting a look at Sandshoes.

'Oh, come on,' says Sandshoes, 'it's not as if we haven't *all* tried it at some time or other.'

'From where I was looking,' replies No-More, 'you *really* went for it!'

'But, child,' says Grandfather, 'you're not interested in a lot of old men quibbling about continuity, are you? Hm?'

She grins at her predecessors.

'Now,' says Grandfather, squeezing what will soon be her – and his – hand, 'it's almost time, as I recall...'

'I'm ready.'

A green-purple scream of agonising light illuminates the mist around them.

'Aye-aye,' quips Fantastic, wiggling his eyebrows irreverently. 'Basil's 'ere.'

'Will I be okay?' she asks. 'Will I be good?'

'You'll be fantastic,' they chorus.

Dazzling in gold and rainbows, she steps through the thirteenth door, into his world.

The Doctor's world.

Her world.

Your world.

THIS OTHERSTIDE:

'Of course my name's not Orlando. But then it's not John Smith. Or Doctor, come to that. See, I'm not the Doctor. I'm not a Time Lord and I'm not from Gallifrey. I tell myself, over and over, when I look in the mirror, when I feel scared or challenged or threatened or found out: *I. Am. The. Doctor.* But I'm not. I killed the Doctor a long time ago. Before the TARDIS, before Susan. None of you ever knew him. I took his experiences, his memories, his future, his Selves, and I played the part. In a very long game. Lying low. And now, finally, I've got something like my *real* body back – at last. The Doctor was a sickening game. Nothing more. And this, incidentally, isn't the real universe. Now. You were saying?'

Gillian Anderson

is

THE DOCTOR...?

WHOBLIQUE STRATEGIES: SPECIAL FEATURES

A collection of related writings by Elton Townend Jones

FICTION: The Blurred Man

On an icy, sparkling morning in what was clearly the British countryside, I stepped from the TARDIS into deep snow.

Locking the doors, the Doctor joined me. Pointing at my bare, pink legs he laughed before ploughing off, in fur coat and wellies, towards a dark, bare wood.

'D'ye know where we are, then?' I asked, my breath forming clouds.

'Of course I do, Jamie,' he said, dismayed that I should question his navigational skill. 'This is Norfolk. Mid-twenty-first century.'

I took him at his word. 'And we're here why?'

He pointed upwards. 'Because They want us to be.'

'Why's that then?' I asked.

'Usual sort of thing. Someone mucking about with their temporal monopoly. Though quite why Norfolk has them in a tizzy I've no idea.'

'And They want you to stop whoever's doing the mucking about?'

He sighed. 'As much as it pains me to stamp on the creative butterfly, yes.'

I thought quietly as we skirted the skeletal trees.

'What?' asked the Doctor.

'Eh?' I asked, confused.

'Jamie,' he said, halting abruptly. 'That brain of yours is ticking away like an impatient time bomb. You want to know why I don't just walk away and leave them to it. Am I right?'

He was a canny wee fellow.

'Well,' he said, steepling two fingers of one hand against the palm of the other, 'as you know, these occasional... assignments... allow you and I to roam the temporal cosmos with impunity. It's the price we pay, Jamie.'

'Aye, but supposing you *could* walk away, would you?'

He glanced sheepishly at the sky.

I wagged a finger at him. 'You know what curiosity did.'

'No, Jamie, that was Schröedinger,' he replied, though I'm not entirely sure what he meant. 'But yes, I am curious. This is what you might call an "extra-historical" situation. Time experiments weren't uncommon in this period, but never anything this significant.'

'Perhaps your historians missed it?' I suggested.

'Jamie,' he said seriously, 'had time travel been developed in twenty-first century Norfolk, I rather think the Time Lords might just have got wind of it, don't you?'

'Hang on. I thought we were here because they *had*. Either it happened or it didn't?'

'Both,' he replied. 'And neither. I'll explain as we go.'

'Imagine you're a rail commuter. Every day you board a carriage and go to work. Today, for no reason discernible to you, you board carriage five. For your part, this is an entirely random action. Tomorrow you might board carriage three. You never notice the number; you don't care. Each day seems like any other. Therefore, what you've failed to noticed is that space-time events are constantly occurring around you, and apparently random factors have set themselves into the wobbly jelly of history. Because nothing is random, Jamie: everything is causally bound. You're in carriage five because the driver overshot the platform slightly, because he was tired, because his eight-year-old daughter was up all night with nightmares, because two years ago her mother died in a traffic accident, because a motorist was drunk, because so on and so forth. And if the "random" boarding of carriage five can be unthreaded into the past like this, then what threads will spin from it, into the future? This is what I mean when I talk about the web of time. Trouble is, once you've grasped the concept, it becomes worryingly easy to assume that all your actions are pre-determined. Ah, we've arrived.'

We'd turned a corner on the wintry woodland to face the dark ruins of a castle.

'Will ye look at the size of that?'

This was my habitual contribution to any brand new escapade. Normally the Doctor would offer a comforting response. Today he was having none of it.

'You are paying attention, aren't you, Jamie?'

'Och! D'ye even have to ask? I might not be the sharpest...'

'Dirk in the sock?' asked the Doctor, with an impish grin.

'Very funny.'

'So, where was I?'

'"Once we've grasped the concept of a web in time..."'

'*Of* time,' he corrected.

'"...It becomes worryingly easy to assume that all our actions are pre-determined."'

The Doctor gasped. 'James Robert Macrimmon! Shall wonders never cease?'

'Aye, well, I picked up the words all right, but I don't have a clue what you're rattling on about.'

I trudged towards the slumped castle.

'"Rattling on?"' asked the Doctor.

He appeared in front of me just as I was about to knock upon a great weathered door.

'What do you know about free will?' he asked.

'Never heard of him,' I admitted.

The Doctor winced. 'It's a philosophical position, Jamie. It suggests we can mentally access possible futures – Action A or Action B – and choose between them to manifest a desired outcome.'

'Sounds all right,' I said.

'Oh no, it's quite unacceptable, and this is down to the illusion of choice.'

'Can I help you?' asked a warm voice.

The Doctor spun around like he'd been booted up the backside.

In the now open doorway stood a tall, broad fellow with a mop of wild, grey hair. His twinkling eyes and carpet slippers suggested he was both friendly and harmless.

'Thank goodness!' said the Doctor, suddenly acting breathless. 'Sorry to trouble you, Mister, ah...'

'Professor,' responded the man, looking us over with evident confusion.

'Professor!' cried the Doctor, shaking his hands and winking at me. 'I was caught out by the snow yesterday and managed to get myself dreadfully lost.'

'Oh dear,' muttered the Professor.

I was about to add myself to the Doctor's subterfuge, when he kicked me slyly in the shin.

'Having spent the night in your wood,' he pressed, fixing the Professor with puppy-dog eyes, 'I wondered if I might trouble you for a glance at a map and a cup of something warm?'

I'd like to say that this was when the Professor let us in, but if I'm honest, we were already through the door and backing him along a narrow passage towards the happy sound of a whistling kettle.

The castle had long since fallen into disrepair and was now being used by the Professor in discreet pockets, partitioned by plastic sheets on wooden frames.

'All that's left of the family pile,' he said, fussing around a teapot in his makeshift living quarters.

As we warmed our hands by the stove, the Doctor eyed some hand-written papers spread across a table.

'Nice place,' I said, affording him more reading time.

'It was boarded up for years,' said the Professor, laying out cups. 'When I returned here to work, it was a devil to get clean. All sorts of mess.' He poured the tea and gave us both a cup. 'No milk or sugar, sorry.'

'Thank you,' said the Doctor, 'Professor, ah, Blinovitch, isn't it?'

This astonished me. Had the Doctor known the man's name all along or had he just read it in his notes?

'Oh,' he said, bowing a little. 'John Smith.'

'Jamie McCrimmon,' I offered.

The Professor coughed. 'Please, call me Ronnie. You chaps must be famished. Sandwiches?'

This was more like it.

'Cheese or ham?' he asked.

The Doctor clapped. 'A choice! Excuse us, Professor; we were putting the world to rights just now. So, Jamie: you're offered a choice in what we call the present. The outcome of which lies ahead, in the future. Cheese or ham?'

I chose ham.

'And now, one of the futures you were asked to choose between has become the present.'

'Ham it is,' said Ronnie.

'And,' continued the Doctor, 'as the present becomes the past, your choice, is etched in time, immutable. But genuine free will would mean that you *did* choose ham and *could also* have chosen cheese.'

I was none the wiser.

'Don't you see? "Did" refers to a now actual event – a temporal fact – and "could" refers to an option offered but not taken – a temporal fiction. This is how time works.'

Ronnie looked at him curiously.

'When Jamie chose ham, Professor, could he ever have done otherwise? Before the choice was made, it seemed so, but now his choice has become a matter of historical fact, we know he was always going to choose ham.'

'Ask me again,' I said. 'I'll pick cheese.'

The Doctor smiled. 'That would only prove that Highland legs are hollow as well as hairy. You couldn't have chosen otherwise because your existence is confined to a single temporal continuum. Before William conquered Britain in 1066, he would have made a choice: invade or not invade? Action A or Action B? Cheese or ham? But what he didn't know before he made his decision was that the historians of his future recorded that he chose Action A. The web of time was just waiting for him to spin that choice into being. But sometimes that's not enough. Or, to put it another way, what exactly are you working on, Professor?'

'I beg your pardon, Mister Smith?' asked Ronnie, handing me a sandwich.

'I'm just a traveller,' said the Doctor, 'but Jamie here is from the village, where they're very concerned about the power fluctuations. And it's "Doctor", by the way.'

I cleared my throat.

'What's going on?' asked Ronnie nervously.

The Doctor nodded at the Professor's papers. 'Solid light mapping? Bubble engrams? You're obviously a pioneer, but you're frightening the neighbours. Now, if you were to let me take a quick look, I'm sure I could lay their fears to rest.'

Ronnie shifted uncomfortably.

'Please,' said the Doctor, fixing Ronnie with deep, unfathomable eyes.

The castle hall was vast and impressive. Daylight shone through stained glass windows, painting everything in rainbows. It felt strangely sacred.

The Doctor sniffed the air. 'Copper,' he muttered.

I was transfixed by a motionless blur that stood in the centre of the room, surrounded by rigs of technology. Cameras whirred and clicked, monitoring the weird shape with curious eyes.

Squinting, I realised it was a man.

'He appears blurred,' explained Ronnie, 'because he's travelling back, through time, from the future. That device he's holding has wrapped him in a relative time cocoon, sending him through non-relative time towards the past.'

'The two kinds of time repel each other,' said the Doctor, stepping back slightly. 'Fascinating.'

'The day I cracked the theory,' said Ronnie, 'and opened up the castle to get on with building such a device, there he was, waiting. Just as you see him now.'

'Just a minute,' said the Doctor, eyes suddenly wide with surprise. 'He's–'

'Me,' chuckled Ronnie. 'Yes.'

'That's you?' I asked. 'Travelling back in time from the future?'

'*Through* time, Jamie,' corrected the Doctor.

'Via this present,' enthused Ronnie. 'And look at his wristwatch.'

I squinted hard. 'It's stopped.'

'No,' said Ronnie. 'He is, in fact, moving in extreme slow-motion, but if you film him and play it back, sped up, the hands of the watch are moving in reverse.'

Ronnie turned a computer screen in our direction. An image of the blurred man's watch played over and over, time rolling ever backwards over its face.

'Can he see us?' I asked.

'Judging by the speed of that second hand,' said the Doctor, 'I doubt it, Jamie. If anything, we're just arcs of colour.'

'The time device is handheld,' explained Ronnie. 'It generates pocket warps, which means the traveller needs no vehicle. Anchored to a spatial location, he passes through every moment that transpired there between his future departure and his past arrival. See the departure date on his wristwatch?'

Ronnie pointed at the computer screen. The date read: 08.04.33.

'Twenty days from now,' said the Doctor.

'And the date of arrival...' said Ronnie, touching the screen, which provided him with a big picture of a tiny counter on the time device. 'The 12th of March 1972: my birth date. Bit obvious, I suppose. He's travelling through about a year per second. This means that, as we see him here, he's only just started his minute-long journey.'

I still wasn't making head nor tail of this.

Ronnie smiled kindly at me. 'Imagine you'd been alive on March the 12th 1972, Jamie. Imagine you saw me *arrive*. Suppose a car then knocked me down and killed me. You'd still be able to return the next day and see me here, alive, travelling from the future but *not yet* arrived. You could return every day for the next 60 years and still see me standing there, blurred. But return to the castle on March 12th 2033 and you'd catch me preparing for the journey you'd seen me finish when you were sixty years younger.'

260

'Quite brilliant,' said the Doctor. He took a swig of tea. 'As long as Jamie doesn't mention the car accident.'

'Eh?' asked Ronnie.

'How will you know when you've reached your temporal destination?'

'It'll be programmed into the chronometer,' said Ronnie. 'I will arrive at twelve noon.'

'And I take it you've already started building such a device,' said the Doctor, looking about him.

Ronnie lifted a dustsheet from a battered workbench and revealed a device just like the one his future self was holding.

'So,' said the Doctor, 'with the means at your disposal, you copied your own work. You'd already got the theory, but seeing the finished device in front of you helped no end. Whenever you wandered up a theoretical cul-de-sac, all you had to do was ask yourself, What would *I* do in this situation; how would *I* build such a device?'

'Quite so,' said Ronnie, perhaps guiltily.

'But it won't work, Professor,' said the Doctor, rather darkly.

'Really, Doctor?' asked Ronnie, gesturing at the figure from the future. 'And what do you see there? A glass half empty or a glass half full?'

'I usually wonder if the glass is there at all,' said the Doctor, thinking hard. He waved his hand dismissively. 'Come along, Jamie. It's time we left the Professor to his work. It's probably nothing.'

We pretended to make for the door.

'Wait,' said Ronnie, taking the bait. 'Please. Explain.'

'Basic physics,' said the Doctor, to me.

'What *about* "basic physics"?' asked Ronnie.

'Two objects can't occupy the same space simultaneously, Jamie. It's all to do with the electrical fields that normally prevent matter from passing through matter. As far as I'm aware, no one's entirely certain how catastrophic a temporal-physical collision would actually be. It's not the kind of thing even a mad scientist would deliberately attempt. Till now.'

'What?' asked Ronnie.

'Your time device,' said the Doctor to Ronnie, 'is anchored to a single spatial location. And your future self is travelling back through every moment of intervening time to March the 12th 1972.'

Ronnie nodded.

'Imagine,' said the Doctor. 'You're looking at the chronometer, which reads 12:01pm and counting; in a few chronometer seconds you'll arrive at 12:00pm...'

'In one possible world,' says the Doctor, 'the March sun shines through the stained glass of a Norfolk castle. Dust dances a mocking waltz along solid shafts of light that illuminate a blurred figure and highlight the chaos and devastation wrought earlier that week at the centre of this blood-soaked hall.'

'In one possible world,' says the Doctor, 'the swirling flux of instants boils about your haloed form, Professor. The chronometer counts the final frantic seconds to noon, March 12th 1972; flashing faster than physics should deem proper. Soon you'll arrive. Ten. The cocoon is holding. Nine. Never mind the mad meanderings. Eight. Of that annoying. Seven. Little Doctor Smith. Six. The cheek of the man! Five. Oh, to see his face now. Four. And young Jamie's. Three. It's so pretty in this cocoon. Two. So very pretty. One. Is that me screaming?'

'In one possible world,' says the Doctor, 'a rainbow-hued figure holding a small electronic device makes a sudden, contradictory appearance at noon, March 12th 1972. Instantaneously, this figure explodes, to be replaced by another – the same figure – and another – the same – and another – the same – and another – the same; each one a pluming ball of blood and bone, continuously replaced by an arriving other – the same – exploding over and over and over for the next fifty-nine years. When the chaos finally ends on April the 8th 2033, the walls, ceiling and floor of a Norfolk castle hall are caked in a scabby brown crust and studded with ivory fragments that glisten with oily jelly, slaughterhouse thick, abattoir red. It smells like fear. Fear and copper.'

'It was a devil to get clean. All sorts of mess.'

Ronnie gasped his understanding.

'By the time you reach twelve noon,' said the Doctor, 'you'll be crashed into by your twelve-noon-and-one-nanoseconds self. And so on and so on, because you all occupy the same space and time. The whole lot of you just won't be able to do that. Temporal pile-up! Very messy.'

'No,' said Ronnie, whitely. 'No.'

'But it gets worse...'

'On the 8th of April 2033, Aaron Blinovitch finishes work on a handheld device of paradigm-crunching simplicity. Looking up from his wristwatch, he admires a blurred man: himself but seconds from now. It's time to be off.

Now we'll see who knows his basic physics, he thinks, and moves towards the future by stepping towards his future self.

His present-self activates the time device and stands in his future self's place, and in that instant, the two Aaron's merge, becoming a single rainbow blur that promptly explodes in a time-crash of blood, bone, cloth and metal.'

'Doctor,' I whispered.

'Yes?'

I pointed to where the blurred man had been standing.

There was nothing there now, just computers and cameras peering curiously at nothing. It was as if the man from the future had never been there, never would be.

'What happened?' I asked.

'I have decided not to complete my work,' said Ronnie.

His eyes were full of tears as he walked from the hall.

He'd made a choice.

We walked back to the TARDIS through melting snow.

'If you could view time in its entirety,' the Doctor told me, 'you'd see a tangled web of immutable facts; some of them catalysed by living beings, all of them catalysed by universal causation; and some of them catalysed by those of us with the persuasive ability to stamp all over everything I've just described.'

Originally published in the charity anthology *A Target for Tommy* (summer, 2016).

REVIEW: Sleep No More

It's beginning to feel like a long time since Steven Moffat's first golden season, and much seems to have come loose since the joie de vivre of *The Eleventh Hour* or *Vampires of Venice*. The dialogue's become self-aware and showy – juvenile – and everyone's making fast with unrealistic quips. It starts with Amy's weekly attempts at staying on top of 'sassy' (a mutation of yesterday's 'feisty') then contaminates the entire cast until we now no longer hear real characters in real – stressful – situations. Now, we hear the leak-through voices of middle-aged men hunched over laptops, trying to top their last witty line (always good on paper); middle-aged men who need a firm editor to tell them 'no' and point out the dampened drama, the diluted product. On the increasingly unenjoyable journey towards Clara (with such exceptions as *A Christmas Carol*, *The Power of Three*, and *The Girl Who Waited*) Amy begins to look like the most amazing drag act ever conceived by a shy but brilliant writer from Paisley. When Clara arrives, unintentional non-reality settles with a distracting thud. The quips are the dialogue now and the plots are the lexical panic-vomit of a man whose ever-increasing workload has tattered his self-confidence, forcing his insecurities to overcompensate. Ideas are developed and abandoned, incomplete; implicit promises to attentive viewers are ignored. Plots begin to think themselves intriguing and clever, though the adults who've seen other television and movies or read the odd book or comic know otherwise. But, as the other adults who enjoy being in the 'cleverness' club for a change often tell them, it's not for adults anyway. This sugar-rush drama – still the best kid's show on the box, then – is beautiful to look at but hard to love.

Then comes Capaldi, the great new hope, replacing probably the most fascinating yet poorly served actor to ever play the Doctor. *Deep Breath*, however, is the strongest debut of any incarnation, yet what follows is a season of 1985-style varying quality. There's the sublime (*Listen*, *The Caretaker*, *Flatline*) but there's also much drivel (robots in Sherwood, forests enveloping London, that moon egg, mummies in space, a tasteless finale – despite Missy being brilliant – and the 'meh' *Last Christmas* with its wasted poignant departure for Jenna Coleman). Up next, Series Nine, opens with an almost excellent Davros story, sadly undermined by its sugar-richness. It's quipped to the max and devoid of restraint. What follows is weaker still: Viking Girl stories, tedious and forced with a guest actor incapable of effectively delivering the material (yet another redundant variation on the River Song format; itself destined never to be adequately utilised); the dull, undeservedly smug Lake story; the worthy but crass Zygon two-parter (lauded for its one good moment); and an appalling mess with a Lion King...

But then comes fresh air – and from an unexpected source: Mark Gatiss (who has offered diminishing returns since his much-overlooked moment of genuine terror in the pre-titles of *The Unquiet Dead*). Yes, Heaven Sent will soon get everyone's attention, but its lofty status won't be quite so magnificent to those who crack what's going on before the titles even roll, solid though it is (thanks to a fabulous lead performance and a Beethoven-filching score). And around it squat the amateurish *Face the Raven* and the superfluous *Hell Bent*, spoiling it, undermining it.

The true gem of Series Nine, hiding away under rags and garments of previous eras and conjuring the essential atmosphere of *Doctor Who* is Gatiss' *Sleep No More*. Immediately subverting the usual form – no title sequence (and, astoundingly, no end credits) – telling the story through a thoroughly unreliable narrator, it dares to pare down previous excesses. When the Doctor and Clara wander into the middle of the narrative, their dialogue is immediately more like that of real people in a real situation. Free of their endless quipping, it's like being with the Doctor and Sarah, say, rather than Chandler Bing and, well, Chandler Bing. And the story isn't theirs – it's not about them for a change, or the overblown, top-heavy legend of them. It's about Doctor Who – that series we used to watch about a bloke and his mate having adventures in space and time. It's also a beautifully made episode; possibly superior in production terms to any other this season. Everything sings: the directorial style, the camera-work (chaotic and disorientating), set design (especially the sleep pods) and effects (amazing, yet unfussy), sound design...

Stand-out visuals include the holograms – not just the singers, but the information hologram (amusingly holding another hologram on its palm) – and stunning Neptune as viewed from the station window. The whole production is confident, smart and slick with an understated brilliance that doesn't scream 'look at me' for a change; the story – and its audience – are afforded time and room to breathe. The jokes work, the details are exquisite and everything is precise, scary and funny without bludgeoning the viewer into loving it. Similarly, the Doctor's not bragging, left, right and centre and is actually placed at a narrative disadvantage: incidental, not focal.

The adventure itself, is pure old-fashioned Who: a scary re-interpretation of *The New Adventures*, played for keeps, with a tangible 'real world' ambience often missing in recent episodes. With its black and white sequences and echoes of radiophonic and library music in Murray Gold's score (particularly in the larder sequence), this base-under-siege tale is, for my money, the best Troughton story ever made. So, the 'sleep' monsters are bizarre, but like a lot of naff ideas in *Doctor Who* (robot yetis whose guns shoot webs, say) they're not the purpose of this instalment. The central monstrous idea is potentially very real: that a time will come when the leisure, pleasure and necessity of sleep will be taken from us by corporate and personal greed; 'an inconvenience to be bartered away' (making this episode very much a piece with the later, equally excellent, *Oxygen*). Deliciously, though, mad scientist Rasmussen (Reece Sheersmith, looking like he's wandered in from the Graham Williams era) finally confesses that the sleep infection is a phantom distraction from the true threat – an electronic signal that will, when transmitted, affect all who watch Rasmussen's testimony: the episode itself. Though no narrative participant sees it, the suggestion lingers that the *Doctor Who* viewer has been infected. It's no *Blink*, but then episodes like that are few and far between; and it's for kids, remember?

It may seem astounding that the Doctor simply leaves (as he arrived) in the middle of the action, flustered and confused by Rasmussen's lies, but he destroys the grav shields of the station, crashing it, before heading for Triton to scupper Rasmussen's plans. And that's all we're allowed to see, because we're being told a story by a different medium than usual (prompting us to wonder, 'What kind of dust usually transmits *Doctor Who* to us?'). The story remains elusive, like a modern-day *Warriors' Gate* or *Ghost Light*, leaving us wanting, but not dissatisfied, and the final visual representation that 'sandman' Rasmussen hasn't been what he claimed to be is one of the most well-executed and chilling moments in *Doctor Who*'s history.

Sleep No More may appear pedestrian when placed against the convoluted spaghetti of its parent season, but it's easily the most re-watchable episode; a place you go, not something you simply watch. Tying itself to nothing but its own narrative, it's entirely independent – an utterly faultless piece of *Doctor Who*, for the first time in a while. And Capaldi is brilliant in it.

Recently, *Doctor Who* seemed to undergo a depression or a crisis of self-confidence. Steven Moffat has confessed that his overwhelming schedule sent him to a dark and difficult place, but at time of writing, Series 10 has begun and the crisis seems to have abated. The show has its sincerity and wonder back, having seemingly discarded the defensive pretence that made it appear smug. Which is good, we're going to need that in our own dark times. *Doctor Who*'s now back to telling stories that can be watched in isolation not as an arc, episodes that keep the viewer's attention without drawing it to the mechanisms and methods utilised in making it. By not persistently yelling 'Look – I'm clever and spectacular' (which only ever invites criticism) stories like *Sleep No More* allow us to get on with noticing *Doctor Who*'s brilliance for ourselves.

Previously unpublished (2017)

REVIEW: Once-the Musical (starring Arthur Darvill)

We knew him best as Rory Williams and took him to our hearts as Mr Pond, but actor Arthur Darvill is a man of many faces, many roles, and talents that his more 'casual' fans may not yet be aware of. Right now – but only until 10 May of this year – you can see him at the Phoenix Theatre in *Once – the Musical*.

Based on the 2007 Oscar-winning film, *Once* is the story of a struggling musician (Darvill) who fixes hoovers for a living. When he meets a Czech girl (played with great warmth by Zrinka Cvitešić) they connect, intensely, through a love of music, and she ignites in him a motivating spark that, over the course of one week, changes their lives for ever.

In many ways, it strikes me as though it might be similar to the hugely successful *The Commitments* (though I've never seen that show). But it's about that search for success, with a big ensemble cast and lots of guitars and fiddles about the place, with misadventures in bars and recording studios.

Now, if you're not a fan of the West End musical – and believe me, I am avowedly not – don't be put off by the genre in this particular instance. *Once* is couched at a very different level. The entire drama takes place on a single Dublin bar-room set, that, by relying on the audience's participant imagination, becomes a music shop, a couple of homes, a bank, and even an interval bar for the audience (should they be brave enough to use it). It's clear, from this, that the budget is perhaps smaller than that of equivalent West End fare, but the focus here isn't on spend and spectacle, but rather on story and talent.

The music that makes the show a musical, is not so much a series of 'numbers' (in which people suddenly start singing at each other for no definable reason) as a selection of works created by the two lead characters to play to each other, to record in studio and perform in pubs. The songs are integral to the show and to the lives of the characters, and, what's more, they're very good. There is, I must qualify, an occasional danger that they might descend into being the kind of wistful 'hipster' tripe that turns up on TV and cinema adverts for phones and computers, but over-all they are strong and often interesting works somewhere in that vein tapped by the likes of Damian Rice (which made one of the show's jokes at the expense of the execrable James Blunt seem somewhat akin to shooting oneself in the foot). The most out-standing song is an acapella/harmony piece in Act 2, as the characters look down on Dublin early one morning (though the bar-room set isn't lit sympathetically enough to allow the audience to fully believe this).

Arthur Darvill offers a solid interpretation of 'Guy', often betraying the truth that Rory Williams wasn't so much a complete performance as, rather, a selection of Arthur's own acting tics, many of which are on display here (unless, and this is not unlikely, the director said 'Give 'em a bit of Rory, love'). However, it is when he performs the songs (playing acoustic guitar), that he fills the theatre with a magic that few of his fellow cast members can come close to equalling. Arthur is an incredible singer – and I don't say that lightly. His vocal range is pretty astounding and it spans generations of mainstream rock and pop crooning. In another life he would surely be pursuing a recording career, though this may have been stemmed somewhat by the fact the he looks like, well, Rory Williams and not, say, Captain Jack. But what a revelation Arthur Darvill is – a truly mesmerising vocal talent. This guy *sings* – and I don't mean he gives it the West End Wendy – Arthur Darvill gives it *soul*.

All that said, I hope that after 10 May, Arthur will go on to work better suited to his strong talents. As a complete piece, *Once* seems to be a reasonably strong – if sentimental – script (though some of the lines are a little groan-inducing, but that could be poor delivery on the part of some of the often weak ensemble) with powerful songs, desperately in search of better direction and tighter production. Sometimes it tries too hard to impress when it really doesn't need to (the incongruous Czech stomping dance bit which looked like it was happening to some people far away, having a better time than the audience) and other times it tries to be a bit too clever (the unfocused opening that doesn't so much jump into the drama as meander). What it really needs is focus and perhaps a fresh eye on things like lighting (generally unimaginative), sound levels (the differential between the actors and the music was often appalling), basic performances from the ensemble (that often killed the comedy, though it got laughs) and actor projection, the latter of which was pretty dire throughout. There's a great piece in here somewhere, but it's not quite making its way out (and even though the audience seemed to love it, there were sleepy heads in the auditorium).

There is an open-endedness to the script, which resolves the story in a brave and unexpected manner, and even suggested the possibility of a sequel. I'd joke and say the producers ought to call it *Twice*, but on this viewing of an undeniably vast talent lost in a murky production, I'd say that *Once* was more than enough.

Originally published under the pseudonym Jon Ritelli by Kasterborous. com (April, 2014)

REVIEW: The Web of Fear DVD

If you've read my review of the DVD release of *The Enemy of the World*, then you'll perhaps understand why this is yet another tough release to cover.

To summarise briefly, *The Web of Fear* has long been acknowledged as a 'classic'; as, perhaps, Patrick Troughton's best ever story (once *Tomb of the Cybermen* ruined all our previous illusions by having the Telosian temerity to be re-discovered in 1992). That only its first episode remained in the BBC archive added to its power and mystique. The opening instalment was, all told, pretty atmospheric and solid – if the other five were as good, then it was bound to be a 'classic' through and through, wasn't it? Douglas Camfield directing, Nicholas Courtney making his debut as Lethbridge-Stewart, Yeti with web guns, and so on – bound to be brilliant. Well, at the end of last year, four of its 'lost' episodes came back in from the cold. In a flurry of insane activity, this most desirable carrot was dangled over we 'missing episode' hungry fans and was quickly and hurriedly consumed as we all went and downloaded it. By now, it's probably the most watched Troughton story in all fandom. But is it any good?

Well, yes. It is.

Having seen *The Enemy of the World*, one is able to make much more sense of the opening sequences of characters sliding about the TARDIS floor in the desperate hope of giving us the impression they're about to be sucked out into space. Quite why this superfluous sequence is tagged on to the beginning of the story (rather than the end of the last one) seems to be a throwback to *Enemy* writer David Whitaker's tenure as script editor on the show, but it's oddly out of place. It would doubtless have been a heck of a lot spookier to open with Travers in Silverstein's 'museum' for that creepy film sequence in which the Yeti (and the Intelligence, presumably) are once more reanimated.

In case you don't know, the bulk of the story takes place some months later when the Intelligence has forced an evacuation of London by filling it with thick fog, a creeping, curiously foam-like fungus and scraggy looking Yeti robots with guns that shoot cobwebs (and we old-school fans accept this, but do ideas get much battier than that?). The army are tasked with trying to control this menace, which is lurking in the London Underground, and it is into this web of fear (get it?) that the Doctor and co rock up.

The Web of Fear is one of Season Five's 'base under siege' stories, but it is probably so well remembered because it's the best of its kind. Ultimately, the story is about the soldiers trapped beneath the city, and because these soldiers are portrayed as 'real people', it's an incredibly effective piece of work that stands head and shoulders over tedious dross like season-mate *The Ice Warriors* because the characters are imbued with real opinions and real motivations rather than 'space/sci-fi' ones.

As monsters go the Yeti are reasonable opponents; they are mobile and threatening in size, although, somewhat strangely, Camfield elects to chuck them straight into the limelight. No hiding in the shadows for these creatures, which makes them, in visceral terms, not especially scary. Perhaps this is a deliberate decision, a warning to the viewer that the enemy does not need to creep about to bring you death – death is there, up front and coming at you with violence in mind. The creeping about is given to the fungus – which, as it passes through the tunnels in both film and studio sequences or even in model shots (as at the end of Episode 5), always looks amazing – and the sinister menace comes from the hissing sibilance of that disembodied possessor of human bodies (dead or alive), the Great Intelligence.

Another reason *The Web of Fear*'s reputation has endured since it was broadcast, might simply boil down to one thing: Episode 4. Whatever you might think of it as a whole, Episode 4 is an astonishing and quintessential bit of Doctor Who. The filmed shoot-out in Covent Garden is a piece of sustained action unlike any seen in the series before (even if you want to quote *The War Machines* or *The Gunfighters*), and in studio, the claustrophobic attack on the electrical shop is brutally effective. Throughout the story, Troughton gives his usual sufficient yet elusive performance, but in Episode 4, he gets some incredible close-ups when telling his companions what the Intelligence is – all of which serves to make him look quite alien.

Many will note, of course, that this is, in effect, the first UNIT story. When Lethbridge-Stewart turns up in Episode 3 it comforts the modern viewer with 45 years' hindsight. But at the time, the Doctor's future ally was portrayed as a mysterious, conspicuous figure whose sudden arrival and subsequent actions were as questionable as those of Harold Chorley (played by second *Avengers* 'girl' and Ian Hendry surrogate Jon Rollason), Professor Travers (Jack Watling, reprising his role from *The Abominable Snowmen* earlier in the season), Driver Evans (the story's most outstanding and multi-layered character, brilliantly played by Derek Pollitt) and Staff Sgt. Arnold (played with great texture by John Lydon lookalike, Jack Woolgar). *Colonel* Lethbridge-Stewart is credulous, pragmatic and often cold, and although these qualities would remain in his later stories (even after his transformation into Pertwee's sidekick buffoon), here they are used to crank up the paranoia that there is a traitor in the Doctor's midst.

If you can suspend your knowledge of the Colonel's future life when you watch this, you will see what viewers saw in 1968 and that will add to the suspense. Once you have, however, and the Intelligence has trundled off into who-knows-where, it's worth re-remembering that Lethbridge-Stewart would go on to found UNIT: United Nations Intelligence Taskforce. Now read that again. Lethbridge-Stewart, as a consequence his involvement in these events, goes on to found the United Nations *Intelligence* Taskforce. Just sayin'.

Ultimately, *The Web of Fear*'s failings are few: it sags a bit in the middle because there's too much repetition (I confess I didn't even realise I'd not skipped Episode 4 when I bought the download) and some of the storytelling is not particularly clear – I still have no idea who is sabotaging what and when – but this might all be to the advantage of the suspense the story is aiming for. But Hitchcock it's not. This lack of clarity or satisfactory explanation may fall at the feet of Camfield or writers Mervyn Haisman and Henry Lincoln (though, given the great and awkward pains the dialogue goes to in explaining to the viewers stuff we've already been able to work out thanks to direction and performance, I suspect the latter). Camfield's direction is, in fact, incredibly accomplished. Here, he proves himself not only to be the master of stylish film work, but also the king of the electronic studio; I note in particular some excellent and highly unusual camera set-ups and cross-fades in Episode 6. He is also backed up by some top-notch set design from David Myerscough-Jones whose tube tunnels and platforms could easily be the real thing and whose Intelligence 'centre' in Episode 6 even features a ceiling (it's the details, folks). The real atmosphere of this story, however, comes from Clive Leighton's realistic and yet often expressionistic lighting, probably unrivalled in any other *Doctor Who* story since Season One.

Those of you who've seen the download, though, will probably agree with me that the most amusing moment comes when we see a chocolate bar emblazoned with the words 'Camfield's Dairy Milk' and that the most frightening things in the whole six episodes are actually Victoria's disturbingly weird legs.

Writing a review of *The Web of Fear* seems an odd thing to be doing so long after we all downloaded it and realised with astonishment and joy that it was great but nowhere near as good as *The Enemy of the World* – but, hey, the BBC are releasing it on DVD this month.

I seem to remember you all took it on the chin when they put out the *Enemy* DVD with no Extras, other than a trailer for this release. You stoic lot, you. I seem to recall the hope was that, as *The Web of Fear* would be released several months hence, there'd be time to record a commentary track, or maybe sling together a little documentary. And, oh how exciting if the BBC were holding back the *real* Episode 3 for the DVD release as a treat for all our dedication and love and pie-in-the-sky daydreaming.

Nah.

As I wrote on my review for *The Enemy of the World*:

Extras

A single shiny disc with a picture on it and words that tell you what it is you're putting into your player.

A plastic case in which to keep your shiny disc safe.

A cover with words and pictures on it telling you all about the shiny disc you're putting into your player.

An insert with words and pictures on it telling you all about the, yeah, you get the picture...

So, there you go.

No Production Subtitles, no Commentary track.

No 'real' Episode 3 – just John Cura's telesnaps (I say 'just', at least we've been spared another poorly-executed cartoon...).

And, yeah, for the wag that asked me last time, it looks like it's been VID-Fired.

But, if you don't already have *The Web of Fear* (unlikely!) then this is a great story and well worth owning. If you have the download, though, I'd advise you against conning yourself again.

Originally published by Kasterborous.com (February, 2014)

OPINION: Game of Rassilon

Ah. Right. Video games. I must have walked into the wrong column. I may as well be up-front: I am no kind of 'gamer'. So, ah, bye.

Oh. You want a full column?

Hm. Well I could witter on, more generically, about games in the TV show. I mean, *Marco Polo* (which we're all hoping we'll see soon) is a big game of chess, isn't it? And who could forget dear old Fenric? The seventh Doctor is all about chess, or so we like to think; he certainly is when he's in the *New Adventures*. The Black and White Guardian are very 'chessy' too... The plot of *Destiny of the Daleks* hinges on a parlour game, and there are seaside puzzle-book games writ large in *Death to the Daleks* and *Pyramids of Mars*. But even in decent stories, puzzle/game sequences are a bit like watching paint dry. Sadly, genre telly has always had a thing for 'game' episodes (a '60s psychedelic fetish; I blame *Batman*'s Riddler). They've all done one: *The Avengers*, *The Prisoner*, *Star Trek*, *Deep Space Nine*, etc – and they were all, largely, crap. Even our very own *The Celestial Toymaker* (and anyone who still thinks it's a classic, ought to read the novelisation, or, better still, the latest Dulux colour chart).

In spin-off merchandise, the Doctor has played plenty of (non-video) games. The 1970s Top Trumps were largely memorable for featuring such villains as the Sea Devils (mislabelled as Ogrons, I believe), the Ogrons (mislabelled as Sea Devils, I believe) and, er, Annie Oakley. Around that time, I owned a bagatelle (a brittle, hand-held pinball game) emblazoned with a World Distributors style Tom Baker who looked malformed. Obviously, World Distributors had their own snakes and ladders style games in their bewildering annuals, but the crème de la crème of dice/counter games came on the back of Weetabix packets in 1977, along with stand-up monster cards. I LOVED them. I still do. But I never PLAYED any of these games - did you? Same goes for Denys Fisher's *War of the Daleks* with its beautiful, tiny Dalek counters. Much later, I even collected some of those Colin Baker *Choose-Your-Own-Adventure* books, but, as with all these things, I couldn't get into *Doctor Who* 'narratives' that weren't prescriptive: I want *his* adventures, not mine.

Okay, so I did play a lot arcade games in the early '80s, mostly on a Colecovision console, which I still own (I'm ace at *Time Pilot*!). But when we got to that cassette-loading phase, I tried Marvel's painful *Questprobe* and didn't bother again until *Tomb Raider* – to which I became addicted. Now, you could have replaced the locales and even Lara Croft and repackaged the whole thing as a *Doctor Who* game and I'd still have been addicted, not because it was *Who*, but because it was just *fun*. You see, when *Destiny of the Doctors* came out I didn't care that there was a new *Doctor Who* video game; I was much more thrilled that there was new footage of Anthony Ainley's Master.

Ultimately, I love *Doctor Who* as a set of stories. I love the TV show, the novels, the comics, the audios and so on. That's where the ideas that attract me to it live. I'm not too fussed about *Doctor Who* pencil cases, Easter eggs, t-shirts, underpants or dollies. And I lump video games in with that lot, I'm afraid. To me, *Doctor Who* doesn't *need* to be any of them. I like *Doctor Who* to tell me a story, *give* me a story; a single, progressive narrative that culminates in a finite ending.

But, hey, whatever floats your boat. I have noticed, however, that designers haven't found it easy to make a *Doctor Who* video game that's actually 'any good'. It occurs to me, then, that *Doctor Who* video games might do well to recreate TV stories and take us into already 'existing' worlds, allowing us to play within well-established, definitive narrative parameters which are then open to our involvement and intervention – a bit like changing a timeline. Any story would do (obvious candidates for 'game' form include *The Keys of Marinus, The Chase, The Daleks' Master Plan, The War Games, The Five Doctors,* and the Key to Time season). And a relaxation in branding might allow us to pick our Doctor/companion team or allow us 12 lives/levels, with regeneration – achieved by adherence to specific rules – given as a reward rather than a penalty.

But what do I know?

Originally published in *K-Mag* (February, 2014)

REVIEW: Terror of the Zygons DVD

If, like me, you have all of *Doctor Who* at your fingertips, you're probably aware that it's easy to take segments of this amazing body of work for granted. In the case of *Terror of the Zygons*, I probably never will.

I started watching *Doctor Who* in February 1974. I was three years old. Pulled in by the electric thrill of Daleks in sandpits and giant metal snake things setting them on fire, I was hooked for life. From here I flinched at giant spiders, recoiled from green creepy stuff, and felt a visceral, brutal horror when faced with gas-masks in the trenches of Skaro. By the time Broton, warlord of the Zygons peered out of the telly at me, hissing sibilantly and alarming the Doctor and my other TV friends with his sucker-tipped fingers, I was approaching five – and the stories I was watching were making more and more sense to me. Watching *Terror of the Zygons*, I was, frankly, terrified. If the sofa hadn't been backed against a wall, I'd have been behind it. This really was my first encounter with tea-time terror for tots...

For those who don't know – and if you don't, then it makes no sense for me to spoil all of it here – *Terror of the Zygons* sees the Doctor (Tom Baker), Sarah (Elisabeth Sladen) and Harry (Ian Marter) return to Earth (Scotland this time – although, really, it's filmed in Sussex) to get to the bottom of who or what has been attacking off-shore oil installations somewhere in the vicinity of Loch Ness... What follows is a creepy and intimate tale of strange goings-on in a Scots village, behind which lurk one of *Doctor Who*'s most imaginatively realised 'monsters', the Zygons (and their less-well realised giant monster, the Skarasen; but hey, it does the job).

This Robert Banks Stewart tale opened Tom Baker's second season (although it was planned to close his first), and is, essentially, the last true UNIT tale. Ian Marter and John Levene (Benton) will return mid-season in *The Android Invasion*, but here it's time to say a sudden and unexpected farewell UNIT's heart and soul, Nicholas Courtney (the Brigadier). It'll be almost a decade before we see him again, turning up several times in that hyper-real fan-fest we've come to know as 'the 1980s' (but only because William Russell wasn't available. That's the weird thing with Courtney; his career only seems to happen because first choices are never available...).

271

It could be argued that under Barry Letts, say, and with a different costume designer, *Zygons* might be average fare – but this is perfect Philip Hinchcliffe (on Jon Pertwee's manor, if you will). Some stories stay in the memory because the writing's good, but others – and *Zygons* is a case in point –stay because they look and sound astonishing. From Douglas Camfield's atmospheric direction to Geoffrey Burgon's haunting music, this is a delicious slice of Robert Holmes Gothic. But what really makes this a special story is the thrilling alliance of John Friedlander and James Acheson in designing the eponymous villains. Ably supported by production design and lighting (Nigel Curzon and John Dixon), and sibilant vocal mannerisms best displayed by *Who* legend, the late John Woodnutt (Broton), the Zygons are astounding to look at. There's been nothing quite like these half-embryo/half-octopoid creatures before or since and to cap it all, they're orange! They're bloody ORANGE! What a triumph they are. If only the new ones looked anywhere near as good...

Extras:

If you've been waiting what feels like ages to own this one on DVD, you won't be disappointed with this 2-disc set. Of most interest to hard-core fans will be the option to view 'The Director's Cut' of Part One, which was trimmed prior to transmission for timing reasons. It's only a tiny scene that's been restored, but it's a lovely one and features 'new' Ian Marter, which can't be bad. The missing footage (some of which only existed in monochrome) has been brilliantly and effectively restored by Peter Crocker and colourised by fan favourite Stuart Humphryes – alias Babel Colour – who recently revived the chromatically impaired *The Mind of Evil*.

Humphryes tells me that the restored footage originated from a cutting copy, the quality of which was very poor and grainy. On an incredibly tight timescale, Humphryes was unable to focus too much on colourising all 300 frames and so employed some short cuts, such as using flat colour washes on the companions' clothing and the TARDIS – not a course of action he would normally opt for.

Humphryes: 'I was sent a couple of dozen reference frames of the recovered colour sections so that I could match my palette to those. They were faded but incredibly useful! Because they required a heavy grade to match the broadcast colours of the episode's film sequences, my colourised shots had to be similarly graded, which had a few odd effects on the colours. But that's the nature of archival material and the constraints of working with poor quality prints. We should all rejoice that it exists at all and I'm proud to be associated with the reinsertion of such a legendary lost scene.'

'Scotch Mist in Sussex' is a 30-minute 'making-of' documentary that wonderfully draws on archive footage of real-life attempts to catch a glimpse of Nessie. Banks Stewart talks of the story in terms of *The Avengers* and Hinchcliffe offers a marvellous elegy for late Production Assistant Edwina Craze. Woodnutt appears in what looks like old Myth Makers footage offering a 'hero theory' of villainy, while that uber-eccentric oddball John Levene (highly ubiquitous on this release) offers thoughts on breast-fondling scenes and the size of Tom Baker's ego.

'Remembering Douglas Camfield' is a 30-minute retrospective of the late director (and Christopher Walken lookalike) which includes his PA work on *An Unearthly Child*, Celia Imrie, an interview with Wogan on the set of *Beau Geste*, and a lovely clip of Katy Manning in his 'Big Elephant' episode of Hinchcliffe's post-*Who* series, *Target*.

Other extras include 'The UNIT Family Part Three' (with Terrance Dicks, Richard Franklin and Nicholas Courtney) and two 'Doctor Who Stories' featuring Tom Baker and Lis Sladen. Recorded in 2003 – just after the return of *Doctor Who* was announced – the latter beautifully has Sladen discuss her enthusiasm and hopes for its return, as footage from 2006's *School Reunion* plays alongside. It was while watching this that I only just realised she's carrying her *The Sontaran Experiment* sou'wester with her when she leaves in *The Hand of Fear*. This wet weather item also appears in the wonderful 1977 *Merry-Go-Round* programme made for schools in which Sladen visits a working oil rig (this appropriate curio has an amazing radiophonic theme tune, too). Also included are: an 'on location' interview with Tom Baker from 'South Today' (the inexperienced reticence of the more well-known Wookey Hole clip gradually warms up to discuss 'bachelor benders'), a couple of pertinent Easter Eggs (one for fans of restoration, one for fans of Disney), and a trailer for the forthcoming release of *The Moonbase* – not a cell of animation in sight, though...

(Thanks to Stuart Humphryes for his generosity and time)

Originally published by Kasterborous.com (November, 2013)

REVIEW: The Enemy of the World DVD

You're a *Doctor Who* fan, so it probably won't have escaped your notice that two 'lost' *Doctor Who* stories from the much-lionised Patrick Troughton era were recently recovered amid a flurry of press and publicity that almost threatened to melt the internet – twice. Back from wherever telly-we're-never-going-to see-again lives came the all-time most-wanted 'lost story', the apparently unassailable *The Web of Fear* (yeah, some might say, just like *Tomb of the Cybermen* was unassailable – until we *saw* it...) and its intriguing but less well-regarded season-mate *The Enemy of the World*.

They were back and it was about time and we were so, so lucky to be able to have them again. Even now, it's pretty hard to tell whether or not we'd know they were back at all just yet, if not for the press leak that fuelled the so-called 'omni-rumour' (of 109 recovered episodes, apparently) and the wildfire press and fan attention (Internet Melt 1) that pinned down the BBC and those-in-the-know-that-didn't-mind-lying-about-it-to-those-not-in-the-know and practically forced them to reveal that *something* had been returned. What follows, as you no doubt know, was a very twenty-first century development, and that was the 'rush release' of said stories onto iTunes for download into the hand of hungry – perhaps even greedy – fans such as you or I before any whole or part of them could find themselves pirated onto YouTube or whatever, but mostly because they wanted to be kind to us and make sure we had them as soon as possible (Internet Melt 2). Yeah, that just might be true, that they had our interests at heart. Who could, in all faith, deny that? I mean, it's not like they were going to be releasing them on proper DVDs any time soon, was it?

Well, it's been about a month, maybe six weeks since we all downloaded these recovered stories and realised that the ugly sister – *The Enemy of the World* –

was actually *way* better than its much-feted sibling. You've shelled out your hard-earned and those without Apple computers have growled and cursed at the inadequacies of the i-tunes experience, but in the end, those nice folks at the BBC rewarded you with perhaps one of the most striking bits of 1960s telly you're ever likely to see, let alone one of the most accomplished bits of *Doctor Who*...

The Enemy of the World, written by David Whitaker – perhaps the biggest influence on early *Doctor Who* – and directed by future producer Barry Letts, marking his place as one of the series' most inventive and creative directors, is relentlessly and magnificently *epic*. Those who read Ian Marter's excellent 1980s novelisation might have suspected as much, but this one just keeps on moving, full of intrigue, excitement, double-cross, red herrings, and twists and turns aplenty. At its simplest – because you've all seen it, so not much point in me telling you at great length – the Doctor, Jamie and Victoria arrive in Australia in the year 2018, where it turns out the Doctor is the exact double of would-be world dictator Ramon Salamander. At the request of Salamander's enemies, the Doctor impersonates Salamander and travels across continents in an attempt to expose the villain's dark secrets and reveal the hand behind a number of volcanic disasters to recently have beset the world.

Letts uses every directorial and visual trick in the book to keep the story moving at an exciting pace – the helicopter P.O.V in episode one is jaw-dropping on its own (yes – they have a helicopter! And a hovercraft!), as are the back projections used to fill out the park and the jetty, the model shots and visual effects used to effectively portray Salamander's 'lift' into his underground base, and the final TARDIS effects sequences. All of this stuff, if you've never seen it before, elicits whoops and coos of wonder.

Whitaker's script is weighty and powerful, recalling his historical tales from the William Hartnell period more than anything else, and the cast is varied and as original a bunch of characters as *Doctor Who* will see at this point in its history. Comic actor Bill Kerr fills Giles Kent with a desperate edgy steel, Milton Johns is deliciously sadistic as Benik, Carmen Munroe eats up the screen as the gorgeous and impressive Fariah, while Reg Lye's Griffin is just adorable. The real acting kudos must of course go to Patrick Troughton, who does do an amazing job as both the Doctor and Salamander – he really does make them *utterly* distinct.

There are some beautiful production designs from Christopher Pemsel and costumes from Martin Baugh, both of which combine to give us an almost *Captain Scarlet*/Gerry Anderson near-future. If you want to be picky, perhaps the only things that let the production down are Colin Douglas as Donald Bruce and the fact that some of the underground dwellers (Adam Verney and Margaret Hickey) are a little wooden, wet, or just too earnest. But in terms of the allegedly brilliant Season Five, *The Enemy of the World* wins out by the sheer freedom it allows its creators – no boring base under siege for six weeks here (and this comes as a refreshing change after the one-note dross of *The Ice Warriors*); this is an exciting, varied epic adventure that spans *a world* and is rich with very *Who*-ish ideas – and, most noticeably, some of the sudden deaths and acts of violence are actually rather striking, if not downright shocking. *The Enemy of the World* is *Doctor Who* doing a proper theatrical drama – a full-on Revenge Tragedy – and doing it incredibly well.

But like I said at the top of this review, you already know this, because you've already spent £17 downloading it and gorging yourself on it because, like me, you didn't want to be the only fan who hadn't seen it when the buzz was happening a few short weeks ago.

Well, now the Beeb want to sell you it again. They want you to shell out £20rrp and do it all over again. And who can blame them? I mean, it's what you want, isn't it? The DVD? So it can sit on your nice, chronologically organised shelf? Not like that messy downloady thing cluttering up your laptop files, no thank you...

But that's OK, buying it twice is fine because you're a completist and you're looking forward to the Extras. Quite right too.

Extras:

A single shiny disc with a picture on it and words that tell you what it is you're putting into your player.

A plastic case in which to keep your shiny disc safe.

A cover with words and pictures on it telling you all about the shiny disc you're putting into your player.

An insert with words and pictures on it telling you all about the, yeah, you get the picture...

Coming Soon Trailer for *The Web of Fear* (which you've seen three times now and already own).

I'm being a little sarcastic, of course, but there aren't even Production Subtitles or a Commentary track. I don't expect miracles – I know these things take time – but am I alone in thinking I would have been happy to wait a year or so until such items could be assembled? Surely you think the same?

On the plus side, if you manage to get hold of the 'Limited Edition' with an alternative cover, you don't get any other DVD content, but you do get a nice, specially commissioned *Enemy of the World* t-shirt. Which is nice. If you're not interested in proper clothes.

All in all, then, an undeniably disappointing release of Patrick Troughton's finest hour (or three) as *Doctor Who* and one of the series' most epic and satisfying adventures. This – if you don't already have it (*really?!*) is a Must-Own.

Originally published by Kasterborous.com (November, 2013)

REVIEW: The Ice Warriors DVD

Let's get a few things cleared up from the outset. All *Doctor Who* is brilliant. All *Doctor Who* deserves to be loved and enjoyed and adored. Any new *Doctor Who* needs to be embraced, and any old *Doctor Who* that we once thought lost deserves to be given a new lease of life that we might enjoy it all over again, praising it and covering it with petals of joy. *Doctor Who* is the best thing on telly, the best thing in the world, the most amazing thing ever; that a randomly formed universe could come up with *Doctor Who* and then come up with me so that I could enjoy it in my own lifetime still astonishes me.

So, we're agreed? *Doctor Who* is ace. I say all this because it gets boring when people respond to a critical view of a bit of *Doctor Who* with uncritical reasoning. This is going to happen with this DVD review. You're dying to see *The Ice Warriors*, you see, and you're dying to enjoy those two 'lost' episodes that have been turned into cartoons to make your enjoyment of them much easier. I am, too. Thing is, though, relative to the rest of *Doctor Who*, I don't really like *The Ice Warriors* much.

I never saw it on first transmission – too young – but when I had the Target book, I found it dull, plodding and laborious (in spite of an amazing Chris Achilleos cover). I always guiltily felt that I *should* like it – it is after all the first 'Martian' story – but it just didn't grip me. As the years passed by, I finally saw the *Peladon* stories and then *The Seeds of Death* – all quite enjoyable, but I realised I wasn't that thrilled by the scaly green men from Mars. Eventually, they came to life for me in the *New Adventures* books, so I found myself re-appraising them and hoping one day to see their debut story.

When the VHS of *The Ice Warriors* finally arrived in 1998 (in a lovely box with a book, and a CD of the missing episodes), I was delighted. I loved that video and watched it several times in one sitting. It seemed like a great story, Peter Sallis was fab, the linking telesnap edit for the 'lost in all but audio' Two and Three was beautifully done (I still tingle when Victoria stops being a photograph and starts to move at the end of Three) but most of all the eponymous villains looked amazing. *The Ice Warriors* became my favourite Patrick Troughton story for many years.

Hm. Well, I watched *The Ice Warriors* again last year and felt very disappointed. The novelty of seeing the original Martians with their weird mouths and their tendency to cogitate whilst huddling their heads into their carapaces had worn off. Peter Sallis was still good, and there was still some lovely filmed stuff with Victoria (Deborah Watling) trapped by Martians in the ice tunnels, but the story really did plod.

Brian Hayles was responsible for the equally plot-thin *The Celestial Toymaker* and his second script for the series, while full of great characters and innovative ideas (a plant museum, a city in a dome, a science base in an Edwardian mansion) isn't a patch on his later, much funnier, warm and genuinely thrilling *The Seeds of Death*. Though that might simply be that *Seeds'* director Michael Ferguson is one of the series' best and stands head and shoulders above even this tale's director, Derek Martinus.

It did occur to me that because I was re-watching the whole series in transmission order that maybe the 'base-under-siege' formula was already wearing thin by the time we got to *The Ice Warriors*, but this story actually comes early in that era, and none of the other stories around it had bored me quite so much. And I felt the same watching this preview DVD – I felt impatient.

What it boils down to is that *The Ice Warriors* has too many episodes for the amount of story at its disposal. It's just too long. Some stories, whether you watch them episodically or in one sitting – like *The War Games* or *The Ambassadors of Death* – have enough story and, perhaps more importantly, enough lightness of touch to carry you smiling to the end without undue pain. *The Ice Warriors* is, undoubtedly lovely in places – in acting and design if not in atmosphere – but it outstays its welcome.

The addition of animated episodes Two and Three to this release is a lovely and welcome thing that shouldn't be scoffed at. But while the artwork is an improvement on *The Reign of Terror*, this is not The Invasion. In fairness, the budget on these DVD cartoons is tiny, but they are, quite simply and unavoidably, the *Thunderbirds* equivalent of animation – puppet-like bodies and puppet-like mouths and eyes that jig about awkwardly and pay very little courtesy to the original production. A telesnap reconstruction would have been the more effective way of delivering these episodes. And then there's that issue of story length. Do the cartoons add anything to the DVD that the VHS didn't have? Well, yes, they add about 35 minutes – to something that already seemed too long.

But there's lots to enjoy in *The Ice Warriors* if you've never seen it before, as I should know: stylish set and costume design, great acting, ice warriors with hair, Troughton being silly (and fluffing his lines), some eerie music, and even a polystyrene computer.

In terms of DVD Extras, there's a lively commentary featuring Deborah Watling and Frazer Hines – who is always good value and thoroughly entertaining. The second episode features a fascinating mix of archive recordings from various 'lost' voices, and the third features a commentary from Patrick's son, Michael Troughton. These are the real highlights of these discs.

For those like me who might want to speed up the viewing experience, the lovingly crafted VHS telesnap links are also included. The documentaries 'Cold Fusion' and 'Beneath the Ice' are enjoyable if a little thin. Best of all is a delightful selection of *Blue Peter* clips detailing various stages of their Design-A-Monster competition, and the second part of Frazer Hines' 'Doctor Who Stories' interview – which twinkles and sparkles throughout.

The Ice Warriors is probably over-rated, and clearly not my favourite *Doctor Who* story, but I'll keep on watching it, because all *Doctor Who* is brilliant. This double-disc set is a 'must-have' for any serious fan of the Troughton years.

Originally published by Kasterborous.com (August, 2013)

INTERVIEW: My Mate John... *IS* the Doctor!
(John Guilor, voice of the first Doctor in Day of the Doctor and Planet of Giants DVD)

This week sees the DVD release of the 1964 William Hartnell story *Planet of Giants*. As you may know, this story was originally recorded as a four-parter and – to add pace – almost immediately truncated to three parts. That edited material was apparently 'junked' at the time of that decision, but one of the much anticipated, discussed and intriguing aspects of the DVD release is a special feature in which the story is once again re-instated to four parts, utilising existing footage, animation, the vocal talents of surviving cast members and modern voice artists. It is to one of these voice artists that the weighty task of recreating William Hartnell's Doctor has fallen. That man is John Guilor, a jobbing actor and lifelong *Doctor Who* fan. He is also my mate; we met in 1989 at a screening of Tim Burton's *Batman* and we've known each other ever since. So, as Kasterborous' man on the inside, it seemed only right that I get together with John and find out what it was like to become the new old Doctor and how to avoid being poisoned by DN6...

ETJ: I've known you for almost quarter of a century, but for those who haven't... Who is John Guilor?

JG: Good grief! Now that's a difficult opening question. John Guilor is a forty-year-old man – currently – born in Wakefield, West Yorkshire in 1972. Those are the facts. Open to conjecture is the following: he is an actor and voice artist. Anything deeper, and you'll have to delve...

ETJ: We were born in the same hospital, as I recall. We even went to the same school for a time – not that we knew that then – and we both became actors. What I *never* did that you did was only go and be bloomin' Doctor Who on a DVD. So how did you come to be involved in *Planet of Giants*?

JG: I had been recommended as a voice artist to (special features producer) Ian Levine by Toby Hadoke. Ian was, at the time, engaged in numerous private projects requiring the voices of several Doctors, some with us, some no longer with us. We worked together on various things for about eight months before *Planet of Giants* was mentioned. But during that time, I voiced six different Doctors.

ETJ: That's twelve very big boots to fill. How do you think you did?

JG: It was quite a learning curve. I insisted that I could perhaps only achieve Tom Baker and William Hartnell with any degree of satisfaction – personal satisfaction that is – but Ian being Ian, he pushed and pushed me. I'm grateful for that, because he made me work hard and well outside my comfort zone, which is the only way you get good or *amazing* results. I had *never* thought of myself as an impressionist, and always hated stand-up routines by impressionists – but I guess I'm doing something different here, so that's okay.

ETJ: From my own experience of recording with you, you'd been very good at Tom Baker for a long time – had you used that voice in other work previously?

JG: I discovered quite early on that I could achieve a very convincing Tom. Now, as I get older, people often say 'Christ, you even *look* like him'. I've been asked

278

to 'do Tom' for the past ten years – although I avoided adverts and anything else that may upset the man himself!

ETJ: Who is the hardest Doctor to pull off?

JG: I would never attempt to pull off any Doctor!

ETJ: Glad to hear it. You passed my little test.

JG: Joking aside – Troughton! I can't do a convincing Troughton! Or a McCoy, beyond caricature.

ETJ: I'm imagining Davison is tough, am I right?

JG: I actually played Davison's Doctor opposite Janet Fielding for a private project – having her there helped the performance enormously. That is one voice I find I have to settle into.

ETJ: Hartnell, however, is no problem?

JG: I wouldn't say 'no problem'. It takes a good couple of minutes or so to settle into him too.

ETJ: Tell me about the *Planet of Giants* DVD?

JG: *Planet of Giants* has been revisited because it was originally made, filmed and completed as a four-part story. Looking at a BBC memo dated 20th October 1964, it seems Donald Wilson suggested cutting it down to three episodes for reasons of pacing among other things. The cut material was originally recorded but destroyed some time shortly after the edit. I have heard strong rumours that the dialogue – audio only – exists, but it hasn't surfaced for this release. I hope it does one day; I'd like to know how close we got! And if I can just say, there really was next to no budget for this. If Ian Levine hadn't stepped in, the special feature would have been limited to a PDF of the scripts for episodes three and four. But the 'lost' material is great.

ETJ: And you're playing the Doctor in the 'lost' scenes?

JG: Yes, I play – no pressure – the first Doctor Who; the original, you might say; the one and only William Hartnell both late and great!

ETJ: As a life-long *Doctor Who* fan, how does it feel to take on the mantle of, in my opinion at least, the definitive Doctor?

JG: It's a kind of dream come true. During one visit to the Blackpool exhibition in 1983, me and my Mum were looking at the Doctor portraits in the TARDIS roundels and she asked, 'Well, which one are you going to be', and I pointed to the eleventh roundel in the sequence, which was, of course, empty at that time. Interesting, though, because here we are with an eleventh Doctor on television, but I'm not the eleventh I'm somehow the first!

ETJ: How did you approach the role?

JG: By watching Hartnell episodes on a loop. The audio soundtracks were on in the car and I'd repeat lines, skip the CD back, listen, repeat, skip back, listen, and so on, before finally making test recordings – some of which even sent a chill down my own spine.

ETJ: Wonderful, because I've seen your spine and it's not the kind that chills easily. What challenges did you encounter?

JG: The main challenge was that I couldn't – and wouldn't want to anyway – give a Richard Hurndall type first Doctor. By which I mean my own interpretation. Because of the nature of the project, I had to get as close to Hartnell as possible. Now, we can perhaps all do a 'silly Hartnell' and 'hmmmppphhh' and say 'Chesterling', but I had to convince the producer, the stars, and finally the audience that this *could well be* William Hartnell speaking the lines we lost so long ago.

ETJ: Did you get to do a Billy-fluff?

JG: I threw in several Billy-fluffs, but I believe only one of the minor ones was kept. I did do a monumental fluff worthy of Bill himself, but I don't think they wanted to go that far!

ETJ: I remember reading a Virgin *Missing Adventure* years ago – possibly by Gareth Roberts – and that had the first Doctor making Billy-fluffs in his dialogue as if it were just another aspect of the character not the actor, which always amused me. Glad you got to keep one in.

JG: I also looked at the film *Will Any Gentlemen* from 1953 to listen to Bill's more natural voice. He had quite a strong voice you know.

ETJ: As do you; whereas Richard Hurndall doesn't. That performance seemed fine when we were about 12, but now it's very odd, isn't it?

JG: I saw *The Five Doctors* yesterday, and yes, it is; very odd. It only worked because it had to, didn't it? But he is very good in his own right. I still wonder whose idea the fingerless gloves were, though…

ETJ: Peter Cushing's?

JG: Speaking of whom, I haven't tried Cushing yet. I think I'd have to reach quite far for that one – if, indeed, I could do it any justice at all.

ETJ: Check with my wife – she's a relation of his. But getting back to Hurndall, he holds his own so well, and I'm led to believe that the other Doctor actors had very little to do with him; but he's also very misleading if you've never seen Hartnell. The teeth are wrong for a start.

JG: Teeth! Funny you should say that! I looked at Hartnell's teeth *a lot* to see if there was anything I could do with my jaw to capture his sound.

ETJ: That's because you're a canny wee fellow.

JG: He keeps his teeth well hidden…

ETJ: Like David Cameron…

JG: But when we *do* catch a glimpse, I noticed he had long incisors and his front teeth seemed slightly set back from them. So, I tried to adjust my jaw to match that. These little tricks can help. I find adopting the mannerisms the greatest help, however.

ETJ: Eyes and hands with Hartnell – old school vamping. That way he turns his head, lots of sidelong stuff. His Doctor is very much a performance.

JG: As you say, eyes and hands, indeed...

ETJ: So who else is providing voices in *Planet of Giants'* reconstructed second half?

JG: There's Katherine Hadoke as Barbara. She did a great job – another difficult voice to mimic. It's more difficult than you think, folks! There's Steve Johnson as Bert and Patricia Merrick as Hilda. And Toby Hadoke as the baddy. And Paul Jones, I think! Not sure if Paul's in it now. I wasn't in the room for every scene, you see. Free mention anyway for Paul.

ETJ: Now I think you're being coy and missing a couple of very important cast members. So I'll come straight out and ask: what was it like working with Ian and Susan?

JG: William Russell is quite simply the nicest man on Earth. He's the kind of man who makes you feel glad to be alive. Carole Ann Ford was wonderful. Her eyes sparkle like a cartoon character's and we got on very well. I loved them. I wanted to stay for a week and record a whole series of adventures!

ETJ: What can you tell us about them that no one else knows?

JG: I discovered that Carole likes Antoine de Clevecy champagne – the empty bottle of which I can see from here – and William Russell is a very early riser! Maybe that's his secret to staying energetic and optimistic: get up before anyone else is there to ruin your day!

ETJ: And how did they react to your Hartnell?

JG: They were both stunned by the voice. But I'm not sure whether they were simply being kind or not.

ETJ: Were you a particular fan of *Planet of Giants* before you were cast in it?

JG: Short answer: yes! I always liked it because it was an odd one. I do like the odd ones!

ETJ: A sideways story...

JG: I thought some of the sets were fantastic and the DN6 sub-plot and various bits of silliness with the phone.

ETJ: I'd have to agree. It's a hidden gem, with some incredible effects work, too. I don't think the Target novelisation did it any favours in the years when no one could see it.

JG: You borrowed my *Planet of Giants* Target book in 1993 and returned it dog-eared. I remember you saying it wasn't much good, and I said 'No, it's not now is it?!'

ETJ: last time you told me off for this it was *The Rescue*.

JG: See – the memory does cheat!

ETJ: Maybe it was both.

JG: Maybe it was?

ETJ: Like me, you're a fan of the Hartnell years. Do you have any favourite stories from that period?

JG: I like *every* Hartnell TV story. Top five off the top of my head: *The Daleks, Marco Polo, The Web Planet, The Myth Makers, The Smugglers*.

ETJ: I remember you had two copies of *The Daleks* on BBC Video and kindly gave me the spares – my first ever Hartnell video.

JG: Really? Gosh, I was generous and kind in those days. I still am. That's why I'm poor. That top five will probably change tomorrow, but *The Web Planet* is *always* there. Make of that what you will.

ETJ: You know what I'll make of that. I was going to ask you about guilty pleasures later, or are you just out and proud about *The* (Utterly Brilliant) *Web Planet*?

JG: *The Web Planet* is the distillation of the Hartnell period. It's stunning in every way – even where the imagination out-stripped the budget, they still did it with utter conviction. Brilliant, irreplaceable, never-to-be-seen-again-type television. True talent and ingenuity at work.

ETJ: I totally concur. What's your favourite *Doctor Who* story bar none?

JG: Bar none? I haven't been able to find an answer to that one. Not even Deep Thought could help.

ETJ: Today, I mean.

JG: Oh, today! Today, it's *The Ambassadors of Death*! Yesterday, it was *The Seeds of Doom*.

ETJ: What's it going to be tomorrow?

JG: Tomorrow, it's likely to be another Hartnell! I love *The Savages*!

ETJ: Another Hartnell impersonator. Frederick Jaeger *is*... the Doctor! And, er, Professor Yaffle. So what was the first *Doctor Who* you ever saw?

JG: My earliest memory is Bellal in *Death to the Daleks*.

ETJ: Freud would have a field day.

JG: Years later, my memory mistook him for Davros. I though there had been a Pertwee/Davros story for at least a year before *Doctor Who Weekly* put me straight.

ETJ: Knowing you well, I know you are unashamedly in love with *Doctor Who* – at what point did you realise this?

JG: From the beginning of Season 15, I really didn't think about much else. Other than going out on my bike and wondering where the next fish fingers were coming from.

ETJ: What story would you like to have been in?

JG: If I can change that to a season, can I say Season 13? To be there when the series was rising in popularity almost weekly; watching Tom Baker transform from a humble, grateful actor into an egomaniac – I'm sure he'd agree – would have been something to behold. I would have liked to have known Lis Sladen, too. Yes, I'd liked to have replaced Harry!

ETJ: Doctors aside, do you admire any particular performances in *Doctor Who* over the years?

JG: Peter 'Are you going?!' Miles from *Doctor Who and the Silurians*, Christopher Gable as Sharaz Jek, and Terry Molloy's Davros.

ETJ: Do you have a guilty pleasure?

JG: *The Web Planet*! Other than that though, I absolutely *adore* Meglos! Tom's great! It's colourful! And it still retains that Season 17 silliness.

ETJ: Great music. Actually, you're a jobbing actor; you drive around the country going from job to job - do you listen to *Doctor Who* music in your car? Dare you confess to listening to radiophonic music for pleasure? I will if you will.

JG: I perhaps would if I had that stuff on CD, but I don't. I'd listen to Dominic Glynn if my *Black Light* tape hadn't died years ago.

ETJ: That was a good one. Mine died too. But then I think mine was a copy of yours.

JG: I have the 60's stock music, but it's not something to drive along to.

ETJ: So from the '60s back to the present day. *Doctor Who* is about to hit 50. What would you like to see for the anniversary?

JG: I'm nervous about the anniversary because I don't see how they're going to please everyone. A bit like *Planet of Giants*, it's something that will be loved, hated or simply tolerated. It would have to be a good story to explain ageing and missing Doctors, therefore I'm not sure I'd like to see that. They could have me with Hartnell's persona trapped inside me trying to get a message to the others!

ETJ: What about the Dominators? Krotons? Wirrn? Adric?

JG: Do you know, I'd really like to see *all* of them included!

ETJ: All the old z-listers re-imagined in a Terrance Dicks story directed by Waris Hussein. Done as live.

JG: The Dominators invading Earth – now wouldn't that be a great new story! But seriously, I think it would be a crime if Carole Ann Ford and William Russell are not asked.

ETJ: And with *Planet of Giants* in the shops as we speak, what does the future hold for John Guilor?

JG: The future for John Guilor? Oh, him. Well, I'm currently the voice of a new web series for *The Onion: America's Finest News Source* called *Horrifying Planet*, and I go to Edinburgh in September to film a pilot for a proposed vampire series from Guts 'N Roses Studios, with whom I made *I Chop You*. After that, let's hope the phone rings.

ETJ: Here's a scary thought - you're only 15 years younger than Hartnell was when he did *Planet of Giants*.

JG: That *is* a scary thought! But I'm also the same age as Tom when he got *Doctor Who* – for which I invite interest from anyone making a programme about his life!

ETJ: And maybe in 50 years, another as yet unborn actor will be involved in the re-re-re-release of *Planet of Giants*, trying to capture Guilor's Hartnell's Doctor as they re-instate your missing monumental Billy-fluff...

JG: I love the idea of recreating recreations! After a very nasty Kaled war, you mean? When all data discs have been utterly obliterated by the Atomic war...

ETJ: Yes, but all of this can only lead to... Movellans!

JG: The Dominators *and* the Movellans! Get writing!

ETJ: A final word, John?

JG: I dearly hope what I have done on *Planet of Giants* pleases the majority. Knowing what I know about *Doctor Who* fans, I won't please everyone. Not even David Tennant managed that!

Originally published in *K-Mag* (August, 2013)

REVIEW: The Visitation DVD – Special Edition

The Visitation might easily have been the most highly-regarded story of *Doctor Who*'s Nineteenth Season but for the story that would follow it three weeks later. At the time, any badly-read eleven-year-old could tell you that while the first three stories of the season had been intriguing and strange, they didn't really match up to the kind of *Doctor Who* he was pining for (thanks to *Doctor Who Monthly* and Target books). Ask that eleven-year-old now that he's forty-two, having read and seen and felt a thing or two, he'd tell you that *Castrovalva*, *Four to Doomsday* and *Kinda* are all wonderful in their own way and signal a renaissance in *Doctor Who*'s imaginative fortunes, a particularly invigorating one thanks to the arrival of brand new Doctor, Peter Davison. But at the time (February 1982), it was *The Visitation* that thrilled the long-term fan by taking *Doctor Who* back into our past for the first time in over four years – to the plague year of 1666, no less – and pitting the Doctor against proper rubber-suited monsters (the Terileptils); and, what's more, they were animatronic for the first ever time.

The Visitation is a solid and confident adventure in history, with a beautiful muted green colour palette and an extraordinarily small guest cast. Well, with four regulars to write for, this is no bad thing. And while Janet Fielding does her usually brilliant job as Tegan, alongside Matthew Waterhouse's equally solid Adric (I've no idea why you hate him – did someone tell you you were supposed to, or were you just jealous at the time?), it is Peter Davison that is, as always, utterly sublime as the Doctor. He might even be the best Doctor after Hartnell. What's that, you say? I omitted Sarah Sutton? Well, look; Nyssa is lovely and all that – and Davison's always bigging her up and saying how she's much the best companion for his Doctor – but, really, she's actually rather dull. Not that Sarah Sutton doesn't always give a reasonable performance, it's just that she's just a bit, well, flat. Given that she went to drama school and the ever-inventive Waterhouse didn't, why are we always sticking the boot into Adric? I'm sure you'll tell me.

Of the guest cast, Corrie's Fred Elliot (John Savident before he made a household name for himself) gets a lovely part in the tense and scary prologue, while former EastEnder Michael Melia plays the rubber-covered fish/lizard villain with utter relish and exquisite diction. But companion-of-the-week/month Richard Mace – thespian, highwayman, raconteur and discretionary coward – steals every scene he's in. With his fruity voice and utter confusion/fascination at the events he has become embroiled in, he really is one of the best characters to turn up in any *Doctor Who* story. Ever. That Michael Robbins was immediately identifiable at the time of broadcast as a balding, middle-aged comic character from a notoriously 'dodgy' but popular sitcom (*On the Buses*) must have made suspension of disbelief somewhat difficult for some viewers. I wonder now, though, with that context long gone, just what new viewers would make of him. He makes the story. He's utterly bloody wonderful, in fact. The Doctor should have dumped the others in 1666 and taken Mace with him.

If you know the story of *The Visitation* then you know how it all pans out and I'm not going to spoil it here for anyone who doesn't know. At the time, the conceit – once revealed – was very thrilling. For four episodes we were treated to a tale of atmosphere and dread. Oh, and disco robots and music from the BBC Tudorphonic Workshoppe (okay, so Tudor's wrong, but you get my drift). It was a deliciously well-written script from newcomer and future/current (it's complicated) script editor Eric Saward, who would later be famous for bringing blood and guts and mayhem to the series that culminated in the sadistic festivities of Colin Baker's inaugural season. And that's the thing about *The Visitation*. It was amazing at the time – and it's still amazing – it's just that three weeks after it finished, its writer rocked up again with a little number called *Earthshock* and that changed the course of *Doctor Who* for the next five years, both in tone and what it was actually talking about. In a way, *The Visitation* was exactly the kind of *Doctor Who* that the aforementioned eleven-year-old had wanted to see, but then *so was Earthshock*, and because that later story had its tongue firmly down the throat of the series' past, it became the story we would always remember (alongside *Kinda* when we got older and more pretentious), so *The Visitation* had to slink back into the shadows wondering why no one was talking about it anymore. Some 30 years on, we look back at this gem of a story and we see it wedged somewhere between two 'classics' of very different colours (*Kinda* being the other) and it looks a bit dowdy and traditional. But at the time, *Doctor Who* hadn't been quite so traditional for a while. In many ways it was 'proper' *Doctor Who* come back at last. So, don't overlook it. Give it another go and enjoy its utter *Who*-ness. If you're one of those nutters that's watching the series in order, you'll love it.

The Visitation returns to DVD on May 6th. I say 'returns' because you probably already bought it in 2004. This is, of course, yet another Special Edition of a DVD that's already out and as I've recently complained about that cynical bit of capitalist methodology in my The Aztecs review, I won't bother going on about it here. All the special features you had on your old disc are present on Disc 1: five minutes of film trims; interviews with director Peter Moffatt, writer Eric Saward and composer Paddy Kingsland; picture gallery; isolated score and a commentary from all the regulars. Of course, the new release has also been cleaned up and does look rather lovely.

In terms of new special features, Disc 2 has three fairly worthwhile features you won't find anywhere else. One of these is a seemingly out of place feature about Big Finish's work in keeping *Doctor Who* alive over the years. At only 27 minutes it's a bit brief, and the most notable thing about it is how old Nicholas Briggs suddenly looks. Then there's a *Doctor Who*-related tour and retrospective of BBC TV Centre. Here, *Blue Peter*'s Yvette Fielding is joined by her namesake, Janet, Peter Davison and Mark Strickson for a just about interesting trip down memory lane. Well, as far back as 1983. It really shouldn't warrant more than half an hour, but this is only Part One... It is notable, however, for Yvette's creepy hogging of the leading man and seemingly deliberate side-lining of The Actress Formerly Known As Tegan. Oh, and for how tiny Mark Strickson's arms look. Most relevant to this release is a 45-minute documentary that returns the cast of *The Visitation* to its filming locations. Well, by 'its cast' I mean Davison, Fielding, Sutton and... Strickson. Not a sign of the Blue Box Boy anywhere. Maybe he declined, maybe he was unavailable. I suspect they probably never even asked, so eager are they to stick the boot in, yet again, at the runt of the litter just because he was naïve, foolish and, for god's sake, having a bloody good go and doing better than ought to be expected. Intriguingly, throughout this one, the Mouth On Legs barely speaks at all, and I do wonder if Davison's reference to Rolf Harris will have been cut by the time you get to see it.

If you already have this, please don't lose any sleep about not having seen the new material; although I know some of you completists will fall for it. If you haven't seen *The Visitation* before though, then go for it. You'll really enjoy this lovely and elegant bit of *Doctor Who*.

Originally published by Kasterborous.com (April, 2013)

REVIEW: The Power of the Daleks

On the human space colony of Vulcan, a coup is being planned by rebels who want independence from their current masters, while factions within the rebel camp are making plans for their own gains. Meanwhile, the colony's leading scientist has unearthed a long-hidden space capsule from the mercury swamp – a capsule containing Daleks who have their own, secretive ambitions. Into this chaotic struggle for ultimate power, stumble Polly, Ben and the Doctor...

Hang on a minute. Did I say... the Doctor?

Last week on *Doctor Who*, the Doctor defeated some men whose old bodies had worn thin and been replaced with medical-mechanical parts, only to slump to the floor of his TARDIS in an op art frenzy of light and sound and be replaced by a complete stranger. Gone is the elderly, white-haired grandfather we have come to love over the last three years (the original, the greatest, the definitive Doctor, William Hartnell) and in his place lays a slightly younger-looking imposter with a Beatle haircut and a craggy, mysterious-looking face. The credits and posterity will tell us that this is The Doctor, now played by Patrick Troughton. We have to believe it's the Doctor because we saw him change with our own eyes, or we think we did, but our viewer-identification characters of the last three months – Ben (Michael Craze) and Polly (Anneke Wills) – really have no idea who he is.

'What was that the Doctor said in the Tracking Room,' asks Polly. '"This old body of mine is wearing a bit thin..."?' Ben makes the logical deduction that the Doctor's made himself a new one... somehow. 'I've been renewed,' says the newcomer. 'It's part of the TARDIS. Without it I couldn't survive.' But even his clothes have changed! The dusty Edwardian garb of our lovely, reassuring, bumbling Doctor have transformed into a gaudy, scruffy, clown's interpretation of that familiar attire.

And this new Doctor doesn't play by the usual rules. He's far more oblique than the man we thought we knew. He is unsettling, infuriating and, at first, often frightening. He cannot control his new body at first, but soon he is dancing jigs, playing the recorder (amateurishly and annoyingly) and cultivating an obsession with hats (as evidenced by his sporting of a stovepipe hat and his new catchphrase 'I should like a hat like that.') He also has conversations with himself, which might be an affectation or perhaps he is talking to the old Doctor, active somewhere still in his mind? However this change occurred, it is not merely a change of features, height or clothes, it is a change of everything. This is an entirely different person (even if he sees his former features looking back at him from an old mirror). He no longer needs the Doctor's reading spectacles and he even speaks of the Doctor as someone else. So, it seems we did not know 'our' old Doctor quite as well as we had thought. That this ability to renew himself was a secret previously unshared (almost the final punch line to three years of asking 'Doctor ... who?') as was his keeping of a 500-year diary...

But just like 'our' Doctor, this new one soon finds himself at the centre of political shenanigans when the TARDIS lands on Vulcan. By Episode Two, he is more avuncular, playful and naughty (he even fluffs his lines just to make us feel at home) – but he's still impishly annoying. By pretending to be the Examiner from Earth (tasked with surveying the efficacy of the colony), he gains access to the seemingly impenetrable space capsule only to find a dark chamber occupied by eerily dormant and cobweb-coated Daleks – and, worse still, a slithering Dalek mutant scuttling about in the shadows. Even independent of their travel machines, it seems the Dalek mutants can create havoc. And, as more Daleks appear, fooling the colonists into blindly assisting them in their bid for power (both literal and figurative) with child-like cries of 'I am your ser-vant!', it is disturbingly clear that they immediately recognise this new Doctor for who he is. Proof then, if we needed it by Episode Three, that this man is exactly who he claims to be.

These Daleks – there appears to be but three of them initially – want to set the colonial factions against each other in a fight to the death, after which they will use the colony to provide materials and power for their building of an army in their hidden factory, deep inside their dimensionally transcendental capsule. They profess to know how the human mind works and seem to have concluded that it is fuelled by greed – indeed, the bulk of the guest cast falls victim to its own schemes and desires. Complementing this Dalek vision of humanity is a nice moment in Episode Five, wherein a puzzled Dalek asks, 'Why do human beings kill human being?' – a damning indictment of what these colonists have become.

In terms of realisation, director Christopher Barry hopes to achieve much on famously limited budgets. Derek Dodd's mercury swamps are a little one dimensional (but no worse than many other planet-scapes in this period of the series' history); the colony is functional but effective with its long metallic corridors (perfect conditions for Daleks oddly still reliant on static electricity – well, odd until you realise that this is a David Whitaker story); and the capsule is impressive but also relatively functional. The film sequences of the Dalek factory are classic, legendary and scary *Doctor Who* (if perhaps too brightly lit). The masses of wobbly mutants are very much welcome three years after the Daleks' debut, but while the voices screaming in unison is a triumph of sound design (as is the use of sound cues from their original 1963 adventure), the factory conveyor filled with toy Daleks and the capsule control room filled to bursting with blatantly cut-out/cardboard/standee Daleks aren't as effective as they should be. This is a shame because these sequences undermine much of the rather sparse tension and threat that the actors have been building for the previous month. I won't say they're not still lovely sequences, though. They're just not as good as you might be expecting them to be. And this could be true of the story as a whole...

The Power of the Daleks has become very fashionable in *Who* circles in recent years, and I must admit that, until late, I had fallen prey to its cold glamour. It is, of course, the first second Doctor story and for Episode One alone it is of inestimable historical importance, but Episodes Two – Five, while full of solid 'Doctor Who', do amble along a little slowly and are nowhere near as tense as they could be. The story is now much lauded for its 'scheming' Daleks, and scheme and plot they do, but when you watch it – and the Daleks POV shots are a brilliant idea, I admit – they do shout rather a lot. In particular, the 'I am your ser-vant!' thing wears thin very quickly (though the pay-off when barmy scientist Lesterson uses the same phrase in Episode Six is wonderfully chilling). It is also currently fashionable to suggest that having 'scheming' Daleks that watch and wait is the best way to utilise the Doctor's most legendary foes. I'm not sure I agree with this anymore, particularly when the humans in this story manage to do quite enough of that on their own, thank you. It strikes me that the Daleks didn't become the Doctor's greatest enemy by serving drinks and supressing their feelings – surely they're far more effective when chasing you and shooting at you and screaming that they're going to kill you – preferably through some space jungle. Isn't that what monsters are supposed to do? Isn't that what the Daleks are for? And that they are almost incidentally defeated here by the Doctor's accidentally pulling out the right wire to withhold their power is an insult to them and the Doctor himself.

On the plus side, Episode Six is an exciting shoot-out with Daleks up against machine-gun carrying colonists. It's all rather macho, but still very impressive and perhaps more visceral than many other *Doctor Who* stories of this time. The death count is very high and even 'innocent' colonists (one seen carrying a swaddled baby on production photos) die in the conflict. The murder is wholesale and Polly is particularly distraught by the carnage. Indeed, both companions do a brilliant support job throughout this story, as do guest cast members Bernard Archard (Bragen), Robert James (Lesterson), Pamela Ann Davey (Janley) and Peter Bathurst (Quinn).

So now there's a new Doctor in the TARDIS and he's already defeated his arch enemies. Whatever next?

Originally published by Kasterborous.com (April, 2013)

REVIEW: The Underwater Menace

A kidnapped highlander joins the Doctor on an adventure west of Gibraltar and south of the Azores in what little remains of lost Atlantis – just in time to be sacrificed to hungry sharks at the Festival of the Vernal Equinox and to witness the end of the world...

Geoffrey Orme's *The Underwater Menace* has a very poor rating amongst *Doctor Who* fans. Until very recently only one of its four episodes survived in the BBC archive, so perhaps it failed to penetrate fan consciousness in any significant way. What did survive was unkindly summed up as ephemeral and daft; a camp-fest with silly costumes and an even sillier villain whose most famous line, delivered in a vibrant Teutonic accent had become a by-phrase for all that was stupid about *Doctor Who*. Another episode turned up last year, so now fifty per cent of this story available to us (the soundtrack for the other fifty per cent still exists and is scheduled for an animated DVD release in the near future), so do we still think this story is just camp, b-movie naffness? Well, yes. But its status as such shouldn't be interpreted as something negative. Eclipsed by the stories that precede and follow it, *The Underwater Menace* is in fact deliciously fabulous.

Its production values are some of the very best this season, with well-directed location sequences (hello, Julia Smith) and dramatic 'water-tank' flood sequences, not least of which is that in which the villainous Zaroff drowns in his own laboratory. Jack Robinson's sets are vast, creepy and alien, from stylish caves to gleaming laboratories whose vast windows open onto the depths of the sea. The Atlantean market place is busy and exciting (recalling the historical settings of *The Crusade* or *The Romans*), while the Temple of Amdo looks like it's been hewn from bedrock, with a striking stone idol, part woman/part fish.

There are great ambient vocal chants in the temple (akin to the later Exxilon chants). Dudley Simpson's temple themes are also beautifully and eerily realised. In terms of music, this story features some of the '60s' best; mostly electronic, often crunchily discordant, it is undoubtedly strange and psychedelic. Who couldn't love the amazing Fish People music (or Brian Hodgson's special sounds)? Sonically and visually, the underwater 'Chinese whispers' ballet is a dazzling example of *Doctor Who*'s ability to impress.

Sandra Reid and Juanita Waterson pull out all the stops on costume duties, doing daring things with the Doctor, realistic/contemporary with Sean and Jacko, outrageous temple costumes, seashell swimwear for Polly and Ara (Catherine Howe) and, of course, the beautifully expressionistic Fish People costumes. These latter creatures are, essentially, 'survivors from shipwrecks who would otherwise be corpses' that have been operated on and given plastic gills – which is what they look like. So, are they zombies? I ask this because they are clearly distinguished from 'normal' people like Sean and Jacko (Paul Anil), who shore up the TARDIS team quite nicely.

P.G. Stephens' Sean is very colourful, but he's not the best of the guest cast, as we are treated to quality turns from wonderful Colin Jeavons as Damon; the great Noel Johnson as Thous; and Peter Stephens playing Lolem (just as Stewie from *Family Guy* might). 'May the wrath of Amdo engulf you,' he curses Zaroff. 'I'll take my chance,' replies the crazy scientist. It's a chance that doesn't pay off, so – quite poetically – that's the end of Zaroff. But where to begin with this villain?

Zaroff is such a mesmerising creation, played to perfection by Joseph Furst (his confrontation with Thous in episode three is perhaps the best scene).

Furst plays Zaroff for camp keeps – but scarily so ('I could feed you to my pet octopus,' he threatens, amusingly) and he's a lovely foil for the new Doctor. Patrick Troughton and Furst clearly have a blast playing off each other. 'You come with me, eh?' asks Zaroff. 'I come with you,' replies the Doctor. 'You, ah, like my laboratory, yes?' asks Zaroff. 'You find it all very impressive, no?' 'No,' replies the Doctor. Zaroff's crazy scheme is to raise Atlantis from its sunken air pocket existence, by drawing the planet's oceans into the Earth's core. When the Doctor astutely asks him why he wants to blow up the world, Zaroff replies that he wants to achieve 'the scientist's dream of supreme power.' – which is quite a dream for someone who's failed to invent the fridge...

The regulars are, of course, brilliant. Ben (Michael Craze) and Polly (Anneke Wills) are always lovely and the addition of Jamie (Frazer Hines) does dilute their efficacy somewhat, but it's great to have them all together. Jamie is still new to the TARDIS, wondering 'What have I come upon?', but he's impressed with the Doctor throughout. Hines still speaks with a soft lilt and his hair is longer than it'll soon become and, trivia-fans, he speaks Gaelic.

Ben sees himself and Jamie as the muscle of the crew, and is very protective of Polly and the Doctor. His desperation when Polly is kidnapped by Zaroff is tangibly played by Craze. His sincerity and loyalty mark him out as one of the series' best companions, but he's not without his rougher edges. He's lovingly irreverent to the Doctor: 'Blimey, look at him. He ain't normal, is he?' He's also cheeky to Jamie, pointing at his kilt and suggesting that he 'might be mistaken for a bird'. And he's less than eloquent, when needing a translator and turning to his oldest companion with the words 'Polly, you speak foreign...'

Polly does indeed 'speak foreign' – three kinds in fact: French, German and Spanish. We also learn that she's very keen to return to Chelsea 1966. Given the tortures she'll endure in this story, who could blame her? By the end of the tale – having endured injections and harassment that even hardy Antipodeans balked at – she is practically hysterical as the caves are flooded. Interestingly, it is Jamie – not Ben – that helps her through this ordeal...

It's still early days for the 'second Doctor', but Troughton's performance is busy and rich, making you wonder how manic his work in the previous two stories must be. The new (perhaps more superficial) aspects of his character are at the fore; this is still the fey pixie-child Doctor that will swiftly be replaced by a much calmer, more avuncular figure, forever groping bits of Jamie. Here though, he's often a little boy, hoping to encounter prehistoric monsters, playing his recorder or fetishizing costumes and hats. He may wear his stovepipe for the last time, but he still manages to dress up as a guard – whose hat he adores – and also dons a sou'wester which allows him to spend a quarter of the second episode looking like a sit-com fisherman. From here he dives giddily into ceremonial robes and the most outrageous bit of headgear you'll ever see him in. 'How do I look?' he asks. 'I would like a hat like that', indeed. However, his most revealing bit of extra-curricular cosplay comes in the third episode's market place sequence. In a groovy headscarf and Ray-Bans, with bells on his wrists, it becomes quite clear that this is the first contemporary Doctor to hit our screens. It's 1967 and this new Doctor looks like a refugee from Greenwich Village or the Haight – he even has a tambourine for Dylan's sake!

While he still channels something of the previous Doctor – eyes darting all over the place assessing the strengths and weaknesses of his foes – comedy and capers are ever-present now. He knocks at his head like it's a door and looks to see if anyone's home when demonstrating how barmy Zaroff is. When the companions leave the Compression Chamber, he says, 'Women and children last'. In arch response, Ben and Jamie leave first. Another lovely in-joke comes just as Polly is to undergo the fish person operation; the Doctor's first plan of action is to disconnect the power supply – the basic but radical solution he employed to somewhat anti-climactic effect at the end of his first story.

This new incarnation is not infallible. He assumes he's been captured by troglodytes, which is wide of the mark, and that the bracelet Polly finds is 'Aztec', when it's actually a souvenir of the 1968 Mexico Olympics. Close, perhaps, to one who has all of time and space to choose from, but still no cigar. When Ben asks him if he knows what he's doing, he says that of course he doesn't but there's no rule against trying. When Ramo (Tom Watson) asks why he should trust him, he replies with sincerity: 'That's a very good question. I wish I could think of a good answer'. Ultimately, he convinces with actions not words.

In the end, the Doctor solves Atlantis' woes by instigating industrial action, using Sean's 'gift of the gab' to convince the food-farming fish people to go on strike. He then halts Zaroff's plans by flooding the already diminished kingdom and leaves, having shocked a complacent, superstitious, immoral society into a new way of living and caring (not that he adequately checks on the success or otherwise of his endeavours).

The Underwater Menace is, on the surface, cartoon, comic strip *Doctor Who*; very b-movie, full of chases and faces full of pepper, but there are dark undercurrents. Zaroff's unfairly maligned 'Nothing in the world can stop me now' (and I'm not going to denigrate Furst's native accent by writing that in the customary phonetics) might appear silly or funny, but for the fact that the funny/silly man in question has just plunged a spear into another man's guts, shot a man and overseen the execution of two others. But this fusion of silliness and seriousness – dare I suggest black comedy? – provides the series with a blast of psychedelic pop colour that is a step forward from, say, *The War Machines'* *Rubber Soul*, sending us off into *Revolver* territory. *The Power of the Daleks* and *The Highlanders* are great stories, but here we touch base with the kind of white heat/psychedelic thinking we last saw in the closing moments of *The Tenth Planet*, and it's beautifully refreshing.

Originally published by Kasterborous.com (April, 2013)

REVIEW: The Aztecs DVD – Special Edition

The Aztecs is one of *Doctor Who*'s finest stories and certainly one of the jewels at the heart of its very first season. When the Doctor (William Hartnell) and his companions become stranded in fifteenth century Mexico at the time of the sun-worshipping, blood-sacrificing Aztecs, Barbara (Jacqueline Hill, who steals the show) is mistaken for the reincarnation of High Priest Yetaxa. In order to prevent her friends from becoming victims of a thoroughly dangerous, alien society, she finds herself playing a dangerous game of cat and mouse with the bloodthirsty Tlotoxl (a deliciously nasty turn from John Ringham). Inspired by her gentle ally,

Autloc (Keith Pyott), Barbara finds herself also hoping to save the Aztecs from imminent conquest by the Spanish and this puts her at loggerheads with the Doctor who insists that she must not attempt to re-write history – not a single line...

John Lucarotti's fabulous script has all the magical, astral charm of a story that has passed under the gaze of editor David Whitaker. The strong guest cast also includes Ian Cullen, Margot van der Burgh and Walter Randall. It has delicious sets by Barry Newbery, delightful music by Richard Rodney Bennett, and great action sequences by David Anderson and Derek Ware. It even gives us a Doctor that (inadvertently?) gets engaged. It's wonderful stuff – some of the very best, in fact. But you might seem to recall having bought this DVD before...

This is, of course, yet another Special Edition of a DVD you've already got; something that happens with increased frequency these days, when all you really want is the Zygon one and not a lot of useless little odds and ends they forgot to give you when you bought your DVDs the first time around. Maybe it's just me, but *Doctor Who* seems to be a pleasure I have, in recent years been priced out of. Since the recession began and finances got tighter, the amount of *Doctor Who* product, simply in terms of audios and books and such, seems to have quadrupled. I love *The Aztecs*, I really do – it's a gem – but I wouldn't buy it twice if it wasn't for addition, this time around, of the Rills...

No, the Rills haven't been added into the shadows of the temple of evil, but there can be few of you who aren't aware that this 2-disc release features a 'reconstruction' of the mostly junked and missing 1965 story, *Galaxy 4*, whose third episode ('Air Lock') was the most recently recovered 'lost' episode. Here, Hartnell's Doctor finds himself caught up in the struggle between two shipwrecked and ideologically different alien space crews – the Drahvins and the Rills – on a planet facing imminent disintegration.

The Rills are confined to a spaceship 'compartment' due to a biological aversion to the planet's atmosphere. They cannot speak, communicating only by thought, and their translated communication via their robot avatars is inspired. The creatures themselves are part-walrus/part-Mr Potato Head and very big (but unwieldy and inanimate-looking). The all-female Drahvins are bouffant blondes, all Bingo hall chic with futuristic Bjork-style eyebrows. Not so much 'beautiful' (like the Thals if you squint) as 'attractive' – and terrified of Maaga, their commander. Believing themselves perfect, they view the world from a dogmatic humanoid paradigm, interpreting the Rills' physical lumpiness as 'evil'. Maaga (Stephanie Bidmead) is precise and clinical; crisply attractive, but fervent and fanatical; a vicious bureaucrat. After playing her opening moments with her back to us, she regularly displays her unabashed mania directly to camera, boldly staring directly into the viewers' eyes in stark and seductive close-up. She is a wonderful, wonderful *Doctor Who* villain.

All in all, *Galaxy 4* is better story than most would have you believe; all it really lacks is a few more natural, planetary expressions of impending oblivion to sell the stakes, which most of the time don't seem that high.

The recon itself seems to have been taken from a fan version produced around a decade or so ago by someone like Loose Canon. It is largely composed of stills from this and other stories, with some nice model shots and early CGI sequences for the Rill robots. Into this is added the extant six minutes of 'Four Hundred

Dawns' and all of 'Air Lock' and it's rather nice given the somewhat dissatisfying results of recent animated episodes. What rankles, though, is that while we have a whole 'new' episode we seem to have a truncated recon. Why episodes one and two are elided without a cliff-hanger or credits or an opening titles sequence is hard to fathom; and the final episode is about half as long as it once was.

So even if you're re-buying *The Aztecs* for *Galaxy 4*, you might still have cause for disappointment. Or perhaps you're buying it for the Disc 2 extras? Because the ones on Disc 1 are ones you already have (actors remembering; Barry Newbery; *Blue Peter*; TARDIS Cam 3 – all of which are as adequate here as they always were).

The 1969 *Chronicle* documentary The Realms of Gold examines Cortez's conquest of the Aztecs in dry BBC colour. It's charming but inessential. It has some music by the BBC Radiophonic Workshop for you completists and John Julius Norwich wears some fabulous glasses.

Doctor Forever is the 'new' documentary on here, looking at *Doctor Who* toys. It has a sweet titles sequence and looks at some great memorabilia like the Weetabix cards, but it drags out all the usual tedious rent-a-heads with their largely orthodox sound-bites and has an astoundingly lacklustre presenter.

The clip from Michael Bentine's *It's a Square World* seems to offer promise with its claim of being the first ever *Doctor Who* skit. Well, OK, Clive Dunn turns up as a batty scientist dressed like Hartnell's Doctor. But it's nothing whatever to do with our favourite TV series. It's inclusion on this DVD release seems, in fact, to be merely the consequence of a whim taken one morning in 1965 by some joker in the costume department; it really has nothing at all else to do with *Doctor Who*. Nice to see TV Centre being abused again, though, as it launches into space. Lovely little cameo from Wilfrid Brambell as Albert Steptoe, too.

A Whole Scene Going takes us (very briefly) behind the scenes of the second AARU Dalek movie with a surprisingly young, chain-smoking and perhaps defensive Gordon Flemyng – who also wears great glasses.

So, it looks like you're getting a lot for your buck, and certainly, if you've never bought The Aztecs before, then you really are. But if you have, then *Galaxy 4* is the thing you'll buy this for. Other than that, this re-issue – which apparently has an even better restoration of *The Aztecs*' print plus new Production Notes (how you'd know that without having this release and the original playing on two tellies at the same time, I have no idea…) – seems like a very strange and cynical release indeed.

Originally published by Kasterborous.com (March, 2013)

REVIEW: *Running Through Corridors, Volume 1: The 60s* (Shearman & Hadoke)

I know my *Doctor Who* inside out. In fact, the only person I've ever met whose own knowledge of my favourite TV show has the power to unnerve me is a certain Mr Toby Hadoke (he of *Moths Ate My Doctor Who Scarf* fame). On the few happy occasions we've met, his copious understanding of the series, on screen and off, has left my own *Who*-related depravity oddly inhibited. That's not Toby's fault, it's mine; I know when respect is due. But since January 2004, inspired by *Doctor Who Magazine*'s Time Team, I've been watching all of *Doctor Who*, in order, from the start – twice (once for entertainment, once for analysis – and if there's a commentary, then three times). Even before 2004, I'd seen/ heard every episode of the original TV run several times, but never in order. To spice things up, I've been listening to the audios, reading the comics, annuals and novels; cross-referencing with the Target books, and topping up my knowledge with evaluations from the reference guides. And what a journey! So, believe me, I know my *Doctor Who*. And I think Toby is the only other person I've ever met that has seen/heard every episode. What all of this means is that he is eminently qualified to be a co-author of this new reference book, and I'm reasonably qualified to read it.

The subtitle of the book is 'Rob and Toby's Marathon Watch of *Doctor Who*' – and that's exactly what *Running Through Corridors* is. Toby joins forces with New Who scribe Robert Shearman to spend a year watching all of *Doctor Who*, two episodes a day, come rain or shine. After each episode, Robert e-mails Toby with an evaluation of what he's seen and Toby responds.

This is a book for people who have spent time with the series and put some effort into appreciating it. A good friend of mine (he's the interviewer in that clip from *Music Arcade*, fact fans, asking Peter Howell how he made the 1980 theme tune) once lamented that the art of appreciation was dead. Ever since he said those words to me, I've made certain that appreciation is something I do with gusto, and it's certainly something Rob and Toby do in this book. One of the most encouraging aspects of the whole enterprise is that they wish to appreciate and examine what's good about *Who*; not pick holes in its (allegedly) less successful moments. But be warned, this is no beginner's guide...

This first volume deals with that most enchanting and magical period of the series, the 1960s. For those who don't know, this is the Hartnell/Troughton period, when the series was made in atmospheric black and white. On my own viewing odyssey, this proved to be the most beguiling and thrilling period of the series – I just couldn't believe how simply brilliant it was when watched in some kind of narrative and cultural context. I count William Hartnell not so much my 'favourite Doctor' but, quite simply, '*THE* Doctor' because of this. It is clear throughout this book that Rob and Toby are also bewitched by this period of the series.

However, as fans, we all 'own' *Doctor Who*; we all have our own vision of what it should or shouldn't be; what works and what doesn't. Personally, I'll forgive the series pretty much anything, as long as it stays on the right side of its own concepts and continuity, while Rob and Toby – in spite of looking for the good in the show – seem to writhe a little nervously when their favourite programme seems to fail or betray their requirements of it (or, perhaps more specifically, the requirements of some abstract 'casual viewer' that might not get it). Like all devotees of this wonderful series, they can be utterly objective one minute and frighteningly subjective the next.

At first, it seems that Rob will be the optimistic voice and Toby's the more pessimistic, but this gradually changes. Rob pulls 'The Velvet Web' apart for being too shabby, but Toby defends its ambition. Toby puts up a spirited defence of how we fans watch the series and how we're able to mentally compensate for its shortcomings (he does this, appropriately, during 'The Sea of Death').

By Season Three, too much death and destruction has deprived Rob of the joy and thrills, while Toby has open-heartedly welcomed a more thoughtful, edgy approach. I think Toby's observations are – even when I disagree with them – perhaps a little more astute than Rob's. They are very strong and well considered (especially when he's in a relaxed mood), and he also flags up some of the show's more 'hidden' details – things I'd certainly noticed and considered upon my own viewing that never get mentioned anywhere else. But it really is impossible to permanently 'side' with one of the authors, and that's a good thing.

Throughout the book, each author's distinctive personality emerges. Toby, for example, has a continuing obsession with getting the programme's facts right (see his entry for 'Mission to the Unknown' for a lovely bit of detective work on the alien delegates). Rob, on the other hand, has a lovely turn of phrase (my favourite being his description of The Rescue as 'an elderly dog by a radiator'). His use of the phrase 'wet fart' has an amusing effect on Toby. Oh, and speaking of wet farts, Toby loves the surviving episode of The Underwater Menace – and quite right, too. It's brilliant. That he has to 'come out' on this (very amusingly) says a lot about fan fashion over the last 30 years. I've never met anyone else who adores this episode as much as I do – and I only realised I did some five or six years ago.

It's when the authors love something you thought you were alone in loving, or notice the tiny moment only you seemed to notice, that you feel like you're on the same journey of exploration, not just the usual tick-box guided tour employed by other works. For me, this was very rewarding, but then I'd done the legwork – if you haven't seen these episodes, or spent time appreciating them, then I don't know if this book will be quite as thrilling as it is informative. You see, even though Rob and Toby have their curmudgeonly moments, it is the love on display here that delights the reader. And it's what they love that certainly makes this reader believe that we're watching the same *Doctor Who*, and that our perception of it is (mostly) free from the shackles of the dogmatic orthodoxy that infected fandom during the 1980s (Rob seems to fall prey to the 'old ways' when his expectations of *The Massacre* are compromised by an old paradigm, and he still thinks *The Celestial Toymaker* is actually good). Here are just some of the things they seem genuinely and unexpectedly enthusiastic about (and I applaud them for this): William Hartnell; Jacqueline Hill; Alethea Charlton; Brian Hodgson; 'The Ambush'; 'Five Hundred Eyes'; John Lucarotti; 'Dangerous Journey'; Maureen O'Brien; 'The Space Museum'; Peter Purves; Barrie Ingham; *The Gunfighters*; *The Power of the Daleks*; Anneke Wills; *The Abominable Snowmen*. I could go on, but these were the things I'd also found myself loving that no one had hitherto told me I should.

If you can watch the episodes as you read this book, you'll have a wonderful time. You'll find yourself not simply agreeing or disagreeing with Rob or Toby's opinions, but identifying with observations that can only be made through appreciative viewing. If you don't, well that's okay, you'll definitely learn something and you'll have a very enjoyable read. But will you be able to appreciate their musings on: the schoolgirls in 'An Unearthly Child'; Hartnell dropping his scarf in the TARDIS during his first episode; *Marco Polo* as a 'road not taken'; Hartnell flying a spaceship in 'Strangers in Space'; Barbara's self-denial at her DN6 infection; the sheer brutality of the Daleks in their second story; Peter Butterworth's prototype second Doctor; the unheeded lessons of *Galaxy Four*; Ben's finest hour; Reg Lye's delightful Griffin in *The Enemy of the World*; the guilty pleasure that is The Krotons!

Whether Rob and Toby like something or not, their opinions, observations (and arguments) are usually fresh and new. We're lucky to have such enthusiastic and intelligent commentators with whom to take this journey. Mad Norwegian must be praised for commissioning this book (they've always been ahead of the game, certainly in terms of their *Who* output), but the genius of Toby Hadoke, Robert Shearman and Lars Pearson lies in the publication of the first ever book that treats *Doctor Who* episode by episode rather than story by story. If the book has a unique selling point then that is it. Quite simply, this is one of the best books about 1960s *Doctor Who* you're ever likely to read. This is what the word 'essential' was coined for. I look forward to Volume 2.

Originally published by Kasterborous.com (January, 2013)

REVIEW: Asylum of the Daleks

Doctor Who is back and *Asylum of the Daleks* is its best season opener in a long, long time. This might even be the best opener since the series returned in 2005. Not only was it 50 minutes of exciting, thrilling, scary, stylish, tense, colourful and utterly brilliant television, this was *Doctor Who* looking mythic and shameless, expensive and bold, confident and cocky.

The Daleks are back, bringing with them all kinds of fannish thrills and new continuity that include a visit to Skaro, a Dalek shaped building, a parliament with a prime minister (!), 'duplicates' with eye-stalks and that eponymous asylum. The parliament sequences were impressive in terms of sheer scale and design - how many Daleks? How many flashing lights? But then the planet sequences and the asylum itself were tremendously pleasing on the eye (if a little cold on the spine...). The production design and colour palette seem to have leapt on somewhat since last season, and the flashes of bright burnt orange, red and green lifted the images right out of the screen.

Following a very poor Christmas special and now the delightful comedy high jinks of *Pond Life*, this new story was a complete and powerfully told slice of sci-fi drama; quintessential *Doctor Who*, I would suggest. It moved at a cracking pace using multiple environs, it had meaty dialogue (notably in the sequences of the Doctor pouring out his disgust at the Dalek love of hatred and their response that this love has thus far prevented them from killing him), atmospheric and genuinely spooky, nay, downright scary sequences (see the zombie 'duplicates' in the claustrophobic shipwreck or the mad Daleks that Rory makes the mistake of getting chummy with); utterly magical moments (the Doctor's first appearance in shadow, the dancing ballerina or Oswin alone in her mind cage); wonderful special effects; perfect lighting and stellar performances from regulars and guest cast alike.

Matt Smith is always brilliant, but he may not have been very well served by his stories. This story didn't let him down at all. Karen Gillan and Arthur Darvill were also quite splendid, especially the latter in his asylum sequences. The biggest surprise was the earlier-than-anticipated arrival of Jenna Louise Coleman as Oswin. Almost instantly one is thinking the best thing would be for her to turn out to be a nano-machined dupe who doesn't know she's a Dalek agent. The reason we don't get too carried away with this notion is that we know she's going to be the new companion, so what transpires is jaw-droppingly wonderful but also a shocking tragedy that brings a tear to the eye. A real tear, mind, brought on by a good story and a human moment, not a tear you're sledge-hammered into having because the music's nice and the script is yelling 'Cry now! Cry now, you buggers! Cry, I tell you! Cry!', as has been the norm in Doctor Who of late. Oswin-Dalek's involvement leads of course to questions of whether or not the Doctor will meet her earlier in her time-stream come the Christmas special and prevent this future from happening and also to questions regarding his removal from the Dalek memory systems (and the consequences of altering that too). 'Doctor who?' ask the Daleks. 'Doctor who,' laughs the Doctor. Doctor ... who? Hang on. Wasn't there some foreshadowing last season about the ancient question that will lead to the Time Lord's ultimate fall? The question is being asked. So, has that sequence of cascading dominoes begun to fall? Let's see...

I feel like an old curmudgeon (and I ought to because I am one), but it's been a long time since there wasn't something to criticise about an episode of Doctor Who – usually a minor niggle here, a lost opportunity there or a bloomin' great reset button all across space and time – but *Asylum of the Daleks* was probably without fault. I – and many others like me – grinned the whole way through (except perhaps for the occasional thrill of dread or terror). A lot of the time I found myself saying to myself that this was proper, proper *Doctor Who*, and I'm not the kind to make that sort of 'distinction', but this felt *so* like the 'classic' series (or a dream of the 'classic' series) in terms of atmosphere and plotting that such a moment of thrilled joy was probably unavoidable. That said, I know that this is but an illusion created by a production team at the top of its game. Sometimes you can watch this show and feel like you're watching the best *Doctor Who* episode ever, even if you know it's not *really*, but the journey is *so* thrilling it can't feel like anything else. It may not be true that this is the best ever story, but boy did it feel it was – all the way through – and this hasn't really happened for a long time. This was definitely Steven Moffat's best story, certainly as a producer and possibly even as a writer. He does Daleks very, very well; so well that they are without doubt once again *Doctor Who*'s premier villains. Big thanks to him and director Nick Hurran.

So, *Doctor Who*'s back and it's in great shape. If they can keep this up for the rest of the season then things are going to be wonderful. This is the stuff of future legend.

Originally published by Kasterborous.com (September, 2012)

REVIEW: Toby Hadoke's *My Stepson Stole My Sonic Screwdriver*

Toby Hadoke returns to the Edinburgh Fringe with what is generally described as a sequel to his hugely popular hit of some years ago now, *Moths Ate My Doctor Who Scarf*. I say generally described because I'm in denial about its status as a direct sequel, having thoroughly enjoyed Toby's 2010 show *Now I Know My BBC*, which has been lost a little in the melee. That last show was indeed a 'difficult second album' and although I found every moment of it funny, exciting and engaging, I guess its appeal was never going to be as broad as something with a *Doctor Who* theme. The irony, of course, is that *Moths* and now *My Stepson Stole*

My Screwdriver pride themselves on being aimed equally at *Doctor Who* fans and those who just like a really good laugh.

This new show, for my money, actually exceeds the previous two in both performance, writing and overall enjoyment. Played out in PowerPoint, *Screwdriver* takes us into a variety of tender and beautiful personal moments from Toby's life since the success of *Moths*. We experience his split from his former partner (precipitated by a text that went to the wrong mobile), we meet his children from that marriage (Harry Potter lovers would you believe? Tut.), we meet his new wife and her son who is hearing disabled, we experience Toby's anxieties about his absent and estranged father, and we go to hospital with him when he suffers a debilitating attack of psoriasis. Doesn't necessarily sound funny, does it? But it is – and it's often hilarious.

Non-fans will love the ins and outs of family life and the funny but also wonderfully romantic moments shared between two old friends coming together after 20 years to discover that they are perfect together; but as a *Doctor Who* fan, I have to say that most of my enjoyment came from Toby's acerbic critical assessment of his own fan gene which placed my own (and that of others) into rather stark relief and had me laughing, quite giddily and almost painfully, with self-aware embarrassment throughout. We're a lovely bunch, but god we can be so anal and so selfish – even unashamedly so, and Toby pulls no punches about this.

The show pretty much opens with Toby recalling how thrilled he was after *Remembrance of the Daleks* aired. His non-stop, no breathing, autistically precise recitation of the entire plot of part one had the whole audience in fits. And even though I'm four years older than Toby, my inner geek knew that my 18-year-old brain had been reciting something equally similar and breathless that happy continuity-rich week in 1988.

Okay, so he's unforgivably hard on *The Underwater Menace* (which I know he actually likes) and equally so with *Meglos* (fair enough), but it's nice to know he's picked such stories because they can get a good laugh from the audience (a talking cactus?) and even though they're turkeys, they're way better than The Only Way Is Essex. My wife watched the show with me and when it came to Who facts – of which Toby is a master – she said she suspected he hadn't told me anything I didn't already know. No, he didn't, but the familiarity of them and my identification with him for knowing all the nonsense I know left me – and presumably many others – with a warm geek-reflecting-mirror of a glow.

Throughout, Toby's love for *Doctor Who* and our fannish impulse to wrestle with the thing we love is fully on display. I am particularly fond of the line (when talking about the 'collector's item' screwdriver of the title) 'like a lot of things associated with our experience of *Doctor Who*, it's not to be enjoyed' (I'm paraphrasing, but you get the idea).

Perhaps the high point for me is Toby's description of his engagement with his stepson, and I must confess to a tear of genuine sadness when he describes the moment at which he is watching subtitled *Doctor Who* and the words (Doctor Who Theme) come on screen. His realisation that his stepson will never hear the *Doctor Who* theme tune touched me more deeply than I might have imagined. This piece of music fills the majority of fans with a wonderful sense of anticipation, dread or excitement and it's one of the best bits of music ever recorded (No.3 in *Mojo*'s top electronic music recordings of all time), and it means so much to all of us – it's our national anthem – but it will never be heard by Toby's wonderful young stepson. I'll be surprised if there was a dry eye in the house.

But it's not all hearts and flowers; there are bags and bags of self-deprecating laughs and jokes in here; not just about *Doctor Who*, but about politics and other topical subjects. If you've seen Toby before, you know what to expect, but I'll say this about him – as a performer he's matured a thousandfold in the last two years. He was endearingly bumbling in the last two shows, but here he has a smart, invigorating confidence that works very well indeed. He looks smarter, the show's more focussed and specific and in Edinburgh terms he's in a more suitable venue. His audience interaction is now utterly sublime and contagiously warm. Oh, and the deliberate choice not to use swear words doesn't harm the gags (or the laughter we give them) one jot.

This show is a must-see for all fans of *Doctor Who* and that belly-achy thing we call laughter. Intelligent, charming, incisive, naughty but above all generous and funny – don't let even the Daleks prevent you from seeing this.

Originally published by Kasterborous.com (August, 2012)

REVIEW: Galaxy 4

The Doctor find himself caught up in the struggle between two shipwrecked and ideologically different alien space crews on a planet facing imminent disintegration (presumably somewhere in a galaxy numbered 'four'...).

As the opening story of one of *Doctor Who*'s most experimental and intriguing – some might say 'turbulent' – seasons, *Galaxy 4* begins in an amusing if low key fashion, with Vicki (Maureen O'Brien) giving Steven (Peter Purves) a haircut in the TARDIS console room. Appropriately then, what follows is a story that is neither radical nor ground-breaking, but well told and entertaining.

That said, it does appear to have been made on a relatively small budget, certainly in terms of the incidental music which is the same as that used in *The Web Planet* (albeit with some previously unused passages). The planet itself is realised in studio, mostly through use of painted backcloths, the vistas of which are sometimes a little wrinkled, but still offer a decent impression of vast, parched plains. There are odd-looking plants too with flowers that are 'not quite roses, but almost'; and a caption shot of three suns to groove things up a bit. Richard Hunt's designs are not poor by any standard but generally they are workmanlike and functional, leaving little impression for the long-term.

One does wonder if the Doctor's dismissal of the Drahvin ship as 'trash' is an apology for the (adequate if a little, well, room-shaped) interior set, and a set-up for the particularly un-ship-like construction that is the Rill ship. Or perhaps – given the references to *The Space Museum* – we are meant to imagine Drahva as a tired empire along the lines of Morok. After all, it is over-populated, its 'human born' female elite rule a population of women-products grown in test tubes to fight and kill, while men are kept as slaves...

The Rill ship is intriguing and elegant – but not much of a ship; more like an art installation. Devoid of anything remotely resembling efficient bulkheads, it must have a hell of a force-field arrangement going on, but then the Doctor does describe it as highly advanced. However, its ability to convince is put to the test when Vicki becomes trapped behind its main door in 'Trap of Steel'. The door is described as 'immovable' and it might well be, but it's a foot off the ground and it's got holes in it.

The Rill robots – better known as Chumbleys – resemble tiered, robotic crustaceans or optimistically redesigned woodlice. They have vestigial arms (like their more successful but equally also-ran – or not-even-ran – predecessors the Mechonoids), light-beam guns and are effectively blind. More importantly, though, one of them is played by Angelo Muscat, the ubiquitous butler in ITC's *The Prisoner*.

The Chumbleys are the Rills' robotic avatars, as the Rills themselves are confined to a spaceship 'compartment' due to a biological aversion to the planet's atmosphere. They cannot speak, communicating only by thought ('60s sci-fi short-hand for wisdom and advancement), and their translated communication via the robots is inspired and brilliantly executed, decoding language from Vicki's protests. Even so, Robert Cartland's pontificating Rill Voice (surely a misnomer) is perhaps just a little too fruity (far better if Maureen O'Brien could have done them). The creatures themselves – whose image had all but eluded *Who* historians until recent years – are realised by Daphne Dare through costume; boldly designed but clumsily built, these part-walrus/part-Mr Potato Head beings are very big, but unwieldy and inanimate-looking. One assumes they are judiciously obscured by smoke effects ('ammonia gas') for more than simple plot reasons (much as the Macra will be...). We are told there were originally 12 of them, but eight died in the crash – so it's possible (although perhaps unlikely) that four actual costumes were made for this story.

The Drahvins have great costumes with a lovely '60s white trim, and are white-heat bouffant blondes, all Bingo hall chic with futuristic Bjork-style eyebrows. Not so much 'beautiful' (like the Thals if you squint) as 'attractive'. Idiots, mind – like killer cattle – and terrified of Maaga, their commander. For vegetarians, they are surprisingly bloodthirsty and sadistic. Believing themselves perfect, they view the world from a dogmatic humanoid paradigm, interpreting physical lumpiness, say, and walrus-like attributes as 'evil'. Worse, their whole societal philosophy seems to stem from a kind of inverted of utilitarianism – illustrated by Maaga's willingness to sacrifice one of her own to start a war.

But where does one really begin with Stephanie Bidmead's Maaga? She is precise and clinical; crisply attractive, but fervent and fanatical; a vicious bureaucrat. She perceives friendliness, sacrifice, alliance and honour as alien, almost mythical things to be snarled at and avoided. To Maaga, *Galaxy 4* is all about 'a fight to the death for existence itself', and after playing her opening moments with her back to us, she goes on to regularly display her unabashed mania directly to camera. Her evil and icy speech in 'Air Lock', as she sadistically anticipates the joy she will derive from knowing the Rills have been obliterated, is a revelation. Maaga utterly savours the fear, the horror, the suffering and the death to which she will condemn her foes. The whole piece is played as some Shakespearean soliloquy, with Bidmead moving from camera to camera and boldly staring directly into the viewers' eyes in stark and seductive close-up. Maaga has been overlooked, Whovians. Maaga is a wonderful, wonderful *Doctor Who* villain and we should put her in our Top Ten. Oh, and she immediately knows when the Doctor is lying...

The regular cast is on top form, and let's not forget that this is the first season to open without Ian, Barbara and Susan (this is also the last story with the Doctor in it to be produced by inaugural visionary Verity Lambert). William Hartnell's Doctor is as authoritative and charming as ever, but we discover very little that's new here, other than that he's personally equipped the TARDIS with a force barrier resistant to Rill firepower and can use the TARDIS to jump-start a spaceship. Oh, and that he's not keen on bathing...

This last suggestion is made by Vicki who, feisty as ever, challenges Maaga with the beautifully delivered line: 'You want to kill us, don't you? You want to.' She is also plucky enough to choose herself as the Drahvins' hostage/bargaining chip when the Doctor and Steven must return to the TARDIS. She even gets a crack at an early version of the 'bung a rock at it' gag, later used to better effect by Patrick Troughton in *The Abominable Snowmen*. It is, of course, she who names the robots 'Chumbleys' after their 'chumbling' motion (she has form here; remember 'Sandy' the Sand Beast and 'Zombo' the Zarbi?).

Peter Purves, only three stories in, is already wonderful. He has often remarked that his character fails to emerge in this story because most of his lines were apparently written for former companion Barbara (who left two stories earlier). This might well be true, but one cannot help asking whether some of his material wasn't also intended for Ian. Certainly, the lusty and horribly sexist comments he makes about the Drahvin soldiers in 'Four Hundred Dawns' don't represent the Steven we're going to one day love, but neither would they appear to belong to his predecessors. As evidence for his grievance, Purves' cites the scene in which Steven is overpowered by a woman. But why shouldn't he be bested by the commanding officer of a warrior race that has subjugated all its males? Sadly, until we are again able to see how Derek Martinus directs that sequence, we'll never know if Purves' objections are justified. But I would suggest that Steven has much to do here, often displaying glimpses of the brilliant, honest and direct character that will soon become the solid big brother of Season Three. Mind you, he should get a t-shirt printed for the line: 'I'd rather face the Chumbleys than you any day'.

A lot of reviews dwell on *Galaxy 4*'s apparently thinly-veiled discourse on racial intolerance or its re-iteration of themes perhaps more effectively discussed in *The Daleks*, but the nice thing about *Galaxy 4* is that for over three episodes what it's really about is the confidence to trust. The Drahvins describe the Rills as 'things' that crawl and murder, but they're so evidently bigoted that we just don't believe it. So, when the Rills actually do turn out to be 'things', we are surprised and – in spite of our best liberal intentions – required to pause and check our belief that they might not actually be a threat. For much of the story, they are so oblique and mysterious that there is nothing to certify that they are any less heartless than the Drahvins. But then comes the flashback sequence. It's not unique in this period of the series (see *An Unearthly Child*), but it's certainly a rarity, and is shot 'as live' in another part of the studio during the Rill explanation of events leading to the space-crash and the following conflict which paints Maaga as the prime villain. Note that Maaga does not get a flashback when describing her version of events – blaming the Rills – and I think the technique is employed to help convince the viewer of the Rills' verisimilitude. Pressing the point further is Steven's 'trilemma' at the end of 'Air Lock' and the lynchpin scene (in 'The Exploding Planet') in which he challenges the Rill agenda (see – Purves has loads to do!). It's only here that we genuinely realise the Rills are in fact *the opposite* of the Drahvins. They are willing to die if it means the Doctor will survive: 'The Doctor *must* go, he travels further than we can; and everything ... he stands for is what we believe in. So, it is better that he goes.' All of which is *very* Season Three. And then when all the nice, friendly, good-hearted people have helped each other escape the destruction; the horrible people are left to suffer the consequences of their nastiness.

All in all, a better story than most would have you believe; it won't make any lists because there's other *Doctor Who* that works much harder and is much better, but really all this story lacks are a few more natural, planetary expressions of the impending oblivion to sell the stakes. An earthquake or a rock-fall wouldn't have gone amiss. But it has a great segue into 'Mission to the Unknown', with a proper *Doctor Who* jungle that reeks of Terry Nation and Brian Hodgson; and look, there's that assassin bloke from The Romans saying 'Must kill ... must kill...'

(Kind thanks to Toby Hadoke.)

Originally published by Kasterborous.com (July, 2012)

REVIEW: The Massacre

Against a backdrop of religious persecution in 16th Century Paris, Steven is separated from the Doctor, who then reappears in the guise of an Abbott and is then murdered on the eve of a horrific genocide...

The Massacre is a difficult one to review because, although its soundtrack thankfully remains, it doesn't even have a single telesnap to show us what was what. Thankfully there are a number of production stills, which allow me to say Daphne Dare's costumes are lovely and Michael Young's sets are serviceable but cramped; even so, I am left me with less to review than I would normally like. I can only hope the entire programme is as excellent as its relics would seem to suggest.

And yet, even before anything particularly dramatic has happened, The Massacre is instantly atmospheric; the simple ambient sounds of Paris, offering an undercurrent of tension, possibly because they recall and conjure the similar atmospheres of *The Reign of Terror.*

Delightfully, the Doctor (William Hartnell) and Steven (Peter Purves) go native, raiding the TARDIS wardrobe for the right period costumes, looking up historical figures (germinologist Charles Preslin) and hanging out in bars. 'Landlord, wine,' demands the Doctor, as if entirely at home in Paris (a consequence perhaps of his untelevised adventures during the Terror...). Yet, before we know it, an innocent trip into the history of science sees Steven dragged into a world of spies, corruption and horrible tensions over superstitious practice. We are thrust into the narrative without a map or guide and expected to cope – which is refreshingly adult. The Preslin storyline doesn't dumb down at all (and despite his obfuscations, the Doctor recognises the apothecary immediately), while the court politics and intrigues, although more complex than we are used to, are engagingly and wittily presented; at one point as a debate about wine. Whichever writer is most responsible for *The Massacre* (Donald Tosh or John Lucarotti) he is supremely confident of its subject.

Apart from Preslin (*The Deadly Assassin*'s Erik Chitty) and the fabulous, corrupt Landlord (Edward Finn), the guest cast fall into two simple camps: Catholics and Huguenots. Both sides are full of hot-headed bullies; the ostensibly sympathetic underdog Huguenots for example are not even close to being as likeable or sympathetic as Renan's rebels in *The Reign of Terror*. Nicholas Muss (David Weston) is obviously pleasant enough, but Gaston (Eric Thompson) is horribly arrogant. At the top of the political tree are a pair of solid performances from the wonderful Leonard Sachs as Admiral de Coligny and the utterly brilliant Leonard Sachs as Marshall Tavannes; actors who bring such great conviction to the story that, certainly in theatrical terms, they place this story on a higher plane than most other *Doctor Who* of this period. Also bringing weight are the royals. Charles IX (Barry Justice) is a bit of a mummy's boy – more interested in playing tennis than governing his people – allowing his bigoted, fundamentalist-Catholic matriarch to rules from the side-lines. Unfortunately, Catherine De Medici (Joan Young), much like Maaga in *Galaxy 4*, is utterly merciless and determined to have every opponent die to fulfil her selfish, narrow ambitions.

But the specifics of the historical situation don't actually matter; what really matters is that, separated from the Doctor, Steven is adrift in a time of perilous and potentially deadly turmoil, utterly unable to exert any kind of tempering control. Before long, a casual drink at an inn leads to his having to prove to his new friends that he's not conspiring against them. Throughout this story, every fact or truth Steven accepts falls away and begins to make less and less sense.

Most commentaries would have it that The Massacre is Steven's story and that's quite right, because the Doctor is absent for much of it. But it's a mistake to imagine this is any less Hartnell's story than Purves'. I'll digress for a moment, by pointing out that each episode of *The Massacre* opens without reprise and commences on the day after that of the previous episode. And it seems to do this in order to confound the audience's ability to control or quantify what it's seeing. This story, you see, is not without some cracking cliff-hangers... 'War of God' ends astonishingly, when the previously unseen face of the Abbot of Amboise is revealed to be that of the Doctor. I mean: WOAH! Did we really see that? I don't know, they're not showing us it again, and now it's the next day; things are moving fast, and this is how Steven must feel...

When Steven meets the Abbot (William Hartnell), he sees the same thing – it's the Doctor. He might not be telling us why he's disguised as the Abbot, but we, like Steven, trust that there must be some grand method in his madness. What he's up to, we have no idea, but there can be little doubt that this is he, particularly when he excuses his staff in order to be alone with Steven. I've heard it said that Hartnell gives an astounding performance that is utterly unlike his Doctor, but I would disagree. The Abbot is pretty much just a stilted version of the Doctor at his most imperious (he even says 'Very well' like the Doctor). The thing is, though, he *needs* to be like the Doctor for Steven's confusion to work. Unlike Patrick Troughton's Salamander, say, the Abbot has to come across as a set of performance choices the Doctor would make if pretending to be a high Catholic official. In short, we, like Steven, have to believe that this *is* the Doctor, and until episode four, we have no reason to believe otherwise...

The deteriorating situation for the Abbot, following Steven's discovery of the plot to assassinate Tavannes, only serves to reinforce our conviction that we are watching the Doctor becoming hoist on his own petard. It reads for all the world as if he is caught up in some unexplained intrigue that has quite spiralled beyond his limited control. When he is killed in 'Priest of Death', we are as shocked as Steven to see his body lying disregarded in a Parisian gutter. In a time before regeneration, this must have been the best, most shocking cliff-hanger ever: the Doctor is dead! Actually dead.

When it is revealed in the following episode that the Abbot *wasn't* the Doctor, I have no idea if it feels like a cheat or not. What I do know is that your brain does a funny thing when he walks in for the first time since the first episode: for an instant you're scared that the Abbot has returned, and then your brain says 'Oh, Hartnell's back from his fishing then...', which in itself might say a lot about how truly effective an actor he's been in this story (and will be again, for different reasons, in *The Gunfighters*). When he does return, he gives no explanation as to what he's been up to; he is however fully aware of the historical importance of this particular St Bartholomew's Day – unlike the contemporary viewer who has no idea that these four episodes will one day obtain the umbrella title of *The Massacre*. Thus, 14 minutes into 'Bell of Doom', the massacre storyline abruptly ends. The Doctor sends Steven's new friend Anne Chaplette (Annette Robertson) to find safety with her persecuted people just as the massacre – realised through woodcut depictions of the slaughter and martial music – begins. The question is 'Does Anne survive?' Even new companion Dodo 'A Taste of Honey' Chaplet's arrival doesn't answer this question adequately, although Jackie Lane looks enough like Robertson to be a convincing descendant.

But this brings us to something magical. Steven's belief that that something could have been done to avert the massacre sets itself against the Doctor's conviction that he could not alter this 'terrible page of the past'. 'I cannot change the course of history,' takes us right back to his arguments with Barbara in *The Aztecs*. Steven is also dismayed that Anne appears to have been beneath the Doctor's notice.

His decision to leave brings with it the contemptuous line, 'If your ... 'researches' ... have so little regard for human life, then I want no part.' And maybe he's not merely thinking of doomed companion-that-never-was Anne but also of those other companions-that-never-were: Katarina, Bret Vyon and Sara Kingdom. And maybe he's also thinking of Vicki, all but abandoned to history.

And with Steven gone, the Doctor's own convictions hang heavy upon his aged shoulders. Hurt at Steven's suggestion that he is responsible for history's wrongs, he sits alone amid the humming, tick-tock clockwork of the TARDIS; truly alone for the first time in the series. Introspective and empty, he misses his former companions, none of whom were able to understand the limits of his involvement in the temporal universe (not even Susan); all of them, in his opinion, too impatient to get back to their own times. 'Perhaps I should go home, back to my own planet,' he says. 'But I can't.' The old time-traveller is weary and broken. 'I can't.'

What more can I tell you? This is a sophisticated and intelligent piece of *Doctor Who* performed by two of its best ever regulars and a sparkling guest cast. Let's hope we all live long enough to see it returned to the BBC vaults.

Originally published by Kasterborous.com (July, 2012)

OPINION: Kisses to the Future – a vision for the 50th anniversary

A few months ago, I had a bit of a brainwave about *Doctor Who*'s impending 50th anniversary. People were beginning to wonder how the series might best celebrate itself within its own narrative and none of the ideas that were coming up thrilled me very much as a long-time fan. The much talked about meeting of five Doctors at a recent convention has only fuelled the notion of another multi-Doctor story in the vein of *The Three Doctors* and its offspring, something that in practical terms seems like a bit of a non-starter, something potentially disappointing and, more significantly, something a bit retrograde. So, what *are* the best and most forward-looking options within the programme's narrative, I wondered. And that's when I had what I think would be a great idea, which, just for fun, I'd like to share with you.

Actually, I shared my idea in a letter to *Doctor Who Magazine*. *DWM* very kindly printed it, but, well, only half of it. I have no argument at all with their editorial policy – I love that magazine and won't hear a word against it. However, they didn't print the meat of the matter, so here it is in full (with a few extras thrown in).

Been thinking/worrying about the notion of a multi-Doctor story for the 50th anniversary. In 1966 when Patrick Troughton became a second Doctor rather than a poor impersonation of the first, an unwritten rule of the show came into play (that if the lead actor could no longer play the role, then his Doctor would be discontinued and a new one would replace him) and, ever since, each actor to play the role has done it his own way, his name becoming synonymous with his Doctor's number.

To this end, I would suggest that the first three Doctors are irreplaceable, and should remain so. Having them played by other actors (physically or vocally) in some anniversary special would defeat the object of what was achieved at the end of The Tenth Planet *(and in 1983's* The Five Doctors *it wasn't immediately obvious to those of us who had no access to older stories how utterly unlike Hartnell Richard Hurndall's performance actually was). Additionally, the remaining Doctors from the series' original run look like very different men now. With pretend Doctors and unrecognisable Doctors what would any of it really mean? The point of the celebration would become lost under the weight of its own wibbly-wobbly convolutions. So, might I suggest that the kind of multi-Doctor story we're used to might not be the best way to celebrate the series – especially a series that continues to stride ever forward.*

This is where *DWM* cut me off, but we can continue here (again with extras).

So, I have three suggestions. Kisses to the past: a Back to the Future *style romp in which the eleventh Doctor and co are caught up in some wibbly-wobbly madness that has them interacting 'behind the scenes' with classic episode footage from each era of the programme (lost in Skaro's Dalek city at the same time as the first Doctor, etc). We already had something of a practice run when we watched Matt Smith dancing with Laurel and Hardy, so the technology is available; and new versions of old sets and costumes could allow us to have parallel stories running alongside adventures we believed we knew intimately – what a joy to see them subverted. It'd be great fun, and wouldn't corrupt our memories of the series (but what a thrill if it could challenge them).*

The second option, kisses to the present, would involve casting previous Doctor actors in new roles, knowing cameos (I fancy Tom Baker as the Doctor's father in this scenario) – but that doesn't help if you're a fan of the first three Time Lords.

Better by far, is the really big idea: kisses to the future. Let the Doctor discover the 12 regenerations thing really is nonsense and isn't going to apply to him, this will allow the series a scope that's been hitherto unprecedented. This will give us an opportunity to have a multi-Doctor story with, for example, the 600th Doctor, the 950th Doctor, the Millionth Doctor, and loads of other far-into-the-future Doctors we're in no danger of ever seeing in this (or any other) lifetime. Perhaps they come back to prevent their potential erasure from the timeline; quantum Doctors if you will. What a spectacular opportunity to use today's top actors, preferably those who'd never get a crack at the part under normal circumstances – women, older actors, teen actors, huge stars, all those people who've been dying to give it a go – and maybe even old TV Doctors in new versions of their previous bodies (imagine white haired Tom Baker as the Millionth Doctor), giving us a new take on the character (thus providing that 'something wittier' that Tom seems to want). It would be a confirmation of the show's on-going, forward-thinking agenda, and it would also open up merchandise and spin-off opportunities. An active multiverse of spin-off Doctors available alongside the incumbent TV Doctor would be a hugely commercial new take on the series. To steal a title, it could be called The Infinity Doctors. *And wouldn't it be brilliant?*

Am I mad, or does the third option sound like the *real* way forward *Doctor Who* needs? I think this would see the series' time-travel basis, so crazily broadened under Steven Moffat, expand to finally reach its true potential.

Originally published in *K-Mag* (June, 2012)

REVIEW: The Web Planet

Caught up in the struggle to free a once magnificent world from the cancerous clutches of a life-sucking spider, the Doctor and his companions are set upon and aided by four species of outer space insect-people...

The Web Planet is *Doctor Who* Marmite (Garmite? Maramite? Kate O'Maramite?) – some love it, some hate it. This, as if you didn't know, is the story that probably had Sydney 'No BEMs' Newman choking on his Camp because it's the only *Doctor Who* story ever made in which every 'non-regular' character is a 'monster' in full monster suit, with monster mannerisms, monster dialects, monster shuffles and monster bleeps. Apparently, it's a tough watch if you think *Doctor Who* should be more like *Star Wars* or *Star Trek* (or any other inappropriate comparison series with 'star' or 'space' in the title). It's also been alleged that the costumes look stagey and theatrically literal; the performances seem over-the-top and strange; the sets look cramped and flat. But *The Web Planet* – what a title! – is quite possibly the most outstanding and expressionistic example of imagination and creativity in the series' black and white period, and everything about it is designed to scream 'alien' or 'bizarre'.

From the opening of the eponymous first episode, it is clear that this is something the series hasn't done before. The 'atmosphere' of Vortis is made visible on screen thanks to liberal smearings of Vaseline across the camera lenses (allegedly), lending a glaucomic otherness to the place; there are strange aurora borealis-like lights in the sky; voices echo oddly across the landscape; stock music sounds like it has literally been beamed in from another world (the music sounds *so* like Vortis that when it turned up the 1973 series *The Lotus Eaters*, this reviewer fully expected giant ants to enslave the ex-pat populace of Crete!).

John Woods' planet sets suffer slightly from being painted backcloths and flat-looking outcrops, otherwise there is much to see and enjoy here. The Carsenome is fittingly dark and claustrophobic, while the temple of light is modestly but effectively realised, with director Richard Martin shooting actors through apertures in the set to allow for weird pictures (with some shots seemingly taken from above). There's also a huge TARDIS control room the likes of which we haven't seen for a while and the menacing hum of its environs is actually quite unsettling. On the subject of the TARDIS, it's worth mentioning the stuff that no longer grabs our attention but should be noted for its inventiveness. We take for granted the ease with which the Doctor and Ian bring the Astral Map from the Ship, but in reality, it's too cumbersome and large to fit through the police box prop doors, so Martin achieves the transition by use of a clever, but unfussy camera angle (the kind of thing that will be employed all the time when K9 joins the series). This sort of thing gets lost because we're too busy watching poor John Scott Martin bump into the cameras (What's that? You'd condemn a whole story for that?!).

Of course, what we're really looking at in this story is the 'monsters'. The Zarbi (bi-Zar – get it?) are stunningly realised gi-ants with mammalian hind legs who look their best in film sequences, most notably when the TARDIS is stolen. The weirdest thing about them is that Richard Martin chooses to reveal them so early. Then again, he has more than one card to play and the first sight of a Menoptra is all the more startling for being full-on. These part-man/part-bee/part-caterpillar/part-moth people are a triumph of Daphne Dare's expressionist costume design (foreshadowing the work of such later luminaries as Jim Acheson) – and Sonia Markham's make-up design is also beautiful. The Optera are also excellently costumed – with compound eyes no less! Both of the more 'humanoid' races benefit from Roslyn de Winter's quirky 'insect movement' and the accompanying vocal tics which see the aliens use innovative bastardisations of the lead characters' names and speak in evocative and metaphorical language patterns.

Throughout this story it's just as much the spectacle you can't see as the spectacle you can – writer Bill Strutton paints great mental images: a sky full of moons; thousands of bee-people massing a space fleet above Vortis; long-lost flower forests. There is some genuine world-building going on, both on screen and in the dialogue ('light was our god'; 'silent walls'; 'speak more light'). Even so, there are plenty of action sequences. The best part of the whole story comes when the Menoptra attack force lands. It's a great battle sequence and the Menoptra look incredible in beautifully designed cowls and silvery facial close-ups.

The best cliff-hanger comes at the end of the best episode, 'Invasion', and sees the Doctor and Vicki mummified in alien web – one of *Doctor Who*'s most horrifying images so far. And this is another thing those who don't rate this story tend to forget: it can be scary; it can be horrifying. Yes, the Carsenome sounds like an end of the pier amusement arcade where someone's always scoring three cherries; yes, the sight of Menoptra leaping about yelling 'Zar-bi!' is a bit silly, but a lot of what happens here is quite mature and well thought out. The clipping of Menoptran wings is very disturbing; the death of the Larvae Guns (Venom Grubs to you Target fans!) when crushed against walls or under other creatures is quite grisly; Nemeni's dutiful self-sacrifice is particularly moving and comes as a shock on first viewing; and let's not forget the deliciously remote and horribly voracious vocal talents of Catherine Fleming as that proto-Great Intelligence, the Animus.

William Hartnell's Doctor remains wonderfully charismatic. He might seem odd to modern audiences who like their heroes young and pretty, but his definitive Time Lord is truly alien, truly mysterious. His reactions in any situation are amazing and never by the book (see the scene with Ian's pen). Hartnell always does his own thing, pushing his character in strange and alien directions. He's clever enough to know that even though he's not always line-perfect (there are many Billy-fluffs in this story) he will win the battle to convince us of the Doctor's deep and powerful intelligence by skilful use of his darting eyes. And he does. Oh, and his despair when the TARDIS is 'lost' at the end of episode one is tangible.

Ian is brilliant, as usual. William Russell is a master of intimate naturalism and is wonderfully tender and supportive when encouraging the Doctor to remove his Atmospheric Density Jacket; taking the smallest scene and bringing it to life. He is a great, great actor. As always, he gets to do plenty of action hero stuff, but his finest moment comes at the start of 'The Zarbi', when Ian emerges from his web-weed induced slumber. He is clearly disturbed by the experience and seems, for once, oddly un-heroic and it is fascinating to see his vulnerabilities exposed like this.

Barbara (Jacqueline Hill) is also as splendid as ever. Her resourcefulness knows no bounds as she leads the Menoptra to victory and one cannot help but feel that the spirit of Yetaxa lives on in her. She is the heart and energy of this TARDIS crew and it's lovely to see that her need to spring clean the TARDIS' instruments shows how much the Ship has become her home. Early on, there are lots of lovely character moments between Barbara and new girl Vicki (Maureen O'Brien), highlighting their cultural differences and picking up on matters left over from the last two stories, re-emphasising *Doctor Who*'s on-going serial nature.

At one point, Ian refers to Vicki as 'that kid', making you wonder if he actually likes her yet – or maybe he's just jealous of her instantly special place in the Doctor's affections? She is, after all, a better foil for the Doctor than Susan was.

All the regulars play to their strengths and get something meaty to do, each one contributing something valuable to the liberation of Vortis.

So, would *The Web Planet* be better if it had been filmed in a quarry? No. Would it be improved by having humanoids rather than alien insects? No. Now if you're of a mind to do so, it is possible to interpret this adventure as more like Lewis Carroll than Arthur C Clarke and use that as a stick to beat the story with. But it was possible for *Doctor Who* to come to a place like this in 1965. And *how* original and brave is this even then? Perhaps we just don't give *The Web Planet* the love and respect it deserves because we've always had it. If we hadn't seen it since 1965 and it turned up tomorrow in a boot sale we'd be evangelists praising its originality and its verve. We might have been all along – and let's be honest, if nothing else, it's always going to be better than *The Celestial Toymaker*. Given the scope of its technical ambition, it's a miracle that it's as good as it is.

Its images and textures, its electronic sounds, watery music and expressionist performances are actually very beautiful – if you allow them to be. We sometimes run away from it because everything about it is 'alien', but isn't that what the series set out to be? And it's BIG – actually BIG – on the screen BIG, in the TARDIS BIG, in the Carsenome BIG; in its ambition BIG. And, by and large, it all works. In the context of all of *Doctor Who*, *The Web Planet* is unparalleled. It is quite possibly the most imaginative *Doctor Who* story ever made and sometimes, when no-one's looking and it can just get on with being brilliant, it might even be the best.

Originally published by Kasterborous.com (June, 2012)

REVIEW: *Marco Polo*

After 13 episodes of (essentially) sci-fi adventure, the time travellers find themselves in the 13th Century, where TARDIS (no definite article) is taken as a prize for the mighty Kublai Khan by Venetian merchant Marco Polo. Forced to follow it and him on a perilous six-month journey across medieval Asia, they befriend bride-to-be Ping-Cho and fall foul of the scheming warlord Tegana...

Fan convention has it that this is the series' first true 'historical' story, but this wouldn't have been obvious at the time – after three months of sci-fi scares, who's to say that some big ugly BEM won't pop up at any second? That no such thing occurs is a matter for hindsight, but in 1964 this was a series where anything could happen at any moment, and given the time travellers' anachronistic presence in the Polo caravan this story is just as sci-fi as anything we've seen so far. In the consistently magical world of exploration and explanation that is David Whitaker's *Doctor Who*, a journey along the Silk Road to Cathay is just as alien as any expedition across Skaro. Venusians/Venetians – what's the difference?

For the first time in the series, Barbara (Jacqueline Hill) is in her history teaching element, often ahead of the others when it comes to understanding Polo and his travels (although much of what occurs here is actually the fantasy of writer John Lucarotti). While strong and outspoken, she endures a horrible scene in which bandits play dice to win the cutting of her throat. Meanwhile, Ian (William Russell) uses his science know-how to educate the viewer regarding the boiling point of water at high altitude and the use of bamboo firecrackers in scaring off baddies. He has also warmed to the Doctor, showing admiration for his kidnapper's technical abilities.

Despite making amends with his companions at the end of the previous story, the Doctor (William Hartnell) is as antagonistic as ever in episodes 1 – 5. Often ill, he contributes very little to the thrust of the tale and is overcome by bouts of hysteria whenever the pickle he finds himself in goes from irretrievably bad to irretrievably worse. In the last two episodes, Hartnell settles into comedy mode – perhaps for the first time –charming himself both into the company of the great and the good (another first) and a delightful double-act with Martin Miller's irascible Kublai Khan. Built up over five episodes as the 'warlord of warlords, mighty and ruthless in his strength', the Khan is the perfect character to bring out the Doctor's lighter side: a withered, gambling administrator, suffering with gout and a comedy accent.

Susan – now saying things like 'fab', 'crazy' and 'I dig it' – is the most pro-active regular in this story; she wants to get on with escaping. Her friendship with Ping-Cho (Zienia Merton) is the bedrock of this tale and serves as a medium for the idea that most of the characters in this story are exiles. 'I've had many homes in many places,' she tells us, and her home is 'as far away as a night star', but she's not the only one who's lost now. We know the Doctor is lost in the fourth dimension and that Ian and Barbara are castaways from 1963, but Polo cannot return to Venice and Ping-Cho misses Samarkand. The underlying theme of Season One is writ large here – a bunch of people have been cut off from home and they want to get back, yes, one day. Here, perhaps more than in any other story, TARDIS is the key to that ambition.

Mark Eden's titular performance is solemn and noble; a fair man – a man of words (narrating and documenting the adventure) – and more advanced than the Doctor's insults will allow. He has strength and integrity, but is desperate to use TARDIS – a 'magic caravan' – to bargain for his freedom. That he is effectively 'owned' by the Khan causes him much anguish; it's his whole life. Ironically, the Khan sees Polo as nothing more than a trifle; a petty inconvenience to be hurried along. Ultimately, it is fitting that Polo realises his selfishness in taking TARDIS and placing his own pains upon its crew. Quickly afterwards, he prevents Tegana's assassination of the Khan (using Tegana's own weapon – the sword – against him) and sets our heroes free – all at the risk of his own life.

Tegana is *Doctor Who*'s first proper villain. Dark and bearded, all charm and supressed violence, this old sly-boots is a prototype Master, imbued with 'the power of persuasion'. To him, the Doctor is a magician who should be staked through the heart. His indignant appeal to Polo when Barbara accuses him of lying is a master class of deceit and manipulation. Derren Nesbitt plays his silent menace for keeps, and there won't be another villain like this until *Galaxy Four*. It's also worth noting that he may be a user of prostitutes. In 'The Wall of Lies' Polo calls a curfew, and Tegana discreetly tells him, 'I want to go into town'. It's an innocuous line, but delivered to suggest a matter of delicacy; Eden plays Polo's response with complicit understanding.

Even counting the Thals, these new characters are the strongest since 'An Unearthly Child' and, effectively, become regulars during this sci-fi road movie; it's beautifully unsettling then that they are swiftly and unceremoniously left behind as the story ends.

Obviously, we're unable to see this story now, but one expects it will look as good as it sounds. Waris Hussein returns for 6 of the 7 episodes (episode 4 is directed by John Crockett) and given that 100,000 BC is a staggering piece of television, then this is just as likely to follow suit. Some of Barry Newbery's desert sets are no doubt cramped (with floors of sacking covered in sand) making them perhaps only as effective as those in, say, *The Chase*. The cave of Five Hundred Eyes looks suitably spooky and garish, but the Khan's palace is unlikely to live up to the ostentatious requirements made of it. The way-stations at Lop, Tun Huang and Cheng-Ting are perhaps more successful, although these are all redressed versions of the same set, becoming more exotic the closer they are to the palace (Cheng-Ting features hanging gardens and a fish pond). Props and costumes are beautifully designed and the companions look great in Oriental garb. Polo's palace robe looks very much like it might be re-used by Michael Gough in Season Three...

Perhaps certain special effects might fall short of some expectations. The sandstorm is achieved, not by chucking lots of sand about and turning a fan on, but by electronic camera interference akin to TV static. It is accompanied by radiophonic howls which are exactly as Ian describes them: 'like all the devils in hell'. Perfect *Doctor Who* if you ask me! Throughout the story, Tristram Cary's music vacillates between electronic throbbery and more tuneful works that are beguiling and magical, telling us just as much about the medieval as they do the Orient.

John Lucarotti does a marvellous job of off-screen world building, placing us in a land where monks levitate cups of wine and evil spirits disguise themselves as men. It often puts me in mind of the novelisation of *The Crusades*, and has me wondering how much of this story belongs to script editor David Whitaker (later editors suggest Lucarotti's scripts needed much work); the language is poetic, often ethereal and dreamlike – not just the Asia stuff but also the talk of metal seas on Venus – and, as with *The Crusades*, the female characters are incredibly strong. The Ian of this story is the future knight of Jaffa; in his attempts to escape and regain the freedom of TARDIS, it is only the fateful interference of others that prevents him from resorting to desperate measures like hostage-taking or even murder. *Marco Polo* also introduces the series' first three deliberately comic characters: Khan, Empress (Claire Davenport) and the amusingly named Wang-lo (Gabor Baraker) who bears more than a passing resemblance to Whitaker's own Ben Daheer. Whitaker's educational remit is here, too, with viewer lessons in arranged marriage, altitude sickness, condensation and chess (the origin of the phrase 'checkmate' grows in import as the story develops).

Whoever's responsible, this is a beautiful story – a glimpse of *Doctor Who* as it might have been, but never would be. It's full of magical moments: the Doctor showing his affinity for the young as he shares beansprout soup with Ping-Cho; Susan and Barbara bonding in the Gobi desert ('One day we'll know all the mysteries of the skies and stop our wandering'); the backgammon match in which the Doctor wins a staggering amount of livestock (and, more wonderfully, 'all the commerce from Burma for one year'). The best cliff-hanger is that of episode 4 when Ian finds that the guard *he might just have to kill* is already dead. The best scene, however, belongs to Ping-Cho and the storytelling sequence in 'Five Hundred Eyes'. Her story of the Al-Qaeda-like Hashashins adds little to the plot (though it possibly foreshadows Tegana's intentions), but it adds *everything* to the atmosphere and environment of this epic and sparkling adventure. It is a highlight not just of Season One, but of all *Doctor Who*.

Originally published by Kasterborous.com (May, 2012)

REVIEW: Missing Believed Wiped, 2011

I was at the BFI last Sunday (December 11, 2011), for the annual *Missing Believed Wiped* event, where recently recovered 'lost' TV gems are shown to a live audience. I went on the back of a tip from a very good friend who, one happy West End evening in October, urged me to go along because it would be of interest to me and as he did, I sensed he was talking about *Doctor Who*. So, I did.

The place was packed, and I was glad to have booked my ticket a month earlier. It quickly became clear that my tipping friend (unable to make it due to work commitments) had been on to something. Many of the great and the good of the *Doctor Who* fan firmament were in attendance, including: Mark Gatiss, Rob Shearman, Tom Spilsbury, Peter Ware, Gary Gillat, Ben Cook, oh and that Elton Townend Jones of course. Something about smoke and fire...

I'd never been into NFT1 before, but what a lovely venue for such a special occasion; plush red velvet everywhere and very well kept. The buzz in the room was wonderful, and according to Dick Fiddy (the event's organiser) it was much fuller than would usually be the case for such an event. Amazing what a whiff of *Doctor Who* will do. Looking down the programme sheet, I must admit I began to feel a little nervous: a Dennis Potter play (*Emergency Ward 9*), some long forgotten TV puppetry, a dreadful ITV drama about the US press corps (the audience were in tears throughout) and some lost Pete and Dud. Each piece had about a paragraph devoted to it, but nothing was mentioned about *Doctor Who*. The closest it got was a sentence at the bottom of the page: 'BBC sci-fi clips'. Could that be what I hoped it might be? If all these fan-folk were here, then surely it must mean a recovered 'lost' episode?

In the event it was two episodes. Ralph Montagu, who had liberated these gems from an '80s boot sale or some such, had captured lightning in a bottle. Twice. Briefly MC-ing the introduction to these recovered gems, Mark Gatiss did a fine job of keeping us in suspense, snatching the mic away from Ralph if it ever seemed possible that he might reveal episode titles; wisely leaving the programme itself to let us know what we were watching.

I think now it's probably time to get all *Tomb of the Cybermen* on you. When that story was recovered in 1992, those of us who'd been told it was the unassailable Best Story Ever immediately saw reasons why it might not be and perhaps felt a little disappointed. I daresay that if, like me, you were one of these people, you have since come to re-evaluate this tale and now see it as one of the finest examples of a '60s story. This is worth bearing in mind as I describe what we saw today...

As the titles began, we knew we were in Hartnell territory (and I must add that at this point we only thought one episode had been recovered). The first image in this episode – *Galaxy Four*: 'Air Lock' – is that of a vast Rill, a creature whose image had all but eluded *Who* historians until recent years. It is big, but unwieldy and inanimate looking. Then, Vicki finds herself cut off from the Doctor by a wonderfully designed door, but fails to notice that it would be very easy to slip under it as it rests about a foot from the floor. Or to climb through one of the big holes it is full of. In response, the Doctor gets to work on trying to solve the problem, whilst fumbling his lines. But I'm cool with 'Billy-fluffs' (so cool I even made a drinking game out of them). That's what happens in Hartnell stories, I accept that. But do you know what? 'Air Lock' may not be a highly regarded classic, but it's wonderful to see 'new' scenes of the original (and probably definitive) Doctor moving around on an elegantly designed BBC world. And the Chumbleys have arms – I never knew that! Most thrilling of all is Maaga, leader of the warrior Drahvins. Stephanie Bidmead looked great on the surviving 6 minutes of 'Four Hundred Dawns', and sounded great on the audio, but to see her deliver her evil and icy speech, as she sadistically anticipates the joy she will derive from knowing the Rills have been obliterated was a revelation. The whole piece is played as some Shakespearean soliloquy, with Bidmead moving from camera to camera and boldly staring directly into the viewers' eyes in stark and seductive close-up. Maaga has been overlooked, Whovians. Maaga is a wonderful, wonderful *Doctor Who* villain and we should put her in our Top Ten.

And then the picture stopped. We all gasped. Mark Gatiss assured that the episode did exist in full, it's just that there was little time in which to show it as it turned out Ralph Montagu had also found another episode, which we would now see in full – *The Underwater Menace* Episode 2. Not that we knew that when the titles started (still the old Hartnell sequence, see?), but I was overjoyed when I saw what it was. There aren't many of us *Underwater Menace* fans about, you know.

Again, most people are never going to love this story, but if Maaga was a lesson in what we don't see when we listen to the audios, then this was a master class. One word? Troughton. I love all the Doctors, but the second hasn't been one of my favourites for a long time. I recognise Troughton's accomplishment as an actor, but I never felt like I knew his Doctor very well. Like he didn't develop. But his performance in this episode is so full and busy and rich, it really does make you wonder how manic his work in *Power of the Daleks* and *The Highlanders* must be. Certainly, by the time we get to *The Moonbase* he seems to have calmed down – or maybe it's just the full-on nature of this particular story that he's responding to? He is always watching, his eyes dart all over the place assessing the strengths and weaknesses of his foes. He does an incredible bit of business when knocking at his head like it's a door and looking to see if anyone's home as a way of proving how mad Zaroff is. He even dresses in a sou'wester and spends a quarter of the episode looking like a barmy old fisherman before diving happily into ceremonial robes and the most outrageous bit of headgear you'll ever seen him in. 'I would like a hat like that', indeed.

So that's two new episodes back. Maybe the mainstream wanted *Tenth Planet* 4 or *Daleks' Master Plan* 12, and maybe the obscurists wanted *The Massacre* or *The Myth Makers*. It never seemed to occur to me that we might get episodes from the stories we once considered Who's b-movies. But we did. And although these are not 'classics', it is wonderful to see old Doctors in what for many of us are new situations. I mean, to actually see them, and watch them move and speak. When these episodes finally see commercial release we're all going to see something new and exciting in them, but based on the performances of Bidmead and Troughton in these two gems, I find myself reconsidering what classic might actually mean. I can't wait to see them again.

(With thanks to Robert Lewis and Toby Hadoke)

Originally published by Kasterborous.com (December, 2011)

REVIEW: The Wedding of River Song

As usual, I came to *The Wedding of River Song* with no knowledge of what to expect, so I had no wild imaginings as to what this season finale might contain; certainly, no imaginings as wild as those of Mr Moffat.

As episodes go (and we're forced by the narrative construction of recent instalments to use the term 'episode' over 'story') this one was filled to the brim with ideas and images. You couldn't fault it for scope and imagination: from vistas of a London where all Time is happening at once (a very literal interpretation, but a fun one nonetheless), through dark caverns full of hungry and curious skulls to Egypt's Area 52 with its cells full of Silence, this one had it all.

Opening in an elegiac and downbeat manner, the story unfurled to reunite us with recent friends and elements from recent episodes, whilst also spoiling us with mentions of Rose Tyler and Captain Jack. I adored the smashed-up Dalek and got a lump in my throat at news of the Brigadier's demise. This lump grew large enough to force a tear when this revelation tipped the Doctor over the melancholy edge, thus revealing the true extent of his affection for an old friend.

But even though this episode was an ambitious and colourful selection box, it reminded me of over-indulgent Christmas Days as a child, where, unconstrained by the usual rules built into my life, I would glut myself on presents, sweets, TV, puddings and chocolate and come away feeling exactly as I do now – thrilled and bewildered; perhaps even a little regretful and tired.

The Wedding of River Song looked great and it certainly entertained, but was it the best way to tell the story it wanted to tell? Placing the action in a universe that never happened fails to provide solid ground upon which to support an audience's suspended disbelief. It's the reset button in reverse, almost. Nothing of consequence can truly happen in an alternate timeline. Or rather, anything and everything a writer can imagine is free to happen, but with no meaningful consequence. Did the Doctor and River Song get married in any real sense? And, while we're at it, did they even care that they did/didn't? (I'm still not entirely sure why they did/didn't, or why indeed River even thinks she loves him.)

I'm not keen on reviewers who offer opinions on what they wanted a story to be, rather I'd prefer they (and I) dealt with what they saw and looked for the good in it, but I'll fall into the trap and let myself down by simply suggesting that what we got tonight was wonderful but also unnecessarily convoluted. This was an explosion in a story factory (and well done to Moffat for being able to explode so colourfully), a Doctor Who fever dream; but something a little more focussed and a little more specific might have been the real order of the day. It was like a pastiche of a Russell T Davies series finale (don't get me started on the 'Tick-tock' rhyme contrivance), a mad, sugar-high dash from A to B that tripped around the houses, lying to its audience and opting for the simple get-out-jail option that we'd all predicted ten minutes into this season (back in April): 'it wasn't really the Doctor who was killed, folks'. Not the bravest choice for a brave programme with a history of brave stories.

I don't want to have to say this, because I had fun while it was on, but it really did feel like it had been made up as it went along, didn't it? I don't offer any judgement on that being a good thing or a bad thing, but I observe it – and you probably do too. We're now in an era of Doctor Who in which the question 'What pictures are weird?' has over-taken the question 'What ideas are weird?'; a series where the ideas fit the image rather than the other way around. This may be a bold experiment that takes us to some wonderful places. It may well be. I hope so.

Whatever my misgivings, *The Wedding of River Song* was a crazy, fun-filled romp to cap a mixed bag of a season – the best aspects of which have continued to be Matt Smith and the general 'look' of the show – and even featured some teasing 'revelations' regarding the Doctor's future. For all the joy I take from such teasing, I still say it's a shame when the best bits of an episode are the bits that have little to do with the current narrative and are there merely to trail an episode somewhere up ahead. In this case, it turns out (again) that the Doctor's going to die (again) – which means he'll probably just send a pretend version of himself along to take the hit and avoid the whole thing, because he can do that now there are no rules. 'I'm faking my own deaths now. Faking my own deaths is cool.' Already then, probably a good two years before we even see it, his impending death just doesn't matter. Hopefully it'll be made to matter by having him (quite sadly) regenerate. And you all knew that the oldest question, hidden in plain sight was 'Doctor Who?' didn't you? Of course you did. I'd have been gutted if it had been anything else. Oh, and speculate all you like, kids, you'll never be told.

In conclusion then, I'll offer a personal opinion that *The Wedding of River Song* was my least favourite season finale since the series returned in 2005, but on its own terms it was, quite unarguably, a brilliant bit of fluffy fun.

And it all ended very suddenly, didn't it?

Originally published by Kasterborous.com (October, 2011)

REVIEW: The God Complex

Since my glowing review of *Day of the Moon*, I've had much cause to wonder whether my gushing exclamation of 'Doctor Who is brilliant right now' could actually apply to subsequent episodes. And I've repressed these feelings, these dark opinions, because I don't want to sound like Jan Vincent-Rudzki reviewing *The Deadly Assassin* or DWB in the 1980s. I've never been a ranty fan; I've always sought the positive in my favourite waste of time (and shelf space) when others have stuck the boot in and twisted the knife. I've loved *Doctor Who* (and always will) since 1973, but Series Six has tested that love more than any other. But maybe long-term fans like me are just too old for this sort of thing now; maybe *Doctor Who* isn't being made for us anymore. Yeah, right. If I'm not the licence fee paying audience for this show, then I don't know who is. And there are others like me (you, probably) who'll follow this wonderful idea across media and through long and changing years to cheer it on even when it's not as thrilling or as focussed as it once was.

Now, I'm not saying Series 6 has been *bad*, far from it; it features perhaps the best Doctor bar none (the endlessly brilliant Matt Smith); it features one of the series' greatest companions (Arthur Darvill's delightful Rory Williams); and it's the best-looking programme on TV (beautifully designed and gorgeously photographed). But after *Day of the Moon* things really slumped: that pirate story was one of the dullest in the series' history; Neil Gaiman's TARDIS love story was ambitious but stifled, nay, sterile; and don't let's dwell on the tedious ineptitude of that clone story. Fortunately, things picked up mid-season with the 'finale' (great ideas, wonderful characters) and the re-launch (fast, furious and confident, if convoluted). OK, so *Night Terrors* was a little limp, no matter how sumptuous it looked, but *The Two Amy's* took us in a bolder and more philosophically challenging direction, whilst showcasing Karen Gillan excellent acting abilities.

So I turned on *The God Complex* hoping it might retain the previous week's ambition, but fearing it would offer the now worryingly usual ingredients: an annoying kid, an eerie mystery revealed to be a malfunctioning bit of mundane space-kit, a wise-cracking Amy, arch whispers about the Doctor's fate, someone dying but not really (probably Rory), death being treated as something you can resolve with a glass of berocca, and time and reality being bent and rewound all over the place until – you know what? – nothing actually matters any more. And I've had to ask these questions quite a lot just lately. If none of this is 'real', then why are we still watching? If people can die but not be dead after all, then what value can stories have? If events happen but are then erased and so didn't happen, then what are we investing in here? The current production team can big-up these stories up all they want on *Confidential*, telling us this is the best one yet and asking us what's not to love, but sooner or later worlds without internal logic will unravel and cease to have meaning for those who have invested in them. It's not that the stories we've been given should never have made it to our screens, it's just that some of them really needed to be much more specific about the story they were trying to tell. This kind of criticism is frowned upon by the current team, I think. There is a general sense that if we don't like a story, then we're ungrateful or, if we're not making TV shows of our own, we should shut up and get over our own inadequacy; which is a shame, because I'd love, just once, to hear RTD or The Moff tell us not how great everything is, but how crap something might have turned out. Until they do, as one who loves *Doctor Who*, I'll always feel nervous being critical of it out loud, on record.

So, there's the context to my viewing of *The God Complex*, to which I came to with no prior knowledge, no 'Next Week' trailer, nothing. Apart from knowing David Walliams was in it. And I'm more than happy to say that it wrong-footed my jaded expectations more than once. For that I am extremely grateful. For the first third, I worried about the forced surrealism (another mainstay of the Smith era). Some will say that the room full of ventriloquist dummies was scary, but although they presented a lovely image, they offered no real chills because, well, they didn't actually do anything. If you want a truly scary ventriloquist dummy let me point you in the direction of *Talons of Weng-Chiang*; that one's a swine and it'll stab you in the heart. The presence of these dummies seems designed to suggest that we were in a kind of *Celestial Toymaker / Mind Robber* 'sideways' adventure where reality was bent and twisted to serve the whims of some 'exterior' being. To some extent this was, of course, true. Soon though, with a small cast assembled in one closed location, I began to think 'base under siege', which was also partly true. But what a cast: Amara Karan (as Rita) and Dimitri Leonida (as Howie) proved to be brilliantly realised companions to the regular team, offering performances of such focus that it was both a shame and a shock to have them die (although you knew Rita's fate was sealed as soon as the Doctor took a shine to her). And it would have been easy to cast David Walliams as a lead character, a villain perhaps; but instead of chewing up the scenery and filling the screen with his celebrity, Walliams came in as the perfect team player, as equal as the other cast members and as brilliantly believable (my favourite moment of his being the simple 'port-hole' moment: 'See that green planet there…').

So, 'sideways' and 'base under siege': two classic *Doctor Who* story types eliding to give us something claustrophobic and mysterious, and even though I thought I had the measure of it, I could never have expected it to have been so tightly directed. The vision-mixes during the 'Praise him' sequences were new and frantic, as were the eerie juxtapositions when characters faced the camera showing terror that quickly made a jump-cut to laughter. Also, particularly effective were the full-screen sequences taken from the black and white monitors, which provided fractured sense of voyeurism.

So far, so very efficient and technically precise, but the real turning point in Toby Whithouse's story came when we realised that the whole scenario had been created by a 'false god', a simple but effective idea kicked heartily up the backside by *Doctor Who*'s long-running secular philosophy. Here, I was taken fully by surprise and found myself once again thrilled by the series' forward-thinking empiricist approach to the numinous. The most delightful moment of this story strand had to be the Doctor's 'that's enough of that' / pull the plug approach to Howie's blindly rapturous paean to an unseen deity whose sole aim was to prey upon his lack of 'advancement'.

Oh, and once it was clear that everyone 'had a room', all we really wanted to know was 'What's in the Doctor's?' That this answer held the key to the story's resolution was made all the more intriguing because we were never shown what it was. Sure, we heard the tolling of the TARDIS cloister bell, which had me quite unconsciously imagining the Master, but on reflection I'm not sure that he didn't see Adric here. It seems like an odd thing to suggest, but having glimpsed his nightmare, the Doctor goes to great lengths to destroy Amy's faith in him (there's a similar scene in *The Curse of Fenric*). The Doctor must surely have glimpsed some failure that resulted in the death of a companion? But I could be wrong. It's quite possible he simply saw himself, and the cloister bell was what he heard as he drew upon his own faith. The ambiguity of this is what makes it all the more tantalising. And this, perversely, is where *The God Complex* restored my own faith in *Doctor Who*'s ability to truly surprise me. The death of Rita was a powerful and difficult moment for the Doctor, who had to suddenly come to terms with the very new notion that there might be others willing to do the saving, others who do not wish for his interference in their affairs and those who do not desire to be saved. This alone would have been enough to give us one of *Doctor Who*'s best-ever moments, but then the fear / faith revelation and its climactic enactment in Amy's room was one of the most tender and heart-rending in this series or any other. That the whole thing led to the sudden and painful departure of Amy and Rory Williams was something that came right out of left field...

Now, I'm assuming Amy and Rory have *really* left? This could be like Martha's departure at the end of Series 2, and the Ponds could well return next year – or even the week after next... I'd heard Amy would be back next year – and maybe she will – or was that just sleight of hand? It was a sudden and, consequently, shocking way to have them go (think Ben and Polly or Jamie and Zoe), but the more it appeared to be *really happening*, the more sense it seemed to make. The Doctor chose well here; refusing to stand over their dead bodies. Not that he hasn't done so already; most recently with poor Old Amy last week. What had she done to warrant having her life erased just so Rory and the Doc could have a more nubile version to hang out with? In the light of this week's sudden (properly) 'game-changing' climax, the choice not to leave with Old Amy seems odd now. Maybe something that daring and brilliant would be too icky for some viewers? I really don't know any more. But even though the Doctor opted to 'save' Amy and Rory by sending them off on a new and bigger adventure, it seemed that such a moving decision came at an odd place in the overall narrative arc. Sure, Gillan got a corker of an episode to herself last week, but is the Amy story *really* over? Is one of the best TARDIS teams in the series' history now gone, before we've even had the chance to take it all in? Although I've not been the biggest fan of Amy, I don't feel entirely satisfied that her story went anywhere after the mid-season break. But part of me likes that (even if she still doesn't seem *that* fussed about losing her baby). And then part of me wonders if the production team wants part of me to like that, and then that part of me doubts it and another, more jaded, part of me thinks there's no plan here at all and the production team are *still* failing to find any specificity with what this meandering season might be trying to achieve. But I just don't know, do I? How could I? And who am I to second-guess them, when they're able to surprise me with something as beautifully affecting as *The God Complex*? After all, Series 6 isn't over yet. To quote the first Doctor's last (-ish) words: 'It's far from being over...' And given our Nimon-cousin's final elegiac words to the eleventh Doctor – which seem to place us in the kind of territory the tenth Doctor found himself in with a single ghostly Ood – will there be yet bigger, even more shocking, surprises before this season draws to a close?

Originally published by Kasterborous.com (September, 2011)

REVIEW: Day of the Moon

Doctor Who is brilliant. We all know that, but what I'm saying is that *Doctor Who* is brilliant *right now*. You might not necessarily have been able to say that during last year's Silurian story or *The Doctor's Daughter* or *Fear Her* – or any number of stories going as far back as, well, *The Keys of Marinus* (probably) – but right now, Doctor Who is one brilliant TV show.

I don't know about you, but I tend to avoid spoilers (I hear River Song's admonishing voice every time I run away from one). I even stick my fingers in my ears and shout 'la-la-la' when the 'Next Time' trailers come on. So I was thrilled when this week's episode kicked off three months after last week's cliff-hanger. Straight away, we were treated to beautiful, epic sequences that saw the best TARDIS crew ever being hunted across stunning American locations to be seemingly killed (as the Doctor was last week...) in order to regroup in a dwarf star alloy cell and plot against the Silents without their ever knowing. Phew.

From here (with three months' worth of 'knowledge' about the Silents and some handy 'telepathic' trackers), the brilliant Canton 3 accompanied Amy to a 'haunted house'/Arkham Asylum-style orphanage, and the Doctor broke into Apollo 11. In the orphanage, Amy (apparently no longer pregnant) made a shocking discovery about the little girl in the space suit, only to be kidnapped by the scary monsters. Finally, the Doctor defeated the aliens (a little disappointingly, given their utter scariness) by capitalising on their own arrogance and hypnotising the human race into murdering them all, whilst condoning River's own policy of shoot first and ask questions later – which was cool, but also worrying. And that kiss! Just watch the Doctor's arms during that kiss...

And how beautiful did it all look? *Doctor Who* has never looked more like a movie. The camerawork and lighting are exemplary, the direction faultless, the music delicious and the acting superb. Matt Smith's Doctor continues to swallow the screen whenever he's on it, but Karen Gillan's Amy is so perfectly pitched now that she's well on the way to becoming one of the series' best ever companions. Arthur Darvill's Rory is bolder now, too; more focused and balanced than last year (and I mean the character not the performance). But River Song... Oh, River

Song. Don't you just love her? How cool can she get? And at the same time so sympathetic. Her face when the Doctor appeared to be leaving without a kiss... Watch *Silence in the Library* again and you'll see the same emotions – that sense of loss and pain that the man she loves doesn't know her. I've had many theories about River; to me, she's been a future Amy, a future Doctor, the TARDIS, but maybe, just maybe, she's River Song and nothing more. I suspect that when her story finally plays out, the tragedy of it all will be enough to allow her an identity that needs no bells and whistles. That said, she might just be the little girl in the space suit. Who might just be the child of Rory and Amy. Or not. And whoever that kid is, how stunning was that regeneration moment? What a wonderful, iconic image. For me, the most wonderful moment this week was the brief and unexpected appearance of the 'eye-patch woman' who appeared to have burst in on what she interpreted as one of Amy's dreams. Among the many mysteries we're going to have to solve this season (and beyond?), we now have what I assume will be this year's running motif (a la Bad Wolf/Torchwood/Vote Saxon). But what does it all mean?

Following last week's opener, *Day of the Moon* came in the wake of a whole Pandorica full of new questions and mysteries. If you'd hoped that many of these questions would be answered (while suspecting that some might be held back for later on), I hope you were as thrilled as I was to have your expectations quashed when Steven Moffat chose simply to tighten the mystery screws. This series is all about questions now. Until this season opened I thought I had a handle on it all, but now, there have been so many twists and turns in the plot, not least of which include: a Doctor from 200 years in the future being killed in 2011, where a Silent that should have been killed in 1969 watches on; Amy being pregnant, then not, then seeing a photo of herself with a baby who might be the little girl, who's been kept alive because she's important, but who would have to have been born before Amy arrived in 1969, and, oh look, she's bloody regenerating... Well, it's almost as if the River Song mystery hardly matters any more – suddenly we've got bigger fish to fry.

If Steven Moffat has the courage to address the questions he is positing (older questions, too, like whose voice that was in the TARDIS in *The Big Bang* – it didn't sound like a Silent – and what was that Silent ship/TARDIS thing doing in *The Lodger*), then Doctor Who might just have hit a period of epic maturity. There are those of you who worry that 'casual viewers' may be lost the more clever and mysterious this show gets. Agreed, this might not have been the best story in which to instigate non-linear plotting (something fairly new to *Doctor Who*, but commonplace elsewhere), but what better way to have the show's production style complement its content? And I'd rather have one brilliant and challenging season of *Doctor Who* than a hundred unambitious ones – wouldn't you? What you have seen may seem confusing, but it might just prove to be some of the most ambitious television ever made – right there, inside your favourite series.

And this is why *Doctor Who* is brilliant. Right now.

Originally published by Kasterborous.com (May, 2011)

OPINION: The Triumph of Doctor Smith

Following his bravura performance in *The Lodger*, and in the dying moments before the Pandorica opens), it's time to take an overdue look at Matt Smith's Doctor.

The casting of the Eleventh Doctor caused a bit of a stir back in 2009; it seemed possible that we might get David Morrissey (so keen was the misdirection of *The Next Doctor*), but names like Russel Tovey and Paterson Joseph were also mentioned. When the role went to an ex-footballer, soon be known by his full title, Twenty-Six-Year-Old Matt Smith, the fans – in time-honoured fashion – began to worry. The hardcore were frightened because they thought the Doctor should be middle-aged and the shippers began to realise that they were going to lose their pinstriped eye candy. For my own part, I supported Steven Moffat's choice of leading man – in spite of my surprise – but believed it was so unusual that the wider audience would not play along. I genuinely thought it would be Colin Baker all over again – even Matt Smith's enthusiasm recalled Baker's in 1983 – and when the pundits came out in force, telling us that the boots Smith was about to fill were very, very big ones, I thought this was game over.

Almost one Matt Smith season later, it is pleasantly surprising to see how things turned out. Even if you still prefer David Tennant, there's no denying that Smith is a worthy successor to, arguably, the most popular *Doctor Who* ever. Smith – unlike Tennant – isn't an obvious *Doctor Who* fan, but one cannot help feeling that he has picked up this beautiful thing we all adore and promised with all his heart to take the greatest care of it. From that perfect opening episode (surely the best of any Doctor bar Hartnell), Smith gave us something so intricate, so real and complete that a great many of us cheered at the TV and struggled to recall the last feller's name. We chose to move on and Smith led us through the treeborgs with an energy and enthusiasm previously unrivalled.

Moffat's observation that although Smith is vibrantly young he conveys great age is now a cliché, but a wonderfully correct one. From the swaggering cockiness of youth to the gentle, delicate insight of experience – via some mid-life crisis of staying 'cool' and coping – Smith has exceeded all expectations of interpretation to bring us a character so unflinchingly detailed that it feels, perhaps for the first time in the series' long history, that the Doctor is a real person. Smith is both a brilliant 'serious' actor and a splendid comedian, achieving the best results by playing both for keeps. His success derives from his deep intensity and sharply focussed attachment to any given situation (something that his co-star seems yet to learn).

Not only is Smith's characterisation rich, it is also very nicely textured. See, for example, how he sits upon Rosanna's throne in *Vampires of Venice*, all fidgetty and never quite comfortable; see him jump excitedly up and down on his bed in *The Lodger* whilst chatting to Amy through his earpiece. Smith never stops finding things for the Doctor to do, even when only in the background of a shot. There is, for example, a lot of brilliantly understated 'business' in the TARDIS doorway at the start of *The Beast Below*. Smith's skill here is that his character continues to live and breathe out of the limelight, whilst never distracting the viewer or upstaging his co-stars. Those of that love him – and I count myself among them – admire his endless ability to fill the screen with a consistent sense of realism.

Before this season began, it was feared that sticking the Doctor in a bow tie and tweeds seemed too deliberate. It is now apparent that Smith needed such an outfit from which to elicit his performance. He does look so blissfully Doctor-ish, and maybe we all felt a bit nervous and self-conscious about that. Christopher Eccleston's leather jacket and boots deliciously pared down all the costumes that had gone before, and Tennant, to some extent, followed suit, but Smith is a very young man. To put him in something young and funky would have diluted the actor's interpretative tension in his young/old persona, especially now the Time War angst has passed. The real catchphrase of this season – 'bow ties are cool' – tells us so much about this Doctor. Look back at his first episode and, boy, does that suit look wrong.

Possibly the Doctor's most iconic scene this year is the one in *Victory of the Daleks* where the Doctor holds the Daleks at bay with a Jammy Dodger. He looks so right, so perfectly precise – as much a part of the programme's design as the Daleks themselves – and Smith's incredible features make him the best-looking Doctor ever. I said this elsewhere, pointing out that Smith was not a pretty boy, but that he was the most fascinatingly alien-looking Doctor thus far. Yet as the weeks have gone by and his eyes have twinkled at lovers, painters, galactic wonders and thoughts unspoken, I have begun to find him oddly beautiful. I find myself wanting to look at him – and isn't that what attractive is about? And his hair! That, my friends, is real Doctor hair; casting him one minute as mad professor, the next as disaffected teddy-goth and the next as some dark, deliberate monster.

Smith is unarguably great in the role, but the writing of the Doctor is equally great. The best writers for the Doctor this season have been Steven Moffat (of course) and Gareth Roberts (with his best script for BBC Wales so far), but all of this year's scripts have brought some wonderful texture to the character.

When we first meet the new Doctor, he seems suddenly very alien and odd again. The way he looks at people, perceiving young Amelia as a new life form, eating fish custard and so on, is reminiscent of the Sixth Doctor, who operated on equally subjective extremes of mood and contrast. It was easy to assume that this was all down to the regeneration, but these extremes are still intact in *The Lodger* when, for example, he sips Rosé and spits it back into his glass (and in just about any other scene in that episode). But such reactions aren't quite as alien as they at first seem. Looked at from another angle, these are the actions and reactions of a being at peace with itself, unconstrained by societal bounds, open to possibilities and honest with the world.

This newfound openness (the Tenth Doctor equivalent seemed very artificial) sees him display an endless sense of thrilled glee in new situations – including the dangerous ones. But, in common with previous Doctors, he is heroic and bold in his dealings with his enemies. Be they Atraxi, Patient Zero, the Daleks or Rosanna, this Doctor steps right into the lion's den and will even place his head between the beast's jaws in order to sell his determination to protect those around him. Capable of great anger, he castigates the humans of Starship UK, the Daleks and River Song alike.

His confidence in himself, although sometimes shaken (he doesn't brag as much as the Tenth Doctor), manifests in many ways. His confrontation with Rosanna is almost flirtatious. He teases her with a predatory, sexual dance equal to her own, only to pull the rug from her by promising to tear her world apart. This aspect of the new Doctor is truly scary – and he knows it. There is an occasional sense of a truly dangerous and threatening Doctor just waiting to emerge in moments such as the one in which he 'nicely' asks Ambrose to leave her cache of weapons behind. His intentions towards Amy also seem very dark. When he takes her aboard the TARDIS, he lies about his intentions (peeking secretively at the scanner display of the crack in the universe). Even after Rory's double-death, he remains deceptive to Amy – when, as we later learn, he only needs to bump heads with her to explain the truth.

It is strange, but sometimes we like the Doctor to be scarier than the monsters he fights and it is tempting to think his nicer qualities are a front for what the Daleks call The Oncoming Storm. But it's also very obvious that his experiences touch him – not just the thrill of them, but also the pain of them. When he has no choice but to abandon Octavian to the absent mercy of a Weeping Angel, he displays heartbroken tenderness (sensitively performed by Smith). His deepest feelings are also exposed by an enigmatic but pained smile when Alaya asks him what he is willing to sacrifice for his cause. She thinks she has the upper hand because she is willing to die, but we already know him capable of sacrificing not only worlds, but worlds full of people very, very dear to him. It is only by a colossal act of will that he is able to keep his passions in check. This may add to our deepest concerns about the darkness he carries within him, but this is a man who is also capable of error, and the Dream Lord plays upon such vulnerabilities. This Doctor also overlooks stuff and gets things wrong in a way that Seventh Doctor never would (until the moment of his death): by allowing himself to become preoccupied he loses Elliot to the Silurians; whilst sitting on Rosanna's throne, he fails to realise that he's sitting on the key to her power; he is also guilty of a misplaced faith in own abilities: 'Nobody dies today.' Well, Alaya does. Rory does. There are far better stories this season, but the Silurian two-parter allows Smith to display the Doctor's complex moral centre, and he plays it not as stoutly as Jon Pertwee did (in a similar story) but in a manner far more relaxed and intimate – a lot like Patrick Troughton might have.

Ah, Troughton. No discussion of Smith's Doctor is complete without mention of Troughton's. As soon as Smith declared Troughton his favourite – and face it, all the Doctor's from Tom Baker have – the pundits latched on to the Troughtonesque qualities of his performance. Let's put this to bed. All actors like Troughton's work because he is, relatively speaking, perhaps the most accomplished and versatile television and film actor to have taken on the role. If you know your broadcast history, the man is a legend in the way that even Eccleston is not yet allowed to be. But is Smith's Doctor just a retread? Well, they both have craggy faces, wear bow ties and walk like little children. But the broad strokes of Troughton's performance are those of almost permanent self-immersion, indignance and soothing apology. Smith can do these – and is, to some extent, informed by these – but they do not define him. Any apparent influence is just window dressing.

Unlike Troughton's Doctor, Smith's is capable of genuine sentiment and glowing pride in others. He displays sincere warmth towards those he encounters and those in his care. Unlike Troughton – or any other Doctor (except perhaps the Eighth) – he is genuine, open and friendly, and this allows him to be humbled by the humans of the 29th century, thrilled at the prospect of being someone's lodger and eager to join Vincent in listening to colours rather than dismissing him as a madman. Taking *The Lodger* as an example that best covers the season, this Doctor's intelligence is sometimes fierce, sometimes naïve, but always utterly compassionate and thoroughly tactile. Smith inhabits the part, whereas all the others – Troughton included – simply performed it (however brilliantly). Smith's is a fully contemporary take on the role of the Doctor, informed by modern, less theatrical acting techniques and supported by modern televisual grammar; as such, it makes Smith quite simply a better Doctor than Troughton. Put Troughton in *The Lodger* and it would not be anywhere near as good.

It might be just as easy to compare Smith to Peter Cushing – both walk funny, bumble about and have very similar silhouettes – but, in all honesty, the Doctor to whom Smith is closest is actually David Tennant. Certainly, their vocal tones are very similar. Perhaps what makes Smith the most effective New Who so far is his combination of Tennant's exuberance and Eccleston's swagger. But again, his performance is more real, more genuine, less, well, performed than that of his immediate predecessors. Look at those clips of Tennant with River Song on *Confidential* – he suddenly seems oddly wrong in the part.

Whether or not you agree with the points I have made, it is obvious that Matt Smith has made the part his own and that the Eleventh Doctor is one of the strongest we have seen both on screen and on paper.

He manages to combine the Big Doctors with the Little Doctors seamlessly, falling into neither camp and filling the boots of Tom, Jon, Sylv, Pat, Billy, Chris, Dave ... Whoever! But unlike any other Doctor (and only Sylvester McCoy came close) he also manages to be both distantly alien and warmly human. Maybe the portrayal is actually not so alien, but played just as real as any part Matt Smith might play – it's possibly just the context of TV drama that makes him look really weird – more real, less mannered than a Troughton. Unfortunately, Karen Gillan plays up to this but hasn't the same set of skills to pull it off. I have begun to suspect that if anything will hold Smith back from truly achieving greatness in the eyes of every fan, then it will be she for it was only during *The Lodger* that he finally seemed unconstrained by her. Perhaps they should team him up with someone older, someone who doubts his abilities, someone like Donna.

This may not have been the best season ever, but it is perhaps the most truly consistent with every episode being at least workmanlike and several of them being utter masterpieces. What is certain now is that what would once have been a below average episode will always stand tall while we have Matt Smith's Doctor to watch and enjoy. Long may he reign.

Originally published by Kasterborous.com (November, 2010)

OPINION: Operation Platinum Age – The Final Word

Recently, I wrote a two-part observation of Matt Smith and Steven Moffat's first eight episodes of *Doctor Who* (entitled Operation Platinum Age). The purpose of the article was to evaluate the season so far, compare it to previous seasons and speculate upon its story arc. I concluded that, while the Russell T Davies era had been rightly regarded as *Doctor Who*'s 'golden age', it was becoming apparent that Smith and Moffat were ushering us into something greater. Now this season has come to a spectacular end, it seems only proper that I should similarly evaluate the final five episodes and question whether that conclusion still holds.

Five stories ago, I was still raving about the new Doctor (and would rave yet more in a subsequent article entitled 'The Triumph of Doctor Smith'). Frankly, my rave looks as if it may never end. From the outset, I have believed – and still believe – that Matt Smith is playing the best Doctor we've ever had – and what a lovely position for those who love him to be in: to know that the current guy is the best. Now I know how those David Tennant fans felt! Of course, many fans continue to adore Tennant, but some take every comparison in Smith's favour as an attack on something they deem unassailable, but when I suggest that Smith is the best, this is not meant as a dig at ten other quite brilliant incarnations. However, this non-prescriptive opinion is offered by one who has seen/heard every episode of TV *Doctor Who* several times over (and heard/read perhaps 75% of the available audios, annuals, comic strips, novels, etc, etc of the last 47 years). I've loved all the Doctors at some time or other, but Smith seems to offer the most precise and realistic portrayal of the character as set down on paper and pared to its basics. Last time I wrote, my favourite new Doctor moments saw him facing down the new (still gorgeous, sorry) Daleks, jumping out of Rory's cake (again), and telling the Atraxi fleet to run. Now I find myself loving his sermon at Stonehenge, where he seemed to channel both John Lydon and Billy Graham in order to tell an even bigger fleet of ships to run. Add to this his Fez moment and he's beginning to look unassailable himself – and a lot like the Doctor that River Song described in *Silence in the Library*. He looks great and sounds great, and any doubts about his suitability to the role have now, surely, been set to rest.

When I last signed off, my biggest concern about this season was that its middle had been a bit saggy. I suggested that once any given season gets past the premise of the Doctor showing the wonders of the universe to a single, wide-eyed companion, the concept tends to dilute with the addition of multiple companions. Don't get me wrong, Rory is one of the best things about *Amy's Choice* and *Vampires of Venice*, but it seems significant that these are perhaps the weakest stories of the season. This has nothing to do with Arthur Darvill (who is sublime), but the show seems to work best – unless there's an epic storyline to be had – with just two leads. There's some exuberant *joie de vivre* to a Doctor/Rose, Doctor/Donna, Doctor/Martha pairing; but that intimacy and togetherness tends to dissipate when someone crashes the party – particularly if that someone is Jealousy. Maybe *Amy's Choice* and *Vampires of Venice* were just weak stories, but we've seen things fall apart at this stage in previous seasons (*The Doctor's Daughter* and *The Long Game* spring to mind).

Following the seemingly dark tensions of (the then latest episode) *The Hungry Earth*, I suggested the series had moved back on track, having fallen off after the Weeping Angels story. I may have been too hasty. While I would still choose the Silurian story over the preceding two, *Cold Blood* just didn't deliver the goods, moving very slowly and sewing things up with little enthusiasm. The saving grace, of course, was Rory's shocking and sudden death scene, which was infinitely more moving than its dress rehearsal a fortnight before. I also suggested that Chris Chibnall might actually be the 'second-in command' writer to Steven Moffat (as Moffat had been to RTD) but this lacklustre episode dissuaded me from that perhaps over-optimistic position. More controversially, this was the week I lost patience with Amy Pond (see Whatever Happened to Amy Pond?), whose character suddenly seemed to grate with its knowing and implausible smart-ass cockiness. If you want to see how a companion might really react to the possibility of having her guts opened up, I'd point you in the direction of Moffat's own *Sherlock*, the second episode of which sees Watson's date squirming with abject terror at the knowledge of her certain doom. Until this point I was on the same side as Amy Pond the character, but when I also cottoned on to the fact that she'd been effectively missing for a month I began to feel cheated of what had promised to be a brilliant companion. This would eventually change, but it mattered so much at the time because Amy seemed – rightly it turned out – to be the central mystery at the heart of the entire season. Looking back, it seems the inclusion of Rory was a distraction, a stalling device that allowed the production team to put Amy on pause until she was next required.

Oh, and do you know what? I was right about the future Rory and Amy waving at their past selves. At the time, I wrote 'Time can be written, re-written and unwritten, it seems, so how real is that future? Perhaps only as real as the past it came from...' Of course, I had no idea how this would play out, but it was clear that something was going on, and in a way it was an introduction to the concepts that would overshadow the season finale...

With Rory "gone", the season reset to everything it had been for the first five weeks and consequently improved. While I am in no doubt that *Vincent and the Doctor* will prove to be one of those overrated *Doctor Who* stories that people feel they should love to death (see *Blink, The Shakespeare Code, The Empty Child, The Talons of Weng-Chiang, The Robots of Death* – 'How dare he!') while guilty pleasures languish (*Midnight, Love & Monsters, Nightmare of Eden, The Power of Kroll* – 'Has he gone mad?!') there is no arguing that it was a rich and accomplished bit of television. But even though Smith continued to delight and Tony Curran gave us an acutely sensitive Vincent, it was here that I began to doubt Karen Gillan as well as the character she was playing. While we witnessed some wonderful character strokes from the pen of Richard Curtis, I know I was not alone in fearing that Gillan's range of emotional responses was becoming repetitive.

Some fans have found it difficult to see Gillan criticised, but it is important to note that the critic's role is not simply to 'like' or 'dislike' a character/actor, but to examine a performance and evaluate the implementation of a craft from a professional and informed perspective. To pre-empt any further discomfort for Amy/Gillan fans, I am happy to say that the final two-parter saw Gillan seriously up her game and prove her worth in the role. Again, I would suggest that perhaps the problems (and their solutions) stemmed from the writing of the episodes. Gillan's performances were probably only ever going to be as good as the material she had to work with, but I think the jury's still out on this. It's worth noting, however, that she was consistently well served by Moffat. As a caveat (and to avoid further death threats) I should point out that Karen Gillan remains one of the most delightful people to grace the talking heads of *Doctor Who Confidential*, and even though I'd rather she and Rory had left at the end of the season, I look forward to seeing how she develops as both actor and character in 2011. I think we're probably in for a few surprises.

Speaking of which, in *The Lodger* we got to see the Doctor without Amy, and were treated to something so special that the idea of any permanent companion seemed suddenly superfluous. A prompt re-evaluation of the David Tennant specials reminded me that this was not necessarily the case. Even so, this standalone episode was perhaps the best character study of the Doctor we've ever seen and a perfect showcase within which to restate Smith's abundant talent. Where the Doctor had seemed restricted by Amy (or Smith by Gillan?) in the previous episode, here he was quite off the leash. What a joy it was to see him settling into a domestic situation with warmth and charm, popping up from behind the sofa, cooking Craig's breakfast every day and singing 'something Italian' to the tune of *La Donne e Mobile*. I'm not the biggest James Corden fan, either, but wasn't he just beautiful as Craig? Gareth Roberts excelled himself with this utterly delicious episode, which was possibly the best of the season. It's obvious now that Roberts should take the post of 'second-writer-in-command' – and then perhaps that of the series' next showrunner?

When the final two-parter came it was a staggering epic, full of fanboy thrills and incredible wonders. From the various times and places of the opening sequence, it was obvious we were in for a treat. Having watched it a couple of times since, I must admit that while it stands up beautifully as a *Doctor Who* movie, the plot still doesn't quite add up. Not really. Fortunately, it doesn't quite add up in a way that doesn't quite matter and we engage with it on its own terms, but some of the sheer coincidence required to make things turn out well scarcely bears thinking about. It's all very tenuous. But didn't it look great, speeding along with a delirious self-confidence that we've never really seen before? Yes, it was blindingly obvious to the attentive that 'the trickster' in the Pandorica legend was the Doctor (very BBC Books' *Alien Bodies*), but the way in which that legend became manifest was truly shocking. All kinds of theories raced through my mind: would the Doctor actually be in the box? Was this his tomb? Would it be a dead Eleventh Doctor? A future Doctor? A past Doctor? Nothing prepared me for the notion that he wasn't even in there yet. Very *Wicker Man*. And the alliance of aliens! Wow! I never saw that coming. You did, though, didn't you? Probably because you saw last week's Next Week trailer, or heard something on *Confidential*.

Take my word for it as someone who tried it this year: avoid the Next Week trailers. They never give the whole game away but they always ruin three or four potential surprises. And *Confidential*, quite innocently, has a habit of dictating your reading of the show. The amount of party line, agenda and prescriptive reading that comes from this wonderful little show is staggering. If you want to feel the wonder of *Doctor Who*, save these up until the season's finished. You'll thank yourself.

But I digress.

The final episode of the season was similar to the second part of the Silurian story in that it didn't quite pay off in the way expected. This time it mattered less, though, because what we were given was a timey-wimey space romp of roller coaster proportions. Last time I wrote, I wished for more Caitlin Blackwood as Young Amy and I was rewarded here. What a talent, I had thought – and still do – but now I much preferred Grown Up Amy (happy now?). This is not the place to go too deeply into the sheer wall of plot and unplot we had thrust upon us in *The Big Bang*, but, as much as I thoroughly loved it, it was the reset button all over again, wasn't it? Admittedly it was the best such button we've had this century, but one year – just one year – the people who run this magnificent show won't paint themselves into such a corner that they have to pretend they never did or, better still, they'll have the courage of their convictions and run with a shifted paradigm.

Looking back at the last third of the season, I think we were treated not only to some excellent visual effects/images (Vincent's starry night, the upstairs TARDIS, the spaceships over Stonehenge, and the scariest reading of the Cybermen since

1966 – perhaps ever), but also some of the series' most golden moments (Vincent, the Doctor and Amy under the stars, 'It's a Fez, I wear a Fez now', the Pandorica cliffhanger, the Stone Dalek begging River for mercy, the alien alliance – oh, and all of *The Lodger*). A few months ago my Top Three directors were Adam Smith, Andrew Gunn and Ashley Way. I still think Adam Smith should take top spot but, following the season finale, Toby Haynes has nudged Andrew Gunn into third place. I'm no longer sure about Way.

At the end of the last article I speculated on what might be happening 'arc-wise' and where we might be led. The sense I got from the first eight episodes was that they sought to question our perception of 'reality', inviting us to doubt the boundary between what was real and what was not; this would prove to be a thematic rather than a literal matter. I made much of Amy's missing memories (but didn't we all?) and memory did in fact prove to be the key to the season. I was right (to some small extent) that the cracks would prove to be a paradox caused by the Doctor's attempts to prevent their ever occurring. However, I was not able to predict quite how, nor had I factored River Song into the final equation. My obsessive attention to the use of eyes in the narratives proved to be much less accurate. I also suggested that the finale might not be a Dalek story, predicting that Christmas Day would see their next big outing. While I do not count the finale as a Dalek story (the production team were careful not to show much of them – cowed by their detractors, perhaps?), it now seems likely that we shan't be seeing them at Christmas, either. Gosh, they would have been delicious baubles on a BBC Christmas tree ident, wouldn't they? Oh well. I only hope that when we see them next, it will be for something very epic and Dalek-centric.

Which brings me to the future. What happens next? Many questions were answered in the season finale, but we never found out about the Silence – or that duck pond! One would assume that the Silence will provide the scares and action in next year's finale. But what was that voice in the TARDIS? Did anyone else think it sounded like a very mad version of the Dream Lord? Let's not forget that in *Vampires of Venice* there were dark rumblings of dreams, faded and bad, that no longer needed their dreamers. The Silence was also described, as something that could actually be seen. I think (sadly) that the Dream Lord might well return, although I did wonder if the Silence might be something to do with the Vashta Nerada. You know, as in *Silence in The Library*? But maybe I'm just making connections that aren't there. Oh, and I'm still worried about the Doctor's attempt to prove his credentials in *The Eleventh Hour*; giving the scientific community Faster Than Light travel – a scientific development Rory later claimed to have read up on. Oh, and poor Rory! Right now, he can't have the remotest clue what or who he is, having been killed and re-invented more times than a Marvel comics character. And his wife's *still* trying to jump the handsome stranger. Poor sod. I sincerely hope Amy stops being quite so shamelessly rude to the guy next year.

Amy. Hmm. There's still something not right there, either. If Amy was the only one who could return the Doctor to 'reality' by remembering him, how come River Song was one step ahead of her, prompting the remembrance with her diary of spoilers? And did anyone else notice that River wasn't dressed for a wedding? She was dressed for a funeral. Was this merely symbolic, or had she just come from one? The Doctor's about to find out who she is, or so she says, and this is when everything changes. Does this mean she'll be the Egyptian Goddess we may or may not meet at Christmas? Or are we in for a season with Smith and Kingston alone (that would be superb)? Or, given that everything's about to change, are we in for a regeneration next year? In spite of all the (clever?) indications to the contrary, will we see Smith regenerate into the Doctor that River spoke of in her first story? Or, yet more daringly, will Amy somehow regenerate and become River? Are they one and the same? From Pond to River in one crazy season? Frankly, who knows!

What I do know is that – in spite of some bumps in the road – this has been the most consistent and tonally coherent season of *Doctor Who* since about 1964. Whether or not it is 'the best' is a matter of personal opinion, but the perfect fusion of a wonderful Doctor, some cracking stories and an atmosphere entirely its own have shown us that *Doctor Who* is in very good hands. It seems almost inevitable that next season will be even better. Therefore, it seems safe to say that this really is the Platinum Age of *Doctor Who*. Enjoy it while it's still here!

Originally published by Kasterborous.com (September, 2010)

REVIEW: Toby Hadoke's *Now I Know My BBC*

There can now only be a few die-hard *Doctor Who* fans that are not familiar with Toby Hadoke (or, indeed, friends with him on Facebook). Hadoke came to prominence a few years ago with his one-man comedy show *Moths Ate My* Doctor Who *Scarf*, the success of which has facilitated regular 'appearances' on BBC DVD commentaries, Big Finish audios and *DWM* review pages.

Moths was a warm retrospective of Hadoke's formative years, told through his experiences as a *Doctor Who* fan; its immediate success was largely down to Hadoke's genuine and entertaining love for his subject and his sincerity as a comedian; but, straddling the zeitgeist, it came along at exactly the right time and had a ready-made audience. It was probably always going to be a tough act to follow.

Now that *Moths* is winding down, Hadoke has finally released his 'difficult second album', in the form of *Now I Know My BBC*, currently playing in the Edinburgh Festival.

Having read the title some months ago, I did wonder where Hadoke was going with this new show – would it feature clever jokes about Maggie Philbin or Philip Martin? Would it be peppered with references to *Gangsters*, *The Lotus Eaters*, *Jackanory*, *Target*, *Tenko*, *Morgan's Boy*, *The Forsyte Saga*, *Juliet Bravo*, *All Creatures*, *Blue Peter* and *Rentaghost*? Would I be able to nod sagely at witty one-liners about *Top of the Pops* sets in 'Carnival of Monsters' or the *Play School* clock strike of 1979? Would this be *Moths* for the ardent student of all that stuff we old-time *Who* fans already know about (largely through osmosis, Pixley and Bentham)? Would it, in short, only appeal to *Doctor Who* spods of Toby's and my TV generation?

Well, no, it didn't. And that, if you haven't already realised, is actually A Very Good Thing. *Now I Know My BBC* is a delightful piece of work, as engaging and funny as it is thought provoking. If anything, *BBC* is less spoddy than *Moths* in that it doesn't necessarily rely on the audience's deep knowledge of its wide subject. Bumbling along like some barmy media professor, Hadoke covers enough BBC output to fill a small retrospective TV show (but with charming authority).

They're all here: *Grange Hill*, *The Generation Game*, *The Singing Detective*, *Howards' Way* (did I get the apostrophe right, Toby?), *The Clangers*, the shipping forecast, and so on; but you don't need to know anything about them, because Hadoke pulls you right in and gives you everything you need to know. Like the best teacher you ever had, he brings to life the BBC's rich back catalogue, couching things in terms of our modern preoccupations such as the Internet or *Hollyoaks*. That he is able to brilliantly and cleverly elicit sparkling humour from the larger drama inherent in both the production and home viewing of these programmes is nothing short of wonderful.

That said, Hadoke shouldn't be afraid of filling in a few more details. When talking of *The Clangers* he describes Oliver Postgate and Peter Firmin as 'two men in a shed', without ever telling us their names. Given that the audience were cheerily nodding along with other such details when they came, I think this would add to the collective experience of those watching 'in the know'.

But it's not all about the programmes. I'm not sure whether Hadoke has realised that this show is a genuine sequel to *Moths* (nor am I sure that *I* did until I had long left the venue), but by once again using BBC output as a mirror to his own youthful experiences, this is perhaps the second in what will prove many chapters of a life long-lived in the company of Reith's electric baby-sitter. Once again, we meet younger versions of Hadoke in the anecdotes and stories he tells, often touching upon ground covered in the last show but from different angles and with new information.

Consequently, *BBC*, like *Moths* is a love letter to its perceived subject (I say 'perceived' because both shows are really about growing up, or rather 'getting older and having/choosing to change'). *BBC*, however, would appear to be the greater romance. There is a beautiful and delicate little love story at the heart of *BBC* – I won't betray its details here – but there is also a profound passion, which Hadoke displays with exuberance and gravitas. In terms of performance, Hadoke is perhaps never better than when defending the BBC as a treasure we discard at our most shameful peril. His fervour is ignited by despair and disappointment at our complicity in the rise and fall of Susan Boyle and her svengalis; at the Daily Mail; at the BNP; at over-running snooker. But he is never cruel or cowardly; he covers everything from school bullying to the death of Freddie Mercury, but there is no strong language and no one suffers on the receiving end of a Hadoke joke (although the snooker players gag comes close).

Oh, and for those of you that were worried, *Doctor Who* is never far away from the action, whether in the frightening certitude of the Daleks or in Hadoke's cheery confessional about chronological DVD storage.

This is a lovely show, a fine and affectionate piece of work. But it is also a brave and determined piece, unafraid to ask questions about the future of an equally brave and determined institution that we could easily lose and very, very soon. As *Doctor Who* fans, we can only surely agree (for once) that we love the BBC. If anything, Toby Hadoke seems to be perhaps our best hope for leading the vocal appreciation of this wonderful and rich contributor to British life, envied the world over for its unflinching quality. As a clarion call, *Now I know My BBC* is informative and educational, but never preachy. It is nostalgic and romantic – but never sentimental. Above all, it is very, very funny. Miss it at your peril.

Originally published by Kasterborous.com (August, 2010)

OPINION: Whatever Happened to Amy Pond?

At the end of *Cold Blood*, Rory died. It was shocking enough to see this good man (a hero to some) fall victim to Silurian fire, but to also see him erased from the memory of the woman he loved was to witness his double death. And sad though it is to bid farewell to Arthur Darvill, I can't help but wonder if his passing might at last see the return of that other wonderful companion from earlier this season... what was her name, now?

Oh yes, that was it. Amy Pond.

You remember Amy, don't you? That feisty young woman the Doctor first met as a mysterious, almost unearthly child. She handcuffed him to a radiator, remember? Handcuffs, remember? Course you do. She helped him discover his eleventh persona and you thought she was easy on the eye. You loved that screwball comedy thing she had going on. She saw the solutions the Doctor couldn't see and saved the day both on Starship UK and in Churchill's Cabinet War Rooms. Not only did you like the length of her legs and the blue of her eyes, you also managed to look past them to realise she was, quite instantly, one of the most quick-witted and uncannily intuitive of all the Doctor's companions: remember the thing with the Angel on pause? Brilliant. Amy Pond was someone we wanted to unwrap, to discover and learn about.

So, where's she been for the last few weeks?

Okay, okay, before I scare you all away, I'm not taking a pop at Karen Gillan (who, if Confidential is anything to go by, appears to be one of the most delightful people to have ever set foot on this earth), but something 'uneven' has happened to the character she is playing. Obviously, once the dynamic of the TARDIS crew shifted to accommodate Rory, things had to become less romantic and more awkward. The new dynamic duo was replaced by a sketchily drawn love triangle – presumably so we could see Amy wrestle with a love that would be taken from her, thus leading us towards the season's endgame. Sadly, though, Amy took a stretch limo back seat to her fellow travellers. Those of you who simply like a *Doctor Who* girl to fill a pair of incredibly short shorts will wonder what I'm talking about, but aside from two genuinely moving moments (one at the end of *Amy's Choice*, where Amy held Rory and Gillan's eyes communicated so much that her frozen face could not, and the frantic *Cold Blood* sequence where Rory slipped from her memory) she's had nothing truly substantial or dramatically truthful to do for four weeks.

There's been a definite 'cruise control' feel to the middle of this (undoubtedly wonderful) season and Gillan has come out of it the worst. Factions of the viewing public that heartily embraced the new Doctor have begun to spurn Amy. Some have expressed dissatisfaction with the character's moral position (her intended ravishment of the Doctor on the eve of her wedding), but others have criticised Gillan's performance. While the former position is up for some debate, the latter is, I think, unfair. Recent scripts have rarely favoured Amy and when they have they've made her very knowing or ironic (see her response to the 6-foot lizard man who's just delayed her dissection). You could place such dialogue into the mouth of *Runaway Bride*-era Donna and it wouldn't be out of place; it's that grating. Some of the problems do lie in Gillan's delivery, which now seems quite settled (while Matt Smith's grows ever inventive), but the character is in danger of being written out of 'feisty' and 'quirky' into 'shallow' and 'dangerously smug'. Perhaps the real tragedy of recent weeks was watching Amy respond to the Human/Silurian peace talks by acting bored out of her skull. It's hard to imagine Rose, Martha or Donna doing the same; they would have been much more proactive. I'm sure Amy is too, but someone seems to have forgotten.

Or have they?

To some extent, it's easy to feel that we might have been cheated. *The Eleventh Hour* promised us an enigma to be unravelled across the season – but we're still no closer to knowing much about Amy Pond. It's like she's as much a void in the centre of the season as the Cheshire cat grin in time. We know nothing about her family or her lost memories. One can only assume that her parents either died after promising to 'be back in five minutes' or they, too, are/were/will be caught up in the collapse of the universe – but what of her aunt? And where did all her memories go? Was it the crack that took them or something more traumatic? Was she even around for the Dalek invasion? And, hey, we're asking the questions, but does she even know who she is? She could be anyone. And I mean ANYONE (handcuffs, remember? But maybe it won't always end like that?). All we have learnt is that she did love Rory after all. Probably.

But with her reset button pressed (one assumes only temporarily), I'm hoping the Amy we get for the next few weeks is the Amy I remember from the first five. With bits added. One hopes that Rory's narrative presence will ultimately serve some larger dramatic purpose and that their relationship will prove to be the key to the entire season (will she remember him and be given the opportunity to reverse his death – like Anji did with Dave in the Eighth Doctor novels – thus causing universal chaos, etc?). Perhaps Rory was there to distract us from the central mystery of Amy. Which means we haven't been cheated, then, but cleverly manipulated.

Almost ten weeks in and we're still no closer to knowing anything about Amy Pond. And that's probably the point.

Originally published by Kasterborous.com (June, 2010)

OPINION: Operation: Platinum Age?

Right now, the eleventh Doctor is peering down on the deliciously volcanic subterranean metropolis of *Homo Reptilia*. What happens next won't be known for another week, but with five episodes to go before we can safely get back on the sofa, this seems a good time to pause and evaluate what Smith & Moffat have given us so far...

On New Year's Day I felt great trepidation regarding the arrival of the new Doctor. My eyes were still wet with tears for David Tennant; so poor old/young Matt Smith's first moments were never going to feel right. Something seemed to jar, but I now know that it was probably me. It wasn't that I had anything against him – he looked like a terrific choice – I was just very worried, in that fannish way, that the 'general public' wouldn't let him into their hearts. I was scared that the Golden Age of *Doctor Who* was over.

When Easter came, however, not even the most optimistic fan was expecting Smith to debut in one of the most stylish, glossy, confident and complete episodes of *Doctor Who* ever made. From the outset, *The Eleventh Hour* made it clear that we were not on the Powell Estate any more. Spooky direction and the programme's suddenly richer colour palette ensured that Steven Moffat's 'fairy tale' agenda was already in full atmospheric swing when we met seven-year-old Amelia Pond.

The new Doctor's attitude towards the little human girl was one of uncompromising equality, setting a tone for all his relationships this season. Caitlin Blackwood's Amelia was so good that the previously anticipated arrival of Karen Gillan's Amy was somewhat thrown off-balance and while the latter has since proven herself to be a suitably quirky foil for Smith, I don't think I was alone in wishing we'd seen more of the Doctor's pairing with Amelia. Perhaps if I close my eyes and wish really hard I will?

The sublime 'fish custard'/ 'crack in the wall' sequence was only the first Great Moment in a story that saw the newly cooked Doctor telling a fleet of dangerous aliens to 'basically... run'. This staggering mission statement could have been written for previous Doctors, but Smith made it his own with charming ease.

We can argue about this some other time, but a lot of people think it, and some of us said it that night – Matt Smith is the best Doctor ever. He really is. We've already seen him do alien, warm, hilarious, thrilled, ridiculous, confident, apoplectic, flirtatious, irresponsible, frustrated, dangerous and sheepish. And Smith does them all *his* way – inhabiting the part rather than simply acting it – but with great respect and dedication to the tradition of the character. He is also the best-looking Doctor. Not pretty like his predecessor, but easily the Doctor with the most incredible and fascinating face. He looks exactly as the Doctor should. And you know what I *mean* by that, even if you disagree.

Not only is Smith a natural in the role but the show itself has been re-tailored to fit him perfectly; his clothes are spot-on, the new TARDIS is wonderful (inside and out), and – controversially – we now have the most impressive and threatening Daleks the series has ever seen. Pan them all you like, it won't stop them being utterly gorgeous. In this year's Dalek story, the series' three main dramatic pillars look exactly as you once imagined they did – futuristic but retro, timeless and modern.

Speaking of radical departures, we have also been treated to some great new visual effects: the Prisoner Zero 'snake', the beautiful Atraxi (at first quite stunningly viewed through the crack in Amy's wall), a space whale, and the Silurian city. Planets and stars also seem more vibrantly executed this year. Obviously, the spitfires in space were quite wonderful, but three viewings later, I still find myself wondering if I really saw them? That's the thing with limited CGI shots, they become so fleeting that they eye cannot quite contain them. Like a dream.

Like it or not, the programme has undergone a subtle but significant change. Even Murray Gold's music seems different, more understated. While Amy's entering the TARDIS and the last act of *Victory of the Daleks* were lovely, there's been nothing as immediately catchy as his previous Doctor or companion themes. But this could change. Oh, and how we hated that theme tune! But eight weeks in, I'm surely not the only one who's starting to like it. Am I?

As befits such confident retooling, this has been a season of bold stories that has followed a pattern not dissimilar to the 2005 comeback series. But with swearing, a horny kissogram and pensioner whacking.

The Beast Below had many of us clenching and nervous after a great first night. With its McCoy era feel and potentially soppy undertones, it trod some of the ground covered by *The End of the World*, and many thought it was an early misstep. Eight weeks in, it looks like a glittering example of a series at the height of its powers. You wait. In 20 years' time the tabloids will 'debate' its challenge to the moral integrity of a monarch that can comfortably preside over a nation built on subjugation and willingly consumed lies. Only The State Opening of Parliament comes close to instilling such awkwardness in a politically aware audience.

Victory of the Daleks made some fans cry because it was bolder than them in its love for a TV programme called *Doctor Who*. Yes, it's derivative, no it's not deep on *Genesis* style philosophy, but that's because it's about nostalgia (look who wrote it!). This was the ghost of 'old' *Doctor Who* offering its own manifesto in coalition with the new administration. We were promised a classic, and I think Mark Gatiss delivered. Never forget that we saw one Dalek shoot five Nazi bombers out of the sky without batting an eyestalk – not too long ago, we would have savoured that moment again and again.

So far, the jewel in this season's crown – perhaps even the crown of all *Doctor Who* – is the two-part Angels story. I still feel that *Blink* is overrated, but this exciting, scary and cerebral Dantean nightmare came close to perfection; full of great ideas, thrilling set pieces, fanboy continuity and some very intriguing possibilities for the future. It seems obvious now that after something so uncompromisingly excellent, the following weeks were going to feel flatter...

The arrival of Arthur Darvill's excellent Rory meant that the scope for 'comic tension' in the TARDIS increased, but the intimate wonder of the early episodes gave way to something more farcical. Don't get me wrong, *Vampires of Venice* does look lovely. At first, it feels like a lost Hammer film, but once the vampires are exposed as fish from space aesthetic thrill goes limp. Vampires are threat enough, and Toby Whithouse should know this. They shouldn't be reduced to the level of Krillitanes, however wonderful the CGI. Sadly, it was also CGI that failed to sell the Doctor's vertical ascent, relying too much on weak direction and good faith.

Which brings me, reluctantly, to *Amy's Choice*. While the script clearly sparkled with funny dialogue and big ideas, I couldn't help but feel they were being wasted on the wrong story. It was *always* obvious that the Leadworth sequences were *a* dream (if not *the* dream), because director Catherine Morshead never managed to sell them as anything else. That the TARDIS sequences turned out to be a dream also was not so much a twist as a cheat. Other than a desperately needed shot of tension, what did this revelation add? Perhaps two TARDIS dreams would have served the idea much more effectively? Unforgivably, it felt like an episode of *Next Generation*, but 'eccentric'. The TARDIS was the Enterprise and the so-called Dream Lord was Q – just another clichéd 'space Puck' – but with considerably less charm. Toby Jones was fine, but somehow managed to annoy the audience as well as the Doctor. The pointless need to reserve his true identity for an undramatic reveal (to the audience, not the characters) negated the possibility of the Doctor's 'dark side' being played by someone more appropriate

– like Sylvester McCoy. It would still have made the same internal sense to the regulars.

Admittedly *Amy's Choice* was better than most things on the box, but with a pregnant Amy on the publicity stills, this was *The Doctor's Daughter* all over again. Pure stunt telly. More criminally, the directorial failure to convince us that Rory's death was real, or that we ought to care, was caused by an under-utilisation of the television grammar required to sell such moments. In fact, both times I watched it, the whole premise got *really* boring after about 30 minutes. I genuinely wanted to go and do something else. 'Pick a world,' said the Dream Lord, 'and this nightmare will all be over...' I nearly picked ITV.

Fortunately, *The Hungry Earth* has put things back on track. It's been clear throughout the season that Moffat has been the strongest writer for the new regulars, but he also seemed to lack the equivalent of himself that Russell T Davies had. Perhaps Chris Chibnall will come to fulfil this role. The latest episode was strong and visually striking, and Chibnall's handle on the regulars was certainly tight. While it's a shame the production team didn't recreate the Silurians of old – or incorporate the original face into their masks – the new versions are well designed, if a little *Star Trek: Voyager* (although, I suspect the scariest reptile we'll see this year is the '70s lounge lizard' Dream Lord we saw the week before...). Following a slight dip, Ashley Way's lovely direction suggests that the season is now moving towards something very substantial indeed.

I'd put Ashley in third place for this year's directors. Second place goes to Andrew Gunn (*Beast* and *Victory*) who proved his ability with tasty pictures and delicious atmospheres, but first place – and surely we all agree on this – must presently go to Adam Smith. His work on the debut and Angel episodes was outstanding. Look at that golden blue light when the Doctor convinces Amy that he's the man who visited her as a child. We've never seen anything quite so cinematic on *Doctor Who*, and he's certainly up there with Harper, Camfield, Maloney, Sax and Lyn. Having a whole new crop of directors has been good for the programme and great for the audience. We have been given some great moments: 'fish custard', 'basically... run', the Doctor's 'nobody human' outburst, Ambrose being warned by the Doctor to leave her accumulated weapons alone, and the most perfect Doctor facing down the most perfect Daleks in perhaps the most perfectly *Who*-esque scene since Eccleston faced the Dalek Emperor. Possibly the best moment so far was the final scene between the Doctor and Octavian (in the grip of an Angel), closely followed by Rory's stag (Doctor: 'I thought I'd burst out of the wrong cake. Again.').

Alongside the new stuff, there have been some tasty Easter Eggs for long-time fans. I'm not just talking about Silurians, Daleks, River Song and the Angels. The new Doctor was fully revealed amid a montage of old Doctors and old enemies (how everyone cheered at the sight of the Sea Devil, but few pondered the significance – if any – of a Colin Baker era Sontaran). We've also had the Cloister Bell, a William Hartnell library card (I cheer every time I see the guy) and the ongoing TARDIS swimming pool gag.

But what has this series been about and what is it telling us? Where will it take us over the five remaining weeks? From the get-go, we've been presented with abundant mysteries: what's causing the cracks in the universe? What happened to Amy's mum and dad? Where was her aunt? Who was that in the kitchen? Did the Doctor return to Amelia, or didn't he? These mysteries gained serious

334

momentum with the 'is it a continuity error' jacket scene amongst the treeborgs in *Flesh & Stone* (which itself became wonderfully entangled with the ever-perplexing mystery of River Song). Oh, and just what is it about that duck pond?

The sense I get from the first eight episodes is that they seek to question our perception of 'reality', our observation of it (how we alter it and how it alters us) and examine our interactions with it. We have been invited to doubt the boundary between what is real and what is not, because travelling through time 'changes the way you view the universe forever...' There are 'eyes' everywhere, in alien spaceships, in cracks in the wall; retracing their observations across Leadworth green, noticing impossible truths on Starship UK; sitting in the mouths of fabricated pensioners, twitching in polycarbide casings; and on the receiving end of quantum Angels, behind frightened eyelids (fine time for the Silurians to lose that third one!). Reality comes under fire when the mysterious orphan who lives with her aunt in a big dark house claims the Doctor as her imaginary friend. Fairy tales are invoked both lyrically and visually by a terrifying walk through the dark forest, or the suggestion that the dangerous myth that awaits us at the end our journey – the thing that could change the world and kill us all – is only as unreal as we are. Dreams have run amok in word and deed. After a long wait, little Amelia seems to see/hear TARDIS return (or at least *a* TARDIS); this is sold to us as Amy's dream, but it might be much cleverer than that. Memory is important in Amy's story – why can't she remember the Daleks? Can she remember what the Doctor told her when she was seven, or not? Did any of these things happen? Did any of them not? On Starship UK, Amy acts like Little Nemo in Dreamland; dressed in her bedclothes, the perfect lucid dreamer. There are dark rumblings of dreams that no longer need their dreamers, while Rosanna (who, don't forget, *saw* 'silence') speaks of dreams faded and bad. Even the Doctor's own nightmare of self-loathing has become manifest...

What any of this means remains unclear, but we know it will end as it began with the crack from Amy's wall and the opening of the mysterious Pandorica on 26.10.2010. But will that be AD, as we've all assumed, or BC? And what of this 'silence' that seems already to have touched 16th century Venice? Have we encountered this 'silence' before? Having watched the first eight episodes a number of times, I'm beginning to feel that the finale might not involve Daleks (perhaps we'll be getting them for Christmas?), and that the cracks might be a paradox caused by the Doctor's attempts to prevent their ever occurring. But I'm also being niggled by the uncooked Doctor's attempt to prove his credentials in the first episode. Here, he gave the scientific community Fermat's Theorem, an explanation as to why electrons have mass and, perhaps most importantly, Faster Than Light travel – one of the latest scientific developments Rory claimed to have been reading up on when he entered the TARDIS in episode six. Coincidence? Maybe. And what about the couple waving at Rory and Amy from the future? Time can be written, re-written and unwritten, it seems, so how real is that future? Perhaps only as real as the past it came from...

What is certain is that we are now at the endgame for Smith & Moffat's first series, with the thrilling conclusion to the Silurian story to be followed by two richly drawn character comedies and an explosive finale (with yet another new director). Since 2005, the best part of any season has been its last third. Smith has suggested that his Doctor is very different in the later episodes; he says his performance has improved. Like it's all been sub-standard so far? This can only mean that this is, regardless of any faults (Daleks? Dream Lords?), going to be quite possibly the best season of *Doctor Who* we've ever had.

Welcome to the Platinum Age of *Doctor Who*.

Originally published by Kasterborous.com (May, 2010)

REVIEW: *Low* by David Bowie

'Sometimes you get so lonely. Sometimes you get nowhere.'

I first heard *Low* in 1986, ten years after it had been recorded. I was 15. I'd 'discovered' Bowie via his excellent *Hunky Dory* album, and had a good idea of who he was and what he'd been doing, but *Low* was something of an unknown quantity; one of those (then) seldom seen albums from what was erroneously known as 'the Berlin trilogy' (alongside "*Heroes*" and *Lodger*). With a head full of Ziggy Stardust and the Jean Genie, *Low* – when I finally tracked it down – was as disorientating to me as it must have been for Bowie fans a decade earlier. You see, in 1986 I wasn't lonely, and I was yet to feel I was getting nowhere. Unlike Bowie in 1976...

In '76, Bowie had finally made it big. Eight albums in, he'd ditched his admittedly sophisticated take on glam rock and re-invented himself as a white soul rebel. Annexing the States with *Young Americans*, his wildest dream came true: he found fame. Genuine, bona fide, trans-Atlantic fame. And then as now, fame's best friend was cocaine.

Snowed under by his new American lifestyle, Bowie quickly lost his grip on reality. He is on record as having no memory of recording of *Station to Station* or filming *The Man Who Fell to Earth*. Fortunately, some part of him knew this wasn't necessarily a good thing. With both his critical faculties and his marriage crumbling, he decided to take control and left for Europe, taking fellow coke addict Iggy Pop with him. They moved to Paris and vowed to get well together.

It is from this period of illness, depression and existential despair that *Low* was born. Hence the title. Calling on musical conspirators old and new (Tony Visconti, Brian Eno, Carlos Alomar) and locked in a French chateau, Bowie vowed to make an album of music that flew in the face of his American success and, in the light of his recent wake-up call, attempted to convey something more meaningful with the tools of what we then knew as rock 'n' roll. And he did.

Side One fades in quickly with electronic fuzz. But no Ziggy! No voice, just a beautiful dance between synthetic noises and almost alien-sounding but somehow traditional pianos and guitars: Joy Division's 'Love Will Tear Us Apart' well before its time. And it's called 'Speed of Life', which makes more and more sense the older you get...

Next up is 'Breaking Glass', one of two tracks you've probably heard of. Ricky Gardner and Carlos Alomar on Beck-like guitars. Dennis Davis on industrial percussion. Bowie singing in the mature Scott Walker style he developed on *Diamond Dogs*. Androids playing the blues.

Somewhere beneath the bleeping barrage of 'What in the World', an edgy love song tries to break free. It's so edgy that Iggy provides the backing vocals.

Then comes the other song you've heard of, with a title that would come to encapsulate the great man's career. 'Sound and Vision' is the futurist sci-fi soundscape that Ziggy Stardust and Aladdin Sane could only dream about, but it's gloriously and ironically put in its place by the folk vocals of Mary Hopkin.

'Always Crashing in the Same Car' (another title that gains in relevance the older one gets) offers an instrumental flirtation between Eno's synthetic backgrounds and Alomar's foregrounded guitar, inventing Duran Duran, Gary Numan, OMD, Visage, Ultravox!, Human League, The Cure, U2, Bloc Party, Arcade Fire and Hot Chip along the way.

'Be My Wife' ups the game with Roy Young's slammed piano offering up more ivory than a pre-historic mammoth. Here, Bowie's vocal sounds like Adam Ant would for the bulk of his career.

'A New Career in a New Town' is a work of genius. Bowie's absent vocal spaces are amply filled by his incredible harmonica. Eno's synthesisers astonish, and the drum break predicts the coming age of New Order's 'Blue Monday'. For just under three minutes a sense of yearning is created, a sense of reflection that finally gives way to a joyous optimism when the longing mouth organ defers to the jollity of the synths.

Side Two opens with 'Warszawa'. Eno creates a magnificent backdrop to Bowie's vocal lamentations; this wailing for an old soul, a past life, a former self, must surely rank among his best vocal performances.

'Art Decade' feels organic, fluid. Like Kraftwerk if they'd been cultured in a laboratory. It's amniotic, like the music of the womb, but at the same time airy, transcendental; the sound it makes is astounding.

'Weeping Wall' is Bowie all by himself, pushing this new sound even further, but presenting the listener with doubt, like something's missing. It conjures that feeling of falling asleep, but suddenly realising something crucial and important, only to lose it again just as quickly. And – things I thought I'd never hear myself say – it's got the best xylophone playing ever committed to record.

'Subterraneans' closes the album with Bowie proving his skill on the sax – an instrument that had and would continue to provide the motif for a number of his albums; pre-figuring X-Ray Spex style punk on *Pin-Ups*, recalling urban city sounds on Black Tie White Noise, and heralding his ascension to Starman heaven on the blissful, elegiac *Blackstar*. But we're not talking jazz on *Low*. The playing here is something stranger, and yet it leaves us with a sense of having come in from the cold. It allows us the realisation that no matter how much we think we might have failed in life, we have actually achieved so much. It touches our humanity without being pious or pretentious. Okay, maybe just a little bit. But then we all recognised that bit of ourselves in Bowie, didn't we?

For an album recorded in a healing environment, as a form of creative therapy, *Low* should, by title and definition, be depressing. On first listen you might be mistaken for thinking it's having a bloody good go. But you should own it, and listen to it and play it over and over as you move into the future, because its total effect is catharsis, and one day it will heal you. Tony Visconti's textured production builds a cocoon where your heart can hide from chaos (in 1977 it was the perfect antidote/accompaniment to punk) and it's great for being alone with when you're going through ch-ch-ch-changes. Listening to *Low* again, I realise that in the 20-odd years since I was first thrilled and alienated by its unpredictability, it's become an old and familiar friend. A friend that makes me smile. There's never been a time when I couldn't listen to it, be uplifted by it, be amazed at it. It's like it's always been there, like I was never without it. And it will grow ever more timeless and ever more amazing the further from 1976 it gets. And it will live forever, because it's an album you can – and will – grow to.

Originally published in *Music-Zine* (September, 2007 – updated January 2016)

ABOUT CHILDREN IN NEED

Children in Need is the BBC's UK corporate charity. Thanks to the support of the public, it is able to make a real difference to the lives of children all across the UK. Children in Need's vision is that every child in the UK has a childhood which is safe; happy and secure; allows them the chance to reach their potential.

Children in Need provide grants to projects in the UK which focus on children and young people who are disadvantaged. It is local to people in all corners of the UK and support small and large organisations which empower children and extend their life choices. It currently supports 2,400 projects all across the UK. The projects it funds helps children facing a range of disadvantages, for example poverty and deprivation; children who have been the victims of abuse or neglect or disabled young people. Its grant programmes are open all year round for applications. It gives its small grants awards four times a year and main grants three times a year.

The BBC Children in Need Appeal Night takes place every year in November. The Appeal show is a whole evening of entertainment on BBC One with celebrities singing, dancing, and doing all sorts of crazy things to help raise money. There are also plenty of one-off specials of popular programmes, which in the past have included *Doctor Who*, *Strictly Come Dancing*, *The One Show*, and *EastEnders*.

You can find out more about Children in Need at
www.bbc.co.uk/corporate2/childreninneed

Printed in Great Britain
by Amazon